Her Sweet Surrender

NINA HARRINGTON

First Published in Great Britain 2016
By Mills & Boon, an imprint of HarperCollins*Publishers*
1 London Bridge Street, London, SE1 9GF

HER SWEET SURRENDER © 2016 Harlequin Books S. A.

The First Crush Is the Deepest, *Last-Minute Bridesmaid* and *Blame It on the Champagne* were first published in Great Britain by Harlequin (UK) Limited.

The First Crush Is the Deepest © 2013 Nina Harrington
Last-Minute Bridesmaid © 2013 Nina Harrington
Blame It on the Champagne © 2013 Nina Harrington

ISBN: 978-0-263-92084-0

05-1016

Our policy is to use papers that are natural, renewable and recyclable products and made from wood grown in sustainable forests.The logging and manufacturing processes conform to the legal environmental regulations of the country of origin.

Printed and bound in Spain
by CPI, Barcelona

Nina Harrington grew up in rural Northumberland, and decided at the age of eleven that she was going to be a librarian—because then she could read *all* of the books in the public library whenever she wanted! Since then she has been a shop assistant, community pharmacist, technical writer, university lecturer, volcano walker and industrial scientist, before taking a career break to realise her dream of being a fiction writer. When she is not creating stories which make her readers smile, her hobbies are cooking, eating, enjoying good wine—and talking, for which she has had specialist training.

THE FIRST CRUSH
IS THE DEEPEST

BY
NINA HARRINGTON

CHAPTER ONE

AMBER DUBOIS CLOSED her eyes and tried to stay calm. 'Yes, Heath,' she replied. 'Of course I am taking care of myself. No, I am not staying out too long this evening. That's right, a couple of hours at most.'

The limo slowed and she squinted out at the impressive stone pillars of the swish London private members club. 'Ah. I think we have arrived. Time for you to get back to your office. Don't you have a company to sort out? Bye, Heath. Love you. Bye.'

She sighed out loud then quickly stowed her phone in a tiny designer shoulder bag. Heath meant well but in his eyes she was still the teenage unwanted stepsister who he had been told to look after and had never quite learnt to let go. But he cared and she knew that she could rely on him for anything. And that meant a lot when you were at a low point in your life.

Like now.

Amber looked up through the drizzle and was just about to tell the limo driver that she had changed her mind when a plump blonde in a purple bandage dress two sizes too small for her burst out of the club and almost dragged Amber out of the rain and into the foyer.

She looked a little like the mousey-haired girl who had lorded over everyone from the posh girls' table at high school.

Right now Amber watched Miss Snooty 'my dad's a

banker' rear back in horror when she realised that the star of the ten-year school reunion alumni had a plaster cast over her right wrist, but recovered enough to bend forward and air kiss her on both cheeks with a loud *mmwwahh*.

'Amber. Darling. How lovely to see you again. We are so pleased that you could make our little get-together—especially when you lead such an exciting life these days. Do come inside. We want to know everything!'

Amber was practically propelled across the lovely marble floor, which was tricky to do in platform designer slingbacks. She had barely caught her breath when a hand at her back pushed her forwards into a huge room. The walls were covered with cream brocade, broken up by floor to ceiling mirrors, and huge gilded chandeliers hung from the ceiling.

It was a ballroom designed to cope with hundreds of people.

Only at that moment several clusters of extremely bored-looking women in their late twenties were standing with their hands clasped around buffet plates and wine glasses.

Every single one of them stopped talking and turned around.

And stared at her.

In total silence.

Amber had faced concert audiences of all shapes and sizes—but the frosty atmosphere in this cold elegant room was frigid enough to send a shiver down her spine.

'Look everyone. Amber DuBois made it in the end. Isn't that marvellous! Now carry on enjoying yourself. Fabulous!'

Two minutes later Amber was standing at the buffet and drinks table with a glass of fizzy water in her hand. She smiled down at her guide, who had started to chew the corner of her lower lip. 'Is everything all right?' Amber asked.

The other woman gulped and whimpered slightly. 'Yes—

yes, of course. Everything is just divine. I just need to check something—but feel free to mingle, darling…mingle.'

And then she practically jogged over to a girl who might have been one of the prefects, grabbed her arm and in no uncertain terms jabbed her head towards Amber and glared towards the other side of the room.

Amber peered over the elaborate hairstyles of a cluster of chattering women who were giving her sideways glances as though scared to come and talk to her.

This was so ridiculous. So what if she had made a name for herself as a concert pianist over the years? She was still the quiet, lanky, awkward girl they used to pick on.

And then she saw it. A stunning glossy black grand piano had been brought out in front of the tall picture windows. *Just waiting for someone to play it.*

So that was the reason her old high school had gone to such lengths to track her down with an email invitation to the ten-year school reunion.

Amber sighed out loud and her shoulders slumped down. *It seemed that some things never changed.*

They had never shown the slightest interest in her when she was their schoolmate—far from it in fact. Amber Du-Bois might have had the connections but she was not one of the posh clique of girls or the seriously academic group. She was usually on the last table and the back of the bus with the rest of the eccentrics.

Well. If there was a time to channel her inner diva, then this was it. One final performance—and the only one they would be getting from her that evening.

Cameras flashed as Amber strode, head high, canapés wobbling, across the polished wooden floor towards the ladies room.

Behind her back, Amber heard someone tap twice on the microphone but the squeaky posh voice was cut off as she stepped inside the powder room, pushed the door firmly closed with her bottom and collapsed back against it for a moment, eyes closed.

Sanctuary! If the speeches had just started she might have the place to hide out for a few precious minutes—it could even be a chance to escape.

She was just about to peek outside to check for options when the sound of something falling onto the tiled floor echoed from the adjoining powder room, quickly followed by a colourful expletive.

Amber's heels clattered on the tiles as she strolled over and peered around the corner to see where the noise was coming from.

A short brunette was standing on tiptoe, straddling two washbasins, with her arms outstretched, trying to reach the handle of the double-glazed window which was high on the wall above her. A red plastic mop bucket was lying on its side next to the washbasin.

'What's this? Kate Lovat running out on a party? I must be seeing things.' A short chuckle escaped from Amber's lips before she could stop it, and instantly the brunette whirled around to see who it was—and screamed and waved her arms about the instant she saw who had asked the question.

Which made her wobble so much that Amber rushed forwards, slid her buffet plate onto the marble counter, flipped up the bucket to create a step and then wrapped her left arm around the waist of a compact bundle of fun in a stunning cerise vintage cocktail dress.

Kate Lovat was one of the few real pals that she had made at high school.

Irrepressible, petite and fierce, Kate used to have a self-confidence which was as large as the heels she wore to push her height up to medium and a spirit to match. Today her short tousled dark hair was slicked into an asymmetric style which managed to make her look both elegant and quirky at the same time.

'Kate!' Amber laughed. 'I was praying that you were going to turn up at the reunion. You look fabulous!'

'Why thank you, pretty lady. Right back at you. You are even more gorgeous than ever.' Then Kate's mouth fell open, her eyes locked onto the floor and she gave a high pitched squeak as she grabbed Amber's arm. 'Oh my...those shoes. I want those shoes. In fact if you were not several sizes bigger than me, I would knock you down and run off with them.'

Then Kate took one step back and peered into Amber's face, her eyes narrow and her brow creased. 'Wait a minute. You look peaky. And a lot skinnier than the last time I saw you... Did I tell you that I have suddenly become clairvoyant? Because I foresee chocolate and plenty of it in your very near future.'

Then she pointed at the plaster cast on Amber's wrist. 'I have to know. Wait.' She held up one hand and pressed the fingertips of the other hand to her forehead as though she was doing her own mind-reading act. 'Let me guess. You slipped on an ice cube at some fashionista party, or was it a yacht cruising the Caribbean? It must make playing the piano a tad tricky.'

'Kate. Slow down. If you must know, I tripped over my own suitcase a couple of weeks ago. And yes, I have cancelled everything for the next six months so my wrist has a chance to heal.' Then she paused. 'And why do you need to sneak out of the window at our school reunion when you could be catching up on the gossip with the rest of our class?'

Kate took a breath, her lower lip quivered and she seemed about to say something, then changed her mind, broke into a smile and waved one hand towards the door. 'Been there. Done that. This has been one hell of a rotten day and the kidnappers have blockaded the doors to stop us from getting out.'

Then Kate lifted her chin. 'But here is an idea,' she said, her dark green eyes twinkling with delight. She gestured with her head towards the red velvet chaise at the other end of the powder room. Two buffet plates piled high with pastries and cocktail skewers were stashed on the floor.

'Who cares about them? We have a sofa. We have snacks. And the really good news is that I crashed into Saskia five minutes ago and she is now on a mission to find liquid refreshment and cake. The three of us could have our own party right here. What do you say?'

Amber's shoulders dropped several inches and she hugged her old friend one-handed. 'That. Is the best idea I have heard in a long time. Oh, I had forgotten how much I missed you both. But I thought Saskia was still in France.'

Kate winked. 'Oh, things have certainly changed around here. Just wait until you hear what we have been up to.' Then she waved both hands towards Amber and grabbed her around the waist. 'It is so good to see you. But come on, sit. What drove you out from the chosen few? Or should that be who drove you out?'

Suddenly Kate froze and her fingers flew to her mouth. 'Don't tell me that snake in the grass Petra dared to show her face.'

Petra. Amber took a sharp intake of breath. 'Well, if Petra was in there, I didn't notice, and somehow I think I would have recognised her.'

'Damn right.' Kate scowled. 'Ten years is not nearly long enough to forget that face. A friend does not jump on her best pal's boyfriend. Especially at that pal's eighteenth birthday party.' Her flat right hand sliced through the air. 'For some things there is no forgiveness. None. Zero. Don't even ask. Oh—is that a mushroom tartlet?'

'Help yourself,' Amber replied and passed Kate her plate. Strange how she had suddenly lost her appetite the moment

Petra's name was mentioned. The memory of the last time she had seen the girl she used to call her friend flittered across her brain, bringing a bitter taste of regret into her mouth. 'It takes two to tango, Kate,' she murmured. 'And, from what I recall, Sam Richards wasn't exactly complaining that Petra had made a move on him. Far from it, in fact.'

'Of course not,' Kate replied between bites. 'He was a boy and she bedazzled him. He didn't have a chance.'

'Bedazzled?'

'Bedazzled. Once that girl decided that Sam was the target he was toast.' Then Kate coughed and flicked a glance at Amber before brushing pastry crumbs from her fingers. 'He's back in London now, you know. Sam. Working as a journalist for that swanky newspaper he was always talking about.'

Amber brought her head up very slowly. 'How fascinating. Perhaps I should ring the editor and warn him that his new reporter is susceptible to bedazzlement?'

'Careful.' Kate chuckled. 'They'll be saying that I am having a bad influence on you.'

'Well, that would never do! Hi Amber,' a sweet clipped voice came from the bathroom.

'Saskia!' Kate instantly leaped up from the sofa and grabbed the plate of mini chocolate cakes that was threatening to topple over at any second. 'Look who's here.' Then she caught her breath. 'What happened to your dress?'

Saskia slid onto the sofa and lowered a screw cap bottle of Chardonnay and two glasses onto the floor in front of them so that she could give Amber a hug.

It was only then Amber noticed the red wine stain which was still dripping down the sleeve of Saskia's cream lace dress. It was almost as if someone had thrown a glass of wine at her.

Maybe things had changed? Because if Kate was the petite quirky one of their little band and Amber the lanky American, then Saskia was the classic English beauty. Medium brown hair, medium height and size. And the one girl who would never cause a scene or make a fuss.

'Excuse me for a moment.' Saskia nodded. And, without waiting for an answer, she clenched her teeth and picked up one of the paper hand towels and tore it violently into strips lengthways. Then into smaller strips, then more slowly into squares. Only when the whole towel was completely shredded into postage stamps did Saskia exhale slowly, gather up all of the pieces and toss them into the waste basket.

'Well, I feel a lot better now.' She smiled and brushed her hands off.

Kate was still choking so Amber was the one who had to ask, 'Do you want to talk about it?'

Saskia sat bolt upright on the sofa, too proud to slouch back against the cushion, and casually mopped the stain with a paper napkin. 'Apparently I am all that is bad in the world because I refused to let the school alumni committee use Elwood House for free for the weekly soiree—you know, the one I have never been invited to? You should have seen their faces the moment I mentioned the going hourly rate. That's when the abuse started.'

She sniffed once. 'It was most unladylike. Frankly, I am appalled.'

Kate pushed back her shoulders and her chin forward. 'Right. Where are they? No one disses my pal and gets away with it. There are three of us against the whole room—no contest.'

'I have just finished ten years of training as a full-on concert diva,' Amber added. 'Want to see me in action? It can be scary.'

Saskia shook her head. 'That would be playing right into their hands. They would just love it if we made a scene. It gives them something to talk about in their shallow little lives.

Let it go. Seriously. I have decided to rise above it.' Then her face broke into a smile. 'I am already having far too good a time right here. Kate. Would you be so kind as to twist open that bottle? I want to hear everything. Let's start with the obvious. My love life is on hold until Elwood House is up and running, but what about you, Kate?'

Kate looked up from pouring the wine. 'Don't look at me,' she replied in disgust. 'I seem to have an inbuilt boy repellent at the moment. One taste and they run. Unlike some people we know. Come on, Amber. What's the latest on that hunky mountain man we saw you with in the celeb mags?'

'History. Gone. Finished,' Amber replied and took a sip of wine before passing it to Saskia. 'But I live in hope. If I ever get out of this powder room I am going to start fund-raising for my friend Parvita's charity in India and, you never know, I might meet someone over the next few months. I visited the orphanage with her a few months ago and I promised the girls that I would go back if I could.' Her eyes stared over their heads at the large white tiles. 'It is the most fabulous place and right on the beach,' she added in a dreamy faraway voice.

Then her shoulders slumped. 'Who am I kidding? Heath would be furious with me for even thinking about going back to India.'

'Heath? You mean, as in your stepbrother Heath?' Kate whispered. 'Why should he object to you going to India?'

Amber took a breath and looked over at Saskia and then back to Kate. 'Because he worries about me. You see, I didn't just fall over my suitcase and break my wrist. I had just got back from India and I sort of collapsed. There was an outbreak of...'

The sound of raucous laughter cut Amber off mid-sentence as a horde of noisy chattering women burst into the ladies room. Their voices echoed around the tiled space in an explosion of sound.

Amber pressed both hands to her ears. 'Sounds like the speeches are over and I have just heard the word karaoke.' She gestured towards the entrance. 'We might be able to sneak out the side entrance if we are quick. My apartment is the nearest. Then I'll tell you what really happened in India and why Heath is as worried as I am.'

CHAPTER TWO

'Tell me what you know about Bambi DuBois.'

The question hit Sam Richards right between the eyes, just as he was swallowing down the last of his coffee, and he almost choked on the coarse grounds in the bottom of the cup.

Frank Evans strode into the corner office as though he had a hurricane behind his back and waved a colour magazine in front of Sam's nose.

Sam sniffed and gave his new boss a one-handed hat tip salute. Frank had made his name in the media company by being one of the sharpest editors in the business who only worked with the best, but Sam had already been warned that Frank had not earned the editor's desk through his personnel skills.

'And good morning to you too, Frank,' Sam replied. 'And thank you for your warm welcome to the London office.'

'Yeah, yeah.' Frank shooed a hand in Sam's direction and pointed to the desk. 'Take a seat. Monday madness. Worse than ever. You know what it's like. The chief is on my back and it's not nine o'clock yet. Time to rock and roll. You talk. I listen. Let's hear it. Show me that you're not completely out of touch with the London scene after all those years out in the wilderness.'

Sam stifled a laugh. *So much for an easy first day in the new job.*

Frank settled the seat of his over tight suit onto the wide leather chair on the other side of the modern polymer table and ran his short stubby fingers through his receding grey hair before drinking down what must now be cold milky coffee.

His cheap tie was already tugged down a couple of inches and his shirt sleeves had missed the iron, but in contrast his eyes sparkled with intelligence as he leant his arms on one of the cleanest and most organised desks Sam had ever seen.

Bambi DuBois? The shock of hearing her name kept Sam frozen to the spot, cup in hand, before his brain kicked in and he frowned as though thinking about an answer. A few manly coughs gave him just enough time to pull together a casual reply to the editor who he had previously only spoken to twice on the telephone.

The editor who had the power to decide whether he had a future career in this newspaper—or not.

This was definitely not the perfect start to his dream job that he had imagined!

Lowering his cup onto a coaster, Sam assumed his very best bored and casual disinterested journalist's face. His career depended on this man's decision.

'Do you mean Amber DuBois? English concert pianist. Blonde. Leggy. Popular with the top fashion designers, who like her to wear their gowns at performances.' He shrugged at the newspaper editor and new boss who was staring at him so intently. 'I think she was the face of some cosmetic company a few years ago. And I would hardly call Los Angeles the wilderness.'

Frank slid a magazine across the desk. 'Make that the biggest cosmetic company in Asia and you are getting close. But you seem to have missed something out. Have a look at this.'

Sam took his time before picking it up and instantly recognised it as the latest colour supplement from their main competitor's weekly entertainment section. And any confusion he might have had about Frank's question vanished into the stiflingly hot air of the prized corner office.

The cover ran a full colour half page photograph of Amber 'Bambi' DuBois in a flowing azure dress with a jewel-encrusted tiny strapless bodice.

The shy, gangly teenage girl he had once known was gone—and in her place was a beautiful, elegant woman who was not just in control but revelling in her talent.

Amber was sitting at a black grand piano with one long, slender, silky leg stretched out to display a jewelled high heeled sandal and Sam was so transfixed by how stunning she looked that it took him a microsecond to realise that his new boss was tapping the headline with the chewed end of his ballpoint pen.

International Concert Pianist Amber DuBois Shocks the Classical Music World by Announcing her Retirement at 28. But the Question on Everyone's Lips is: Why? What Next for 'Bambi' DuBois?

Sam looked up at his editor and raised his eyebrows just as Frank leant across the desk and slapped one heavy hand down firmly onto the cover so that his fingers were splayed out over Amber's chest.

'I smell a story. There has to be some very good reason why a professional musician like Amber DuBois suddenly announces her retirement out of the blue when she is at the top of her game.'

Frank aimed a finger at Sam's chest and fired. 'The rumour is that our Amber is jumping on the celebrity bandwagon of adopting a vanity charity project in India to spend her money on, but her agent is refusing to comment. As far as I am concerned, this is a ruse to get the orchestras begging her to come back with a solid platinum hello. And I want this paper to get in there first with the real story.'

Frank sat back in his wide leather chair and folded his arms.

'More to the point—I want *you* to go out there and bring back an exclusive interview with the lovely Miss DuBois. You can consider this your first assignment.'

Then Frank shrugged. 'You can thank me for the opportunity later.'

The words stayed frozen in the air as though trapped inside an iceberg large enough to sink his new job in one deadly head-on collision.

Thank him?

For a fraction of a second Sam wondered if this was some sort of joke. A bizarre initiation ceremony into the world of the London office of GlobalStar Media, and there was a secret camera hidden in the framed magazine covers behind Frank's head which were recording just how he was reacting to the offer of this amazing *opportunity.*

Sam flexed out the fingers of both hands so that he wouldn't scrunch up the magazine and toss it back to Frank with a few choice words about what he thought of his little joke, while his normally sharp brain worked through a few options to create a decent enough excuse as to why Frank should find another journalist for this particular gig.

Sam inhaled slowly as each syllable sank in. It had taken him three months to arrange a transfer from the Los Angeles office of the media giant he had given his life to for the past ten years. He had worked himself up from being the post room boy and sacrificed relationships and anything close to a social life to reach this point in his career.

This was more than just a jump on the promotion ladder; this was the job he had been dreaming about since he was a teenager. The only job that he had ever wanted. *Ever*. No way was he going to be diverted from that editor's chair. Not now, not when he had come so far.

Sam blinked twice. 'Sorry, Frank, but can you say that again? Because I think I must have misheard. I've just spent the last ten years working my way from New York to Los Angeles on the back of celebrity interviews. I applied to be an investigative journalist not a gossip columnist.'

Frank replied with a dismissive snort and he bit off a laugh. 'Do you know what pays for this shiny office we are sitting in, Sam? Magazine sales. And the public love celebrity stories, especially when it concerns a girl with the looks of Amber DuBois. It's all over the Internet this morning that orchestras have been lining up and offering her huge bonuses to come and work for them for one last season before she retires. And then there is her publicity machine. The girl is a genius.'

He raised one hand into the air and gave Sam a Vee sign. 'She has only ever been seen with two dates in the last ten years. *Two.* And not your boring classical musician—oh, no, our girl Amber likes top action men. First there was the Italian racing car driver who she cheered on to be World Champion, then that Scottish mountaineer. Climbing Everest for charity. With the lovely Amber at Base Camp waving him farewell with a tear in her eye. She is the modelling musical sweetheart and her fans love her—and now this.'

The pen went back to some serious tapping. 'Think of it as your first celebrity interview for the London office. Who knows? This could be the last fluff piece you ever write. Use some of that famous charm I've been hearing about—the lovely Miss DuBois will be putty in your hands.'

His hands? Sam's fingers stretched out over his knees. Instantly his mind starting wheeling through the possibility that someone had tipped off this shark of an editor that ten years ago those same hands had known every intimate detail about Amber 'Bambi' DuBois. Her hopes, her dreams, the fact that she always asked for extra anchovies on her pizza and had a sensitive spot at one side of her neck that could melt her in seconds. The way her long slender legs felt under his fingertips. Oh, yes, Sam Richards knew a lot more about Amber DuBois than he was prepared to tell anyone.

This job was going to make or break his career, but he had promised himself on the night they'd parted that, no matter how desperate he was for money or fame, he would never tell Amber's story. It was too personal and private. And he had kept that promise, despite the temptation—but the world he worked in did not see it that way.

Sam had seen more than one popular musician or actor pull celebrity stunts to get the attention of the media, and he had learnt his craft by writing about their petty dramas and desperate need for attention, but Amber had never been one of them. She didn't need to. She had the talent to succeed on her own, as well as a body and a face the camera loved.

Frank shuffled in his chair. *Impatient for his reply.*

Sam took one look into those clever, scheming eyes and the sinking feeling that had been in the bottom of his stomach since he had walked into the impressive office building that morning turned into a gaping cavern.

He was just about to be stitched up.

What could he do? He did not have the authority to walk into a new office and demand the best jobs as though they owed him a future. Just the opposite. But Frank might have waited until his second day as the new boy.

'I'm sure you're right, Frank. But I was looking forward to getting started on that investigation into Eurozone political funding we talked about. Has it fallen through?'

Frank reached into his desk drawer and handed Sam a folder of documents.

'Far from it. Everything we have seen so far screams corruption at every level from the bottom up. Take a look. The research team have already lined up a series of interviews with insiders across Europe. And it's all there, waiting for someone to turn over the stones and see what is crawling underneath.'

Sam scan read the first few pages of notes and background information for the interviews and kept reading, his mind racing with options on how he could craft a series of articles from the one investigation. And the more he read, the faster his heart raced.

This was it. This was the perfect piece of financial journalism that would set him up as a serious journalist on the paper and win him the editor's job he had sacrificed a lot to achieve. And it had to be the London office. Not Los Angeles or New York. London.

'Does your dad still have that limo service in Knightsbridge? We've used them a couple of times. Great cars. Your dad might get a kick out of seeing your name on the front page.'

Might? His dad would love it.

His father had sacrificed everything for him after his mother left them. He had been a single parent to a sullen and fiercely angry teenager who was struggling to find his way against the odds. Driven by the burning ambition to show the world that he was capable of being more than a limo driver like his dad.

Sam Richards had made his father's life hell for so many years. And yet his dad had stuck by him every step of the way without expecting a word of thanks.

And now it was payback time.

This promotion to the GlobalStar London office was a first step to make up for years of missed telephone calls and flying Christmas visits.

Shame that his shiny new career was just about to hit an iceberg called Amber DuBois.

Aware that Frank was watching him with his arms crossed

and knew exactly how tempting this piece was, Sam closed the folder and slid it back across the desk. This was no time to be coy.

'Actually, he sold the limo business a few years back to go into property. But you're right. He would be pleased. So how do I make that happen, Frank? What do I have to do to get this assignment?'

'Simple. You have built up quite a reputation for yourself as a hard worker in the Los Angeles office. And now you want an editor's desk. I understand that. Ten years on the front line is a long time, but I cannot just give you a golden story like this when I have a team of hungry reporters sitting outside this office who would love to make their mark on it. All I am asking you to do is show me that you are as good as they say you are.'

Frank slid the dossier back into his desk drawer. 'If you want the editor's desk, you are going to have to come back with an exclusive interview from the lovely Amber. Feature length. Oh—and you have two weeks to do it. We can't risk someone else breaking Amber's story before we do. Do we understand each other? Excellent, I look forward to reading your exposé.'

Sam rose to shake hands and Frank's fingers squeezed hard and stayed clamped shut. 'And Sam. One more thing. The truth about "Bambi's Bollywood Babies" had better be amazing or you will be back to the bottom of the ladder all over again, interviewing TV soap stars about their leg-waxing regime.'

He released Sam with a nod. 'You can take the magazine. Have fun.'

Sam closed the door to Frank's office behind him and stood in silence on the ocean of grey plastic industrial carpet in the open-plan office, looking out over rows of cubicles. He had become used to the cacophony of noise and voices and telephones that was part of working in newspaper offices just like this, no matter what city he happened to be in that day. If anything, it helped to block out the alarm sirens that were sounding inside his head.

This was the very office block that he used to walk and cycle past every day on his way to school. He remembered looking up at the glass-fronted building and dreaming about what it must be like to be a top reporter working in a place like this. Writing important articles in the newspapers that men like his dad's clients read religiously in the back seat of the limo.

The weird thing was—from the very first moment that he had told his dad that he wanted to be a journalist on this paper, his dad had worked all of the extra hours and midnight airport runs, week after week, month after month, to make that possible. He had never once doubted that he would do it. Not once.

And now he was here. He had done it.

The one thing he had never imagined was that his first assignment in his dream job would mean working with Amber.

Sam glanced at the magazine cover in his hand. And reflected back at him was the lovely face of the one woman in the world who was guaranteed to set the dogs on him the minute he even tried to get within shouting distance.

And in his case he deserved it. The nineteen-year-old Sam Richards had given Amber DuBois very good reason to never want to talk to him again.

He might have given Amber her first kiss—but he had broken her heart just as fast.

Now all he had to do was persuade her to overlook the past, forgive and forget and reveal her deep innermost secrets for the benefit of the magazine-reading public.

Fun might not be the ideal word to describe how he was feeling.

But it had to be done. There was no going back to Los Angeles. For better or worse, he had burnt those bridges. He needed this job. But more than that—he wanted it. He had worked hard to be standing on this piece of carpet, looking out, instead of standing outside on the pavement, looking in.

He owed it to his dad, who had believed in him when nobody else had, even after years of making his dad's life a misery. And he owed it to himself. He wasn't the second class chauffeur's son any longer.

He had to get that interview with Amber.

No matter how much grovelling was involved.

CHAPTER THREE

'AND YOU ARE quite sure about that? No interviews at all? And you did tell Miss DuBois who was calling? Yes. Yes I understand. Thank you. I'll be sure to check her website for future news.'

Sam flicked down the cover on his cellphone and tapped the offending instrument against his forehead before popping it into his pocket.

Her website? When did a professional talent agency direct a journalist to a website? No, it was more than that. His name was probably on some blacklist Amber had passed to her agent with instructions that she would not speak to him under any circumstances.

He needed to think this through and come up with a plan—and fast.

Sam wrapped the special polishing cloth around his fist and started rubbing the fine polish onto the already glossy paintwork on the back wheel arch of his dad's pride and joy. The convertible vintage English sports car had been one of the few cars that his dad had saved when he had to sell the classic car showroom as part of the divorce from Sam's mother.

It had taken Sam and his dad three years to restore the sports car back to the original pristine condition that it was still today. Three years of working evenings after school and the occasional Sunday when his dad was not driving limos for other people to enjoy.

Three years of pouring their pain and bitterness about Sam's mother into hard physical work and sweat, as though creating something solid and physical would somehow make up for the fact that she had left Sam with his dad and gone off to make a new life for herself with her rich boyfriend. A life funded by the sale of his dad's business and most of their savings.

But they had done it. *Together.* Even though Sam had resented every single second of the work they did on this car. Resented it so much that he could cheerfully have pushed it outside onto the street, set it on fire and delighted in watching it burn. Like his dreams had burnt the day his mother left.

In another place, with another father and another home, Sam might have taken his burning fury out in a sports field or with his fists in a boxing ring or even on the streets in this part of London.

Instead, he had directed all of his teenage frustration and anger and bitterness at his father.

He had been so furious with his dad for not changing jobs like his mother had wanted him to.

Furious for not running after her and begging her to come back and be with them—like he had done that morning when he came down for breakfast early and saw her going out of the front door with her suitcases. He had followed that taxi cab for three streets before his legs gave way.

She had never even looked back at him. Not once.

And it was all his dad's fault. The arguments. The fights. They were all his fault. He must have done something terrible to make her leave.

Sam's gaze flicked up at the thin partition wall that separated the cab office from the workshop. Just next to the door was a jagged hole in the plaster sheet the size of a teenage fist.

Sam's fist.

It was the closest he had ever come to lashing out at his dad physically.

The screaming and the shouting and the silent stomping about the house had no effect on this broken man, who carried on working as though nothing had happened. As though their lives had not been destroyed. And to the boy he was then, it was more than just frustrating—it was a spark under a keg of gunpowder.

They'd survived three long, hard years before Sam had taken off to America.

And along the way Sam had learnt the life lessons that he still carried in his heart. He had learnt that love everlasting, marriage and family were outdated ideas which only wrecked people's lives and caused lifelong damage to any children who got caught up in the mess.

He had seen it first-hand with his own parents, and with the parents of his friends like Amber and the girls she knew. Not one of them came from happy homes.

The countless broken marriages and relationships of journalists and the celebrities he had met over the years had only made his belief stronger, not less.

He would be a fool to get trapped in the cage that was marriage. And in the meantime he would take his time enjoying the company of the lovely ladies who were attracted to luxury motors like free chocolate and champagne, and that suited him just fine.

No permanent relationships.

No children to become casualties when the battle started.

Other men had wives and children, and he wished them well.

Not for him. The last thing he wanted was children.

Pity that his last girlfriend in Los Angeles had refused to believe that he had no intention of inviting her to move into his apartment and was already booking wedding planners before she realised that he meant what he said—he cared about Alice but he had absolutely no intention of walking down an aisle to the tune of wedding bells any time soon. If ever.

No. Sam had no problem with using his charm and good looks to persuade reluctant celebrities to talk to him—and he was good at it. Good enough to have made his living out of those little chats and cosy drinks.

But when it came to trust? Ah. Different matter altogether.

He placed his trust in metal and motor engineering and electronics. Smooth bodywork over a solid, beautiful engine designed by some of the finest engineers in the world. People could and would let you down for no reason, but not motors. Motors were something he could control and rely on.

He trusted his father and his deep-seated sense of integrity and silent resolve never to bad-mouth Sam's mother, even when times had been tough for both of them. And they had been tough, there was no doubt about that.

But there had always been one constant in his life. His dad had never doubted that he would pass the exams and go to university and make his dream of becoming a journalist come true.

Unlike his mother. The last conversation that they ever had was burned into his memory like a deep brand that time and experience would never be able to erase.

What had she called him? *Oh, yes.* His own mother had called him a useless dreamer who would never amount to anything and would end up driving other people around for a living, just like his father.

Well, he had proven her wrong on every count, and this editor's job was the final step on a long and arduous journey that began the day she left them.

It was time to show his dad that he had been right to keep

faith in him and put up with the anger. Time to show him that he was grateful for everything he had done for him.

All of which screamed out one single message.

He needed that interview with Amber. He knew that she was in London—and he knew where her friends lived. He *had* to persuade her to talk to him, no matter what it took, even if it meant tracking her down and stalking her. He had come too far to let anything stand in his way now.

Amber DuBois. *The girl he left behind.*

His hands stilled and he stepped back from the car and grabbed a chilled bottle of water from the mini-fridge in the corner of the workshop and then pressed the chilled bottle against the back of his neck to try and cool down. Time to get creative. Time to...

The bell over the back door rang. Odd. His dad didn't like customers coming to the garage. This was his private space and always had been. No clients allowed.

Sam turned down the radio to a normal level and was just wiping his hands on a paper towel when the workshop's wooden door swung open.

And Amber 'legs up to her armpits' Bambi DuBois drifted into his garage as though she was floating on air.

He looked up and tried to speak, but the air in his lungs was too frozen in shock. So he squared his shoulders and took a moment to enjoy the view instead.

Amber was wearing a knee length floral summer dress in shades of pastel pink and soft green which moved as she walked, sliding over her slim hips as though the slippery fabric was alive or liquid.

Sam felt as though a mobile oasis of light and summer and positive energy had just floated in on the breeze into the dim and dingy old garage his dad refused to paint. The dark shadows and recesses where the old tins of oil and catalogues were stored only seemed to make the brightness of this woman even more pronounced.

She took a few steps closer, her left hand still inside the heart-shaped pocket of her dress and he felt like stepping backwards so that they could keep that distance.

This was totally ludicrous. After all, this was his space and she was his visitor.

His beautiful, talented, ridiculously lovely visitor who looked as though she had just stepped out from a cover shoot for a fashion magazine.

She was sunlight in his darkness—just the same as she had always been, and seeing her again like this reinforced just how much he had missed her and never had the courage to admit it.

Amber looked at him with the faintest of polite smiles and slipped her sunglasses higher onto her nose with one fingertip.

'This place has not changed one bit,' she whispered in a voice what was as soft and musical and gentle and lovely as he had remembered. A voice which still had the power to make his blood sing.

Then she glanced across at the car. 'You even have the same sports car. That's amazing.'

Sam had often wondered how Amber would turn out. Not that he could avoid seeing her name. Her face was plastered on billboards and the sides of buses from California to London. But that was not the real Amber. He knew that only too well from working in the media business.

No. This was the real Amber. This beautiful girl who was running the manicured fingertips of her left hand along the leather seat of the sports car he had just polished.

Maybe she had decided to forgive him for the way they had parted.

'My dad kept it.' He shrugged. 'One of a kind.'

Amber paused and she sighed. 'The last time I saw this car

was the night of my eighteenth birthday party and you were sitting in the front seat with your tongue down the throat of my so called friend Petra. About twenty minutes after you had declared your undying love for me.'

She gave a strangled chuckle. 'Oh, yes, I remember this car very well indeed. Shame that the driver was not quite as classy.'

Or maybe she hadn't.

Sam pushed his hand down firmly on the workbench behind him.

So. *Here we go.* In her eyes he was *still* the chauffeur's son who had dared to date the rich client's daughter. And then kissed her best friend.

Goodbye editor's desk.

Time to start work and turn on the charm before she chopped him into small pieces and barbecued him on the car's exhaust pipe.

'Hello, Amber. How very nice to see you again.' He smiled and stepped forward to kiss her on the cheek but, before he got there, Amber flipped up her sunglasses onto the top of her head and looked at him with those famous violet-blue eyes which cut straight through any delusion that this was a social call.

Her eyes might have sold millions of tubes of eye make-up, but close up, with the light behind her, the iridescent violet-blue he remembered was mixed with every shade from cobalt to navy. And, just for him today...blue ice.

The contrast between the violet of her eyes and her straight blonde hair which fell perfectly onto her shoulders only seemed to highlight the intensity of her gaze. The cosmetic company might have chosen her for her peaches and cream ultra-clear complexion, but it had always been those magical blue eyes that Sam found totally irresistible. Throw in a pair of perfect sweet soft pink lips and he had been done for from the first time he had seen her stepping out of his dad's limo with her diva mother screaming out orders from behind her back.

She didn't seem to know what to do with her long legs, her head was down and she peered at him through a curtain of long blonde hair before brushing it away and blasting his world with one look.

Now she was standing almost as tall as he was and looking him straight in the eyes. The smile on her lips had not reached her eyes and Sam had to fight past the awkwardness of the intensity of her gaze.

'My agent mentioned that you were back in town. I thought I might pop in to say hello. Hope you don't mind.'

Her gaze shifted from the casual trainers he had found stuffed in the bottom of the wardrobe in the spare bedroom, faded blue jeans and the scraggy, oil-stained T-shirt he kept for garage work. 'I can see that your fashion sense hasn't changed very much. Shame, really. I was hoping for some improvement.'

Sam glanced down at his jeans and flicked the polishing cloth against his thigh. 'Oh, this little old outfit? Don't you just hate it when all of your chiffon is at the dry cleaner's and you can't find a thing to wear?' He crossed his arms. 'And no, Amber, I don't mind you popping in at all, especially since my editor has been harassing your agent for weeks to arrange an interview. He will be delighted to hear that you turned up out of the blue, expecting me to be here.'

Amber floated forward so that Sam inhaled a rich, sweet floral scent which was almost as intoxicating as the woman who was wearing it.

A whirlwind of memories slammed home. Long summer days walking through the streets of London as he memorised routes and names and places for the limo business. Hand in hand, chatting, laughing and enjoying each other's company as they shared secrets about themselves that nobody else knew. Amber had been his best friend for so long, he hadn't even realised how much she had come to mean to him until they were ripped apart.

'Don't flatter yourself. May I sit?'

Sam gestured to the hard wooden chair his dad used at the makeshift desk in the corner. 'It may not be quite what you're used to, but please.'

She nodded him a thanks and lowered herself gracefully onto the chair and turned it around so that she was facing him.

Sam shook his head. 'You are full of surprises, Amber Du-Bois. I thought that it would take a very exclusive restaurant in the city to tempt you to come out of your lair long enough to give me an interview.'

Her reply was to lift her flawless chin and cross her legs. Sam took in a flash of long tanned legs ending in peep toe low wedge sandals made out of plaited strips of straw and transparent plastic. Her toenails were painted in the same pale pink as her nails, which perfectly matched her lipstick and the colour motif in her dress.

She was class, elegance and designer luxury and for a fraction of a second he wanted nothing better than to pick her tiny slim body up and lay it along the bonnet of the car and find out for himself whether her skin felt the same under his fingertips.

'What makes you think that I am here to give you an interview?' she replied with a certain hardness in her voice which plunged him back into the cold waters of the real world. 'Perhaps I am here to congratulate you on your engagement? Has your fiancée come with you from Los Angeles and my wedding invitation is in the post? I can see that you would want to give me heads-up on that.'

He reeled back. 'My what?'

'Oh—didn't you announce your engagement in the Los

Angeles press? Or is there another Samuel Patrick Richards, investigative reporter and photojournalist of London, walking the streets of that lovely town?'

Sam sucked in a breath then shrugged. 'That was a misunderstanding. My girlfriend at the time was getting a little impatient and decided to organise a wedding without asking me first. Apparently she forgot that anything to do with weddings brings me out in a nasty rash. It's a long-standing allergy but I have learnt to live with it. So you can save your congratulations for another time.'

Amber inhaled very slowly before speaking again. 'Well, it seems that this garage is not the only thing that hasn't changed, is it, Sam? You do seem to make a habit out of running out on girls. Maybe we should all get together and form a support group.'

She raised both of her arms and wrote in the air. '"Girls Sam Richards has dumped and ran out on." We could have our own blog. What? What is it?'

Sam crossed the few steps which separated them and gently tugged at her cardigan. 'Your arm is in plaster. Hell, Bambi, what happened? I mean, you have to play the piano...'

She pulled her cardigan over the plaster, but lifted her left arm across her chest.

'I broke my wrist a few weeks ago and I'm officially on medical leave. And that is strictly off the record. My career is fine, thank you. In fact, I am enjoying the holiday. It is very restorative.'

Sam shook his head. 'Must make your daily practice interesting...but are you okay? I mean there won't be any lasting damage?'

She parted her lips and took a breath before answering, and for some reason Sam got the idea that she was about to tell him something then changed her mind at the very last minute. 'Clean break, no problem. The exercises are working well and I should be as good as new in a few months.'

'Glad to hear it. This brings us right back to my original question. What are you doing here?'

He stepped forward and stood in front of her, with one hand on each arm of his dad's old wooden chair, her legs now stretched out in front of her and trapped between his. He was so close that he could feel her fast breath on his cheek and see the pulse of her heart in her throat.

Her mouth narrowed and this time it did connect with the hard look in her eyes.

But, instead of backing away, Amber bent forward from the waist, challenging him, those blue eyes flashing with something he had never seen before. And when she spoke her voice was as gentle and soft as a feather duvet. And just as tempting.

'Okay. It goes like this. I understand that you want to interview me in the light of my recent press release concerning my retirement. I'm curious about what it is that you think you can offer me which is so special that I would want to talk to you instead of all the other journalists who are knocking at my door. You have never been the shy or modest type, so it must be something rather remarkable.'

'Absolutely. Remember that dream I used to talk about? The one where I am a big, important investigative journalist working at that broadsheet newspaper my dad still reads every day? Well, it turns out that to win the editor's desk I have to deliver one final celebrity interview.' Sam pointed at Amber with two fingers pressed tight together and fired his thumb like a pistol trigger.

Amber nodded. 'I thought it might be something like that.' Her eyebrows went skywards. 'I take it your editor doesn't know about our teenage fling?'

'Fling? Is that what you call it? No. He certainly doesn't,

or he would have sent me to your last known address with a bunch of supermarket flowers and a box of chocolates as soon as I walked into his office. No. That part of my life is filed under "private". Okay?'

She gave him a closed mouth smile. 'Why? I know you must have been tempted. I can see the headline now. "The real truth about how I broke Amber Du Bois' heart"? Yes, there are plenty of television reality shows who would love to have you on their list. I could hardly sue, could I?'

'I suppose not, but let's just say that I was saving that for a financial emergency. Okay?'

'An emergency? You were saving me to get you out of some money crisis? I don't know whether to be flattered or insulted. Or both. I'm not sure I like being compared to a stash of used notes which you keep under the mattress.'

'Oh—is that where you keep yours? I prefer banks myself. Much more secure.'

Her eyes narrowed and she licked her lower lip as though she was trying to decide about something important.

He could remember the first time he'd kissed those lips. They had just come out of a pizza restaurant and got caught in a heavy rain shower. He had pulled her under the shelter of his coat, his arm around her waist and, just as they got to the car, laughing and yelling as the rain bounced off the pavement around them, she had turned towards him to thank him and her stunning face was only inches away from his. And he couldn't resist any longer. And he had kissed her. Warm lips, scented skin, alive and pungent in the rain, and the feeling of her breath on his neck as she rested her head on his shoulder for a fleeting second before diving into the warm, dry car.

Not one word, but as he'd raced back to the driver's door, there was only one thing on his mind.

She was the passenger and he was the driver. Her chauffeur. The hired help. And that was the way it was always going to be. Unless he did something to change it.

Which was precisely what he had done.

Except to Amber he would always be the rough diamond she broke her teeth on. Girls like this did not date the help.

Sam stepped back and chuckled as he tidied away the polishing kit.

'Relax, Amber. It takes a lot of hard work to become a journalist in today's newspaper business. I earned this new job in the London office. Besides, I don't need to trawl through my past history to score points with my editor. Frank Evans is far more interested in what you are doing in your life right now. Not many people retire at twenty-eight. That's bound to cause some interest.'

'And what about you, Sam? Are you interested in what I am doing in my life right now?'

He looked up into her face, which was suddenly calm, her gaze locked on him.

Was he interested? A wave of confusion and a hot, sweaty mixture of bittersweet memories surged through Sam. His breathing was hot and fast and for a fraction of a second he was very tempted to lean back and give her the full-on charm offensive and find out just what kind of woman Amber had become by being up close and personal—and nothing to do with his job.

Fool. Eyes on the prize.

'The only thing I am interested in is the promotion to the job I have been working towards for ten long years in the trenches. Sorry if that disappoints you, but there it is.'

'Ah—so your editor needs a story and you thought you could use our teenage connection to wangle the real truth from my lips. Tut, tut. What shameful tactics. And if I even hear the words "for old times' sake", I promise that I will pretend to cry my eyes out and sob all the way home to my good friend Saskia's house and my girl gang will be round with my legal team in an hour. And I will do it. Believe me.'

'Oh—cruel and unnecessary. I think I just cut myself on your need for revenge. Well, think again, because I have no intention on wandering down memory lane if I can avoid it.'

Just for a second her lips trembled and the vulnerability and tender emotion of the girl he used to know was there in front of him but, before he could explain, her lips flushed pink and she chuckled softly before answering.

'I'm pleased to hear it, because I have something of a business proposition to put to you. And it will make things a lot simpler if we can keep our relationship on a purely professional basis.'

'A business proposition? Well, there's a change. The last time we met your stepbrother and your mother were doing a fine job running your life. As I remember, you didn't have much of a business sense of your own back then.'

And the moment the words were out of his mouth Sam regretted them.

How did she do that?

He made his living out of talking to celebrities and teasing out their stories with charm and professionalism, but one look at Amber and he slotted right back into being an angsty teen showing off and saying ridiculous things. Trying to impress the girl he wanted.

Yes, Amber's mother had been furious when she found out that her musical prodigy of a daughter was sneaking out to see the chauffeur's son, but he didn't have to listen when she told him how a boy like him was going to hold her daughter back and ruin her career.

He was the one who'd taken the cheque Amber's mother had waved in front of him.

He was the one who'd marched out of Amber's eighteenth

birthday party alone, only to find a warm and receptive Petra waiting for him in the car park.

Maybe that was why it still smarted after all of these years? Because the young Sam had fallen for her mother's lies, just as she had planned he should. Because she'd been right. What hope did Amber have if she was trapped with a no-hoper like Sam Richards?

It did not excuse what he'd done. But at least her mother cared about what happened to her child. Unlike his mother.

Amber's head tilted to one side and she peered around his side to focus on the sports car that he had just been polishing before answering in the sweetest voice, 'Well, some of us have moved on in the last ten years.'

The silence between them was as rigid as steel and just as icy.

Then Amber shuffled forwards in his dad's chair and raised her eyebrows. 'Do you know what? I have changed my mind. Perhaps it was a mistake coming here after all. Best of luck with the new job and please say hello to your dad for me. Now, if you will excuse me, I have an appointment with the features editor at another newspaper in about an hour and I would hate to be late.'

She pushed herself to her feet and waved a couple of fingers in the air. 'See you around, Sam.'

And, without hesitating or looking back, Amber strolled towards the garage door on her wedge sandals, the skirt of her floaty dress waving back and forth over her perfect derrière as she headed out of his life, taking any chance of a career in London with her.

CHAPTER FOUR

'AREN'T YOU GOING to ask me what it feels like to finally work in that shiny glass office I used to drag you down to ogle every week?' Sam called after her. 'I would hate for you to stay awake at night wondering how I'm coping with being a real life reporter in the big city. Come on, Amber. Have you forgotten all those afternoons you spent listening to my grand plans to be a renowned journalist one day? I know that you're curious. Give me another five minutes to convince you to choose me instead of some other journalist to write your story.'

Amber slowed and looked back at Sam over one shoulder.

And her treacherous teenage heart skipped a beat and started disco dancing just at the sight of him.

Just for an instant the sound of her name on his lips took her right back to being seventeen again, when the highlight of her whole day, the moment she had dreamt about all night and thought about every second of the day, was hearing his voice and seeing Sam's face again. Even if it did mean sitting in the back of the limo and in dressing rooms around the country as her mother's unpaid assistant and general concert slave for hours on end.

It was worth it when Sam took her out for a pizza or a cola for the duration of the concert she had heard so many times she could play it herself note perfect.

She had adored him.

He had not changed that much. A little heavier around the shoulders and the waistline, perhaps, but not much. His smile had more laughter lines now and his boyish good looks had mellowed through handsome into something close to gorgeous. She was sorry to have missed the merely handsome stage. But, if she closed her eyes, his voice was the same boy she used to know.

And the charm? Oh, Lord, he had ramped up the charm to a level where she had no doubt that any female celebrity would be powerless to resist any question he put to them.

Sam had always had a physical presence that could reach out and grab her—no change there, but she had not expected to feel such a connection. Memories of the last time she came to this very garage flooded back. His ready laughter and constant good-natured teasing about watching that she didn't knock her head on the light fittings. The nudges, the touches, the kisses.

Until he betrayed her with one of her best friends on her eighteenth birthday. And the memories of the train wreck of the weeks that followed blotted out any happiness she might have had.

Amber turned back to face Sam and planted her left hand on her hip.

'Perhaps I am worried about all of those hidden tape recorders and video feeds which are capturing my every syllable at this very moment?'

He smiled one of those wide mouth, white teeth smiles and, in her weakened pre-dinner state, Amber had to stifle a groan. What was wrong with the man? Didn't Sam know that the only respectable thing for him to do was to have grown fat and ruined his teeth with sugary food? He had always been sexy and attractive in a rough-edged casual way, as relaxed in his body as she had been uncomfortable in her tall gangly skin. But the years had added the character lines to his face, which glowed with vitality and rugged health. Confidence and self-assurance were the best assets any man could have and Sam had them to spare.

'In this garage? No. You can say what you like. It's just between us. Same as it ever was.'

The breath caught in Amber's throat. Oh, Sam. Trust you to say exactly the wrong thing.

She flicked her hair back one-handed and covered up the bitter taste of so much disappointment with a dismissive choke. He must be desperate to go to such lengths for this interview. She had no idea how much journalists earned, but surely he didn't need the job that much?

Drat her curiosity.

Of course she remembered the way he used to talk about how he was going to work his way through journalism school at all of the top London newspapers and be the star investigative journalist. His name would be on the front page of the big broadsheet newspapers that his dad read in the car as he waited for his clients to finish their meetings or fancy events.

Maybe that was it?

Maybe he was still hungry for the success that had eluded him. And this interview would take him up another rung in that long and rickety ladder to the front page.

She was a celebrity that he wanted to interview for his paper to win the extra points he needed for the big prize. And the bigger the story the more gold stars went onto his score sheet.

And that was all. Nothing personal. He had walked—no, he had *run* away from her at the first opportunity to make his precious dream of becoming a professional journalist a reality.

She did not owe him a thing.

'Same as it ever was? In your dreams,' she muttered under her breath, just loud enough for him to hear. 'That editor of yours must really be putting the pressure on if you're resorting to that line.'

Sam shrugged off her jibe but looked away and pretended to tidy up the toolbox on the bench for a second before his gaze snapped back onto her face.

'What can I say? Unlike some people, I need the job.' Then he laughed out loud. 'You always had style, Amber, but retiring at twenty-eight? That takes a different kind of chutzpah. I admire that.'

He stepped forward towards her and nodded towards her arm, his eyes narrowed and his jaw loose. 'Is it your wrist? I know you said that it was a clean break, but...'

'No,' she whispered. 'It's nothing to do with my wrist.'

'I am glad to hear it. Then how about the other rumours? A lot of people think that you are using this announcement to start a kind of bidding war between rival orchestras around the world. Publicity stunts like this have been done before.'

'Not by me. I won't be making a comeback as a concert pianist. Or at least I don't plan to.'

Amber swallowed down her unease, reluctant to let Sam see that she was still uncertain about where her life would take her.

She had made her decision to retire while recovering in hospital and she'd imagined that a simple press statement would be the easiest way to close out that part of her life. Her agent was not happy, of course—but he had other talent on his books and a steady income from her records and other contracts—she was still valuable to him.

But the hard implications were still there on the horizon, niggling at her.

Music had been her life for so long that just the thought of never performing in public again was so new that it still ruffled her. Playing the piano had been the one thing that she did well. The one and only way that she knew to earn her mother's praise.

Of course Julia Swan would have loved her daughter to choose the violin and follow in her footsteps, but it soon became obvious that little Amber had no talent for any other instrument apart from the piano.

For a girl who was moving from one home to another, one school to another, one temporary stepdad to another, music had been one of the few constants in her life. Piano practice was the perfect excuse to avoid tedious evenings with her mother and whatever male friend or violin buff she was dating at the time.

The piano was her escape. Her refuge. It was where she could plough her love and devotion and all of the passion that was missing in her life with her bitter and demanding, needy and man-hunting mother.

So she had worked and worked, then worked harder to overcome her technical problems and excel. It was her outlet for the pain, the suppressed anger. All of it. And nobody knew just how much pain she was in.

Because there was one thing that her mother never understood—and still did not understand, even when she had tried to explain at the hospital. And then in the endless texts and emails and pleading late night phone calls begging her to reconsider and sometimes challenging her decision to retire.

Amber had always played for the joy in the music.

She was not an artist like her mother, who demanded validation and adoration. She just loved the music and wanted to immerse herself in the emotional power of it.

And Sam Richards was the only other person on this planet who had ever understood that without her having to explain it.

Until this moment she had thought that connection between them would fade with the years they had spent apart.

Wrong.

Sam was looking at her with that intense gaze that used to make her shiver with delight and anticipation of the time that they would spend together and, just for a second, her will faltered.

Maybe this was not such a good idea?

Getting her own back on Sam had seemed a perfectly logical thing to do back in the penthouse, but here in the garage which was as familiar as her own apartment, suddenly the whole idea seemed pathetic and insulting to both of them. She had made plenty of poor decisions over the past few years—surely she could forgive Sam the mistakes he had made as a teenager desperate to improve his life?

Amber opened her mouth and was just about to make an excuse when Sam tilted his head and rubbed his chin before asking, 'I suppose this is about the money?'

And there it was. Like a slap across the face.

Her lower lip froze but she managed a thin smile. 'Are you talking about the blood money you took from my mother to leave me alone and get out of London? To start your new career, of course.'

His mouth twisted and faltered. 'Actually, I was thinking more about the generous donation the paper will be contributing to your favourite charity. Although I should imagine that we are not the only ones to offer you something for your time. Not that you need the money, of course. Or the publicity.'

'You don't think that I need publicity?'

'Come on, Amber, your face was on billboards and the sides of buses, your last CD went into the top ten classical music charts and you have set new records for the number of followers you have on the social media sites. Publicity is not your problem.'

'It goes with the job—I am in showbiz. Correction. Was in showbiz. That doesn't interest me any longer.'

'Okay then. So why are you even talking to me about doing an interview? Seeing as you don't need the publicity.'

'Logistics. I thought that the press would get bored after a couple of weeks and move onto the next musician. Wrong! I was almost mobbed outside the record company this morning. So it makes sense to do one comprehensive interview and get it over with.'

She waved one hand in the air. 'One interview. One journalist.'

Sam shoved his hands deep into the pockets of his jeans, his casual smile replaced by unease.

'Wait a minute. Are you offering me an exclusive?' he asked. 'What's the catch?'

'Oh, how suspicious you are. Well. As it happens, I might be willing to give you that interview.' She cleared her throat and tilted her head, well aware that she had his full attention. 'But there are a few conditions we need to agree on before I talk on the record.'

'Conditions. This sounds like the catch part.'

'I prefer to think of them as more of a trade. You do something for me, I do something for you. And, from what I have seen so far, you might find some of them rather challenging. Still interested?'

'Ah. Now we have it. You know you have the upper hand so you decided to come down here to gloat?'

'Gloat? Do you really think I would do that?' she repeated, her words catching at the back of her throat. Was that how he thought of her? As some spoiled girl who had come to impress him with her list of achievements?

'I haven't changed that much, Sam. We've both done what we set out to do. You need an interview and I have a few things I need doing which you might be able to help me with. It's as simple as that.'

'Simple? Nothing about you was ever simple, Amber.'

Sam leaned back against the workbench and stretched out his long arms either side of him so that his biceps strained against the fabric of his T-shirt across his chest and arms. The sinewy boy she had known had been replaced by a man who knew his power and had no problem using it to get his way.

And the tingle of that intense gaze sent the old shivers down the back of her legs and there was absolutely nothing she could do to stop them. Her heart started thumping and she knew that her neck was already turning a lovely shade of bright red as his gaze scanned her face.

She could blame it on the hot May sunshine outside the garage door, but who was she trying to kid?

What had Kate said about Petra? That she had bedazzled Sam that night? Well, the Sam who was scanning her body was quite capable of doing his own bedazzling these days.

Sam had been the first boy who had ever given her the tingles and there had only been two other men in her life. All god-handsome, all rugged and driven and all as far removed from the world of music and orchestral performance venues as it was possible to imagine.

And every single one of them had swept her off her feet and into their world without giving her time to even think about what she was doing or whether the relationship had a chance. Little wonder that she had ended up alone and in tears, bewildered and bereft, wondering what had just happened and why.

But one thing was perfectly clear. Sam had been the first, and there was no way that she was going to go through that pain again, just to score a few points on the payback scoreboard.

Decision time.

If she was going to do this, she needed to do it now, and put the tingles down to past stupidity. Or she could turn around and run as fast as she could back to the penthouse and lock the door tight behind her. Just as her kind friends thought that she should. Just as she would have done only a few months earlier, before her life had changed.

'I hadn't planned to give any more interviews after the press release. That part of my life is over,' she said, her chin tilted up. 'But I have a few things you could help me with and you need this interview to impress your editor and make your mark in the London office. Am I getting warm?'

He shrugged and tried to look casual. But there was just that small twitch at the side of his mouth which he used to have when things were difficult at home and he didn't want to talk about it. 'Warm enough.'

'Warm? If I was any hotter I would be on fire. If I go to another paper, you will be waiting on the pavement for movie stars to stagger out from showbiz parties wearing their underpants as hats.'

Sam's hands gripped onto the bench so tightly that his knuckles started to turn white. 'Ah. Now I am beginning to understand. You want to see me suffer.'

Amber winced and gave a small shoulder shrug. 'You walked out on me and broke my heart. So yes, it would be a shame to miss the opportunity for some retribution. And I am not in the least bit ashamed.' She took a breath. 'But that was a long time ago, Sam. And I am keen to put that away in a box labelled "done and dusted". I think this will help me do that.'

Sam closed his eyes and shook his head from side to side before blinking awake and laughing out loud. 'Done and dusted, eh? I am almost frightened to ask what form my punishment is going to take. But please, do continue, let's get it over with.'

He stood to maximum height, pushed his shoulders back and lifted his chin. 'Hit me.'

Amber strolled into the garage and focused her attention on the sports car, her fingertips lingering on the old leather seats, her face burning with awareness that Sam's gaze was still locked onto her. 'I want to get this done as soon as I can, but time is tight. I'm redecorating my apartment and the girls want to celebrate my birthday this week.'

She almost turned around at the sound of Sam's sharp intake of breath. 'May eighteenth. Hard to forget.'

Amber flung her head up and twisted around at the waist, ready with a cutting remark, but bit it back when she saw the look on Sam's face was one of sadness and regret.

His lips twitched for a second before he replied. 'Busy week. No problem. Just give me your email address and I can send over some questions so you can work on them when you have time.'

'Email questions? Oh, no. This interview has to be in person.'

Sam coughed twice. 'Are you always so awkward?'

She tilted her head slightly to one side before replying. 'No. Just with you.'

He laughed out loud and planted a fist on each hip. 'Don't try and kid me, girl. You have been planning this for ages and are having way too much fun teasing this out.' He flicked his chin in her direction. 'You could have asked your agent to make the call and organised the interview over the phone. But that wouldn't have been nearly so satisfying, would it?'

He waved her spluttering away. 'And I understand that perfectly. Really. I do. I made a horrible mistake and treated you badly, and now you're going to make me pay.'

Then his stance softened and his gaze darted from side to side. 'I'm not proud of what happened the last time we met. Far from it. But that was ten years ago and we're different people now. At least I am. I'm not sure about you.'

'What do you mean?'

'You never had a vindictive thought in your life, Amber DuBois. So why don't you just take me through that list of little things you want me to help you with and we can get this over and done with, and we can put the past behind us?'

Amber inhaled slowly and turned to face Sam, her head tilted slightly to one side, and she carefully pushed the slip of paper deeper into the heart-shaped pocket of her dress.

'What makes you think I have a list?' she asked in the best innocent and surprised voice she could muster at short notice.

'Amber. You always had a list. For everything. A list of things to do that day, a list of how long you practised that week. You are a listy type of person and people don't change that much. So it makes sense for you to have a list of all the things I am going to have to do in exchange for one interview.'

He shot her a glance which made her eyes narrow. Why did he have to remember that small detail, of all things? There was no way she could talk him through her list now.

'I prefer to think of them as challenges. But you are right about one thing—I have thought about what you could possibly give me in exchange for an exclusive, and you can take that smirk off your face right now. You would not be so lucky. So I came up with a new approach.'

She crossed the space between them until her face was only inches away from his and licked her lips before speaking.

'Look, Sam,' she said in low, calm voice as her gaze locked onto his. 'I know people are interested in why I decided to retire when I did, but my reasons are very personal and very close to my heart.' She took a breath and swallowed before rolling her shoulders back a little. 'It would be very easy for a reporter to do a hatchet job with some crazy headline just to sell more papers. So…I need to know that I can trust the journalist I go for to give me a fair hearing.'

'That's not going to be easy,' he replied in a voice which sang with resignation and disappointment.

'I know. This is why you are going to have to prove to me

that you are the right man for the job before I say a word on the record.'

His eyebrows went skywards. 'Any ideas on how I do that?'

'Oh, yes,' she sniffed. 'You are going to have to pass an audition before I give you the job. You see, this week is crazily busy and my wrist is a problem. So I need someone to be my Man Friday for the next few days. Unpaid, of course, and you provide your own uniform. But all refreshments are provided by the management. And I just know how much Saskia and Kate are looking forward to having you around the place.'

'A Man Friday,' Sam repeated, very, very slowly. 'So, basically, I have to be your man slave for the next week before you'll even think about giving me the interview?'

Amber picked her business card out of her dress pocket with two fingers, gave Sam her sweetest camera-ready smile and looked deep into his startled eyes as she held the card high in the air. 'Well, it's good to know that your powers of deductive reasoning are as sharp as ever. The audition starts at my apartment at ten tomorrow morning. Oh—and just to make it a little more interesting, I'll have a new challenge for you every day. See you there, Sam. If you are man enough to accept the challenge.'

The air bristled with tension for all of ten seconds. Then Sam took two powerful steps forward, his brows low and dark-eyed, his legs moving from the hips in one smooth movement. Driven. Powerful.

And, before Amber had a chance to complain or slip away, Sam splayed one hand onto her hip and drew her closer to him. Hip to hip.

Amber's breath caught in her throat as his long clever fingers pressed against the thin silk of her dress as though it was not there. She could feel his hot breath on her face as she inhaled a scent that more than anything else she had seen or experienced today whipped her right back to being held in

Sam's arms. It was car oil, polish, man sweat, dust and ambition and all Sam. And it was totally, totally intoxicating.

His gaze locked onto her eyes. Holding her transfixed.

'Bambi, I am man enough for anything that you have to
offer me,' Sam whispered in a voice which was almost trembling with intensity, one corner of his mouth turned up into a
cheeky grin as though he knew precisely what effect he was
having on her blood pressure. And there was not one thing
she could do about it.

Then, just like that, he stepped back and released her, and
it took a lot to stay upright.

And then he winked at her.

'See ya tomorrow—' he smiled with a casual lilt in his
voice '—looking forward to it.'

CHAPTER FIVE

'NO MOTHER. SERIOUSLY. I don't need another expert medical opinion. Every specialist I have seen recommends six months' recovery time. Yes, I am sure your friend in Miami is excellent but I am not pushing my wrist by trying to practice before it is ready.'

Amber closed her eyes and gave her virtuoso violinist mother two more minutes of ranting about how foolish she was to throw away her career before interrupting. 'Mum, I love you but I have to go. Have a great cruise. Bye.'

Amber closed the call, strolled over to the railing of her penthouse apartment and looked out over London. The silvery River Thames cut a wide ribbon of glistening water through the towering office blocks of glass and exposed metal that clung to the riverbanks. Peeking out between the modern architectural wonders were the spires and domes of ancient churches and imposing carved stone buildings that had once been the highlights of the London landscape.

Even five storeys up, the hustle and bustle of traffic noise and building work drifted up to the penthouse, creating the background soundtrack to her view of modern city life.

Everywhere she looked she saw life and energy and the relentless drive for prosperity and wealth. Investment bankers, city traders and financial analysts jostled on the streets below her on the way to their computer trading desks. Time was money.

The contrast to the tiny beachside orphanage in Kerala where Parvita was celebrating her wedding could not be greater.

The seaside village where the girls' orphanage was based had running water and electricity—most of the time.

She would love to go back and see them again. *One day.* When she was not so terrified of catching another life-threatening infection.

A cold shiver ran across Amber's shoulders and she pulled her cashmere tighter across the front of her chest.

Heath and her mother were right about one thing. *As always.* Even if she wasn't scared, she *could* raise more income for the orphanage by staying in London or Boston or Miami and fund-raising than risk returning to Kerala, where she had caught meningitis only a few months earlier.

Now all she had to do was come up with a way of doing precisely that.

Not by playing the piano. That was for sure.

No matter how much her mother nagged her to reconsider and plan a comeback concert tour. A year ago she might have gone along with it and started rigorous training but that part of her life was over now.

Wiped away by meningitis and a few months of enforced bed rest when she had to ask some hard questions about the life she was living and how she intended to spend it in the future.

Amber closed her eyes and inhaled and exhaled slowly a couple of times. *No going back, girl. No going back. Only forward. This was her new start. Her new beginning.*

The sun was warm on her face and when she opened her eyes the first thing she saw was the braided cord bracelet that

Parvita had made and woven onto her right wrist that last day she was at the orphanage.

She was so lucky.

Heath and her mother loved her and that was what she had to focus on. Not their nagging. She would go back to Boston and start work with the fund-raising committee for Parvita. Benefit concerts were always popular and between her mother and their network of professional musicians they could pull together some top name soloists who could raise thousands for the charity.

This was her chance to do something remarkable. And she was going to grab hold of it with both hands and cling on tight, no matter how bumpy the road ahead was.

First hurdle? Talking to Sam.

Amber glanced at her wristwatch and a fluttering sensation of apprehension blended with excitement bubbled up from deep inside. In another place and time she might have said that the thought of seeing him again face to face was making her nervous. That was totally ridiculous. This was her space and he was here to help her out, as he had promised.

This was not the time to get stage fright.

She was an idiot.

They had agreed to make a trade. His time in exchange for one interview. Nothing more. *What else could there be?*

Her thoughts were interrupted by a petite bundle of energy.

'One good thing came out of that whole school reunion fiasco.' Kate laughed and threw her arms around Amber's waist. 'The three of us haven't been in the same city at the same time for far too many years. And that is a disgrace. So all hail school reunions.'

Amber laughed out loud and stepped back to clink her mug of coffee against Kate's. 'With you on that. I still cannot believe that it's the middle of May already. April was just a blur.'

Kate groaned and slumped into the patio chair facing

Amber. 'Tell me about it. London might be suffering from the economic recession but bespoke tailoring is booming and I have never been so busy. It's great. Really great. But wow, is it exhausting.'

'Well, here is something to keep you going.' Saskia Elwood came out from Amber's penthouse apartment with a tray of the most delicious-looking bite-sized snacks, which she wafted in front of Amber. 'Test samples for your birthday party. I need you to taste them all and tell me which ones you like best.'

Kate half rose out of her chair. 'Hey, don't I get to try them too? I could scoff the lot. And breakfast was hours ago.'

'You're next but the birthday girl has first pick. Besides, she needs fattening up a bit. What did they feed you in that hospital, anyway? I can't have you coming to my dining room looking all pale and scrawny.'

Amber munched away on a mini disc of bacon and herb pizza and made humming sounds of appreciation before speaking between bites. 'No appetite. It was so hot and I was asleep most of the time. And the food certainly wasn't as good as this. These are fantastic.'

'Thought you would like it and there are lots more to come. So tuck in.'

Kate snatched a tiny prawn mayo sandwich and chewed it down in one huge bite before sighing in pleasure. 'Oh, that is so good. Amber DuBois, it was a genius idea to have your birthday party at Saskia's house.'

'It was the very least I could do. Ten years is a long time and all three of us have come a long way,' Amber replied and raised her coffee as a toast. 'I missed you both so much. To the goddesses.'

'The goddesses,' Kate and Saskia echoed and all three of them settled back in their chairs in the sunshine with the tray of snacks between them, hot Italian blend coffee and the sound of the city way below to break up the contented sighs.

'So what have you been up to, Amber?' Saskia asked, her eyes shielded with a hand as she nibbled on a fresh cream profiterole drizzled with chocolate sauce. 'It must get you down when you're unable to practise for hours like you usually do.'

Amber waved her right arm in the air and turned the plaster cast covering her wrist from side to side. 'Frustrating more than anything, but the exercises are keeping my fingers working and I have to get used to being one handed for a few more weeks. Only that isn't the problem. There is something missing and somehow...' Then she gave a chuckle and shook her head. 'Oh, ignore me. I'm just being silly.'

'Oh, no, you don't,' Saskia said in a low voice. 'We can tell that there is something bothering you. And you know that we're not going to let it drop until you tell us what the problem is. So come on. Spill. Out with it.'

Amber focused her gaze on the terrace. Bright flowering plants and conifers spilled out of colourful planters in front of a panoramic view across the London city skyline.

'Yesterday I was feeling down in the dumps so I pulled out my favourite music scores. If I have a spare hour or two on tour I can usually visualise the performance in my head and it is the one thing that is always guaranteed to cheer me up and have me bouncing with excitement.'

She paused and sighed low and slow. 'But not this time. I didn't feel a thing. There was nothing that made me want to tear off this plaster cast and play. *Seriously.* It's as though all of my passion for the music has gone out of the window.'

She paused and looked from Saskia to Kate and then back to Saskia again. 'And that's scary, girls. I don't know how to do anything else.'

The silence echoed between the three of them before Kate put her mug down on the metal mesh table with a dramatic thud.

'Amber? Sweetie? It might have something to do with the fact that you have just spent months in hospital recovering from the infection you caught in India. And yes, I know that it is still our secret. We won't tell anyone. But you have to give yourself time to recover and get your mojo back. Maybe even be kind to yourself and let your body heal, instead of running from place to place at top speed. How about that for a crazy idea?'

Amber blew out long and slow. 'You're right. This is the first time in years that I have been in London long enough to take stock. I just feel that I am lost and drifting on my own. Again.'

Saskia slid over to the end of Amber's lounger and wrapped her fingers around her arm. 'No, you're not. You will always have a home at Elwood House. And don't you dare forget that.'

Amber smiled into the faces of her two best friends in the world. Friends who had somehow got pushed lower and lower on her priority list over the past few years, and yet they were the very people who had come running the first time she asked.

'I don't know what I did to deserve you two. Thanks. It means a lot. But I won't put you out too much.'

'Decision made, young lady,' Saskia said in a jokey serious voice. 'You are coming to stay with me at Elwood House as my birthday present, and you are going to be cosseted, whether you like it or not.'

'Oh, that sounds good,' Kate said, and snuggled back further onto the soft cushion of the patio lounger. 'Can I come over and be cosseted in exchange for making curtains and cushions? I could use a good cosset.'

'You and your needlework skills are welcome any time.'

Saskia laughed and gestured towards Amber with her head. 'I'm going to need some help keeping this one from wearing herself out getting ready for her birthday party.'

Amber dropped her head back and closed her eyes as bright warm sunshine broke through the light cloud cover. Then she turned back to face Saskia and Kate, who were looking at her. 'It's going to be like old times. The three of us, camped out at Elwood House. But at least this time I'm not running away from home to spite my mother by eloping with Sam Richards.'

Saskia peered at her through narrowed eyes. 'Ah, yes. Sam.' She nodded. 'Were you okay? With seeing him again? Because I still cannot believe that you went there on your own.'

'Ah. So you think I would be safe from the evil clutches of the teenage boy who broke my heart and betrayed me with one of my best friends if I stayed here in my ivory tower penthouse like a fairy tale princess waiting to be rescued.'

She laughed and said with a snort, 'Not a chance, gorgeous. I refuse to be turned into some kind of recluse just because the press want to know why I decided to retire. Besides, I've been working with reporters like Sam Richards for years. He doesn't bother me.'

Kate shuffled to the edge of her seat, her bottom jiggling with excitement while Saskia just chuckled softly to herself. 'Really?'

Amber pushed out her famous moisture lipstick slicked lips. 'Oh, yes. My musician friend Parvita runs a wonderful charity in India who could certainly use the fee, only…' she sighed with a slight quiver in her voice and Saskia and Kate instantly leant closer towards her '…I've had enough of that circus who think that they can make up any kind of story and get away with it. I have helped the media sell newspapers and magazines for the last ten years. And now I'm done with it.

I am not playing that game any more. And they are going to have to get used to the idea. This time I call the shots.'

Kate's eyebrows lifted. 'I knew it! You're going to charge them megabucks for a full page nude shot with you sitting at a white grand piano with only discreet pieces of sheet music and fabulous jewels to cover your modesty? That could be fun.'

Amber and Saskia both turned and stared at Kate in silence.

'What? So I have a vivid imagination?' Kate shrugged.

Amber frowned at Kate for a moment and then blinked. 'Not exactly what I had in mind and no, it wouldn't be fun, not even for the megabucks. But do you know what? The more I thought about it, the more I got to thinking that maybe Sam does have something we can trade with after all.'

Kate drew back and squinted at her suspiciously. 'Go on.'

'I need to get the past off my back. Parvita's charity and my birthday party are going to take all of my time and energy, and the last thing I need is a troop of paparazzi making my life even more of a nightmare.'

'You really are serious about retiring?'

'Totally,' Amber replied and smiled at Saskia. 'But talking to you two has reminded me where my real priorities lie.' And then she reached out and squeezed Saskia's hand for a second. 'Your aunt Margot gave me a sanctuary at Elwood House, and I haven't forgotten it. I owe you. This is why I'm thinking of doing something rather rash.'

'What do you mean by rash?' Saskia asked in her low, calm, gentle voice.

Amber took a long drink of coffee, well aware that both of her friends were waiting for her to speak.

'When you told me all about your plans to convert Elwood House into a private meeting and dining venue I was amazed that we hadn't thought about it before. Your dining room is stunning.'

Her voice drifted away dreamily. 'I gave my first piano re-cital in that house. I'll never forget it. The crystal chandeliers. The flickering firelight. It was magical. This is why I want to do as much as I can to help make Elwood House a success.'

Saskia shook her head. 'You have already invited half the fashion models in London, their agents, their posh friends and the music industry to your birthday party this week. I couldn't ask for better publicity.'

'And yet you still don't have a decent website or booking system or photo gallery to showcase the house. And that. Is where I come in. And you can stop shaking your head; I know that you won't take my money. So I am going to ask a professional photographer to come over and put together your full marketing package and organise the website. Free. Gratis. Won't cost you a penny.'

'Really?' Saskia replied and lifted her mug towards Amber in a toast. 'That's fantastic. Is he one of your fashion pals?'

Amber licked her lips and took a sip of water before an-swering.

'Not exactly. I think Sam Richards is calling himself a photojournalist these days. More tarts, anyone?'

Amber paused and looked at Kate, who was groaning with her head in her hands. 'Don't worry about Sam. He knows that he has to be on his very best behaviour if he has any chance of that interview. Saskia needs those photos and Sam seems to know which end of a camera to point. And no, I haven't for-given him yet. Think of this as part of the payback. So please don't kill him. At least not in front of the party guests. Saskia does not want bloodstains on her nice carpet.'

The words had barely left Amber's mouth and the shouts were still ringing in her ears when the oven timer bell rang and Kate shook her head slowly from side to side before div-ing back into the kitchen to get fresh supplies of snacks.

'Don't burn your mouth by eating them straight out of the

oven,' Saskia called out to Kate, but then her mouth relaxed into a half smile. 'Payback. I suppose that is one way of looking at it and I have no doubt that he would do a good job. But sheesh, Amber. I am worried for you.'

Amber was just about to rattle off a casual throwaway remark, but instead she paused before answering one of her few real friends in the world. The old Amber would have laughed off her friend's concern with a flippant gesture as some sort of silly joke, but the new Amber was slowly getting used to opening up to people she loved and trusted. 'You always did like Sam, didn't you?'

Saskia gave a brisk nod. 'I suppose so. Not in any sort of romantic way, of course, nothing like that, but yes, I did. His dad had driven my aunt Margot around for years and sometimes he brought Sam along with him. I suppose that's why I suggested that your mum use his limo service to take her to venues.'

Saskia lifted one hand. 'I think I might even have introduced you. So blame me for what happened. But yes, I thought he was okay.' Her brow squeezed together. 'Why do you ask me that now?'

'Because it was so weird. Over the years I sometimes imagined what I would say if I met up with Sam unexpectedly at some airport or hotel, or if he came to one of my performances. But when I saw him yesterday? All those clever, witty put-downs just fled. He was still the same Sam, working in his dad's garage. And I was right back to feeling like a gawky, awkward, six feet tall seventeen-year-old with big feet who was trying to sound all grown-up and clever around this handsome, streetwise city boy.'

Amber looked up at Saskia and shrugged. 'I trusted him then and he let me down just when I needed him the most. How do I know that I can trust him now? The orphanage in India is too important to me to see the real message buried under some big celebrity exposé which is around the world in seconds. Can you imagine the headlines? "Brave Bambi DuBois cheats death from meningitis. Career in tatters." Oh, they would love that.'

'Which is why you are taking control. Maybe there is too much history between the two of you for him to be objective. But we agreed that we would give him an audition for the job, and that is what we are going to do. Okay?'

'Absolutely okay. If he can stand it, then so can I.'

'Right. And on the way you can make sure that Sam gets the message that you have moved on to even more handsome and successful boyfriends. But fear not. Kate and I will make sure that we rub it in at regular intervals that he made a horrible mistake when he let you go and you are so totally over him.'

'Saskia! I didn't say anything about being cruel. And as for being over him? Sam only had to smile at me yesterday and I got the tingles from head to toe. Which is so ridiculous I can hardly admit it. The last time that happened I ended up on a plane to Kathmandu with a suitcase full of evening wear and piano music and no clue about what I was going to do when I got there.'

'Mark the mountaineer?'

Amber nodded. 'And three years before that it was Rico. Racing car driver. One kiss on the cheek and a cuddle in the pits and I smelt of diesel fumes for months.'

Amber sighed dramatically and slumped back. 'I am a hopeless case and I know it. I mean. *A mountaineer*? What was I thinking? I got the tingles and that was that.' She blinked a couple of times. 'The only scientific explanation is that I was cursed at birth. You know how it goes. The good fairy godmother blesses me with some musical talent, and the evil one says, "Oh, that's sweet, but in exchange you are going to fall for men who will only ever be interested in their obsession. So you had better get used to the idea.'"

'You weren't thinking. You were taking a chance on love with remarkable men,' Saskia replied wistfully. 'You know. Not all of us have had a chance to be cuddled by racing car drivers or kissed at Everest base camp. I envy you for having the courage to take that risk.'

Amber instantly sat up and wrapped her arm around Saskia's shoulder. 'You'll meet someone—I'm sure of it. Especially now you're opening up Elwood House. Think of all the handsome executives who will be queuing up to sample your tasty treats.'

'From your lips… But in the meantime, where does that leave our Sam Richards? Because, to me, this little plan of ours could go in one of two ways. Either you keep your cool and freeze out his tingle power so that you can finally get Sam out of your system and your life. Or…'

Saskia smiled and pushed out her lips. 'You might be tempted to try out the new and improved version to see if the quality of those tingles has improved over the years. And don't look at me like that. It's a distinct possibility. Dangerous, scary and not very clever, but a possibility…and that worries me, Amber. I know how much you cared about Sam. I was there, remember? I don't want to see you running back to Elwood House in tears over Sam Richards.'

'Sam?' came a squeaky voice from the bedroom and a second later its owner appeared on the patio and she was not carrying more snacks.

Kate was wearing a huge fascinator in the shape of a red tropical flower on her head and several strings of huge beads cascaded below bundles of silk scarves. 'You don't have time to think about boys, woman!'

Kate gestured with her head towards the dressing room, which had long since given up any hope of being used as a second bedroom. 'Amber DuBois, you are officially one of the worst hoarders I have ever seen. And I make clothes for women who are still wearing their mother's hats. You have been crushing stuff into those cupboards for years. I am frightened to open those wardrobes in fear of avalanche.'

Amber waved one slender hand in the air. 'I know. I spent most of yesterday trying to root out casual day clothes to wear and ended up going to the shops. I have got so used to just dumping my stuff here that when I want something I cannot find it.'

Amber frowned and pushed her lower lip out. 'Is it normal to have more performance dresses than pants? I love dressing up for my audiences, but I find it so hard to refuse when designers start giving me free gorgeous things to wear. Most of those dresses have only had to survive one recital. It does seem a shame to just stash them until they gather dust. Unless, of course…'

She grinned and looked from side to side. 'Ladies. I have been looking for some way of raising funds. What do you say to a spot of dressing up in the name of decluttering? I am talking Internet auctions and second-hand designer shops.' A wide grin creased her face as she was practically deafened by shrieks from Saskia and Kate. 'I'll take those screams as a yes. Right. Then let's get started on those ball gowns. But girls—there is one condition. You do not touch the sacred shoes. Okay? Okay. Let's do it. I'll race you.'

CHAPTER SIX

SAM RICHARDS LEANT against the back wall of the elevator, propped his camera bag against his foot and crossed his arms as he enjoyed the view.

Two tall, very slender brunettes dressed from head to toe in black had rushed in at the last minute from the cream and caramel marble reception area to Amber's apartment building, gushing thanks and flooding the space with giggling, floral perfume and an empty garment rail which took up the whole width of the elevator. Judging by their sideways glances, indiscreet nudging and body language, they were not too unhappy with being crushed into the space with him, and any other time and place he might have started chatting and enjoying their company.

But not today.

His morning had already got off to a poor start when his dad had phoned from France saying that he was going to stay on a few more days because for once the weather in the Alps was perfect for a spot of touring.

Perhaps it was just as well. His dad had not exactly been sympathetic when Sam had told him about Amber's little scheme. In fact he had laughed his head off and told him to behave himself.

As if he had a choice.

Sam pressed his hands flat against the cool surface of the elevator wall.

Amber had the upper hand and he was going to have to go with it, but it didn't mean to say that he liked it. One. Little. Bit. He had stopped being at other people's beck and call the day he'd left London and there was no way he was going to step into the role of Amber's fool and like it.

But he would get through it and move on. He could survive being pulled back into Amber's high class life as a diva for a few days.

If she could stand it—then so could he.

Sam inhaled the perfumed air, which was suddenly overheated and cloying. He had no interest in this world of fashion and celebrity—he never had. The A-list party and clubbing circuit had long lost their appeal for him. It was his job and he worked hard to create something interesting and new out of the same old shallow gossip and the relentless need for fame and riches fuelled by the public obsession for celebrity—an obsession he helped to foster, whether he liked that fact or not.

Past tense. He had paid his dues and earned the right to sit behind that editor's desk, doing the job he had been trained for. And he wasn't going to let that slip away from him without a fight.

He had come a long way from the raw teenager with a fire in his belly that Amber had known.

Man enough for the job? Oh, yes, he was man enough for the job all right.

Even if he had no clue what the actual job was. Her text message had asked him to bring his camera bag and a screwdriver over and they were all the clues she had given him.

Sam rolled his shoulders back as the elevator slowed and the girls starting fidgeting with the clothes rail.

The elevator doors slid open on the floor number Amber had given him but, before he could stride forward with his bag, the girls swept out into the wide corridor of pale wood and pastel colours.

Interesting.

Unless, of course...

With a tiny shoulder shrug Sam slowly followed the girls towards the penthouse apartment. Lively disco dance music drifted out through an open door towards him, the beat in perfect tune with the rattle of their high heels on the fine wooden floor.

Disco music? If this was Amber's place, she must be out shopping for the morning. The only music Amber DuBois liked was written by men with quill pens and dipping ink hundreds of years ago.

The girls rolled the garment rail into the apartment, waved at someone inside, then swept back past Sam out into the hallway, arm in arm in a flutter of perfume and girly giggles.

He paused for a second to admire them, then turned to face the door.

This was it. Show time. He took a deep breath, pushed the door open another few inches, stepped inside the apartment and instantly went into sensory overload.

What looked like the entire contents of a large fashion boutique was scattered over every surface in the living room. Handbags, shoes, hats and assorted female fripperies were draped across sofas, chairs and tables in a wild riot of colours and patterns, illuminated by the daylight streaming in from the floor to ceiling patio doors at the other end of the room.

His first reaction was to step back into the corridor and call the whole thing off. Right then and there. Apparently there were some men who enjoyed going clothes shopping with their wives and girlfriends. He had never understood how they could do that. There was probably medication for that kind of mental self-affliction.

He had never done that kind of crazy and he had no intention of starting now.

But he couldn't leave. And she knew it. Which meant that Amber had to be here to witness the payback in person.

Time to get this over with.

Sam sniffed, pushed his shoulders back, stashed his bag behind the sofa so that it was out of the mayhem and by stepping over the entire contents of a luggage department, he wound his way through the obstacle course that was the corridor towards the source of the disco music.

He had been on racing circuits which had fewer chicanes than this room.

Sam paused at the open bedroom door and leant casually on the door frame, his arms crossed.

It was a long, wide room but surprisingly simply furnished with a large bed with an ivory satin quilt, a small sofa covered in a shiny cream fabric with flights of butterflies painted on it and a wide dressing table next to more patio doors.

One complete wall was covered with a floor to ceiling mirror.

And standing in front of the mirror were three girls he had last seen together at Amber's eighteenth birthday party, what felt like a lifetime ago.

Amber, Saskia and Kate were wearing lemon-yellow over-sized T-shirts with the words 'ALL SIZES' printed on them in large black letters. Kate was in the middle, moving her hips from side to side and jiggling along to the disco music and holding a hairbrush to her mouth as a microphone. Saskia and Amber were her backup singers. Kate could not be more than five feet four inches tall in heels, Saskia was a few inches taller in flat shoes and Amber—Amber had been six feet tall aged sixteen.

It stunned him to realise that he could recognise Amber's voice so easily. She could sing like an angel and often had at

Christmas concerts and birthday parties. Kate was the best singer in their little schoolgirl clique so Amber had left her to it and stayed on the keyboard, but she had such a sweet, clear voice. He had missed that voice. And whether he liked it or not, he had missed the sound of Amber whispering his name as she clung on to him with her arms looped around his neck.

Sam pressed back against the door frame.

A memory of those same three girls wearing those same yellow T-shirts at Margot Elwood's house came drifting back. It was someone's birthday party and the girls had put together a little musical routine for Saskia's aunt and Amber had asked Sam to join in the fun. Strange. He had not thought about Elwood House in years.

These three girls looked the same—but he knew that they had all changed more than he could have imagined. But these three girls? In those T-shirts? It was a blast from a happier time when they all had such wonderful dreams and aspirations about what they were going to do with their lives.

This was a bad time to decide to become sentimental. Time to get this started.

He banged hard on the door with the back of his knuckles and called out in a loud voice, 'Is the lady of the house at home? The help has arrived.'

They were so intent on singing along to the words of some pop tune from the nineteen nineties that it was a few seconds before Saskia even glanced in his direction.

She instantly stopped dancing, put down her can of hairspray microphone and nudged Amber in the ribs before replying, 'Hi, Sam. Good to see you.'

'Hey. We were just getting to the chorus,' Kate complained, then turned towards him and planted a fist on each hip and tutted loudly, but Sam hardly looked at the support band.

His whole attention was focused on the girl who was peeking out at him over the top of Kate's head.

In contrast to the fresh, floral Amber who had waltzed into his dad's garage, this version of Amber had donned the uniform of the full-on casually elegant fashion world.

The T-shirt was V-necked and modest enough to cover her cleavage but fashionably off centre so that a matching azure bra strap was exposed over one shoulder as she moved. Her collarbone formed a crisp outline.

Amber had never been overweight, but it seemed that she was paying the price of working with fashion designers.

She was too skinny. *Way too skinny.*

She had tied her broken wrist into a long blue scarf with pink and gold threads which ran through it to form a kind of halter neck.

The shade of blue matched the colour of her violet eyes. Perfectly. And, without intending to, Sam's gaze was locked onto those eyes as though he was seeing them for the first time.

Her hair was clipped back behind her head in a simple waterfall. She wasn't wearing any make-up from what he could see and did not need any.

He wondered if she realised how rare that truly was. Yes, he had met stunning girls in Los Angeles—the city was full of them.

But Amber DuBois was the real deal.

No doubt about it.

The lanky, awkward girl who had never known what to do with her long legs and arms and oversized feet was gone.

For good.

Replaced by a woman who looked totally comfortable and confident in her own skin.

This was the Amber he had always known that she would become one day, and he was suddenly pleased that she had realised just how lovely she truly was. And always had been.

Now the world had the chance to see Amber the way he

had once seen her. As a beautiful, confident woman with the power to take his breath away. Just by looking at her.

'Hi, trouble,' she replied casually with a bright smile as though she were greeting an old friend, which was about right. 'You are right on time.'

He gave her a mock salute. 'Reporting for duty as ordered.'

Her small laugh turned into a bit of a cough, then she turned back to Kate and Saskia and pressed her cheek lightly to each of them in turn. 'Thanks, girls. I'll see you the same time tomorrow. Oh—and don't forget to check online about the shoes. Bye. Bye for now.'

Amber stepped past Sam and waved to Kate and Saskia as they carefully wove their precious cargo of bags and suit carriers down the hall towards the front door, laughing and chatting as they went, with only the occasional backwards scowl from Kate over one shoulder to indicate how *pleased* they were to see him again. *Not.*

Only then did Amber turn back to face Sam, her hand resting lightly on one hip.

'I cannot believe that you actually came.'

'So you weren't serious about the audition? Great!' Sam replied, pushing himself off the door post and dusting his hands off and patting his pocket. 'Shall we get started now? I have my trusty tape recorder right here.'

Amber exhaled explosively and held up both hands. 'Not so fast. I was perfectly serious—you have to audition for this gig.'

Sam lifted both hands as he grinned at her.

'Well, here I am. This is me proving that you can trust me to keep my word and do whatever it is you need me to do. Your personal slave is ready for action. So let's get started.'

'Oh, now don't tempt me,' Amber murmured under her breath, then she lifted her chin and peered at him through creased eyebrows. 'You had better come into my bedroom.'

Sam blinked several times. 'I am liking the sound of this already.'

She closed her eyes and shook her head. 'And I am regretting it already. Do not even try and flirt with me because it won't work. Okay?'

'Methinks the lady doth protest too much,' Sam replied, then winced at the searing look she gave him. 'Okay, I get the message. I am a snake who cannot be trusted. So. Let's get this game of charades started. What is the first thing on that long list of yours?'

Amber pressed her forefinger to her full, soft pink lips and pretended to ponder.

'You may have noticed that I am having a bit of a declutter at the moment.'

'Declutter? Is that what you call it? I have to tell you that, despite reports to the contrary, my knowledge of female clothing is not as great as you might imagine. So if you are looking for fashion advice...'

Amber jabbed her finger towards the bedroom wall right in front of them, which was covered with a framed collection of artwork, portraits of Amber and old sheets of music manuscripts.

'I need someone to take my pictures down so I can decorate. It is a bit tricky one-handed and some of them are quite valuable. I vaguely recall that you can handle a screwdriver. Think you can manage that?'

Sam stepped forward so that they were only inches apart.

'Bambi, I can handle anything you throw at me.'

She took a step closer, startling him, but there was no way that he was going to let her know that.

'Oh, this is only the start. I have a very, very long list.'

'I expected nothing less.'

He turned to go back into the living room, and then looked back at Amber over one shoulder. 'And don't worry. I won't tell anyone that you couldn't wait to drag me into your bed-room the first chance you could get.' He tapped one side of his nose with his forefinger. 'It will be our little secret.' And with that he strode away from Amber, leaving her wide-mouthed with annoyance, delighted that he had managed to squeeze in the last word.

CHAPTER SEVEN

Two hours later Sam had taken down the framed pictures from the walls of two bedrooms, a kitchen and a hallway, covered them in bubble wrap and packed them into plastic crates already stacked two high along the length of Amber's hall, before starting on the living room.

The barrage of noise, telephone calls and visitors had slowly faded away as the morning went on so that by the time he had unscrewed the last of the huge oil paintings and modern art installations in the living room, he didn't have to worry about stepping on Amber's peep toe sandals as she worked around him, or accidentally brushing plaster dust onto some fabulous gown which had been casually thrown over a chair or garment rail.

It took superhuman effort but for most of that time he kept his eyes on the rawl plugs and loose plaster behind the pictures instead of the long, lean limbs of the lovely woman who brushed past him at regular intervals in the hallway, leaving a trail of scented air and a cunning giggle in her wake.

Decluttering? When he'd cleared out his furnished Los Angeles apartment, he had walked out with two suitcases and a laptop bag. The same way he had found it. All of his car magazines and photos were safely scanned and digitised. The rest had been recycled or passed on to his pals. He never had to go through this palaver.

Sam stood back and tilted his head to look at a pair of large oil paintings made up of small shapes inside larger shapes inside larger shapes which was starting to give him a headache.

And some of the picture frames had sticky notes on the front with the letter S written in purple marker pen. Purple, he snorted. What did that mean?

Right. Finish this little collection. Then it was time to go and find the lady and find out.

No need. Here she was, ambling towards him. Head down, a large garment bag over one shoulder and a cellphone pressed against her ear, oblivious to his presence.

From the corner of one eye he watched her flip the phone back into her pocket and pick up several scarves from the top of the piano. Then Amber paused and ran two fingertips along the surface of the keys without pressing them firmly enough to make music.

Only as he watched, her lovely face twisted into a picture of sadness and regret and pain that was almost unbearable for him to see.

He turned around to face her, but it was too late—the moment was lost as Amber suddenly realised that she was being observed. A bright smile wiped away the trauma that had been all there to see only a few seconds earlier, startling him with how quickly she could turn on her performance face, and she lowered the lid on the piano. 'Plaster dust,' she whispered. 'Not a good idea.'

'Don't let me put you off playing,' Sam quipped and gestured towards the piano with his screwdriver. 'I brought my own earplugs in case you were holding a rehearsal session.'

'Very funny, but your ears are safe. I am not playing today.' She took a breath and raised her plaster cast towards him. 'My wrist is hurting.'

Her chin lifted and she angled her head a little. 'You can

tell your lovely readers that I simply cannot tolerate second best. My standards are just as high as ever.'

'Yeah.' He nodded. 'Right. It's just weird that you haven't even tried to play. It used to be the other way around. I spent a lot of time trying to drag you away from the nearest keyboard.'

Sam looked into her face with a grin but her gaze was firmly fixed on the scarves in her bag.

'That was a long time ago, Sam. People change.' And with that she turned away and strolled back to her bedroom. In silence.

As he watched her slim hips sway away from him, every alarm bell in his journalist's mind started ringing at the same time.

Music used to be the one thing that gave Amber joy. She used to call it her private escape route away from the chaos that was her mother's life.

Well, it didn't look like that now.

Something was not right here. And it was not just her wrist that was causing Amber pain.

And, damn it, but he cared more than he should.

Amber ran her fingers over the few dresses still left in her wardrobe and stifled a self-indulgent sniff. She had loved wearing those evening gowns which were now on their way to a shop specialising in pre-loved designer wear. But she had plenty of photos of the events to remind her what each dress had looked like if she wanted a walk down memory lane.

Which she didn't.

She had never been sentimental about clothes like some of the other performers. There was no lucky bracelet or a corset dress which was guaranteed to have her grace the cover of the latest celebrity magazine. They were just clothes—beautiful clothes which had made her feel special and beautiful when she had worn them. But clothes just the same.

So why did it feel so weird to know that she would never wear them again?

Amber sniffed again, then mentally scolded herself.

This was pathetic! She was still Amber Sheridan DuBois. She was still the girl with the first class degree in music and the amazing career. The same Amber who had flown so very high in a perfect sky which seemed to go on for ever and ever.

Until she had gone to India and fate had sent her tumbling back down to earth with a bang.

The sound of an electric screwdriver broke through her wallow in self-pity and Amber shivered in her thin top. All in the past. She was over the worst and her wrist would soon be better. She was lucky to have come through the infection more or less intact, and that was worth celebrating.

So why did she feel like collapsing onto her bed and sleeping for a week?

She was overtired. That was it. *Idiot.* The doctors had warned her about overdoing it, then her mother and Heath and now so had Kate and Saskia—and Parvita, who had offered to delay the wedding because she felt so guilty about inviting her friends to perform a concert at the orphanage. She had had no clue that there was a meningitis outbreak sweeping across Kerala.

Of course she had told Parvita not to be so silly—the astrologers had chosen a perfect wedding day and that was precisely what Parvita was going to have. A perfect wedding back in her home village without having to worry about an exhausted concert pianist who should be in Boston resting in glorious solitude at her stepbrother's town house.

Pity that she had not factored in the mess in her apartment, and surviving a birthday party at Elwood House. And then there was the ex-boyfriend who had suddenly popped into her life again.

Yes. Sam might have something to do with her added stress levels.

Good thing he had no idea how her body was on fire when he was in sight or she would never live it down.

He had no idea that she had tossed and turned most of the night with an aching wrist, wondering would have happened if she had fallen into Sam's arms that night of her eighteenth birthday. Would they still be together now? Or would their relationship have fizzled out with recriminations and acrimonious insults?

She would never know, but there was one thing she was sure about.

Ever cell in her body was aware that Sam Richards was only a few feet away from her in the next room. His boyish grin was locked into her memory and, whether she liked it or not, her treacherous body refused to behave itself when he was so close. Her hands were shaking, her legs felt as though they belonged to someone else and it had nothing to do with the fact that she was supposed to be resting. Nothing at all.

All she had to do was survive a few more days and Sam would be out of her life.

Amber rolled her stiff and sore shoulders and rearranged her sling.

Shaking her head in dismay, she stretched up to tug at the boxes on the top shelf of her dressing room but they slid right back into the corner and out of her reach.

Grabbing the spare dining room chair Kate had used earlier to find the hat boxes, Amber popped the headphones of her personal stereo in her trouser pocket over her ears, and hummed along to the lively Italian baroque music as she jumped up onto the chair and stretched out on tiptoe to reach the far back corner of the shelf.

She had just caught hold of the handle of her old vanity case and was tugging it closer when something touched the bare skin below her trouser leg.

As she whipped around in shock, her left hand tried to grab the chair, which had started to wobble alarmingly at the sudden movement, throwing her completely off balance. The problem was that her fingers were already tightly latched onto the vanity case and as it swung off the shelf it made contact with the side of Sam's head as he stepped forwards to grab hold of her around the middle and take the weight of her body against his.

She dropped the case, and it bounced high before settling down intact.

Not that she noticed. Her fingers were too busy clutching onto Sam Richards as she stared into his startled face.

Time seemed to stand still as she started to slide down the front of his hard body, her silky top riding up as she did.

Sam reacted by holding her tighter, hitching her up as though she was weightless, his arms linked together under her bottom, locking her body against his.

'Sorry about that,' she said, trying to sound casual, as though it was perfectly normal to have a conversation while you were being held up against the dusty T-shirt of the man who had once rocked your world. 'Good thing I didn't hit anything important.'

He bit his lower lip, as though he was ready to hit back with some comment and then thought better of it, then one corner of his mouth turned up and he slowly, slowly, started to bend his knees until her feet were on the floor. But all the time his arms were locked behind her back as though he had no intention of letting her go.

Why should he? Amber thought. Sam was having way too much fun.

Strange that his breathing seemed to be even faster than

hers, if that was possible, and she could see the blood pulsing in his neck. Hot and fast.

His wide fingers slid up from her hips to her waist, holding her firm, secure, safe but being careful not to crush her plaster cast.

Amber inhaled the warm spicy aroma of some masculine scent that had a lot of Sam in the blend and instantly became aware that she could feel the length of his body pressed against hers from chest to groin.

His breathing became stronger. Louder. And his fingers stretched to span the strip of exposed skin below her top, gently at first and then moving back and forth just a little against her ribcage. Amber felt like closing her eyes but didn't dare because his gaze had never left her face.

He felt wonderful. He smelt better.

Sam tilted his head and looked at her. Really looked at her. Looked at her with an intensity that sent shivers and tingles from her toes to the ends of each strand of hair.

It had been such a long time since any man had held her like this, with that fire in his eyes.

Bad fire.

Bad tingles.

Bad, bad heart for wanting him to finish what he had started.

It would be so easy to kiss him right now and find out if his kiss was still capable of making her weak at the knees.

Bad Amber for wanting him, when that was the worst thing that could happen to either of them.

Her back stiffened and she lifted her chin slightly.

'You can put me down now if you like,' she said in a jokey voice which sounded so false and flat. Her words seem to echo around the narrow dressing room until they found their target.

'And what if I don't like?' Sam replied and leant closer to

breathe into her neck while his fingers moved in slow circles at her waist.

Suddenly Amber wished that she had installed air conditioning in the apartment because the air was starting to heat up far too quickly in this small space. And so close to her bed…

Amber lifted her hand from Sam's shoulder and reached behind and gently slid her fingers around his wrist and released him.

And, just like that, the connection was broken, leaving her feeling dizzier than she wanted to admit.

Without his support, her legs felt so wobbly that she had to swivel around and sit down on the chair—anything but the bed. That would be far too dangerous with this man around and she would hate to give him ideas.

His brow creased and Sam crossed his arms in front of his chest as he stared at her, his legs wide, his shoulders back and squared, his gaze locked onto her face. As he stared his eyes narrowed as though they were concerned about something. And her foolish girly heart gave a little leap at the idea that he might still care about her.

'Hey, Bambi. I thought we had a deal. It's time you kept to your side of the bargain.'

'Will you please stop calling me Bambi? Yes, I know you came up with the name in the first place, but Amber will do fine. And what do you mean? My side?'

'Okay, then. Amber, I brought my own work uniform…' Sam waved a hand down his clothing.

'But you promised me refreshments. So far all I have seen are a small plate of girly mini cupcakes and one mug of weak Earl Grey tea.'

He winced and shook his head slowly from side to side. 'That. Is not refreshments as I understand them. What's more, I have just raided your refrigerator and there is nothing more than a couple of low fat yoghurts and some supermarket ready meals.'

He stood back and ogled her, then reached out and pinched her arm.

She wriggled away. 'Hey. Ouch. What was that for?'

'Too skinny and too pale and wobbly. By far. That decides it. We, young lady, are going out to get some food. What is your fancy? Mexican? Pub food? Take your pick.'

Amber looked around the bedroom in horror at the debris. 'I can't leave now. The flat is a mess and it will take me ages to tidy it up.'

'But the girls have gone for the day…right?'

'Well, yes. I don't have any more appointments.'

'Good. Because it is two o'clock in the afternoon and neither of us have eaten since breakfast. Right?'

Amber sighed and checked her wristwatch, and then her shoulders sagged. 'I am flagging a bit. I suppose it would make sense to eat some late lunch…and what are you doing?'

'Looking for your coat. And which one of these is your handbag? Come on, girl. The sun is still shining and there is nothing fit to eat in this apartment. What do you say? We get some lunch and I volunteer to carry your shopping home from the supermarket on the way back. You can't get a better offer than that.'

'Can't I?'

Amber leant backwards and pulled out her mobile phone from her trouser pocket and was about to sling her cashmere wrap over one shoulder when Sam stepped behind her and wrapped it around her shoulders, gently pressing the collar into her neck, his fingertips touching her, and she blinked in delight then cursed herself for being so needy.

'Actually, I might have a better idea, but I need to make a phone call. This restaurant can get extremely busy around lunchtime.'

Sam groaned. 'I might have known. How many awards does it have? Because I have to tell you—I am not in the mood for mini tasting portions served on teaspoons made out of toast.'

She sniffed dismissively. 'Several. But wait and see. You might just like it. And the table has the most amazing view over London.'

'I don't believe that you ordered home delivery,' Sam exclaimed and put down his screwdriver as Amber sauntered into the kitchen swinging a large brown paper bag. 'Don't tell me that the famous Amber DuBois has suddenly got cold feet about being seen out in public. Or were you worried that I would make you pay the bill?'

Amber sniffed dismissively in reply. 'Well, someone has a very high opinion of themselves.' Then she sighed in exasperation and gestured with her head towards the cabinets. 'Only now I am out of hands. Would you mind bringing the plates and cutlery? Have a rummage in that drawer. Yep. That's it.'

'You are avoiding my question,' Sam said as he followed Amber out onto the sunlit terrace and spread the picnic kit out onto the table, where Amber was already pulling out foil containers. 'Why not go out to some fabulous restaurant so the waiters can fawn all over you?'

She looked up at him and gave a half smile. 'Two reasons. First, I want some peace and quiet to enjoy my meal, and the restaurant this food came from is always crushed jam-tight. And secondly—' she paused and looked out towards the skyline '—I have only used this apartment on flying visits these past few years and never stayed long enough to enjoy the view.' She nodded towards the railing. 'Feel free. This is your city, after all. And I know how much you love London.'

Sam took the hint and walked the few steps over to the railing. And exhaled slowly at the awe-inspiring scene spread out in all directions in front of him. The stress of the past few days melted away as he took in the stunning view over the Thames and along both sides of the river for miles in each direction. His eyes picked out the locations which were so familiar they were like old friends. Friends like Amber had once been.

'You always were the clever one. This is a pretty good view, I'll give you that. And yes, London is my city, and it always has been. And what is that amazing smell?'

He turned back towards Amber and instantly his senses were filled with the most amazing aromas which instantly made his mouth water.

'Are those Indian dishes? You used to hate spicy food.'

'That was before I tasted real southern Indian food like this. Home-cooked traditional recipes from Kerala. The restaurant doesn't usually do take out but I know the owner's cousin. Willing to risk it?'

'Are you kidding me?' Sam replied and flung himself into the seat. 'I loved living in Los Angeles, but you cannot get real Indian food unless you cook it yourself. Pass it over and tell me what you ordered.'

'Vegetable curry, chickpea masala, coconut rice and a thick lamb curry for you. And just this once we are allowed to eat it using a fork and plates instead of fingers and a banana leaf. Go ahead and tuck in. I ordered plenty. What do you think?'

Sam held up a fork and dived into the nearest dish, speared some lamb and wrapped his lips around it.

Flavour and texture exploded on his tongue and he moaned in pleasure and delight before smiling and grabbing each dish in turn and loading up his plate with something of everything.

'This is seriously good. But now I'm curious. How do you know the owner of a Keralan restaurant in London? That doesn't seem to fit with a career musician.'

Amber swallowed down a mouthful of vegetables and rice and gave a tiny shrug before taking a sip of water.

'The orchestra I tour with has an amazing cellist who has become one of my best friends in the business. Parvita is one of those totally natural talents who has been winning awards all over the place—but it was only when I got to know her that I found out just how remarkable she really is.'

Amber topped up her plate as she spoke, but there was just enough of a slight quiver in her voice to make Sam look at her as he chewed. 'Parvita was left at an orphanage for girls when she was only a toddler. Her widowed mother was too poor to feed another daughter. She needed her boys to work their farm in Kerala and knew that the orphanage could give a little girl an education and a chance to improve her life.'

Amber chuckled. 'I don't think that Parvita's family were expecting her to win scholarships to international music schools and then build a career as a concert cellist. But she did it, against all of the odds.'

Amber raised her water glass. 'And along the way my friend introduced me to real home-cooked food from Kerala. The chef who runs this restaurant is one of her cousins and is totally passionate about fresh ingredients and cooking with love. I think it shows.'

Sam lifted his fork in tribute. 'This is probably the best Indian food that I have ever eaten. Although it does make me wonder. Aren't you going to miss your friend Parvita? Now that you have decided to retire?'

Amber closed her lips around the fork and twirled it back and forth for a second before replying. 'Not at all. She is still my friend so I will make the effort to keep in touch. She even invited me to her wedding next week and sent me a fabulous hot pink sari to wear.'

'Now that is something I would like to see. Just tell me which fabulous and exclusive London venue is having the privilege of hosting this happy event and I'll be right there with my camera.'

'Oh, she isn't coming to London. The wedding party is in Kerala. I've already sent my apologies—' Amber shrugged '—but the newlyweds will be passing through London in a few weeks, and we can catch up then.'

'So you are not going to the wedding after all?'

She shook her head as she chewed and pointed to her plaster.

'That's interesting.' Sam nodded. 'If one of my friends was getting married I wouldn't let a simple thing like that stop me from going. Unless, of course, there is more to it than that. Hmm?'

Then he leant back and crossed his cutlery on his plate and shook his head from side to side.

'Well, well. Why do I get the feeling that some things have not changed that much after all? Let me guess. Your mother ordered you not to go, didn't she? Or was Heath Sheridan worried that his little stepsister is going to get sunburnt if she goes to India? How is your stepbrother doing these days? Still trying to interfere in your life? Um. I take that glaring scowl as a yes.'

He sniggered off her rebuke, and dived back into his food. 'You surprise me, Amber. You're twenty-eight years old, with a brilliant career, an international reputation and the kudos to match, and you still cannot get out from under their thumb, can you? Well, shame on you, Amber DuBois. I thought you were better than that.'

CHAPTER EIGHT

'SHAME ON ME? Shame. *On me*?'

Amber felt the heat burn at the back of her neck which had nothing to do with the Indian food and she crashed her hand down onto the table hard enough to make both Sam and the plates jump, and leant forwards towards him.

'*How dare you?* How dare you tell me that I should be ashamed of the fact that my family love me and care what happens to me? No, I don't always agree with what they tell me, but at least they make an effort to be part of my life. But you know all about that, don't you? How are you getting on with your dad these days? And remind me of the last time you saw *your* mum?'

The words emerged in harsh outbursts which seemed to echo around her patio and reflect back from the stone-faced man sitting opposite. And she instantly regretted them.

It shocked her that Sam was capable of making her so spiteful and hard. She was one of the few people who knew how hard it had been for him when his mother abandoned her husband and son. But that didn't mean that she had to throw his pain back in his face.

She was better than that. Or at least she was trying to be.

'In fact I don't know why I am even listening to you in the first place.' She blinked and tossed her head back and calmly sipped her water. 'You are hardly qualified to take the moral high ground. I certainly don't need a lecture on making decisions from you, Sam. Understood?'

'Perfectly.' Sam nodded, then leant forward and rested his elbows on the table while his gaze locked onto her face. 'Is your little tantrum over now, Miss DuBois? Because I would really like to get this so called interview over and done with as soon as possible. I have a real assignment waiting for me back at the paper, so can we move on, please?'

'Absolutely,' Amber replied, trying to calm her heart rate and appear to be more or less in control again. 'But it does make me wonder. What are you *really* doing back here in London? Because whatever it is must be very important to persuade you to go through with this little game of charades.'

Sam tried to savour more of the delicious food as slowly as he could while his brain worked at lightning speed, trying to form an answer, but his appetite was gone and he pushed his meal away.

Amber had fired her arrow and hit her target right in the centre.

Strange how this girl was one of the few people alive who knew just what his emotional hot buttons were and was not afraid to press them down hard when she needed to.

Just as he had pressed hers.

That was the problem with working with people who understood you.

Touché Amber.

If this was a game, then it was one point to each of them.

Sam sat back in his chair and watched Amber as she turned away from him and looked out over the city, all joy in her food and apartment forgotten.

The warm sunlight played on her pale skin and delicate features. Up close and personal, she was even lovelier than the girl on the magazine cover. Her chest rose and fell and he could sense the emotional strain these last few minutes had cost her.

Strain he was responsible for.

Shame on him.

Amber DuBois was gunpowder and those few minutes they had just shared in the dressing room had proved just how explosive getting within touching distance could be.

Any ideas he might have had about staying distant and professional had just gone out of the window the instant his fingers touched her skin.

He might be over his teenage crush but this woman he was looking at now had the power to get under his skin and bother him.

Bother him so badly that suddenly it felt easier to keep his change of heart towards his father to himself. If she had a whiff that he was some sort of self-sacrificing martyr who desperately wanted to make it up to his dad for all those angry years, she would never let him forget it.

A few days. He could stay cool and professional for a few days for his dad's sake.

His eyebrow lifted. 'I told you. I need the promotion and the boss made it clear that I will only get that if I come back with an exclusive from, and I quote, "the lovely Miss DuBois". That's it, job done,' and Sam went back to the food.

No way was he going to fall into Amber's trap and start spouting on about how guilty he felt about leaving his dad all alone for years on end while he lived the high life in California. This was Amber he was talking to. She would be only too ready to believe that he was a heartless son who had only come back to London for the job and the status.

After what had just happened in the dressing room he intended to keep as far away from her as physically possible.

He had to keep up the pretence that he was still the self-absorbed young man who would let nothing come between him and his career. Which was not so far from the truth. Happy families were for other men. Not men like Sam Richards.

'Job done. Right,' Amber replied and picked up her water glass. 'Come on, Sam. Out with it. From what I hear, you can get a job anywhere you like. Why here? Why now? And why do I suspect that there is a lovely lady involved in the answer?'

'You think I came back to London for a woman? Oh, no. Sorry to burst your romantic bubble, but this was strictly business all the way.'

'Um,' Amber replied. 'Pity. I could have given her a few tips. Such as run for the hills now, before he breaks your heart. That sort of thing. But not to worry, it will keep for another time.'

And she smiled sweetly at him over her water glass. 'But do tuck into your lunch. You are going to need it for this afternoon's opportunity to shine.'

'More pictures?'

'Yes, but that is for later when you deliver the paintings to Saskia and hang them up for her,' Amber replied. 'But in the meantime I have something which is much more suited to your…talents.'

She narrowed her eyes and rested her elbows on the table so that she could support her chin with one hand. 'Did you bring your camera and tripod? I'll take that nod as a yes. Super. My shoes really do need the right angle to look their best.'

Sam spluttered into his water glass. 'Shoes? You want me to photograph your shoes?' he asked in complete disbelief.

'Eighteen pairs of designer loveliness.' Amber sighed. 'Worn once or not at all. Gorgeous but unloved. Kate wanted them but she has tiny feet so I am selling them on the Internet.'

'You are selling your shoes.' Sam snorted and tossed his

head with a sigh. 'Things must be desperate. Cash flow problems?'

Her tongue flicked out and she licked her lips once. And right there and then he knew that she was keeping something from him.

'Don't try and hide your enthusiasm. I knew that you would be excited by the opportunity. This is just part of the modern girl's annual clearing out of last season's couture so that she can buy new ones to take their place—and all the money goes to charity. Oh—and tomorrow gets even better. The lovely Saskia is trying to launch Elwood House as a private dining venue and her online presence is just not cutting it. She needs a professional writer to redesign the website and create a whole new photo gallery—and it has to be complete in time for my birthday party on Thursday.'

'Is there any good news in all of this?' he spluttered, while shovelling down more chickpeas and rice.

'Of course. You have a front row seat at my birthday party, hobnobbing with the great and good of the London scene. Even if you are taking the photographs for Saskia's website at the same time.'

Sam blew out slowly. 'I am so grateful for your kind consideration. So that's Saskia covered. Are you sure that Kate Lovat wouldn't like me to stand in her shop window modelling a tartan dinner suit in my copious spare time?'

'Hey, that's not a bad idea. You might be able to fit it in after you have cleaned the spiders and mouse droppings out of her attic tomorrow. Oh. Didn't I mention that? Silly me. And after you have sorted the ladies out, then you can pop back here. By then I should have sorted out my unwanted lingerie. I am sure you can come up with some suitable slogan like "as worn by Amber" when you put together the adverts for the Internet auction.'

Amber tilted her head to one side as he glared at her through slitted eyes.

And this was the girl he was thinking of asking to be his friend.

'Not lingerie. Shoes I can understand. But I draw the line at photographing lingerie unless you intend to model it in person.'

'But this is your audition, sweetie. Have you forgotten so quickly? Of course, if you are refusing to carry out my perfectly reasonable requests, well, I shall have to phone the journalist on the other paper and see if she is still interested... And no, my modelling days are over.'

She leant her chin on the back of one hand and fluttered her eyelashes at him.

'You're looking a little hot under the collar there, Mr Richards.' Amber smiled. 'How about some ice cream to cool you down? It's delicious with humble pie.'

'Well. What do you think? The emerald and diamond drop necklace or the sapphire white gold collar?'

Amber held one necklace then the other to her throat, slowly at first, then faster and then faster, using two fingers of her plastered wrist to prop them up against her skin.

'Hey. Slow down, I'm still thinking about it.'

Kate sat back against Amber's bed pillows in Saskia's best spare bedroom and stretched both arms out above her head.

'Decisions, decisions.' Then she sniffed. 'The sapphires. They are absolutely perfect with that dress. Although, if it was me, I would wear both and go totally overboard on the bling. Especially since you won't be wearing either of them again.'

Amber smiled and dropped the emerald necklace, which had been a present from a fashion designer who had been trying to woo her into being their cover girl, back into the velvet tray. 'True. But the way I look at it, some other girl has the chance to enjoy them and the charity gets the loot. The last thing I need is a load of expensive jewellery in a safety deposit box which has to be insured every year at huge expense. It makes sense to sell it back to the jewellers while it is still in pristine condition.'

Kate shuffled to the edge of the bed. 'Don't let the spy hear you say that. Can you imagine the headlines? "Injured pianist forced to sell her jewellery to make ends meet".' Then Kate pushed herself off the bed. 'Here. Let me help with the earrings. I'm thinking some serious dangle and maximum sparkle and that is a tricky thing to pull off one-handed.'

She peered into the tray and pulled out a pair of chandelier diamond and sapphire drops. 'Ah. Now we are talking...' Then she took another look at the maker on the box and blew out hard. 'Wow. Are these for real? My fingers are shaking. I never thought I would be holding anything from that jeweller. Oh, Amber.'

Amber reached up and wrapped one arm around Kate's shoulders but, as her friend laughed and reached up to fit her earrings, she shook her head. 'Not until you have tried them on first. Go on. I want to see you wear those earrings—and that necklace.'

'What? My neck is too short and my ears are tiny. Nope. These are serious jewels for serious people. I'll stick to my pearls, thanks all the same.'

'Kate Lovat, I won't take no for an answer. I know that my clothes and shoes are huge on you, so please, just this once, be nice and do what I ask. It is my birthday.'

Amber pushed her lips out and pretended to sulk.

'Oh, stop it,' Kate replied with a dramatic sigh. 'You are ruining your make-up and it has taken me the best part of an hour to make it look natural. Okay, okay, I'll try the jewellery on. But only because it's your birthday, Look, I'm doing it. And... Oh, Amber.'

Kate stepped behind Amber and rested her head on her shoulder as Amber smiled back at her. 'Absolutely gorgeous. Told ya. Right, that's sorted. You're wearing the jewels that Heath gave me. Done. Or do you want them to sit in the box up here in the bedroom unused and unloved because you have rejected them?'

Kate replied by reaching for a tissue. 'Oh. Now look what you have made me do. Pest.'

Then Kate peered at herself in the mirror. 'Do you think that Heath would like me in these?'

'Pest right back. And he would definitely like you in those earrings,' Amber replied and wrapped her arm around Kate's waist. 'Does Heath still hold the prize for the best emergency school party date a girl could hope for?'

Kate rested her head on Amber's shoulder before answering with a small shrug. 'Absolutely. Which must make me the stupidest girl in London. Here I am, surrounded by loads of handsome boys, and the only one who comes close to being my personal hero is living in Boston and doesn't remember that I even exist unless you are around. Mad just about describes it.'

'Oh, Kate. Don't worry. You'll find someone special, I know you will.'

Kate grinned and ran a tissue across the corner of both eyes. 'Damn right. Who knows? My soulmate could be on his way to this very party this evening. How about that?'

'Absolutely. Now shoo. I have to finish getting ready and you need to show your loveliness to all and sundry. Go. Have fun at the party. And Kate…make sure that Sam the spy takes your picture. You can't miss him—he'll be the one with the camera around his neck.'

'You've got five minutes, young lady—then the posse will be up here to drag you downstairs.'

'I would expect nothing less,' Amber replied and waved to

Kate as she waltzed across the carpet on her tiny dainty heels and the bedroom door swung closed behind her.

Only when she heard Kate's sandals on the marble floor of the entrance did Amber feel it was safe to flop back down on her bed.

So her best friend Kate was still in crush with her step-brother Heath. Oh, Kate. Maybe it was a good thing that Heath had already spoken to her from his lecture tour in South America and was not turning up for this party after all. He might have brought his lovely girlfriend Olivia with him. Not good. *Not good at all.*

Her wrist was aching, her head was thumping and she could quite easily pull the quilt over her legs right then and there and sleep for days. But she couldn't. She might have or-ganised her birthday party at the last minute, but she was still the star of the show—and she had to make her appearance.

Time to turn up and give the greatest performance of her life.

All smiles and confidence and clear about what she was doing and why. Exploring. Taking a break. Enjoying herself. Fund-raising for charity. What fun!

That was the official line and she was sticking to it. She could count the number of people who knew the truth on one hand—and that was how she wanted it to stay. Until she was ready. And then she would have to add Sam Richards to the list.

Sam.

What was she going to do about Sam?

Was he Sam the spy as Kate called him? Could she trust him again?

He had kept his side of the bargain and worked hard at every ridiculous task that the three of them had thrown at him over the past few days without much in the way of complaint.

He could never know that she had spent two nights tossing and turning in her bed as his words roiled in the pit of her stomach. She did listen to Heath—she always had and probably always would. He was her sensible older stepbrother. But these past two days, every time he had told her to do something rather than ask or suggest, she kept thinking about what Sam had said. Maybe she was still under his thumb more than she liked? Maybe he had a point.

Of course going back to Kerala would be scary. She would be a fool not to be worried. But she had made a vow in hospital that her life would be different from now. She *wanted* to see Parvita married and share her happiness.

She *wanted to* go back and yet it was so risky. Doubt rolled over Amber in waves, hard and choppy, buffeting and threatening to weaken her resolve.

Turning her life around was harder than she had expected.

The jewel tray was still open on the dressing table and Amber slithered off her bed and lifted out the top tray. Hidden inside a tiny suede pouch at the very bottom was a small gold heart suspended from a thin gold chain.

Sam had given it to her at her eighteenth birthday party, just before they had escaped out of the kitchen door and taken a ride in his dad's vintage open top sports car.

Amber smiled as she let the chain slip between her fingers. Sam had let her stand up tall on the passenger seat with her arms outstretched to the sky as they rode through the London streets—the wind in her hair and the sound of their laughter and the hoots from passing motorists reverberating through every bone in her body.

She had been so very, very happy, and she should be grateful to Sam for showing her what true happiness felt like. It was a joyous memory.

The sound of party music drifted up the stairs and Amber grinned. She had survived meningitis more or less intact, she had friends waiting for her downstairs and more on their way.

She looked at herself in the mirror and, without another moment of hesitation, she winked at her reflection and dropped the gold chain back into the pouch and closed the lid down on the box with the rest of her past.

She was a lucky girl.

Time to rock and roll and *enjoy herself.*

Taking a deep calming breath, Sam Richards strolled across the luxurious marble-floored hallway of the Victorian splendour that was Elwood House.

He paused to check his reflection in the Venetian hall mirror above a long narrow console table, and lifted up his chin a little to adjust his black bow tie.

Not bad. Not bad at all.

For a chauffeur's son from the wrong part of London.

At least this time he had been welcomed at the front door!

Which had certainly not been the case ten years ago when he had stood in the hallway of another house and another birthday celebration.

Amber might have invited him to her eighteenth birthday party but her mother had taken one look at him standing on her front doorstep, snorted and closed the door in his face. Just to make sure that he got the message loud and clear.

Sam Richards was not good enough for her daughter. Oh, no. Nowhere near.

Of course he wasn't going to put up with that—he had plans for Amber's birthday and there was no way that her mother was going to thwart his little scheme.

So he'd climbed over the garden fence and sneaked in through the conservatory where the young people were having fun.

Suddenly there was the tinkle of laughter from the kitchen and Sam grinned as he strolled into the warm, light, open space of the huge kitchen sun room that Saskia's aunt Margot had built. Every worktop was covered with plates and bowls and platters of foodstuffs—but his attention was focused on the two women who were walking towards him.

Here come the girls.

Saskia's arm was around Kate's shoulder, which was not difficult, considering that Kate could just about make five feet four inches if she stretched. Although tonight she looked stunning in a dark green taffeta cocktail dress with real jewels. Saskia was in midnight-blue crushed velvet with a real pearl choker and gorgeous lilac kitten heels.

They were like dazzling stars transported from a catwalk fashion show into this London kitchen. English style and elegance. Not too much flesh on show, and all class.

Kate hissed at him, but Saskia nudged her with a glare and moved forward to shake his hand.

'Hello, Sam. Nice to see you again. I appreciate your help with my website—it's ten times better than I could have thought of on my own. We're having a few drinks on the patio before the hordes of locusts arrive. Why don't you come and join us?'

'Perfect. Thanks. And I'm pleased I could help.'

'You go ahead. One more thing to bring out of the oven,' Saskia replied, and waved Kate and Sam onto the terrace.

The second they were out of sight of the kitchen, Kate grabbed Sam's sleeve, whirled around and planted a hand on each hip as she stared up at him with squeezed narrow eyes.

'I'm watching you, Sam Richards. If you step out of place tonight or do anything to spoil Amber's evening I'll be on to you like a shot.'

He raised both hands in surrender.

'I came here to work. And help Amber have a good time along the way. Okay?'

Kate replied by jabbing her second and third fingers towards her eyes then stabbed them towards his face, then back to her eyes.

'Watching you,' she hissed, then broke into a wide-mouthed grin and popped one of Saskia's mini tomato tarts into her mouth and groaned in pleasure as Saskia strolled up with the most delicious-smelling tray.

Kate raised her glass of white wine in a toast. 'Fab. You always know exactly how to pull off the perfect party, Saskia. Always have.'

'Hold that thought, gorgeous. Special order for the star of the show. Mini pizza. Extra anchovies. Okay?'

'Did someone say mini pizza?'

Amber sidled up to Saskia and kissed her on the cheek before biting into the crisp pastry and nodding. 'Delicious.' Only then did she look across at Sam and smile. 'Hello, Sam. What perfect timing.'

And she took his breath away.

Her long sensitive fingers were wrapped around the stem of a wine glass which Kate was topping up with sparkling tonic water rather than wine. A diamond bracelet sparkled at her wrist and flashed bright and dazzling as she moved in the sunlight.

But that was nothing compared to the crystal covered dress and jewelled collar she was wearing.

Sam dragged his eyes away from Amber's cleavage before Kate noticed and stabbed him with the corkscrew.

Her earrings moved, sparkling and bright, and helped him to focus on her face. Stunning make-up showed her clear, smooth complexion to perfection, and her eyes glowed against the dark smudge of colour. Her lips were full, smooth. Her whole face was radiant.

Amber had never looked so beautiful or more magical.

This was the Amber he had always imagined that she

would look when she was happy in her own skin—and she had exceeded his wildest imagination.

He had often wondered over the years if Amber had stayed the sweet, loving girl that he had fallen for, under the surface gloss and razzmatazz, and it only took a few seconds of seeing her now with her friends to realise that she had somehow managed to keep her integrity and old friendships alive.

Now that was something he could admire.

He would give a lot to be here as her date this evening. To know that those lovely violet-blue eyes were looking at him with love instead of tolerance.

He had walked away from a great love.

Maybe his only love. And certainly the only girl that he had ever truly wanted in his life.

Which made him more than a fool. It made him a stupid fool.

The best that he could do was try and capture this moment for ever. So that when they were back in their ordinary worlds on other continents he had something to remind him of just how much he had lost.

She was the star. And he was a reporter who was working for her.

Because that was what he was here for, wasn't it? To work?

Not as one of the guests.

Oh, no.

The likes of Sam Richards did not come to these events as a guest. He was the one parking cars and taking the coats.

Strange to think that he had some standing on the A-list circuit in Los Angeles. But it took London to put him right back in his place.

As one of the help.

Pity that he had no intention whatsoever of fitting in with someone else's idea of who and what he was. He was here because they needed him as much as he needed Amber.

An equal trade. Yes. That was better. He could work with that. He was done with being second best. To anyone.

Instantly Sam smiled. 'You look lovely, Amber—and not a day over twenty-eight. In fact, you ladies look so stunning as a group that I think this would make a charming example of a perfect summer drinks party. Early evening cocktails for a private party? So if you could just hold that pose? Lovely. And a little more to the right, Kate? Gorgeous—and don't forget to smile, Kate. Much better than sticking your tongue out at me. That's it.'

Sam stepped back and by the time the girls had straightened their dresses and rearranged the canapés his digital camera had already captured the trio from several angles, taking in the conservatory, the lovely sunlit garden and the happy women enjoying themselves.

Of course Amber had no idea that he had taken several shots for his personal album. And every one of them was of Amber.

'Fantastic. And a few more with you choosing something from the tray and pouring more wine. Excellent. Now. Saskia. How do you want to showcase the patio? With or without the food?'

CHAPTER NINE

FIVE HOURS LATER, every canapé, savoury and dessert that Saskia had served had been eaten, empty bottles of champagne stood upside down in silver wine buckets and the eighty or so guests had been entertained by some of London's finest musical talent.

One Spanish musician had even brought along a classical guitar and Amber had kicked off the flamenco dancing with great gusto and much cheering. It was amazing that the glass wear had survived the evening.

He had taken hundreds of photographs in every public room, with and without guests, from every possible angle. But there was no doubt who was the star of the show.

Sam could only watch in awe as Amber laughed and chatted in several languages to men and women of all ages and dress styles. Some young and unkempt, some older and the height of elegance, but it did not seem to matter to her in the least. The fashion models and media people were introduced to classical artists and quite a few popular musicians with names that even he had heard of.

Everyone from the costume designers to hairdressers and international conductors were putty in Amber's fingers. He had never expected to hear a sing-song around the grand piano where four of the world's leading sopranos improvised a rap song with an up-and-coming hip hop star.

It took skill to make a person feel that they were the most important person in the room—and Amber had that skill in buckets.

He was in awe of her.

It was only now, as Saskia and Kate chatted away to old friends and lingering guests, that he realised that Amber had already slipped away into the kitchen before he had a chance to thank her and say goodnight.

He quickly scanned the kitchen for Amber and waved to the waiting staff that Saskia had set to work on the washing-up. He had just turned away when he saw a splash of blue on the patio and slowly strolled out of the hot kitchen into the cool of the late May evening.

Amber was sitting on the wooden bench on the patio, humming along to the lively Austrian waltzes being played on the music system in the conservatory only a few feet away.

Her eyes were closed tight shut and her left hand was twisting and moving as though it was dancing in the air, her right arm waving stiffly along in time, the plaster cast forgotten.

Her face was in shadow but there was no mistaking the expression of joy which seemed to shine from inside outwards, illuminating her skin and making it glow.

She was happy. Beautiful. And content. And he yearned to be part of that happiness and share that little window of joy with this amazing woman.

This was the Amber he had fallen in love with ten years ago and then fallen in love all over again in the first ten seconds when she'd walked into his dad's garage and knocked his world off its axis.

And the fact that he had been in denial until this moment was so mind-boggling that all he could do was stand there and watch as she sang along to the music, all alone in the light of

the full moon and the soft glow streaming out from the conservatory where the last guests were mingling in the hallway.

He stood in the shadows, watching her for minutes until
the music changed to a new track and she dropped her hands
onto her lap and clasped hold of her knees and blinked open
her eyes.

And saw him.

'Hi, Sam,' she said, and her eyes met his without hesitation or reluctance. Almost as if she was pleased to see him
there. 'Are we on our own?'

Sam swallowed down the lump in his throat and strolled
over to the bench in the soft light and lifted up her feet and
sat down, her legs on his knees, well aware that he probably
had a huge man crush grin all over his face.

'More or less. The girls are seeing the last of the guests
out. It was a great party. Did you have a good time?'

Amber sighed and snuggled sideways on the arm rest.
'The best. Even though I am now completely exhausted. How
about you?'

Sam half turned to face her and as she shuffled higher,
her legs resting on his thighs and her arm on her lap, he inhaled a wonderful spicy, sweet perfume that competed with
the full musk roses and lavender which Saskia had planted
behind the bench. It was a heady, exotic aroma that seemed
to fill his senses and make him want to stay there for as long
as Amber was close by.

He wanted to tell her that she looked beautiful.

But that would be too close to the truth. So he covered up
his answer and turned it into something she would be expecting him to say.

'I had an interesting evening. Your guest list was inspired.
I suspect the birthday present swag will be excellent.'

'Birthday presents? Oh. No, I only had a few. I asked people to make a donation to Parvita's charity instead.'

She looked at him. Really looked at him. Her gaze moved so slowly from his feet upwards that by the time it reached his face Sam knew that his ears were flaming red.

'Nice suit. You look positively dangerous. Was it safe to let you out on your own? I'm sorry I didn't have much time to talk. Did you get all of the shots Saskia needs?'

'I can usually be trusted to behave myself if the occasion demands. And yes, I think I can do something creative for a website and make the most of the venue.'

'Really? That almost sounds professional. Then things truly have changed. And not just the suit.'

'Oh, no compliments, please; you'll have me blushing.'

'I noticed you working the room with your camera. Hasn't Saskia done a lovely job?'

'I have been to this house so many times with my dad but I'd forgotten how stunning it is. Judging from some of the comments from your guests, I think she might be on to a winner.'

Amber hunched up her shoulders. 'I hope so. She's had a rough time since her aunt Margot died. This is why it's important to me that you do a good job and help Saskia out. Elwood House is her home but it's also her business. She needs a decent marketing and promotional campaign to get it off the ground.'

'There are expert companies out there who could make it happen.'

'Yes, there are. And they cost serious amounts of money. And Saskia won't accept my help. I have plenty of colleagues and casual friends in my life. You met some of them this evening. But nobody comes close to real friends like Kate, Saskia and her aunt Margot. They made me believe that, despite everything that happened with my mother, I could make a real home in London and create something close to a normal school life for myself. And that was new.'

'I know, I was there. Remember?'

Then she laughed out loud. 'Oh, yes, I remember very well indeed. But I refuse to be angry with you on my birthday. Life really is too short. I have had enough of all of that. And yes, you can record that little snippet on your handy pocket tape recorder and do what you like with it.'

He patted his pockets. 'Oh, shame. I seem to have left it at the office. Fancy that. The last time I came to your birthday party I had to climb over the garden fence. It makes a nice change to come in through the front door.'

She chuckled before answering. 'How could I forget?' She laughed out loud. 'You strode into my eighteenth birthday party as though you were the guest of honour and hadn't just climbed over the fence to avoid the security on the front entrance. And then you kidnapped me when my mother was in the salon with all of the stuffy, important guests she had invited who I had never met, and you whisked me away in your dad's sports car. It was magical and you were the magician who made it possible. It was like some happy dream.'

She shook her head, making her chandelier earrings sparkle, and brought her knees up to her chest. 'My mother still hasn't forgiven you for the fact that I missed my own birthday cake, eighteen candles and all. Heath had to blow them out for me.'

'Your mother is a remarkable lady. As far as she is concerned, I will always be the chauffeur's son, but do you know what? I am proud of the fact that my dad used to drive limos for a living before he moved into property. I always have been. No matter what you and your family think.'

Amber inhaled sharply and tugged her hand away from his.

'Wait a minute. Don't you dare accuse me of treating you differently because your dad was our driver. Because I didn't. I never did, and you know that. You were the one who was always defending yourself. Not me.'

'Your mother…'

'I'm not talking about my mother. I'm talking about you and me. I would never, ever have looked down on you because of the job you did. And maybe it's about time to get over that stupid inferiority complex of yours so that you can see all of the amazing things you have achieved in your life.'

'You mean like being an international concert pianist who is able to perform in front of thousands of people? Or my wonderful career as a fashion model and cosmetics guru? Is that what you mean?'

'I was in the right place at the right time and I got lucky. And you are insufferable.'

'And you are deluded.'

Amber glared at him for several seconds before she took a slow breath and shook her head slowly from side to side, before flicking her long hair back over her left shoulder.

'Parents. They have a lot to answer for. And that includes mine as well as yours. It's a good thing that we have both been able to rise above them to become so independent and calm and even-tempered.'

'Isn't it just.'

Amber slowly lowered her legs to the floor and shuffled closer to him on the bench so that there were inches and ten years of lost time between them. So close that he could hear her breathing increase in speed with his.

'Which reminds me…' Sam smiled and released her to dive inside his jacket pocket and pull out a long slim envelope which he passed to her. 'Happy birthday, Amber.'

And, without waiting for her to reply, he leant forwards

and kissed her tenderly but swiftly on the cheek. Lingering just long enough to inhale her scent and feel her waist under his fingertips before he drew back.

She looked at him with wide, startled eyes. 'Thank you. I mean, I wasn't expecting anything. Can I... Can I open it now?'

'Please. Go ahead.'

Sam looked around the garden for the few seconds it took for her to slide a manicured fingernail under the flap of the envelope and draw out a slim piece of faded paper.

'Sam? What is this? It looks like...' And then she understood what she was holding and her breath caught at the back of her throat.

'Is this what I think it is?'

Then she shook her head and sat back away from him, head down, reading the letters in the dim light before speaking again. And this time her voice came out in one long breath.

'This is the cheque my mother gave you to leave me alone.'

She looked up at him and her gaze darted from the cheque to his face and then back to the cheque again. 'I don't understand. She told me that she had offered you enough cash to take you through journalism school.'

Amber dropped the cheque into her lap and took hold of his hand, her eyes brimming with tears. 'Why? Why didn't you use this money, Sam? The damage had already been done.'

Sam raised his hand and stroked her cheek with his fingertips, until they were on her temple, forcing her to look into his eyes.

'Your mother knew the real thing when she saw it. I was dazzled by you, Amber. Dazzled and scared about how deep I was getting into a relationship I never saw coming. She took one look at me and saw a terrified young man who had barely survived his parents' divorce and was determined not to make the same mistake myself. She knew that we cared about each other very much. Too much. You were so beautiful and talented and for some crazy reason you wanted to be my friend and were even willing to sacrifice your music scholarship to stay in London with me. She couldn't let that happen.'

Sam made a slicing motion with the flat of his hand through the air.

'So she did the only thing she knew. She used my feelings for you to break us up.'

The air was broken by the sound of Amber's ragged breathing but Sam kept going. If ever there was a time and a place for the truth to come out, this was as good as any.

'All she had to do was put the idea in my head that you were looking for a ring on your finger and a house and two kids and that was it. She didn't need to spell it out. Staying with me would mean the end of your career as a concert pianist and my grandiose fantasy scheme to be an intrepid international reporter.'

Sam turned to face the garden so that he could rest his elbows on his knees, only too well aware that Amber's gaze would still be fixed on his face.

'That was the weird thing. I didn't believe her at first. I kept telling myself that she simply wanted me to leave you alone because she didn't think that I was good enough or ambitious enough for you.

'The problem was, when I went back into the party, you were talking to your rich friends from the private school who were all in designer gear and real jewels, chatting away about yacht holidays, and the more I thought about it, the more I realised that maybe she had a point. What future did we have together? If you stayed with me, I would be holding you back. You would be better taking the scholarship and spending the next three years in Paris with people who could further your career. People who sat in the back of limos. Not in the driver's seat.'

'Sam—no!' Amber exploded. 'How could you even think that? Why didn't you come and talk to me about what she had said? I would have put that idea out of your head right then and there.'

He shook his head. 'Clever woman, your mother. She knew that my dad was on his own because my mum had walked out on us. All she had to do was plant the idea in my head that if I wasn't good enough for my own mother—then how could I possibly be good enough for her beautiful and talented daughter who deserved the very best in life? The big chip on my shoulder did the rest.'

Amber took his hand in hers and squeezed but he dared not look at her. Not yet. 'It was all too much; my head was thumping with the champagne and I couldn't deal with everything with the sound of the party going on around me. So I slipped out of the kitchen door and into the car park to get some air.'

Sam looked up into the sky, where the stars were already bright. 'And you know who was there, waiting for me in the convertible?'

'Petra,' she replied in a shaky voice.

He nodded. 'She had a bottle of champagne and two glasses and my mind was so racing with all the possibilities and problems and options that it never even occurred to me to wonder why she was outside in the first place. It was only later that I found out—Petra knew that I was going to be coming outside.'

'My mother sent Petra out to wait for you? Is that what you're saying?'

Sam nodded. 'Petra called a few days later to tell me that her folks were taking her to their villa in Tuscany for the whole of the summer before finishing school in Switzerland. I think she was genuinely sorry that she had been used the way she was, but by then it was too late. You had already left for Paris. It was too late. She had done it. She had broken us up.'

Amber pushed off the bench and walked across the patio to the flower beds and stood with her back to Sam, her shoulders heaving up and down with emotion.

Every word that Sam had said echoed around inside her head, making it impossible for her to reply to him.

Her good arm wrapped tight around her waist, trying to hold in the explosion of confusion and regret that was threatening to burst out of her at any moment.

And not just about what had happened on her eighteenth birthday.

She had been so totally trusting and gullible! But the more she thought about it, the more she recognised that Sam was right. She was still dancing to her family's tune eleven years later—and the worst thing was, she was the one who was allowing them to do it.

So much for her great plans to make a new life for herself! She was still too afraid to make her own decisions and follow her heart.

No longer.

That ended tonight.

From now on, she chose what to do and where. And who with.

Starting with Parvita. She wanted to see her friend get married so very much and that was precisely what she was going to do. Risk be damned.

Before Amber could calm her beating heart, she sensed his presence and seconds later a strong hand slid onto each side of her waist, holding her firm. Secure. She breathed in his aftershave, but did not resist as he moved closer behind her until she could feel the length of his body from chest to groin pressed against her back.

She had not even realised that she was shivering until she

felt the delicious warmth and weight of Sam's dinner jacket as he dropped it over her shoulders.

Sam's arms wrapped tighter around her waist, the fingers pressing oh so gently into her ribcage and Amber closed her eyes, her pulse racing. It had been a long time. And he smelt fabulous. Felt. Fabulous.

Sam pressed his head into the side of her neck, his light stubble grazing against her skin, and her head dropped back slightly so that it was resting on his.

Bad head.

Bad need for contact with this man.

Bad full stop.

One of his hands slid up the side of her neck and smoothed her hair away from her face so that he could press his lips against the back of her neck.

'It was all my fault,' he said, and his low, soft voice sounded different. Strained. Hesitant. 'I was trying to do the right thing and in the end I caused you pain. I'm so sorry.'

Amber sighed and looked up at the twinkling stars in the night sky, but sensed her shoulders lift with tension.

'There's nothing for you to be sorry about. It was eleven years ago and we were both so young and trying to find our way. It's just…it never crossed my mind that you were trying to do the noble thing by walking out on me. I wasted a lot of angry tears. And that is just sad, Sam.'

Sam continued to breathe into her neck, and one of his hands slid up from her waist to move in small circles on her shoulders under his jacket, and Amber suddenly began to heat up at a remarkably rapid rate.

'I know you're tired. No wonder. I've watched you dance the night away and I'm glad that I was here to see that. So thank you again for inviting me. Although Kate was watching me like a hawk to make sure that I wasn't making any moves on you.'

And that did make Amber grin. 'Kate the virtue keeper. I like that.'

Sam said nothing, but the hand tracing circles slid down her arm from shoulder to wrist, and he moved impossibly closer, his hand moving slowly up and down her arm.

'And necessary. You look very beautiful tonight.'

Amber smiled wide enough for Sam to sense her movement. 'Thank you. And thank you for finally telling me the truth about what happened.'

She slowly lifted one of Sam's hands from her waist and pushed gently away from him, instantly sorry that she had broken the touch, but turned back to face him.

'It's gone midnight. And I have had a very bad year, Sam. In so many ways. I don't want to start the next year of my life with regrets and bitterness.'

The smile on his lips faded and his upper lip twitched a couple of times. Amber knew that move. He couldn't be nervous. *Could he*?

She looked into his face and smiled a closed mouth smile. 'We both made mistakes. And I'm the last person who should be judging anyone. So how about starting the next year of my life as we mean to go on? As old friends who have just met up again after a long break. Can you do that?'

'Old friends,' he replied and lifted her fingers to his lips, his eyes never leaving hers. 'I'll drink to that. How about…'

But, before Sam could finish speaking, a fat lounger cushion whacked him on the side of the head. And then a second time.

'You can stop that right now, Sam Richards. I mean it. Stop or I'll go and find the rolling pin and wrap it around your ears.'

'It's okay, Kate.' Amber sighed and rolled her eyes. 'Sam has just passed the audition. He'll be coming to India to interview me next week. You can put the pillow down.'

Sam stopped ducking his head and whipped around. 'What did you just say?'

'I have changed my mind about going to Parvita's wedding.' Amber smiled, her eyebrows high. 'Isn't that exciting?'

CHAPTER TEN

From: Amber@AmberDuBois.net
To: Kate@LondonBespokeTailoring.com; Saskia@Elwood-House.co.uk
Subject: Sam Report
Hey Goddesses

Greetings from another gorgeous day in Kerala. The girls are still trying to settle down after all of the excitement of Parvita's wedding so lots to do, but my wrist is feeling a lot better today—despite all of the sitar playing!

Sam's flight was an hour late leaving London so he won't arrive until very late in the evening, which is probably a good thing considering this pre monsoon heatwave. No doubt he is bursting to get this interview over and done with so he can get back to his nice cool London office. Especially since I asked the janitor to pick Sam up at the airport in his rusty old motor, which is definitely on its last legs. Just for Kate.

Will report back tomorrow. Have fun. Amber

SAM RICHARDS SLID his rucksack off his shoulder and mopped the sweat from his brow and neck with one of his dad's pocket handkerchiefs as he strolled up the few steps to the single storey white building. If it was this hot at dusk he was dreading the midday temperature. But he would find out soon enough.

Great! *Not.*

The school janitor, who had picked him up at the airport,

had pointed him towards the main entrance to the girls' home but Sam had barely been able to hear what he said since he kept the wreck of a car engine going just in case it broke down before he made it home.

The last hour had been spent in a bone-shaking car from the nineteen-sixties driven by a friendly janitor who seemed oblivious to the fact that he was hitting every pothole on the dirt road between the local airport and the girls' home in a car with bald tyres and no suspension.

Sam was amazed that the patched up, barely intact motor had lasted the journey without breaking down in a coconut grove or rice paddy. But it had got him here and for that he was grateful.

Slipping his sunglasses into his shirt breast pocket, Sam stretched his arms tall and tried to take in the sensory over-load that was the Kerala coastline at sunset.

And failed.

The sea breeze from the shockingly beautiful crescent shaped bay was blocked by the low brick wall which formed the boundary of the property, creating a breathless oasis of fruit trees, a vegetable garden and exotic flowering plants which spilled out in an explosion of startlingly bright colours from wooden tubs and planters.

The immaculately kept gardens stretched down to the ocean and a wide strip of stunning white sand which glowed in the reflected shades of deep rich apricot, scarlet and gold from the setting sun. His view of the lapping waves was broken only by the thin trunks of tall coconut palms, banana plants and fruit trees.

It was like a poster of a dream beach from the cover of a holiday brochure. Complete with a long wooden fishing boat on the shore and umbrellas made from coconut palm fronds to protect the fishermen and occasional tourists who were out on the beach this late in the evening.

Coconuts. He was looking at real coconut palm trees. Compared to the grey, drizzly London Sam had left the previous afternoon the warm breeze was luxuriously dry and scented with the salty tang from the sea blended with spice and a tropical sweet floral scent.

A great garland of bougainvillea with stunning bright purple and hot pink flowers wound its way up the side of the school entrance and onto the coconut fibre roof, intertwined with a wonderful frangipani which spilled out from a blue ceramic pot, attracting bees and other nectar-seeking insects to the intensely fragrant blossoms. The perfume almost balanced out the heavy red dust from the dirt road and the bio odours from the cows and chickens who roamed freely on the other side of a low coconut matting fence.

He loved writing and his life as a journalist. He always had, but it was only when he came to villages like this one that it really struck home how much of his life was spent in open plan offices under fluorescent light tubes.

Even the air tasted different on his tongue. Traffic from the coast road roared past. Trucks in all colours, painted auto rickshaws and bright yellow buses competed with birdsong and the chatter of people and motor scooters. Everywhere he looked his eyes and ears were assaulted by a cacophony of life.

But as he relaxed into the scene, hands on his hips, the sound of piano music drifted out through the partly open door of what looked like a school building to his left and Sam smiled and wandered over, his shirt sticking to his back in the oppressive heat and humidity.

Amber was sitting on a very frail looking low wooden bench in front of an upright piano which had definitely seen better days. The polish was flaking off, the lid was warped and, from where he was standing, it looked as if some of the black keys were missing at the bottom of the scale.

But it didn't matter. Because Amber DuBois was running the fingers of her left hand across the keyboard and suddenly the old neglected instrument was singing like a nightingale.

She was dressed in a blue and pink long-sleeved cotton tunic and what looked like pyjama bottoms, her hair was held back by a covered elastic band and, as her feet moved across the pedals, he caught a glimpse of a plastic flip-flop.

And, for the first time in his professional life, Sam Richards did not know what to say.

Amber DuBois had never looked more beautiful in her life. Exotic. Enchanting. But at that moment there was something else—she was totally and completely relaxed and content. Her eyes were closed and, as she played, she was humming along gently to the music as it soared into flights of soft and then dramatic sections of what sounded to Sam's un-educated ears as some great romantic composer's finest work.

Her shoulders lifted and fell, her left arm flowing from side to side in brilliant technique while her plastered hand moved stiffly from octave to octave. But that did not matter—the music was so magical and captivating that it reverberated around this tiny school room and into every bone of his body.

The tropical garden and birdsong outside the window disappeared as he was swept up in the music.

This was her joy and her delight. The thing she loved most in the world.

He was looking at a completely different woman from the one who had flounced into his dad's garage, or the fashion model who had haughtily gossiped with the designer goddesses as she decluttered her apartment.

This was the real Amber. This was the girl he used to know. The girl whose greatest joy was playing the piano for her own entertainment and pleasure.

She was back!

And Lord, the longer he looked at her and listened to her

music, the more he liked what he saw and the more he lusted. The fire that had sparked the second his fingers had touched her skin in that ridiculous penthouse dressing room suddenly flared right back into a blazing bonfire.

The heat and humidity of Kerala in May was nothing compared to the incendiary fire in his blood which pounded in his neck and ears.

Did she know? Did Amber have any clue that when she played liked this she was revealing to the world how much inner passion was hidden inside the cool blonde slender frame?

He had thought that he had been attracted to her before, but that was nothing compared to the way he felt now.

He wanted her. And not just in his bed. He wanted Amber in his life, even if it was only for a few days, weeks or months. He wanted to be her friend and the man she wanted to share her life with. The music seemed to soak into his heart and soul and fill every cell with a fierce determination.

Somehow he was going to have to find a way of winning her back and persuading her to give him a second chance, or risk losing her for ever.

His bag slumped onto the floor.

Sam walked slowly into the room and slid next to Amber on the very end of the child-sized wooden bench. She did not open her eyes but smiled and slowly inhaled before giving an appreciative sigh.

'They say you can tell a lot about a man from the aftershave he has chosen. Very nice. Did you buy it at the airport?'

Her hands never missed a note as he gave a short dismissive grunt in reply. 'Then you won't mind if I move a little closer.'

Sam was blatantly aware that the fine wool cloth of his trousers brushed against the loose cotton trousers Amber was wearing as he slid along the shiny wooden surface until the whole side of his body seemed to be aligned against her.

'Hello. How was the flight?'

He started to say something, changed his mind, and left her staring at his mouth for just a few seconds too long. Much too long. His eyes scanned her face as though he was trying to record the images like a digital camera in his memory.

He had been worried about how awkward this moment was going to be. But, instead of watching every word, it was as though he was meeting one of his best friends in the world—and his heart lifted.

'You're playing nursery rhymes. From memory.'

She shook her head slowly from side to side. 'It sounds terrible and I am totally out of practice.'

'But you are trying. In your apartment last week, I couldn't help wonder if the old piano-playing business had lost its appeal. Am I right?'

Her fingers slowed down but did not stop. 'Full marks to the man in the sweaty shirt. You're right. I didn't want to play. No. That's wrong. I didn't want to perform.' She gave a little giggle and her left hand played a trill. 'This is not performing. This is having fun. And I have missed that. Do you know what I spent this afternoon doing? Making up tunes and songs around nursery rhymes these girls have never heard before. We had a great time.'

'Wait a minute. Are you telling me that you don't enjoy performing? Is that why you decided to retire? Because you do know that you are brilliant, don't you? I even splashed out and bought your latest album!'

She stopped playing, sat back and smiled, wide-eyed.

'You did? That was very kind.'

'No, it wasn't kind. It was a delight. And you haven't answered my question.'

Her gaze scanned his face as though looking for something

important and Sam suddenly remembered that he needed a wash and a shave. 'That depends on who is asking the question,' she replied in a low, soft voice with the power to entrance him. 'My old pal Sam who I used to trust once upon a time, or the newest super-journalist at GlobalStar Media who I am not sure about at all.'

He swallowed down a moment of doubt but made the tough choice. Editor be damned. 'Let's try that first option.'

'Okay. Let's.' She looked down at her left hand and stretched out the fingers on the piano keys. 'Well. *Off the record.* These past few years have been very hard going. I haven't given myself enough time to recover from one tour before launching into rehearsals for the next. Combine that with all of the travelling and media interviews and suddenly I'm waking up exhausted every morning and nothing I do seems to make any difference.'

Her gaze shifted to his eyes and locked on tight. Shades of blue and violet clashed against the faint golden tinge to her skin. 'Every night was a struggle to make myself play and dive into the music to try and find some energy. I lost my spark, Sam. I lost my joy.'

'That's not the girl I used to know talking.'

'I'm not that same girl any more.'

'Aren't you?' Sam replied and reached up and touched her cheek. 'Are you quite sure about that? Because when I came in just now you had that soppy girly look on your face like you used to have when you sat down at a piano.'

'What do you mean, soppy?'

'Soppy. It means that you are your old self again—and I am very glad of it. This place seems to be doing you a lot of good.'

He glanced down and shocked her by gently lifting up her left hand and turning it over, his forefinger tracing the outline of the beautiful scrolls and flowers drawn in henna on the back of her hand.

'Take this, for example. I've never seen anything like it. Totally amazing. How was the wedding?'

His fingers stroked her palm, then lifted the back of her hand to his lips so that he could kiss her knuckles and was rewarded with an intense flash of awareness that told him that she knew exactly what he was saying. It was not the henna he found amazing.

She tutted twice, took her hand back then turned to face him. 'It was a fabulous wedding and I wouldn't have missed it for the world.' She gestured with her head towards the window. 'Parvita's family organised a flower arch in the garden and the service was so simple. A few words spoken by a man and a woman from completely different worlds, and yet it was totally perfect. There was not a dry eye in the house.'

'You cried at your friend's wedding? Really? And there is no such thing as a perfect marriage, just a decent wedding day.'

'Yes, I cried, you cynic,' Amber replied and scowled at him and pulled her hand away. 'Because this was the real thing. They didn't need a huge hotel with hundreds of guests who they would never have a chance to meet and talk to. All they wanted was their friends and family to help them celebrate. The little girls were all dressed up and throwing flowers. It was perfect. So don't mock.'

Sam held up both hands in surrender.

'Hey. Remember my ex-girlfriend who tried to lure me into a wedding without asking me first? Not all of us believe in happy endings, you old romantic.'

Amber thumped him on the arm. 'Well, that is just sad and pathetic.'

'Maybe you're right,' Sam replied and looked around, suddenly desperate to change the subject. 'Is this one of your school rooms?'

She nodded. 'The building work is going flat out before the

monsoon rains so this is a temporary teaching room. I like it but I can't wait until the new air conditioned school is ready.'

'Have you decided on a name for the school you are paying for?' Sam asked as he picked up his bag and they strolled out into the evening air. 'The DuBois centre? Or the DuBois School for Girls. What is it to be?'

'Oh, you would like that, wouldn't you? No. I suggested a few names to the board of governors and they came back with one winner: the Elwood School.'

'Elwood? You named the school after your friend Saskia? Why did you choose that name?'

Amber leant back and gestured towards the girls who were playing on the grassy lawn under the mango and cashew nut trees. 'Do you see these lovely girls? They are so talented and bursting with life and enthusiasm. And yet not one of them has a home to go to. They are not all orphans as we would define orphans—far from it. Most of them have parents who cannot look after them or there were problems at home which mean that they only see their parents for a few months every year. But one way or another they have found their way here to this girls' home, where they can feel safe and protected by people who love them.'

Amber turned back to Sam with moisture sparkling in the corners of her eyes and when she spoke there was a hoarseness in her voice which clutched at Sam's heart and squeezed it tight. 'Well, I know just what that feels like. Saskia and her aunt Margot gave me a safe refuge when I needed to get away from my mother and whatever man she was living with who struggled to recall my name.'

Then she shook her head with a chuckle. 'They even let me stay with them after the mega-row I had with my so called parents after the disaster that was my eighteenth birthday party.'

Sam coughed, twice. 'You had a fight with your mother? I haven't heard that part of the story.'

She sniffed. 'I had no idea that those particular terms of abuse were in my vocabulary until I heard them come out of my mouth. Harsh words were exchanged about the expensive education I had been subjected to. It was not my moment of shining glory. And then I stomped out of the house with only my handbag and walked around to Elwood House. And Saskia and her aunt Margot took me in and looked after me as though I was one of their own.'

Amber sat up straight and curled her right hand high into the air with a flourish. 'Ta da. Elwood School.' Then she blinked and gave a curt nod. 'It may surprise you but I do have something in common with Parvita and these girls.'

Then she shivered and chuckled. 'Well, I did tell you that this article was going to be a challenge. I cannot wait to see what you do with that little insight, if it was on the record.'

'Any more like that?'

'Plenty. Just wait and see what tomorrow brings.'

CHAPTER ELEVEN

From: Amber@AmberDuBois.net
To: Kate@LondonBespokeTailoring.com; Saskia@Elwood-House.co.uk
Subject: My fiendish plan
Well, this is turning out to be a very odd week.

I came out first thing this morning to find Sam halfway up a jackfruit tree tossing fruit down to the girls below. He claims that he couldn't sleep because of the heat but he is now their official hero in long pants and is mobbed wherever he goes. I have just peeked outside and he is showing his little gaggle of fans the slideshow of photos on his digital camera. Amazing!

He even had me playing Christmas carols and nursery songs to amuse the girls during meal times in exchange for helping to organise the juniors. They adored him. I think he may never be allowed to leave!

My fiendish plan is to steal Sam away long enough for a walk along the beach at dusk and talk him into working on Parvita's story instead of mine. It is worth a try. Otherwise I don't know how long I can keep him hanging on.

The good news is that my wrist is feeling a lot better and I am enjoying playing for the first time in ages.
Cheers from Kerala. Amber

From: Kate@LondonBespokeTailoring.com
To: Amber@AmberDuBois.net

Subject: Sam Report
Sheesh, that man has no shame when it comes to charming the ladies. Don't be fooled. Glad that your hand is feeling better. Don't forget to drink plenty of water. Love ya. K

SAM WIPED THE spark plug from the janitor's ancient motor
car on a scrap of cotton and held it up to the fading sunlight
before deciding that the plug had lived a very long life and
needed to take retirement, as of right now. He had managed
to find one replacement at the bottom of a tool kit which was
so rusty that it had taken hours to clean the tools to the stage
where he could use them to service what passed as a car.

But at least the work had kept him close to Amber.

They still had a lot of work to do to rebuild that fragile
friendship but she had seemed genuinely delighted when he
helped her collect the girls together and keep them in one
place long enough for her to explain about the keys on the
piano and what the notes meant. With a bit of help from a
couple of coconut shells, three tin buckets and a wrench.

Weird. He had surprised himself by actually enjoying playing on a makeshift set of drums.

The only thing they were not doing was talking about her
career.

She might have trusted him enough to take the risk and invite him here to his magical place to see what she was doing
with her life but that was as far as it went.

So far there had always been some excellent excuse why
this was not a good time to record an interview and after three
days he had all the background photos he might need but not
the exclusive extra material he needed to create a compel-
ling story—her story.

So what was the problem?

The sound of female laughter echoed out from the school
room and he peered in through the window just in time to

see Amber conducting a mini orchestra of five girls playing wooden recorders in tune with some Italian baroque music which blasted out from a cheap cassette player perched on the teacher's desk.

He smiled and dropped back down before she saw him.

It might have been his idea for her to play a few simple tunes, one note at a time, but once she got started the girls and teachers had begged her for more and now there was no stopping her.

Amber had a way with the girls that was nothing short of astonishing. It was as if they knew that she understood what they were going through and wanted to help them any way she could.

And it had nothing to do with her musical talent, although she was playing more and more every day.

Amber was giving these girls the kind of unconditional love he hadn't seen in a long time.

Seeing her with the children, it was obvious that Amber would make a wonderful mother—but how did that happen? Her own parents certainly had not been good role models. No. This came from her own heart and her ability to reach out and touch a child's life and make a little girl laugh.

Perhaps it was a good thing that Amber had thrown herself into working with the girls at the orphanage. Because the longer he spent with her and listened to her sweet voice and shared her laughter, the harder it was to kid himself that he could control this burning attraction to her.

He was falling for Amber DuBois all over again.

And that had to be the craziest thing that had happened to him in a long time.

But the worst thing that he could do right now—for either of them, was tell her how he felt. He had to be patient, even if it killed him.

Somehow he had to stay objective and cool enough to write

an exclusive celebrity interview which gave no hint of how badly he wanted to be with the celebrity, talk to her and tell her how much she meant to him.

No. Forget wanted. Make that *needed* to be with her while he had the chance.

In the past few weeks he had seen Amber the cold, snarky concert pianist, Amber the fashion designers' favourite model, who happened to love Indian food as much as he did, and now he was mending the janitor's car while a stripped down, enchanting Amber taught small girls with bangles on their wrists all about Italian baroque.

And guess which version of Amber was capable of rocking his world just at the sight of her?

Every day she spent here seemed to make her even more relaxed and at ease. Happy and laughing. Enjoying her music again with every note she played and loving every minute she spent with these girls. And she could teach—that was obvious, even if she did roll her eyes at him every time he applauded after a class.

He must have told her a dozen times how good it was to hear her play with such delight—even if it was with one hand and a few fingertips, and his message seemed to be getting through. She had actually admitted over breakfast that she had never enjoyed music so much in a long time.

Maybe retiring from concert performances was not such a bad idea for Amber DuBois?

Everything he had seen and heard so far told him that she was serious about turning her back on the offers streaming in from orchestras all over the world. Frank had got that wrong. She was a lot more interested in the girls here than a prestigious career—for the moment, at least.

Sam jumped into the broken driver's seat and listened as the engine reluctantly kicked into life.

The problem was that after listening to Amber's countless

stories about how wonderful her friend Parvita's wedding had been, it was fairly obvious that her idea of a happy relationship meant a ring on her finger and a house and a garden with children to play in it.

What was it with women and weddings? Why couldn't two people accept that they wanted to share their lives and be happy at that?

A few months before his ex-girlfriend Alice took the initiative in Los Angeles, they had travelled to New York for her cousin's wedding and over a very long weekend at grandiose parties he had fended off at regular intervals the constant ribbing from her relatives about when they were going to make an announcement about their wedding. Alice had done the same, only with a twist. 'Oh, Sam is not the marrying type. You can take a horse to water, but you can't make him drink. Isn't that right, Sam?'

And he had smiled and replied with yet another joke, just a bit of fun to amuse the other guests. Alice had known, even then, that they would never be together long-term, and he had been too complacent to talk to her about it. Too content to accept second best and go with the flow. Until she'd decided to take the initiative and organise the wedding on her own. And he had bolted.

Coward. After he'd left, Alice had found someone she wanted to spend the rest of her life with.

Amber was bound to do the same. She was beautiful, funny and talented and she deserved some happiness in her life. With a man who could give her what she wanted.

He wanted Amber to be happy—why wouldn't he?

The problem was, he had broken the unwritten rule. He cared about Amber. If he went back to London without telling her how he felt he would be walking away from the best thing in his life. And breaking both of their hearts all over again. And that truly would make him a coward.

'Hey there. Good news. You have just won the prize for inventing a new musical instrument. Coconut shells and buckets filled with different amounts of water make different sounds when you hit them with a wrench. Who knew? The girls loved it! What made you think of that?'

'Ingenuity. And drumming on oil cans in my dad's garage. I thought it might work.' Sam chuckled up at Amber, who was waving goodbye to the girls who were streaming out from her classroom. 'Failing that, I could always play the spoons. But I am saving that for an encore. I live in hope.'

Amber gave a small shoulder shrug. 'Either one of those would work for me. It seems that you have hidden talents after all. Are your mum and dad musical?'

'Not a bit. Nobody in our house could sing a note in tune but I like the drums. Not exactly the most subtle of instruments and my mum couldn't stand me making a noise in the house so my dad let me make loose on the oil drums. I hope I didn't scare the girls.'

'Not a bit and I was impressed. But, speaking of hope, are you free to come down to the beach for a stroll before it gets dark? It's lovely and cool down there.'

'Five minutes to wash my hands and I'll be right with you. That's the best offer I have had all day,' he replied with a sexy wink.

'Keep that up and it will be the only offer you have. Meet you under the palm tree. Second from the left.'

'It's a date,' he whispered and was rewarded with a definite flush to her cheeks before she lifted her chin in denial, rolled her eyes in pretend disgust and strolled down the lawns towards the bay.

In the end it took Sam ten minutes to wash then extricate himself from the gaggle of girls who clutched onto his legs as he made his way across the gardens towards the beach.

But it was worth it.

Sam reached for his small pocket digital camera so that he could capture the lovely image of the woman who was sitting on the edge of an old wooden fishing boat on a wide stretch of the most incredible fine golden sand, on a beach fringed with coconut palms.

She looked up as he took the shot and gave him a warm smile which came from the heart.

And he knew. Just like that. This was the photo he would use on the cover of his article—and keep in his wallet for rainy days back in London when the office got too much.

She was wearing a simple tunic and trousers, the plaster cast on her wrist covered with children's names, and her hair was tied back with a scarf. And in his eyes she was the most beautiful woman that he had ever seen in his life.

And then he saw it. Nestling at her throat. It was a gold heart shaped pendant that had cost him every penny of the money that he had been saving for spare tyres for the car his dad was working on for him.

He had given her the necklace in the car the evening of her eighteenth birthday the moment before he had turned the key in the ignition. And it had been worth every penny just to see her face light up with joy and happiness at that moment.

It was the first time she had kissed him without him prompting—and it meant the world to him.

He couldn't drag his eyes away from it. Of all the jewels she must have collected she had chosen to wear his necklace tonight. Had she chosen it to provoke him, or, and his heart swelled at the thought, to show that she had not forgotten how very close they had been?

Sam shuffled closer to her, stretched out his hand and, with two fingers, lifted the gold chain clear of her remarkable cleavage and dangled the heart pendant in the air.

'Nice necklace.'

'Thank you. It was a gift from a boy I was in love with at the time. I wear it now and again.'

'To remind yourself that you were loved?'

'To remind myself that love can break your heart,' Amber replied and reached up and took hold of Sam's fingers in hers. 'And that I was loved. Yes, that too.'

And she took his breath away with the honesty.

So much so that, instead of sitting next to her, Sam knelt down on the sand in front of Amber and looked deep into her surprised eyes before asking the question which had been welling up all day.

'Why are you avoiding our interview, Amber? What is it that you are so afraid of telling me?'

Her reply was to break off eye contact and look out over his shoulder to the sea in silence.

'We were such close friends once,' he went on. 'We used to talk about everything. Our hopes and our dreams. Our great plans for the future. *Everything*. I don't think you have any idea how much it hurts me that you find it so impossible to get past the mistake I made when I listened to your mother and walked out of your birthday party that night.'

She glanced back at him, reached out and plucked a leaf from his shoulder. 'I thought that you were the one who had thrown our friendship away as though it didn't matter.'

'You were wrong. So *wrong*. I was confused about where we could go as a couple—but never about that. You were always the friend I came to when I needed someone. Always.'

His gaze scanned her face from her brow to her chin and back again. 'You were the only real friend I had. Oh, I know that you and your pals thought that I was the popular boy around town, but the truth was harder to accept. I knew everyone in my area, played football and talked big, but I was still too raw from my parents' divorce to talk about what really mattered to anyone at school. So I kept my deep feelings to myself. Even if that meant being lonely.'

'Was that why you talked to me, Sam? Because I was an outsider?'

'Maybe.' He shrugged. 'I may also have noticed that you were not hard to look at. But hey, I was a teenage pressure cooker of hormones and bad skin. Nothing special about that.'

'Yes, you were. You were always special. To me at least.'

'I know.' His brows squeezed together. 'I think that was what scared me in the end, Amber.'

'What do you mean?'

'You took me seriously. You listened to me babbling on about what a successful journalist I was going to become and actually encouraged me to stick my neck out and pass the exams I needed to go to university. You believed in me. And that was one of the reasons why I fell in love with you.'

He heard her sharp intake of breath but ignored it and carried on. 'And it terrified me. I had seen my parents fall apart from all of the fights and arguments which they tried to keep from me, but failed miserably. You were not the only one to be dragged around from new house to new house as your mother found a new partner. I refused to go to see my mum the minute I turned eighteen but she still had the power to make my life miserable.'

Sam paused. He had not thought about that in years. Strange. 'And then you stepped out of a limo with your mother one evening. Amber Sheridan DuBois.' He grinned up into her face. 'And suddenly my life was not so miserable after all. And I will always be grateful to you for being the friend that had been missing from my life and I hadn't even realised that fact. Always. I couldn't have been happier that last year.'

'Until we became more than friends. Is that what you are saying?'

Sam nodded, lips pressed tight together. 'That night of

your eighteenth when we got back to your house after our mini tour of London, and I told you that I loved you—I meant it, Amber.'

He pushed himself to his feet. 'That is why you asked me to come out to Kerala instead of giving your interview in London or over the Internet. You knew that I loved you but I still walked away. And now you are the one with the power to walk away and leave me behind.' Sam shook his head and half turned to look out across the sands to the gaggle of children playing in the surf. 'Strange,' he chuckled, 'I never thought that you would turn out to be such a diva.'

Amber gasped so loudly that Sam whirled back to look at her.

'A diva?' she repeated in a horrified voice. 'You think I am behaving like a diva? Oh, Sam. You have no idea how hurtful it is for me to hear you say those words. A diva?'

She shook her arm away as he reached out to take it and stood up. 'A diva is the very last thing I ever wanted to be.'

Sam started to follow her onto the sand, but she whirled around to face him, her hand clenched into a tight fist by her side. 'I thought that you, of all people, would understand why I despise the very word. That was what they used to call her. Remember? "The loveliest diva in the music business". Julia Swan.'

Sam groaned. 'Yes. Of course I remember. Your mum used to relish it. But I thought…I thought you wanted star billing and your own dressing room. You have worked so hard for so many years as a soloist. Doesn't that go with the territory?'

'Of course it does. And I have worked hard. So very hard. But you still don't understand, do you?'

She stepped up to him and clenched hold of his hand. 'That wasn't what I wanted. It has never been what I wanted. I loved the music. That was the important thing.'

She released him and turned sideways to stand with her

arm wrapped around her waist and look out over the ocean. 'You asked me the other day why I wanted to retire. It wasn't the work. It was me.'

Her voice faded away as though the breeze was carrying it out to sea. 'I didn't like what I was becoming, Sam. And this last tour of Asia was the final straw.'

She flung back her head so that the breeze could cool her neck. 'By the time we got to India, I started demanding things like my own dressing room and quiet hotel rooms and white cushions and stupid things like that. My pals on the tour said that it was because we were all so tired but when we got to Kerala and took a break from the tour I realised that the concert organisers were wary of me—they expected me to be demanding and difficult.'

As Sam watched, Amber closed her eyes. 'And the worst thing was that the complaining and the headaches—they had nothing to do with the love of the music and everything to do with the stress of the performances and the touring. Somewhere along the way my passion for the music had been buried under the avalanche of photo shoots and the press parties and the dresses and I hadn't even noticed. And that was so wrong.'

Amber half turned to look at Sam and she felt the tears prick the corners of her eyes even before she said the words. 'I was turning into my mother and it was killing the one thing that I had loved. I was terrified of becoming that sad and bitter and lonely diva that was Julia Swan. That's when I decided to retire, Sam. I was terrified that I was turning into my mother.'

CHAPTER TWELVE

'No,' Sam replied, resting the palms of his hands on Amber's shoulders and drawing her back to the boat to sit down. 'That was never going to happen. Never.'

His gaze locked onto her lovely eyes and held them tight. 'I've spent the last three days watching you connect with these girls. Where did you learn those skills? Not from Julia Swan and certainly not by being some diva.'

She smiled back at him but her eyes were suddenly sad. 'I can say the same thing about you. Those girls love you. But you don't understand. It had already happened. And do you know the worst thing? The moment it hit me what I was doing was when I finally understood her. After all of these years I finally understood that my mother didn't hate people—she hated her job. She hated it but she didn't know anything else, so she took her frustration out on everyone around her.'

'You might be right. But what did you do? Just walk off the tour?'

She flashed him a look. 'Hardly. No. My friend Parvita had organised a series of charity concerts in small towns and school halls in Kerala and Goa. Until then I had always said that I was too busy, but at the very last minute their solo pianist had to go to New York and Parvita asked me to take his place.'

She raised her hands then dropped them to her lap. 'What

can I say? India knocked me sideways. I love everything about it. The heat, the colours, everything. We travelled with a group of incredible sitar players, and we had the best tour of our lives. And the very last day was a revelation. Can you imagine—the whole musical troupe was in a rickety bus, dodging the potholes, in the middle of nowhere heading for a string of orphanages for abandoned girls?'

She looked at Sam and managed a smile.

'Nothing can prepare you for what we found here. I thought I had seen it all. Wrong again. Same with my friends. I think I cried every night. It was tough going but Parvita worked her magic and for a short while we had a real working music school right here in this village. We had planned to do two nights at the orphanage before heading back to the airport. We stayed a week! Can you imagine? By working all around the area, we raised enough money to pay for hospital treatment for the girls with enough left over to give them a decent meal every day for a month. These girls. Oh, Sam. These amazing girls.'

She broke into a wide grin. 'You wouldn't believe the fun we all had. It was crazy. They are living in the worst conditions and they found happiness. It was very precious. I'll never forget it.'

'I can see how important it is to you. Is that why you decided to come back here for Parvita's wedding?'

Amber nodded. 'Parvita wants to create the music school but she needs help to pay the teachers' wages and keep things going. So when she left on her honeymoon I offered to stay on and help in the school before the monsoon hits.'

She paused and her eyes flicked up at Sam as he held his breath for what she was about to say next. 'I have had the most amazing fun here. You were right when you told me that I seemed happier here. The problem is—until I came here I had no idea how shallow and self-indulgent my life as a concert performer was. These girls have given me a new insight into my life.'

'You worked your whole life for your success, Amber. Hey, wait a minute. Last summer you were the new face of a huge cosmetics campaign. How does that fit in?'

Amber screwed up her face and Sam could almost see hear her jaw clench. Her face creased into a grimace. 'It was a tricky decision. My agent was thrilled and suddenly I had all of these glamorous people telling me what an asset I would be for their cosmetics. But that was not why I did it. Of course my first reaction was to laugh it off as some big joke. But then they offered me a sum of money that made my head spin. A wicked amount of money. Criminal, really. And once I had that sum in my head, it wouldn't go away. I kept thinking about my friend Parvita and all of the fund-raising work she was doing for the charity. And the more I thought about it, the more I realised that what I was actually saying was that my pride was more important than these girls having an education and healthcare. All I had to do was sit there wearing a lovely dress while make-up experts, hairdressers and lighting engineers worked their magic. This was ridiculous. I couldn't walk away from that opportunity to do something remarkable for the sake of a few hours having my photograph taken. That would be so selfish I wouldn't be able to live with myself.'

She chuckled. 'I knew that I would get a terrible kicking from the media. And I did. You and your colleagues were not very kind and it upset me at the time, but do you know what?'

Amber smiled and dropped her shoulders. 'It was worth it. I had to weigh up every cruel comment from the music press and every sniping gossip columnist against seeing a real school going up in place of the slum ruin that was here before.'

'Why didn't you tell them? That the money wasn't going into your own bank account?'

Amber turned to face him. 'You know why, Sam. How long

have you been interviewing television personalities and so-called celebrities? Years, right? And how many times have you ridiculed the charity work that people do with their time and money? It doesn't seem to matter if a famous basketball player wants to visit a hospice for the day to cheer up the boys. Or a bestselling novelist donates a huge amount to a literacy campaign. They are all accused of having so much money that they can splash out on some charity or other for tax reasons and to make them look good.'

She shook her head. 'That's not for me, Sam. I wanted this project to be part of my private life, away from the media and the cameras and the concert halls. It is too personal and important. The last thing I want is my photo with the girls to be splashed over the cover of some celebrity gossip magazine. I would hate that to happen.'

'Now that I simply do not understand. Yes. Those articles help to sell newspapers and magazines, and the charity gains some free publicity at the same time. Don't you want that for the girls?'

He looked back up the hill towards the school. 'They still have a long way to go. And your name could help them get there.'

Amber started chewing on the side of her lower lip. It was an action that he had seen her do a hundred times before, usually when her mother was nagging.

'I know. And I have turned it over in my mind so many times but, in the end, it all boils down to this.'

Her gaze locked onto his face. 'I need you to write a feature article about the orphanage. And if that means using me as a hook to get readers interested—' she took a breath '—then okay, I will have my photo taken in India and splashed all over the internet and wherever the article reaches—as long—' she paused again '—as long as the article makes it clear that I am supporting the charity set up by my friend,

Parvita. I'm just one member of the team working on fund-raising and teaching the pupils for free—and there is a whole long list of other professional musicians who are involved. Small cog. Big charity project. Only...'

'Only?' he asked, his head whirling with what she was asking him to do.

'I have to trust you to tell the truth about why I chose to spend my time teaching here with Parvita instead of performing in some huge concert hall, without turning it into some great fluff piece about how I am lowering myself to be here. And not one word about my mother. Can I do that? Can I trust you, Sam?'

'Amber, you don't know what you're asking. My editor, Frank, is not interested in an in-depth article on a charity in India. He wants celebrity news that will sell papers in London. And if I don't deliver, that editor's desk will go to another hungry journalist and I'll be back at the bottom of the pecking order all over again.'

She closed her eyes and his heart surged that he might be the cause of her pain. She had offered him the truth—now it was his turn.

Reaching out, he took her left hand and held it tight against his chest, forcing her to look at him.

'I need this job, Amber. My dad isn't getting any younger and I've hardly seen him these past ten years. I made his life hell after my mother left us and he had to take the blame. But do you know what? He believed in me when my mother made it clear that I was a useless dreamer who would never amount to anything. And now I have proven her wrong. That's special.'

'Your dad. Of course. How stupid of me. You finally did it. You got there. And I'm not so stupid that I can't see how much of your dad has rubbed off on you. You are terrific with the kids. But...' her brow screwed up '...now it's my turn to be confused. You always said that you wanted to write the long feature articles on the front page, and wouldn't be happy until your name was right there. On the cover.'

Then she shook her head. 'But that was years ago. I probably have got it wrong.'

Sam took a breath. 'You didn't get it wrong. I simply haven't got to the front cover yet.'

'But you will, Sam,' Amber breathed, her gaze locked onto his face. 'From the moment I first met you, I knew that you had a fire in your belly to prove your talent and were determined to be the best writer that you could be. Your passion and energy drove you on against the odds. And you have done it. Your dad should be proud of you. In fact, am I allowed to be proud of you too?'

He felt his neck flare up red in embarrassment but gave her a quick nod. 'Right back at you.'

'Thanks,' she sniffed and then lifted her chin, eyebrows tight together. 'In that case, I have an idea.'

'You always have an idea. Go on.'

'Simple. Write two articles. I will give you enough quotes for a celebrity piece about my broken wrist and taking time out with my friend at the music school—and you have those shots from my birthday party to show me in full-on bling mode. But…' her voice dropped '…the real interview starts here. At the orphanage for abandoned girl children in a wonderful country bursting with potential. You were the one who saw that they needed a teacher more than they needed a fundraiser this week. *You get them. You understand.* That could be the feature which takes you to the front page, Sam.'

'You think I am ready for those dizzy heights?'

'I know that you have the talent—you always did have. But what do you think, Sam? You have been writing fluff pieces for years, languishing in the middle ground and peeking out now and again to write about the bigger world. Are you ready to show Frank what you are truly capable of? That is what he wants, isn't it? Or are you too scared to stick your head out above your comfort zone and take a risk in case you are shot down and rejected?'

She stepped forward and pressed her hand flat against Sam's chest. 'You have an amazing talent. I still believe that you can do this. And do it brilliantly. Do it, Sam. Do it for me, but most of all, do it for yourself.'

CHAPTER THIRTEEN

From: Amber@AmberDuBois.net
To: Kate@LondonBespokeTailoring.com; Saskia@Elwood-House.co.uk
Subject: Sam Report
Sam has just let me read his article about Parvita and it is fantastic! My boy done good! In return I have posed for some cheesy photos on the beach under the palm trees and answered lots of questions about my last concert tour and the building plans for the new school I have decided to fund here at the orphanage. I am calling it the Elwood School—I think that your aunt Margot would have approved, Saskia.

There is so much to do here and the builders are pestering me with questions and paperwork, I am really flagging. Good thing that Sam has been here to help with the tradesmen and architects.

I am going to miss him when he goes back tomorrow. And so will the girls.

This is his last evening. So it is time to have that talk I have been putting off.
Wish me luck. Amber

From: Saskia@ElwoodHouse.co.uk
To Amber@AmberDuBois.net; Kate@LondonBespokeTailoring.com;
Subject: Elwood School

Oh, you wonderful girl—Aunt Margot would have loved it, and I have just spent five minutes blubbing into my tea.

Re Sam the friendly spy. I think it could be time to ask that young man his intentions!

Take a chance on happiness Amber. And tell Sam that he is welcome here any tlme.
Good luck. Saskia

From: Kate@LondonBespokeTailoring.com
To: Amber@AmberDuBois.net
Subject: Sam Report
Love, love, love the name of the school. Do they need a needlework teacher next winter? You should tell Sam what happened pronto. Who knows? He might be okay now you have worn him down a bit with tropical beaches and hot curries.

Big might. Still scared for you.
Best of luck, gorgeous. Kate

AMBER DROPPED DOWN onto the fallen tree trunk that lay among the driftwood on the shore and pressed her hand flat against the weather-smoothed exposed wood before closing her eyes. The warm wind was scented with spices from exotic flowering shrubs and the tang of the ocean waves as they rolled up on the sand in front of her. White foamed and fresh and cool, their force broken by the shallow rocks and reefs under the sand.

Which was pretty much how she was feeling at that moment. Like a spent force.

She desperately needed to calm down and focus on the coming days ahead. But her mind was still reeling from the thousand and one things on her to do list. And Sam.

Maybe things could have turned out differently for them if her mother had not scared him away.

Would they have stayed together in London and stuck it out through university and her concert tours? It would have made a difference to know that she had someone who loved her back in London, waiting for her. Someone who she could give her heart to and know that it was safe and protected.

The sound of children playing made her open her eyes as a group of boys ran across the beach, wheeling a rubber car tyre with a stick, laughing and dancing in and out of the surf. Their mothers strolled along behind them, barefoot, bright in their lovely gold braid trimmed colourful saris and sparkling bangles. Chatting like mothers all around the world.

And somewhere deep inside her body her need to have her own family contracted so fast and so painfully that she wanted to whimper with loss. Being with these girls had shown her how much she loved to share her life and her joy with open minds.

She would willingly give up her slick penthouse for a small family house with a garden and a loving husband who wanted children with her.

Sam was right. Her parents—and his—were hardly the best examples that they could have, but she still wanted to give some love to children of her own one day. At least she knew what *not* to do.

As for Sam? Sam would make a wonderful father given the chance.

'A penny for your thoughts.'

Sam!

Amber whipped around on the sun-bleached tree trunk so fast that her tunic snagged. But there he was. Sam Richards. This man who had come back into her life just when she'd least expected it, and was just as capable of making her head and body spin as he had ten years earlier.

It staggered her that one look at that tanned handsome face could send her blood racing and her senses whirled into a stomach-clenching, heart-thumping spin.

How did he do it? How did he turn back the clock and

transform her back into a schoolgirl being taken out for a pizza and a cola by the chauffeur's son?

But those were on dull evenings back in London. She could never have dreamt that she would be with Sam on a sandy tropical beach with the rustle of coconut palms and tropical birdsong above her head.

Sam grinned and strolled along the sand towards her.

He was wearing loose white cotton trousers and a pale blue linen shirt which matched the colour of his eyes to perfection. He looked so confident and in control it was ridiculous. He moved from the hips, striding forward, purposefully, with his head high. Even on a remote beach in Kerala, Sam managed to look like a journalist ready to interview a big movie star or show business personality for the next big news story.

The Sam she was looking at belonged in the world she had left behind—the world he would be going back to in only a few hours, while she stayed behind.

Was that why she longed to hold him closer and relive the precious moments when he had held her in his arms in the apartment? To feel the tenderness of his lips on hers for one last time before they parted?

No—she dared not think about that! Amber smiled back and patted the log.

'I've saved you the best seat in the house but the show has already started.'

But when she looked up into Sam's face as he drew closer, his ready smile seemed to fade and he stopped and shrugged, almost as if he was wondering what to say to her.

His gaze locked onto her face and the look he gave her sent her body past the tingling stage and way over into melting.

'Sorry to keep you waiting. I have just been phoning London.'

'Parvita told me that you had emailed her with a few questions, even though she was on her honeymoon,' Amber said, trying her best to appear calm and unruffled. 'But you couldn't promise her much in the way of publicity.'

She peered into his face. 'Was that what you were trying to tell me yesterday, Sam? That Frank might not want to know about two crazy women who are trying to build a music school in Kerala? Especially when you are handing over the exclusive on how brave Bambi has survived her terrible trauma of being forced to play on out of tune pianos in the back of beyond?'

'Not exactly. I have just got off the phone with Frank and offered him a very interesting feature for the paper's new current affairs magazine on how girls are still being given up by their parents in some parts of India but are now being trained to be part of the technology boom. Giving them a great education and a future. And do you know what? He loved it. Two sides of an amazing developing country. In fact he loves it so much he wants to bring it forward to next month's magazine, complete with photographs and quotes from the lovely Parvita.'

Amber laughed out loud and gave him a quick one-handed hug. 'Wow. That's amazing! Congratulations. Your first feature in the London paper. And it couldn't be better publicity for what we are trying to do here. Thank you. Thank you, Sam. It means a lot—to all of us.'

Sam tilted his head sideways and grinned. 'My pleasure. And don't make me out to be some kind of hero—it's my job to spot a great story and run with it.'

Then her face relaxed into a smile. 'Of course. You were simply being a professional reporter. So the girls didn't have any effect on you at all. Of course they didn't. You were just doing your job.'

He nudged her with his elbow and she nudged him back.

'What does it feel like to be a feature writer at long last, oh, great journalist?'

'It feels okay. No. Better than okay. It feels grand. Just grand.'

He took a breath. 'There is one thing. Frank gave me a heads up on a couple of rumours flying around the Internet that you have just spent time in hospital in Boston recently.'

The cool breeze on Amber's shoulders suddenly felt icy and threatening.

Boston. Of course. Someone had tipped off the newspapers. Probably one of the hospital team back in Boston. Heath had warned her that she wouldn't be able to keep her hospital visit a secret for long and it looked as though he was right.

Great.

She inhaled slowly, then pushed down hard on the log.

His whole body stilled and he reached out and took her hand in his. 'You are still underweight, still pale despite this glorious sunshine and the other day I felt every one of your ribs. And yes, I know how hard you are working to make this new school possible before the rainy season, but there is more to it than that. Isn't there?'

Amber looked into Sam's face and saw genuine concern in his blue eyes. It was almost as if he was scared of hearing her answer.

Squaring her shoulders, she stared directly into his eyes and said, 'They are right, I was being treated for an infectious disease, but I am absolutely fine now.' She rushed on as Sam tensed up. 'Seriously. I had the all clear before I left London and don't need to take any more antibiotics.'

Then she paused and licked her lips.

'Amber. Just make it fast and tell me. Because my imagination is going wild here and you are killing me. Just how bad was it?'

Taking a deep breath, she met his gaze head-on. This was it. This was what the whole interview jag had been building up to. 'It was bad,' she whispered, her whole body trembling with the emotion and the relief that came with finally being able to tell him the secret that she had been keeping from him. She turned her head and rested her forehead against his, feeling his hot, moist skin against hers and soaking up the strength she needed to say the words.

'The last time I came to Kerala I caught meningitis. And I almost died, Sam. I almost died.'

CHAPTER FOURTEEN

THE SOUND OF motorised rickshaws and the relentless battle of car horns and truck engines from the village road rumbled across the beach towards Amber and Sam but she did not hear them. She was way too busy fighting to keep breathing, as she desperately scanned his face, which was pale and white with shock.

Sam turned sideways, lowered his body onto the log next to her and stretched out his long legs, his arms out in front of him, hands locked together, his chin down almost to his chest.

One side of his throat was lit rosy pink by the fading sun as he twisted his body around from the waist to face her, apparently oblivious to the damage he was causing to his trousers, which stretched to accommodate the muscled thighs below.

The look on that face was so pained, so tortured and so intense that Amber could barely look at him for fear that she would burn up in the heat.

They sat in silence for a few seconds but she could hear each slow, heavy quivering breath that he took, his chest heaving as his lungs fought to gain control.

His fingers reached across and took hers and held them tight to his chest, forcing her to look up into his face.

'Oh, Amber,' he said, his pale blue eyes locked onto her face, his voice low and intense, anxious. 'Why didn't you tell me that you had been so ill?' Then he exhaled very, very slowly. 'You knew where I was working. All you had to do was ask Heath or one of your friends to lift the phone and I would have flown over to see you. Spent time with you. Help you through it, read you books, tell you crazy stories and the latest gossip from Hollywood. Anything. Anything at all.'

She swallowed down hard and took a long juddering breath. 'You would?'

'In a heartbeat, you foolish, stubborn woman,' Sam answered with a faint smile, and reached up and stroked a strand of her hair back over her ear, his fingertips gently caressing her forehead as he did so.

His touch was so tender and so very gentle that Amber almost surrendered to the exhaustion that keeping her secret from Sam had caused.

'You might be right about the stubborn bit. I had intended to tell you before you left,' she whispered through a throat that felt as though she had swallowed a handful of sharp gravel, 'but there never seemed to be a good time. But I had to be sure, Sam. Really sure, before I told anyone the truth.'

'Sure of what? That I would do a good job telling your story? Or that you could trust me enough to be honest with me?'

His brows screwed together and for a terrifying moment Amber thought that he was going to jump up and walk out on her. But instead, Sam closed his eyes and when he opened them she was stunned to see a faint gleam of moisture in the corners.

Moisture she was responsible for putting there by her selfish behaviour.

And the sight sucked the air from her lungs, rendering her speechless.

'That was why you decided to retire,' Sam said, his gaze scanning her face.

All she could do was nod slowly in reply. 'I was already

back in Boston when I collapsed. I don't remember breaking my wrist when I fell over my suitcases. And I only have snatches from that first week in the hospital. I think I scared the hell out of Heath.'

'I'm not surprised. You are doing a pretty good job with me right now,' Sam replied with a tremble in his voice that she had never heard before.

'The doctors told him that I was in danger for the first twenty-four hours—but when I was in the ambulance I made Heath promise not to tell anyone. This was one time I did not want the media following every second of my life. I couldn't hide the fact that I had broken my wrist—but I could hide the fact that I broke it when I collapsed. I don't want the world to feel sorry for me. Pity me. Can you understand that?'

'Not a bit. Why not?' Suddenly Sam's voice switched from desperate and sad to excited and enthusiastic. 'Let me tell the world how you survived this trauma and came out of the other side with a new purpose in life. That's an amazing story. Inspiring. You could do a lot of good for the children's home if you went out and promoted it.'

'Promoted? You mean talking about the trauma of those weeks in hospital on TV chat shows and breakfast television? No. Not for me, Sam. I'm done with talking about how great I am. Because I don't feel brave or inspiring or any of those things.'

She dropped her head backwards, closed her eyes and inhaled slowly several times before going on. 'I remember the afternoon I was discharged from hospital and Heath drove me to his house and I looked out of the window in awe and astonishment. The colours were so vibrant it made me glad to be alive. The air smelled wonderful, fresh, clean, invigorating—especially compared to the hospital. Everything looked amazing, as though I was seeing the streets and the cars and even Heath's old stone house for the very first time.'

Amber raised her hand then dropped it again onto Sam's lap. 'And waiting for me was all of the clutter and admin and mess of details that comes with being a public performer.'

She shrugged. 'And do you know what? I didn't want any of it. The little things didn't matter any longer. All that mattered was being with my friends again. Living my life the way I want. In a world full of colour and hope and laughter and enthusiasm for life. That was what mattered to me now. And I knew that was not in Boston with Heath in stifling luxury, or in Paris with my dad and his new family, or in Miami with my mother on a cruise ship somewhere.'

Amber winced and pinched off a flower blossom from the tree by her side and inhaled the fragrance. 'I wanted to go where I felt at home and loved and welcome. I wanted to come here. Doing what my heart tells me is right, and not what other people and my fears tell me to do. Not any longer.'

Sam shook his head. 'I cannot believe that you came back. Hell, Amber, the same thing could happen again. Or there could be another tropical disease.'

'Or I could get knocked over by a London bus. It happens. And I'm okay with that—because this is where I want to be, Sam. This makes me happy.'

Her fingertips stroked his cheek before she tapped him on the end of his nose. 'I could have woken up with permanent brain damage or deafness, but I didn't. I don't know what I am going to do with the rest of my life but I know that I cannot go back to the life I had been living. I am so grateful for every new day that I am alive.'

She gestured towards the coconut palms. 'I have a roof over my head and food I can pick off the trees if I get hungry. And there is enough work here to last a lifetime.'

'You want to stay here? For good?' Sam asked with a look of total astonishment and disbelief.

'I've decided that I want to be happy. I choose to be happy.

Whatever problems I have in my own life—sharing the magic and beauty of music with these girls and seeing the glow of excitement in my students' eyes makes everything worthwhile again. Small gestures. A hug. A smile. A kiss. A surprise when they are least expecting it. That is how I want to spend my life.'

Amber stopped talking and grinned at him as Sam sighed in exasperation.

'And I have you to thank for all of this, Sam. Now, don't look so surprised. Remember what you said over lunch at the penthouse? You challenged me to come here for Parvita's wedding and somehow I found the courage to take that first step and make it happen. Thank you. It's been a long journey, Sam.'

'Right back at you. We've both come a long way to get to this place.'

Then he looked around him, from the coconut palms to the beach, and laughed out loud. 'And what a place. You always did have great taste, girl, but this would take some beating. In fact, this village had got me thinking.'

'And I thought the burning smell was from the road. What are those trucks burning? Cooking oil?'

'Funny girl. And yes, they might be burning cooking oil, but actually I was thinking more along the lines of a series of articles about regional development and the culture of Southern India. What do you think? It could be a winner and the paper would cover all of the costs. Providing, of course, I could find someone who was willing to put me up around here. Know any local hotels or guest houses?'

Sam was so close that all she could focus on was the gentle rise and fall of his chest and the caress of the warm breeze on her skin. Time fell still so that she could capture the moment.

'What do you say, Amber?' he asked, his pale blue eyes smiling into hers, and with just a touch of anxiety in his voice.

'Could you put up with me if I came back here to stay for a while? Say yes. Say that you will let me be part of your life. And you know that I am not just talking about a few weeks. I want to be with you for the long haul.'

Say yes to having Sam in her life? Here in India at the school?

'Are you sure?' she asked, her voice hoarse and almost a whisper. 'I thought that your life was going to be in the London office from now on. It's your dream job. Don't you want that editor's chair any more?'

Sam replied by sliding his long, strong, clever fingers between hers and locking them there. Tight. His smile widened as his gaze scanned her face as though he was looking for something, and he must have found it because his grin widened into an expression of such joy and happiness that was so infectious that she had to smile in return.

'A clever woman has shown me that it is possible to go beyond your dream and never stop following your passion until you know what you finally want. I like that idea. I like it a lot. Almost as much as I like those girls of yours.'

He snorted out loud. 'You never thought that you would hear me admit to loving kids. But there is something about this place. And about you, Amber DuBois. In fact, this might not be the comfiest chair I have ever sat on,' Sam said as he patted the log, 'but I do know what I want. And I'm looking at what I want at this very minute.'

And just to make sure that she got the message, Sam bent forward and tapped her on the end of the nose with the soft pad of his forefinger.

'That's you, by the way,' he said in a voice that could have melted an iceberg, 'in case you're not keeping up.' And then he sat back up straight and winked at her.

Amber blinked and tried to take it all in.

The school.

Her dream.

Her Sam.

This was a chance of happiness with this man who she thought she had lost ten years ago. This amazing man who had come back into her life only a few weeks ago, and yet at that moment she felt even more connected to him than she had ever done before.

She felt as though they were two parts of one whole heart and soul. She had known happiness in her music and her teaching but nothing compared to this.

Could she do it? Could she take him back and take a risk on heartbreak?

Sam was holding her dream out to her, and all she had to do was say yes and it would be hers.

And that thought was so overwhelming she faltered.

Amber inhaled a deep breath and tried to keep calm, which was rather difficult when Sam was only inches away from her, the fine blue linen of his shirt pressed against her tunic, begging her to hold him and kiss him and never let him go.

'Why me? We tried to be together once before and it didn't work. And we both know how hard long distance relationships can be.'

Amber let out a long slow breath as his fingertips moved over her forehead and ran down through her hair, sliding off her hair barrette before coming to rest on her shoulder.

'You're right. We would be spending time apart. But it would be worth it.'

His forehead pressed against hers. 'You are the only woman I want in my life. I lost you once, Amber. I can't stand the idea of losing you again.'

'I know. And I want you too. Very much. It's just...'

'Just what—go on. Please, I want to know what is holding you back and what I can do to help you.'

'It has taken me ten years to build up all of these heavy

barriers around my heart to protect it from being broken again by being rejected and abandoned. You were the only man that I ever let into my world. The only one. I fell in love with your passion and your fire and I was pulled towards you like a moth to a flame. Rico and Mark had that same spark and I knew that I could get burnt, but I couldn't help but be drawn to them. You had ruined me for ordinary men, and I have only just realised it. I want to give you my heart, Sam. *Truly.* I do. But I'm scared that it would never recover if it was broken again this time. That's why I'm scared of making this leap.'

'All or nothing. It's the same for me. So here is the plan. We both know what hard work is like. So we work at our relationship and make our love part of the joy we find in everything that we do. We might not be in the same room or even the same country but we would still be together. We can make this work. I believe it.'

'All or nothing. Oh, Sam.'

Suddenly it was all too much too soon to take in.

She looked across at the new school building and was instantly transported into what life could be like. The school. Her concerts. And then, maybe, the tantalising prospect of playing with the girls in the lovely garden of the orphanage with Sam by her side.

By reaching up and taking hold of Sam's hand in hers, she managed to regain some control of herself before words were possible. His fingers meshed into hers, and he raised one hand to his lips and gently kissed her wrinkly dry-skinned knuckles before replying.

'I know a good opportunity when I see one and, from what I've seen, we would make a great team. You can do this, Amber. You can teach and run this school. I know you can.'

The pressure in her chest was almost too much to bear as she looked into his face and saw that he meant it. He believed in her!

'You would do that? You would fly back to India just to be with me now and then?'

'If it meant I could be with you and the girls? In a heart-beat. You are bound to spend some time in London, especially over the monsoon season. And the rest of the time we have these amazing new-fangled technical inventions which mean that I can see you and talk to you any time I want. In fact I intend to make myself the biggest pest you could imagine.'

His presence was so powerful, so dominating, that she slid her fingers away from below his and pushed herself off the log and onto the hot sand on unsteady legs. Sam was instantly on his feet and his fingers meshed with hers and held them to his own chest as it rose and fell under her palm.

She forced herself to look up into his face, and what she saw there took her breath away. Any doubt that this man cared about her flashed away in an instant.

No pity, no excuses, no apologies. Just a smouldering inner fire. Focused totally on her. She could sense the pressure. Trembling, hesitant, but loving.

He was the flame that had set her world on fire. Nothing would ever be the same again.

Which was why she said the only words she could.

'Yes, Sam. Yes. You are the only man I want in my life—the only man that I have ever wanted in my life. I want you and I need you and I never want us to be torn apart again. Never again. Do you understand that?'

Sam looked into those perfect violet-blue eyes which were brimming with tears of joy and happiness and fell in love all over again. All of the clever and witty things he had intended to say to make her laugh and look at him drifted away onto the sea breeze, taking doubt and apprehension with them.

This was it. He had finally found a woman he wanted to be with. As a girl, Amber had taught him what the overwhelming power of love could be like. But Amber the woman was a revelation. She was so beautiful his breath caught in his throat just at the sight of her.

And now this woman, this stunning, clever, open and giving woman, had just told him that she wanted to be with him as much as he wanted to be with her.

And, for once, words failed him.

How could he have known that the path to happiness led right back to the first girl that he had ever kissed and meant it? How ironic was that?

Frank Evans and that editor's desk were not important any longer.

All that mattered was this woman, looking at him with tears in her eyes. This was where he wanted to be. Needed to be. With Amber.

He dared not speak and break the magic of that moment, that precious link that bound him to Amber for this tiny second in time. But he could move closer, closer, to that stunning face. Those eyes filled with the love and tenderness he had only imagined was destined for other men. And now she was here. And he loved her. This was no teenage crush but a tsunami of love which was more shocking and startling but destined to last.

He. Loved. Her.

Finally. It had happened. He had known lust and attraction. But the sensation was so deep and overwhelming that the great loner Sam Richards floundered.

He was in love.

The lyrics of every love song he had ever heard suddenly made perfect sense.

Without thinking, his hands moved slowly up from her arm to her throat, to cradle her soft and fragile face, gently, his fingers spreading out wide. As her eyes closed at his touch, he had to blink away his own tears as he moved closer, so that his body was touching hers, his nose pressed against her cheek, his mouth nuzzling her upper lip, as his fingers moved back to clasp the back of her head, drawing her closer to him.

She smelt of every perfume shop he had ever been into, blended with spice and vanilla and something in her hair. Coconut. The overall effect was more than intoxicating; he wanted to capture it for ever, bottle it so that he could relive this moment in time whenever he wanted.

And then her mouth was pressing hotter and hotter into his, his pulse racing to match hers. Her hand was on his chest, then around his neck, caressing his skin at the base of his skull so gently he thought he would go mad with wanting her, needing her to know how much he cared.

Maybe that was why he broke away first, leaning back just far enough so that he could stroke the glint of tears away from her cheeks with the pads of his thumbs.

'Why didn't you tell me that you were still recovering from meningitis when you came to my dad's garage in London? I could have swept you away to a long holiday in California.'

Amber grinned despite the turmoil inside her heart. 'Each day is a new day for me. A new start. It could have been a lot worse. Instead of which, I am here with you. Who needs a holiday? I am just grateful to be in one more or less working piece.'

She pressed her head into his shoulder as his arms wrapped around her body, revelling in the touch of his hands on her skin, the softness of his shirt on her cheek, and the way his hand moved to caress her hair.

'Me too. I understand that you want your independence. I get that. But when you need help, you have to know that I am right here. I am not going anywhere without you in my life.'

He was kissing her now, pressing his soft lips over and over again against her throat, and tilting his head so he could reach the sensitive skin on her collarbone without crushing her plastered wrist and hand.

His mouth slid slowly against her hot, moist skin and nuzzled away at the shoulder strap of her dress. Her eyes closed and she leant back just a little further, arching her back against his strong arm, which had slid down her back to her hips.

Amber stopped breathing and inwardly screamed in frustration when his lips slid away and she could no longer inhale his spicy aromatic scent.

His hot breath still warmed the skin on one side of her neck, and she knew that he was watching her. And her heart and mind sang.

Amber closed her eyes tight shut and focused on the sound of her own breathing. Only it was rather difficult when the man she wanted to be with was holding her so lovingly.

Tempting her. Tempting her so badly she could taste it. She wanted him just as much as he wanted her.

His voice was hoarse, low, intense and warm with laughter and affection, and something much more fundamental.

'I have an idea.'

'Umm,' was all she could manage. His fingers were still moving in wide circles on her back.

'Let's hold our own private concert. Just the two of us. Your place is closer. I'm sure the girls would understand. But, one way or another, we need to get off this beach before we get arrested for bad behaviour and setting a bad example for the girls.'

The girls! The concert!

Amber opened her eyes, shook her head once from side to side and chuckled into his shoulder. 'Are you mad? They would never forgive us! I promised them a little Mozart if they had done their piano practice.'

Then she raised her eyebrows coquettishly as Sam groaned in disappointment.

'Maybe—' she took a breath '—you could escort me home afterwards, Mr Richards?'

The air escaped from his lungs in a slow, shuddering hot breath against her forehead, and he lowered both hands to her waist.

'It would be my pleasure. Do you think they would notice if we skipped dessert? My stomach is not used to those syrupy sweets yet.'

'That sounds wonderful. Although I will have to insist on having an early night.'

The brilliant grin grew wider, although she could still sense the thumping of his heart in tune with hers. 'I'm sure we could manage that.'

Then the reality of what he was asking hit her hard. 'Oh, I'm sorry, Sam. I completely forgot. I arranged a meeting with the local governors after the concert. They are keen to organise some legal guardians for the new babies who are still being brought in every week. They are so adorable I'm tempted to offer to put my name down. But that wouldn't be fair on them with my life being so unsettled at the moment. Looks like I shall have to wait to have my own children.'

As soon as the words left her mouth, she regretted them. 'But we have a few hours tomorrow before you fly back, and I'll be in London in a few weeks. The time will fly by.'

The man who had been holding her so lovingly, unwilling to let her move out of his touch, stepped back. Moved away. Not physically, but emotionally.

The precious moment was gone. Trampled to fragments.

His face closed down before her eyes. The warmth was gone, and she cursed herself for being so clumsy. She had lost him.

It took her a few seconds to form the words of the question she had to ask, but was almost too afraid what the answer would be.

'You don't want children, do you?' Her voice quivered

just enough to form the syllables, but she held her breath until he answered.

Sam shook his head slowly as his chin dropped so their foreheads were touching. His breath was hot against her skin as the words came stumbling out. 'No, my darling, I have never wanted a family. I want you, and only you. Can you understand that?'

Amber took a slow breath and squeezed her eyes tight shut, blinking away the tears. 'And I want you. So very much. I had given up hope of ever finding someone to love. Only I so want to have children of my own. You would be a wonderful father, Sam, and I know that we could make a family. Besides, you're forgetting one big thing. We aren't our parents. We're us. And we can make our own happiness. I just know it.'

'A family? Oh, Amber.'

'I saw you working with the girls, Sam,' Amber replied with a smile. 'You were wonderful and I know that any child would be lucky to have you as their dad.'

His back straightened and he drew back, physically holding her away from him. Her hands slid down his arms, desperate to hold onto the intensity of their connection, and her words babbled out in confusion and fear.

'Let's not talk about it now. You are going to have a busy few days at the paper. And your dad will be back from holiday. That is something for you to look forward to.'

He turned away from her now, and looked out onto the shore and the distant horizon, one hand still firmly clasped around hers.

'Children need stability and love. I saw what happened when my parents divorced and so did you. The kids always suffer when a relationship breaks down and I would hate that to happen to us.'

The bitterness in his voice was such a contrast to the loving man she had just been holding. The world stilled, and the temperature of the air seemed to cool, as though a cold wind had blown between them.

She stepped back and wrapped her arm around her waist, closing down, moving away from the hot flames that would burn her up if she kissed him again, held him close to her again.

'Oh, Sam. Are you really telling me that you don't believe that we could stay together and make our marriage work?'

'I love you so much and I don't want to lose you. But I can't wipe away twenty years of resentment in a few days. Maybe you're right but it's going to take me a lot longer than that. We have each other. We don't need a piece of paper or children to make us a couple. You are all I need.'

She raised both of her hands in the air so that Sam couldn't grab hold of them.

'You're breaking my heart, Sam. Is it wrong to give a child a loving home with two parents, in this hard and cruel world? Can't you see that is part of my new dream?'

'Amber! I need some time.'

She paused and spoke very slowly, with something in her voice he had never heard before and did not ever want to hear again.

'Oh, don't worry. I'll get through the concert tonight and see you off at the airport tomorrow with a smile on my face. I care about you so much, but I have to protect myself from more heartbreak down the road. So it might be best to stop this now. You have your life thousands of miles away, but this in my new home and I don't want to give it up. If you care about me, then let me go, Sam. Let me go.'

The only thing that stopped Sam from running after her was the heartbreak in her words and the unavoidable truth that he did care about her enough to stand, frozen, and watch her walk away across the sand.

CHAPTER FIFTEEN

From: Amber@AmberDuBois.net
To: Kate@LondonBespokeTailoring.com; Saskia@Elwood-House.co.uk
Subject:
Sam left this morning. And I miss him. So very much. Can't talk about it. A

SAM WAITED IMPATIENTLY in the baggage reclaim area as more bags were unloaded from his flight. He slung his laptop bag over one shoulder and rolled back his shoulders as the time difference and lack of sleep started to kick in.

The huge echoing hall was jam packed with families and people of all shapes and sizes from his flight, all jostling to find their luggage and get back to their normal lives.

He closed his eyes for a moment, then blinked them open again. He was used to air travel—that was part of his job, but that didn't mean to say that he liked it.

Especially not tonight.

It was hard to believe that only sixteen hours earlier he had been sitting on the beach looking out over the ocean with the morning sun on his face and the colour and life and energy of India whizzing around him. Now he was back in this white, cold, sterile land in a city of stone and glass which he called home.

And he had never felt as lonely in his life.

Amber had kept her word and travelled with him to the airport but her forced smile and tense face only served to make him feel even more uncomfortable and awkward. Their easy friendliness and connection felt strained to the point of snapping completely.

When he wrapped his arms around her to kiss her good-bye, Amber's gentle tears had almost broken his resolve. It would have been so easy to forget all about the flight and the London job and find some way of working as a freelance in India. Other people did it and so could he.

But how would that change the way he felt? Staying would only prolong the agony for both of them. It was up to him to have the strength to walk away.

Over the past ten restless hours in the cramped aircraft seat where sleep was impossible, he had come to the conclusion that Amber was the strong one. She had the courage to change her life for the better and do something remarkable that she was passionate about, and he couldn't be more proud of her. He counted himself lucky to know her. Care about her. Love her.

He had loved working with those girls at the orphanage. Loved being part of Amber's life and sharing her world.

The fact that she actually cared about him in return was something he was still trying to deal with.

So what was the problem?

He was scared of not being worthy of her love.

Scared about not being the man and husband she wanted and needed.

He was scared of letting her down.

He cared enough for her to leave her and walk away from the pain he would cause if he stayed—but he already missed her more than he'd ever thought possible. An Amber-shaped hole had formed in his heart and the only person who could fill it was thousands of miles away, teaching little girls how to make music.

A huge over-stuffed suitcase nudged his foot and Sam turned around to see a gorgeous toddler grinning up at him, followed by a laughing man about his age who swung the giggling child up into his arms and hugged him and hugged him again then apologised profusely but Sam let it go with a smile and jogged forwards to grab his bag off the belt before it went around again.

He had to smile because at that moment his throat was so tight he wouldn't have been able to talk even if he had wanted to.

That was the life that he had turned his back on.

He glanced back over one shoulder. A pretty pregnant blonde girl had her arm looped around her lucky partner's waist. And just for a second she looked like Amber, and his heart contracted at the sight of her.

Amber wanted to be a mother so much. And she would be.

How was he going to feel when another man had made her his wife and given her children, when he knew that Amber had loved him and offered him her life and her soul?

And he had turned down the chance of a family life with the only woman he had ever loved. Why?

The answer screamed back at him so loudly that he was surprised that the other passengers didn't hear it above the sound of the tannoy.

Because he was a coward.

Which made him the biggest fool in the world.

Sam strolled out through the customs area and peered around the cluster of people waiting impatiently in the arrivals hall at Heathrow Airport, looking for the familiar face of his father. And there he was, one hand raised in a friendly wave.

Sam had never been so grateful to see a friendly face after a long exhausting flight.

A quick back slap and a greeting and they were on their way to the car park and a small family hatchback that Sam had never seen before.

'What's this, Dad? Don't tell me that you have finally got around to buying yourself a little runabout to take you to the supermarket? About time.'

'Don't be so cheeky. No, I borrowed it from your Auntie Irene.'

'Auntie Irene? I thought my lovely godmother was living in France these days?'

'She moved back to London about six months ago, so she's renting out her house in the Alps as a holiday let. And it's a great place. I know I enjoyed it. The views are unbelievable.'

'Ah, so that was why you chose the Alps. And here I was thinking it was all about driving around those hairpin bends and mountain roads. You don't get a lot of that around London. Or are you getting too long in the tooth for that kind of driving?'

His dad snorted a reply as he loaded Sam's bag into the boot and closed down the lid. 'Hey. Watch it on the "too old" bit. And, as a matter of fact, we did squeeze in a driving tour around the lakes, then went over to Switzerland for a few days. We had a great time.'

Sam's eyebrows headed north as he fitted his seatbelt in the passenger front seat. 'We? I thought you went on your own.'

His father started to say something, then paused. 'I'll tell you about that when we get home,' he replied and reached forward to turn the key in the ignition.

Sam rested his hand lightly on his father's wrist and looked into his startled face.

'Dad, I have just had a very long flight after an exhausting few days with Amber DuBois. And I have come to one very startling conclusion. If you need to say something, then just say it. Please. So. What is it? What do you have to tell me?'

'Okay, son,' his dad replied with just enough lift in his chin for Sam to inhale slowly so that he was prepared for whatever was coming.

'It's your Aunt Irene. Over these past few months we have been seeing a lot of each other one way or another. She needed someone to help her settle into the town house I had just renovated and it's just two streets away from the garage, so it made sense for me to show her how things have changed around our part of London in the past twenty years.'

He took a breath and licked his lips before going on.

'Do you remember when Irene used to come around to the house to see your mum and take you out when you were little?'

'Auntie Irene. Yes, of course. She was mum's best friend. I always knew that we weren't related but she liked being called Auntie Irene and I didn't have any other aunties or uncles. I missed her when she went to France. And I still don't see where this is going.'

'Then I'll make it clear. Irene invited me to stay at her home in France to have a bit of a holiday and, well, when we were away, she finally confessed to me that she had been in love with me for years. Before I married your mum we all used to go out in a big group of friends together. But she knew that I only had eyes for your mum, so she didn't tell me how she felt. But in the end it was too hard to watch our marriage fall apart so she moved away.'

He shot Sam a glance. 'She hated leaving you. But she couldn't stay.'

Sam blew out a long whistle. 'Is that why she never married? I always wondered if she had a secret boyfriend in France somewhere.'

'She had a couple of relationships but never met anyone else.'

'So Auntie Irene has been burning a candle for you for thirty years. Did you know? Or even suspect?'

His dad nodded quickly. 'About a year after I divorced your mum, Irene turned up at the garage one day out of the blue. She cooked us both that lovely French meal. Do you remember that? After you had gone to bed, she asked me if I wanted her to stay and take your mother's place. And I said no.'

'You turned her down,' Sam said in a low voice.

'Wrong time. I was still hurting and you needed me to be there for you. So I sent her back to France.'

He banged the heel of his hand against his forehead.

'I was a fool. I lost the woman who loved me and who had always cared about me as a friend. I have spent the last years alone when I could have shared them with Irene and had some happiness. But these past few weeks have shown me that it's not too late. She is a wonderful woman, Sam, and I have decided to take a chance on love for the second time in my life. I hope that is okay with you.'

'Okay? You don't need to ask my permission. I think that it's fantastic. Good luck to you. Good luck to both of you.'

'Thanks, son. Right. Let's get this car started. Because I want to hear exactly what you have done this time to mess up your chance of happiness with Amber. And I won't take no for an answer. Oh, and you had better get used to seeing Irene around—she's moving in. So. Start talking. And there's your first edition of the paper if you want to catch up with the latest. I think I saw something about Amber in it.'

'What?' Sam picked up the paper and turned the pages until he found it. It was the photo he had taken of Amber on the beach.

His blood ran cold and the more he read the more chilled he became.

It might be his photograph but he had not written one word of this article.

Frank had given the fluff piece to someone else to write. And that was so wrong that he didn't even know where to start.

He snatched up the paper and started reading, desperate to find out how bad it was.

He couldn't believe it. Frank had taken the quotes and twisted them around to portray Amber as a shallow, selfish woman who was creating a vanity project for her own glory—just the opposite of what Sam had intended. His idea had been twisted around to focus on Amber and how foolish she was to risk her health and try to teach with a broken wrist.

'Son, are you okay? What's happened?'

'Frank Evans has sold me out,' Sam replied in a low voice, the paper on his lap. 'This is not about Amber, this is about rumours and lies and half-truths for a headline. And it makes me feel sick to my stomach.'

He looked up at his father and took a breath. 'Dad, I need your help. But before that I need to say something and say it now. I was a brat when Mum left. And I am sorry for making your life such a misery. I truly am. Can you forgive me for that?'

His dad shook his head and smiled. 'I've waited a long time for you to grow up. Looks like it's finally happened. Past history. What do you need?'

Sam exhaled long and slow and stared out of the car window. 'A family house with a garden where Amber can play with our kids.'

The silence in the car was so thick that it was hard to breathe, but it was his dad who finally broke it by asking, 'Do you love Amber that much?'

'She is the only woman I have ever loved and ever will love. It has taken me ten years to realise that. I can't lose her again now.'

The instant the words came out of his mouth Sam realised

what he had just said and chuckled. It was the truth and he had been a fool to pretend otherwise.

'Then I have just the house for you. Welcome home, son. Welcome home.'

CHAPTER SIXTEEN

From: Amber@AmberDuBois.net
To: Kate@LondonBespokeTailoring.com; Saskia@Elwood-House.co.uk
Subject: On my way back to London
The June monsoon rains came! At last. And how. We are
flooded out and the girls have either been sent home for a
few weeks or moved to the old school further inland. Any
building work has stopped and the lads have taken off.

I am just waiting for my connecting flight back to London
and should be with you for breakfast tomorrow. Cannot wait
to catch up. See ya soon. Amber

From: Kate@LondonBespokeTailoring.com
To: Amber@AmberDuBois.net
Subject: On my way back to London
Brilliant—but do not read the newspaper at the airport. Se-
riously. Don't. We need to talk first. K

AMBER STROLLED INTO Saskia's kitchen conservatory room,
yawning loudly, her good hand stretched tall above her head.
There was no sign of Kate or Saskia but, instead, stretched
out on a lounger with his feet up and a steaming cup in his
hand was Sam Richards.

He looked as casual, cool and collected as if he had just

come from a business meeting. Come to think of it, he was wearing a suit and a shirt with a tie.

Amber glanced back towards the hallway. 'How did you get in? Saskia is going to have a fit if she sees you here, drinking her coffee.'

'I climbed over the garden gate,' Sam replied with a quick nod. 'They might want to think about making it a little taller. I can still clamber over, even at my age. Although I probably have dirt on my trousers.'

'Which you are now putting onto her favourite lounger. Sheesh. What cheek.'

Amber peered at his jacket, then physically recoiled. 'Has anyone ever told you that you have the worst taste in suits? Our Kate needs to take you in hand.'

He smiled up and waved his coffee mug in her direction.

His gaze slid up from Amber's unpainted toenails to the tip of her bed-head and gave a low growl of appreciation at the back of his throat to indicate how much he liked what he saw.

Amber instantly tugged the front edges of her thin silk pyjama jacket closer together as her neck flared with embarrassment.

'A lovely sunny good morning to you too. And thank you for a warm welcome. And, as for the lovely Miss Lovat? Kate may have called me to let me know that you have come back to escape the monsoon rain, but Kate is not the woman I want to take me in hand,' he whispered, and then spoilt the moment by wagging his eyebrows up and down. His meaning only too obvious.

Amber's heart soared but her head took over.

He seemed determined to make leaving him even more difficult than it would be already.

'Are you always this much trouble in the mornings?' she asked.

'Want to find out?' he replied in a low husky voice.

Amber dropped her head back and rolled her shoulders.

'What? No. You do not do this to me on my first morning back from India. Especially when I am not awake yet.'

She blinked several times. 'Wait a minute. Did you just say that Kate called you? That is not possible. Because you are officially off our nice man list. You snake. Your magazine did a real hatchet job on me. You have no right to interfere with my head like this. In fact, I shouldn't even be talking to you.'

'Of course you should. I am the new media and fund-raising manager for the Elwood School.'

'Oh, no, you are not. We don't need a media… Wait a minute, okay, maybe the school does need a fund-raising manager but the last person I would choose would be an investigative journalist with a chip on his shoulder the size of a pine tree who delights in stitching me up. Sorry.' She peered at him and sniffed. 'Nice tie. Best of luck with your job interview. Are you going to your newspaper today?'

'Already been. I had a little chat with the editor in chief and we agreed that I should leave the magazine to explore creative opportunities outside of GlobalStar Media.'

Her eyes shot open and she slumped down on the edge of the sofa. 'Oh, no, Sam. You've been sacked.'

'Actually, I resigned. I didn't like the way they changed the meaning of your article without asking me first. Let's just say that we had an honest and open discussion.'

'You stomped out.'

Sam touched two fingers to his forehead. 'I stomped out.'

'Oh…but what are you going to do? Your dad is so proud of your new job—this is what you've been working for.'

'My dad is back home and when I left this morning my godmother was making him breakfast and giving him a cuddle. My dad is in heaven and loving every minute of it—and my lovely Auntie Irene is the wealthiest woman I know. The last thing he needs is an out of work layabout of a son cluttering up his love life.'

'Oh, I am pleased; I like him so much. He deserves some happiness.'

Sam raised both hands and gave a flourish from his lounging position.

'At last we have something we both agree on. And in case you were wondering, he has always liked you too. You should be grateful, you know. There are plenty of other job opportunities for a man of my experience in this town. I could even work with my dad in his new property development business. But no, I came here to offer you my services before anyone else snapped me up.'

She flashed him a freezer stare but it was obvious from his smug smile that Sam had no intention of doing anything other than what he wanted or letting her get a word in sideways.

'Your ploy to drive me away will not work. Not listening. We are officially working on this together. Full-time job. Sorted. You see, I have been thinking about our last discussion—' he nodded, his brows tight together '—and it seems to me to point one way.'

'Ah. Thinking.' Amber smirked and pretended to waft away some horrible smoke from in front of her face.

'Funny girl. But not always a clever one. In fact, after several hours of deep consideration, I have come to a serious conclusion.'

Sam swung his legs off the sofa and pointed to Amber. 'Amber DuBois, I have decided to appoint myself the job and save you the time and effort in advertising and then going through a series of tedious interviews before deciding that I am the one and only candidate.'

He flung one hand towards her, palm upwards. 'I know. It is not a job for the faint of heart, and it would mean giving up my dream of joining the astronaut programme, but I am willing to take on the task. I am the man to do it. Starting today.' He beamed a wide-mouthed grin. 'What do you think of that?'

'What do I think?' Amber replied and started pacing the floor, her eyes wide. 'I think you need to cut down on the dose of whatever you are taking because it is making you quite delusional. I have never heard such arrogance in my life—and I'm used to working with prima donnas in major orchestras.'

'It's okay, you can thank me later.' Sam shrugged.

'Thank you? Oh, I don't think so. Now, listen to me when I explain, Are you listening? Good. First, I do not need help finding a project manager. Full stop. I am quite capable of taking care of myself and when my wrist heals I shall be back on fighting form. And second, you never had any intention of joining the astronaut programme. You only sent off for the forms from NASA so that you could impress your science teacher with your knowledge of hydrogen and hydrazine.'

'You remembered—' Sam grinned '—how sweet.'

'Of course I remembered. I think you only did it because Heath was thinking of being a pilot for all of two days and the girls in my school thought that was amazing. Astronaut, indeed. As if anyone would be impressed by that.'

'Did it impress you?'

Amber paused just long enough for Sam to sit back smirking. 'I thought so. And you're missing the point. You need someone to take care of the business side of the project because you are going to be busy with Parvita and the other girls in the school.'

'We already have cooks and housekeepers and an office receptionist, thank you. I'm not sure how many, but plenty.'

'Ah, I had better add that to the job description.' He tugged a smartphone out of his pocket and began keying in as he spoke. 'Sort out staffing. Got it.'

'Job description? What job description?' Amber asked, blinking in confusion.

'The one I came up with during my thinking session—you know, the one you should be writing if you were not so very confident that you can do everything yourself.'

'What makes you so sure that I can't do everything myself? I have managed very well so far, thank you.'

'Have you? Have you really, Amber?' He pointed to her wrist. 'Look at you. Your hand is hurting and you're hardly sleeping. You are worrying like mad about the girls in Kerala, even though you talk to them every day, and now you are intent on going over there and making things worse by barging in with the best intentions when your architect is quite capable of sorting things out himself.'

'What?' Amber called out and raised her hand into the air in a rush, blinking and shaking her head in disbelief. 'He has problems and is asking for answers based on out of focus photographs. I feel so accountable. I need to go there and see for myself and take responsibility for the project. I have to make sure the money isn't wasted on work that has to be repeated and…oh.'

She only wobbled for a fraction of a second before Sam took her hand and half tugged, half helped her across to the dining table.

'Sit. Head between your knees. Deep breaths. Then breakfast. Here. Finish my coffee.'

'Well, this is embarrassing.' She sniffed as she lowered her head and tried to stop feeling dizzy.

'Not for me. It's actually rather satisfying.'

Sam slid onto the fine oak floor and sat cross-legged so that his face was more or less in line with hers.

'Now. About this job interview. I may have just proved my point that you need someone to help talk to the architects and works manager and all of the suppliers and the like while you do what you do best. Teach. Play your piano and fill those girls' heads with the sounds of wonderful music that they will never forget. Because that is what happens when I hear you play. You transport me to a better place. A place where I want to stay and never leave.'

'I do?'

'Every time. You always did. Probably always will. Those girls are going to have a wonderful teacher. The best. And I want to help you to make that happen. If you will let me.'

He turned his head and flashed her a full strength beaming smile. 'Will you let me, Amber? Will you let me work with you and travel with you and be part of your life?'

He nodded towards the sofa. 'I have my laptop in my brief-case and can print out my resumé if you like.'

'You might get bored without your career,' Amber countered. 'It's been your life.'

'No chance. Not around you. And look who's talking.'

Amber sat up slowly in her hard dining chair and stretched out both hands and took hold of Sam, who stayed exactly where he was.

She could tell that his breathing had speeded up to match hers.

This was it. This was where she had to make the decision.

'You know that I want to take over from Parvita some time soon. After what happened…are you ready to move away and be accountable for a whole school-load of children? Because I don't want to bring you into their lives only for you to take off. That wouldn't be fair, Sam. On them or you. On any of us.'

'I know,' he replied in a serious voice that she had never heard him use before. 'And I wouldn't be offering unless I was in it for the long haul. I mean it, Amber. I want to help you run this school. You can do it on your own, I have no doubt about that, but with the two of us…we could achieve some remarkable things.'

'Are we still talking about the project manager's job?' she asked, smiling.

'What do you think?'

'I think that you care about me, but I would need a lot more than that.' Amber took a breath. 'I need to know how you feel before I agree to have you in my life. Working with you is one thing, but more than that is just setting me up for heartbreak, and I don't know if I am up for it.'

'Hate to break the news to you, gorgeous, but I am already in your life. And I am not going anywhere. From the second you walked into my dad's garage that day I have felt an over-whelming sense of recognition and connection. I have abso-lutely no intention of letting you go again. And, from what I saw, that orphanage needs someone who is handy with a car repair kit and those girls could use someone to teach IT and my version of English. I can probably fit all of that in around my freelance writing work.'

'I'm scared, Sam.'

Sam silenced her by pressing his fingertips to her lips. 'I know. But you haven't heard the rest of the offer. My dad has just finished renovating a sweet little two bedroom terraced house within walking distance of where we are sitting.' His lips turned up into a smile. 'The whole place is about the size of your penthouse living room. But it has a garden. A garden fit for children and pets. And all it needs is a little love to make it a family home. It's ours. All you have to do is say the word.'

He stood up and pressed one hand onto each of her shoul-ders.

'I should be going. My dad needs me to help him plaster a wall. But you know where to find me when you decide that you are crazy in love with me after all. And Amber, don't wait another ten years. Be seeing ya.'

And, before Amber had a chance to reply or even move from her chair, Sam had started walking back into the kitchen.

He was leaving.

And this time it was through the front door.

Amber shuffled off her chair and opened her mouth to reply, then closed it again. This was it. Decision time. She had to take Sam as he was, faults and all, or risk losing him for ever.

Wait a minute. He had just offered her a home. A real home. *Their home. With a garden fit for children and pets.*

He understood. He understood everything.

She did need him. But she wanted him more.

'Sam. Wait.'

His steps slowed until he was more shuffling forward instead of striding.

'Stay. Please. Stay.'

Sam turned around just in time to catch her in his arms as she flung herself at him, her arms around his neck.

Her feet swung up into a perfect curve as he lifted her high off the ground, his arms wrapped tight around her waist as he pressed his lips to her forehead, eyes, then onto the waiting hot lips with all of the tender passion that Amber had been dreaming about most of that night.

The energy and passion of his kiss sent her reeling so hard that Amber had to step back and steady herself before leaning into his kiss, focusing her love into that single contact as she closed her eyes and revelled in the glorious sensation.

When she eventually pulled away her eyes were pricking with hot tears.

'It's okay, darling,' Sam laughed. 'It's okay. I'm not going anywhere without you ever again. You want to go to India, I'll go to India. Timbuktu, I'll be there. There's no way you are going to get rid of me.'

She replied with a wide-mouthed grin and her heart sang at the look of love and joy on Sam's face.

'Timbuktu wasn't on my list before but it sounds good to me. Anywhere with you. Oh, God, Sam, I love you so much. I don't care what happens any more. I just know that I love you.'

The tears were real now, her voice shaking with emotion as she forced out the words he needed to hear, afraid that they were getting lost in his shirt as she slid to the ground.

One arm unwound and lifted her chin high enough for their eyes to meet, and her heart melted at what she saw in his eyes as he grinned down at her, eyes glistening in the bright sunlight.

'I've loved you since the moment you stepped out of the limo with your mother at your back all of those years ago. It just took a while for it to sink in.'

He took her face in between the palms of his hands and confessed, 'I never imagined that I could love another human being on this planet as much as the way I feel at this moment. Come here.'

Somewhere close by was the sound of whooping and hooting from Saskia and Kate but Amber didn't care who saw her kissing the man she loved and would go on loving for the rest of her life.

* * * * *

LAST-MINUTE BRIDESMAID

BY
NINA HARRINGTON

PROLOGUE

High school parties were the worst punishment in the world! In fact, there should be a law banning them for all girls who had not managed to find a date—especially on Valentine's Day.

Squeezing in between the gaggles of teenage girls who had formed a tight huddle on the other side of the dance floor, Kate Lovat clutched her empty plastic cola glass with both hands and tried to push her way through to the bar by waggling her hips and elbows.

It would be so much easier if she was a couple of inches taller!

Not even the high-heeled sandals she had bought in the January sales could bring her up to the shoulders of the posh clique of rich girl prefects who had made it their duty to take guard duty on the bar.

From this much sought-after position they could snigger and make snide comments about what every other girl at the sixth form school party was wearing or not wearing, who they had brought as their date and generally act superior in their designer mini dresses, which barely covered their gym-tight assets.

Kate had seen those assets in the school showers many times over the past three years and they still had the power to make her feel that she came from a different species of teenage girl. The kind that hated exercise and would rather eat her own feet than strut around the changing room in only a thong and heels, pretending to look for a hairdryer, which was Crystal Jardine's speciality.

Shame that Kate was providing them with such excellent entertainment.

So far the evening had been a disaster and she could not even rely on her pals to get her out of this one. Kate lifted her chin and tried to look around the crush of bodies to catch a glimpse of her backup crew.

Amber was laughing and chatting away with Sam in the corner, oblivious to anyone else in the room, Saskia was doing her best to entertain a girl cousin who had arrived from France the day before, and Petra was flirting with every boy in the room while her handsome date was at the bar. Nope. For once she was on her own.

'Kate...what a lovely dress,' Crystal simpered as she sneered down at her. 'It was so clever of you to find something second-hand suitable for a petite figure. Is that why you're the only girl in the class to turn up without a date on Valentine's? What a shame. After you've gone to *so* much effort to clean yourself up.'

A ripple of amused snorting ran around Crystal's little band of followers, which had been dubbed the Crystallites by Saskia. Cold and transparent and all the same.

She couldn't help it. Kate had to run one hand down the side of her new strapless dark purple satin prom dress. She didn't have much in way of boobage or hips for a girl aged seventeen years and one month, but she had done what she could with the help of her friend Amber's bra collection. 'Oh, do you like the dress?' Kate looked up with an innocent expression and tried to fling off a casual reply. 'I designed it myself but I wasn't sure about the colour for my evening gloves.'

The tall blonde replied with a dismissive choke, 'Evening gloves? For a school disco? What era do you think this is? It's really embarrassing for the rest of us—in fact I suggest that you should take them off right now.' And with that she reached down and started pulling the sleeve of the glove down from Kate's elbow before she had time to snatch it away.

Kate gasped in disbelief and took a breath, ready to tell Crystal exactly what she could do with her suggestion, but before she had a chance to reply, four things happened in quick succession.

The plastic cola glass in her right hand fell, clattering, to the hard floor, Crystal blinked, pushed out her chest and did the hair-over-one-shoulder flick she reserved for full-on boy entrancement, the other girls in the group stopped yapping and started gawping and Kate instantly knew in every cell of her body, even before she turned around, that a very tall, very gorgeous man boy had just invaded their little world.

Her senses seemed to tune out the noise of the disco blasting out from the stage and the chatter that only forty teenage girls and their assorted friends and dates could make. It was as though she had been waiting all evening, no, all her life, to hear that rustling sound of crisp fabric and a rich aromatic aftershave which smelt of everything that represented old-school class, elegance, wealth and gorgeousness.

But she was still not prepared for the manly arm that wrapped around her waist and practically lifted her off her feet.

'Katherine, there you are. I've been looking for you everywhere.'

Kate half turned in the circle of his arms and slowly,

hesitantly looked up into the face of the one and only Heath Sheridan.

Amber's stepbrother. Captain of the university polo team, heir to the Sheridan publishing empire, top of his business class, the celebrity party favourite, nice to children and animals.

And, to her, the most gorgeous twenty-year-old man *alive.*

He was smiling down at her with the full-on power smile she had seen him use before on the rare occasions that he came over to London from the Sheridan estate in Boston.

But she had never been on the receiving end of it up close and personal before. At this distance she could see the flecks of gold in those amazing dark brown eyes and the small scar on his smoothly shaven chin where, according to Amber, he had fallen off his sledge as a boy.

Well, that boy was long gone.

And hurrah and hallelujah and no complaints from her about that fact.

Heath's neat brown hair was clipped tight around his ears but just long enough at the back of his neck for her hand to touch as she raised both arms and linked them behind his head—just to lay it on extra-thick for the open-mouthed gawping audience, of course.

The fact that he instinctively slid both arms around her middle, forcing her to literally cling to his body, was a truly special bonus.

'Darling, you look wonderful,' Heath said, his gaze totally locked on her face. 'And that dress is divine on you. I am so sorry my flight was late getting into London. Can you ever forgive me?'

His voice was so husky, tinged with a soft transatlantic accent and deep and intimate that she could eat it with a spoon. It seemed to echo back in the small space that separated them, burning up the air and lodging inside her head, making her feel dizzy from lack of oxygen.

'Of course, Heath,' she replied in a low whisper. Her eyes fluttered closed for a second as her chest pressed against the open-necked silky white shirt he was wearing, which revealed just the smallest amount of chest hair but enough to do serious damage to her blood pressure, especially when his lips pressed into the top of her hair.

'Sorry, ladies,' he breathed, scarcely breaking his gaze to flick a look at Crystal, 'but I am going to have to steal my gorgeous girl away from you. We've been apart for far too long. Don't you agree, baby?'

A very unladylike squeak and part giggle escaped her lips and she managed a tiny self-satisfied but apologetic shoulder shrug as she slid back into her sandals, her feet hit the floor and she clung onto Heath's arm.

With a brilliant smile, his arm tightened around her waist, pulling her even tighter against his body and his lips met her forehead this time, claiming her in front of the entire posh clique, who were slowly moving from stunned shock to dagger-looks mode. As they moved away like some romantic three-legged race, Kate flicked her hair back and silently mouthed the words *elbow gloves* to the thunderous face of Crystal Jardine.

Two minutes later, Kate's feet had hardly touched the floor and she found herself standing propped up by Heath, next to Amber and Sam, who were smirking like mad—at her.

'How did I do, Kate?' Heath whispered in his very best husky voice into her ear, with his chin pressed against her temple. 'Do you think those girls got the message? Now why don't I get you that drink before I escort you all home?' Heath grinned and tipped up her chin with a cheeky wink.

'I take my job as a stand-in party date very seriously. So don't you dare go away. I'll be right back.'

She waited until Heath's hand had slid languorously down her arm and his back was turned before grabbing Amber by the arm and flicking her head towards the ladies' room.

'We'll just be a minute,' she absent-mindedly flung at Sam, who simply shook his head, far too used to their little gang of rebels sticking together whenever possible. Petra seemed to have gone outside with a boy—typical—but Saskia didn't even have time to ask what was happening before Kate propelled her into the powder room and as far away as possible from the cubicles where most of the other girls in their class seemed to be either crying or noisily suffering the effects of cheap wine and vodka cocktails.

'What's the emergency? Has Crystal been winding you up again?' Saskia asked, trying not to shout above the ear-damaging background noise. 'I keep telling you that the girl is only jealous.'

Kate swept her two best pals into a tight huddle before taking a breath so that all of her words came out in one long rush. 'Heath Sheridan has just rescued me from the Crystallites and called me darling. And now he has gone to get me a drink. Amber, *help me out here. What shall I do?* I didn't think that Heath even knew my name!'

'Do?' the six-foot-tall stunning blonde replied with a laugh. 'You're asking the wrong person. He might be my stepbrother but Heath has always looked out for me. I say go with it and then accept his offer of a lift home. Your grandfather's place is just a few streets away and, from what I saw, he would be more than happy to see you home safely after he has dropped me off.'

'Safely? This is your Heath we are talking about here. You know, the boy who has his pick of the rich, gorgeous girls at university? And what about those celebrity mags you keep showing me? He always has some flash, sophisticated lady draped over him at some big cheese event or other. Boys like that don't have time for a seventeen-year-old wannabe fashion student.'

Saskia wrapped her arm around Kate's shoulder. 'Stop putting yourself down like that. You're gorgeous and he knows it. Top marks to Heath—and it's not as though he's a stranger. You have met him before and Amber adores him.'

Amber sniffed. 'I do. There is nobody else my mum would trust to deliver me home safe and sound—not even Sam. Go for it, Kate. He won't let you down. Be brave.'

Brave? Brave was fine when she was with her pals but it was a very different matter sitting in the passenger seat of Heath's sports car an hour later.

Alone. With Heath Sheridan.

Listening to his warm deep voice chatter on about the lecture he was planning to attend the next day. The radio was tuned to popular music, the brightly lit streets spun by and it seemed only minutes between leaving Amber's third dad's house and pulling up onto the pavement outside Kate's grandfather's shop. Her brain was spinning to come up with something clever and witty and eloquent to say. No chance! Breathing was hard enough, never mind talking.

Heath must think that she was a complete idiot. It was so humiliating.

And now he was opening the car door for her. If she was going to say something this was the time.

'Thank you, Heath,' she choked through a throat as dry as the Sahara as she took his hand, locked her knees together and swung her legs out of the car with as much decorum as she could manage and lifted her chin. 'It was very kind of you to bring me home.'

His reply was to wrap one arm around her waist, push

the car door closed with the other and half support her all of the four steps to the front door of the shop. Then wait until she had fished her key out of her tiny evening bag.

It was heaven and she sneaked a cuddle before he laughed out loud and whirled her around. 'You are most welcome, lovely lady. Any time.' And before she could reply he had lifted her gloved right hand to his lips and kissed the back of her knuckles. 'It was my pleasure.' He wrinkled his nose up and winked at her. And slowly, slowly, slid his hand from hers and half turned to go.

He was leaving. Heath was leaving. No!

Which was when she did it. Kate Lovat, doing-okay-but-not-likely-to-win-any-prizes high school student, trainee fashion designer and glove aficionado extraordinaire, stepped forward, grabbed the lapels of Heath's jacket with both hands, raised herself as high as she could on tiptoe, closed her eyes and kissed him on the mouth. *Hard.*

The startled and strangely delighted look on his face when she did squint her eyes open made her whirl around, turn the key in the door and hurl herself inside before she had to face him.

'Goodnight, Heath,' she whispered as she pressed her back to the door, heart thumping and lungs heaving. 'Goodnight. And very, very sweet dreams.'

CHAPTER ONE

Eleven years later.

HEATH SHERIDAN WAS going to kill her.

He was going to jump up and stomp around and scowl and say that he knew that he had made a huge, huge mistake trusting her with something as important as making the bridesmaid dresses for his dad's wedding.

Kate Lovat lifted her left arm and squinted at her wristwatch for the tenth time in the last five minutes, then winced, sighed out loud and joggled from foot to foot.

Amber had warned her that Heath hated people being late to meetings. *Hated it.*

After all, he wasn't some heart-throb student any longer. Heath Sheridan was a serious publishing executive running his own media empire. He might have turned up late for that Valentine's Day dance, but this was different. This was business.

And she *was* now officially, undeniably, without doubt, late.

As in already ten minutes late. And that was allowing for the fact that her grandmother's watch always ran slow.

If only she hadn't bumped into Patrick, the friend she shared her loft with, on her way out.

Of course Pat wanted to check that he hadn't left anything behind in the studio, and then they'd got talking about his leaving party and then Leo had arrived to organise the photo shoot and…she'd finally escaped almost thirty minutes later. But it had always been the same. She was hopeless when it came to her friends.

Simply hopeless.

Just like her business management skills.

Good thing that she was a goddess when it came to the actual tailoring.

Kate slumped into the corner of the carriage of the rush-hour train on the London underground with both arms wrapped so tightly around her precious dress box that whenever the carriage lurched to one side, she lurched with it.

Today, of all days, the tube was slow leaving every single station on the route from her lowly design studio to the posh central London address for Sheridan Press. It seemed to be teasing her and the faster she willed it to go, the slower it went.

She had given up apologising to the other passengers after the first few times she had crashed into them and braced herself against the grubby glass partition instead.

The fact that she was too vertically challenged, as her friend Saskia called it, to reach the plastic loop swinging above her head was entirely immaterial when every lurch and rattle of the train seemed to be calling out in a sing-song tune the word *late,* rattle, *late, late,* rattle, *late.* Taunting her.

But it didn't matter. She had worked so hard on these dresses and they *were* lovely.

She would make Amber proud of her and prove to Heath and the wedding guests and their friends, hairdressers, postmen and anyone else they knew, how fabulously professional and creative she was and that they should choose Katherine Lovat Designs to create all of their future outfits.

With a bit of luck this wedding would be exactly the type of promotional opportunity she had been looking for. The first three dresses had already been delivered to the bride and the fourth and final dress had been finished right on deadline. Just as she had promised it would be.

Now all she had to do was go out into a thunderstorm and deliver the final dress—and she would be done.

Kate glanced down at her damp high-heeled peep-toe ankle boots and crunched her toes together several times to get the circulation going again.

Okay, maybe they weren't the most sensible footwear in the world for trudging through city streets on the way to make a special delivery, but it shouldn't be raining in July. It should be sunny and warm and the pavements dry enough to walk on without being in danger of being drenched from passing cars.

The train slowed but Kate's pulse started to race as she peered out at the curved tile walls as they pulled into the tube station.

This was it. She swallowed down a lump of anxiety and nervous tension the size of a wedding hat, and then she lifted her chin and turned on her trademark bright and breezy happy smile.

Nothing to see here, folks. Move along. Everything is fine in Kate land.

No problems at all.

The lease on the warehouse studio which she rented with Patrick had *not* just doubled in cost in the last year, Patrick had *not* just decided to leave London and move to Hollywood as a wardrobe assistant in the movie business and, biggest of all, she was totally, absolutely *not* nervous about meeting the man she was on her way to see at that minute.

Heath Sheridan was Amber's ex-stepbrother. That was all. And her silly teenage crush was over years ago!

So what if she had pounced on Heath the last time that she had seen him? They had both kissed a lot of other people since then. He was bound to have forgotten that embarrassing little incident…wouldn't he?

She had never seen Heath since that night and he certainly hadn't got in touch with her. But of course that was the autumn his mother had been taken ill and coming back to London wasn't included in his plans.

No. This was a straightforward business transaction. Heath needed the last of the four bridesmaids' dresses today and was willing to pay extra to have it delivered in person.

Why should it matter if Heath saw her looking like a drowned rat? With her soggy bare toes sticking out of her damp designer boots?

He probably wouldn't even notice that she was late for their meeting. *And wet.*

Probably.

And if he did, well, she could simply make a joke of her problems. The way she always did.

The glass doors slid open behind her back and Kate exploded onto the crowded platform with the crush of other passengers behind her with such momentum that she had to press one hand against the wall to protect her precious cargo.

And instantly winced.

She had just touched a wall decorated with graffiti, and who knew what else, with her white lace summer gloves.

Well, this day was getting better all the time.

It would actually be funny if she wasn't so nervous.

She sucked in a breath of hot fuel and soot-filled air charged with that tang of electricity from the tracks.

Nervous? Kate Lovat did not do nervous.

Kate Lovat was brave and strong and invincible and courageous.

Kate Lovat was going to exude an aura of total confidence and professionalism and Heath's family would recommend her work to all of their friends.

Kate Lovat had just spent an hour on her make-up so that it looked natural, and much longer choosing a professional outfit which would impress even the toughest of clients.

She clutched the dress box to her chest as she boarded the escalator.

She needed high-profile clients like the Sheridans to adore the bridesmaids' dresses she had created. After all, she had followed the brief Heath had emailed her to the letter.

Okay. Maybe she might have added *a little* something extra. After all, she had to stamp some Lovat flourish on her work. Otherwise, what would be the point of making something unique?

A smile crept up from her mouth to her eyes and a quick chuckle caught in her throat.

Watch out, Heath Sheridan. *Ready or not, here I come. Get ready to be dazzled.*

'The trade fair figures are not what we wanted, Heath. The presentations were brilliant and every buyer I spoke to was impressed with the quality of the hardbacks, but they are dragging their heels when it comes to firm orders,' Lucas explained, his exasperation clear even down the cellphone from a Malaysian hotel. 'The book stores simply don't want to hold a wide range of reference titles which only shift a few copies a year.'

Heath Sheridan scanned through the sales figures that had arrived onto his notebook computer in the past few minutes and quickly pulled together a comparison chart of how book sales were tracking in each region.

No matter how he mapped the data, the results were the same.

Sales were down in every category of reference book that had made Sheridan Press one of the few remaining commercially successful privately owned international publishing houses. The company had made its name one hundred and twenty years ago with high end, beautifully produced reference books. Biographies, dictionaries and atlases. Lovely books designed to last. And they did last. And that was the problem.

Over the past few weeks he had worked with Lucas and his talented marketing team to come up with a brilliant promotional campaign which focused on how Sheridan Press had invested in digital technology to illustrate the books which were still bound by hand so that every single reference book was a unique work of art. A superb combination of the latest technology with the finest handcrafting techniques that four generations of the Sheridan family had created.

Shame that the booksellers did not see it that way.

That was precisely the kind of approach that his father had been looking for when he'd asked Heath to inject some new blood into the company—and save the jobs of hundreds of employees who made up Sheridan Press in the process.

Growing up, he had spent more time watching men embossing gold letters onto beautiful books than he had watching sports. These men had given their lives to the Sheridan family, just as their fathers and grandfathers had done before them.

He could not fail them. He would not fail them.

Heath exhaled long and slow before replying to his father's Far East sales manager, who had lost just as much sleep as he had preparing for this sales trip. 'I know that you and your team did the very best you could, Lucas—thank you for all of your hard work,' Heath said, trying to inject a lighter tone to his voice. 'Let's see what Hong Kong brings! I can just see all of those new undergraduates heading off to university with some Sheridan books under their arms this fall.'

'Absolutely.' Lucas laughed out loud. 'Call you when we get there. Oh—and don't forget to take some time out to enjoy yourself at the wedding of the year. I'm glad I don't have to come up with a best man's speech for my own dad.'

'Hey! I'm going to be a great best man. But, talking about enjoying yourself—why not take the team out to celebrate on Saturday? I'll pick up the tab.'

'Sounds good to me. Call you later in the week.'

The cellphone clicked off, leaving Heath in silence, his quick brain working through the ramifications of the call. Frustration and exasperation combined with resigned acceptance. This promotional tour of the Far East book fairs had to pay for itself in increased sales. This was precisely the market the investment in new technology was designed to attract.

He had been convinced that the techniques that had worked so brilliantly in the commercial fiction line of the Sheridan publishing empire, could be applied to the reference book section. He had taken over a tiny and neglected division straight out of university and transformed it into one of the seven top commercial publishers in the world. The profits from Sheridan Media had been keeping Sheridan Press afloat for years.

Surely it was time to reap the benefits of ten years of driving himself with a punishing workload. When was the last time that he had a holiday? And what about the series of failed relationships and missed family events?

There had to be a way to use all of that hard-won success to save the reference books. And save his relationship with his father at the same time.

His father had reached out to ask for his business advice. It was a small step—but a real step. And an important one in rebuilding their fragile family life. The media loved it and Heath had set up press releases and interviews which had rippled through the publishing world. New technology and traditional craftsmanship. Father and son. It was a golden ticket. Heath Sheridan was the equivalent of calling in the cavalry to save yet another much respected publisher from going to the wall.

He had jumped at the chance, excited by the possibilities. And excited by the opportunity to spend more time with Charles Sheridan. They had never had an easy-going relationship and this was the first time they had worked together as professionals.

Of course he hadn't counted on being asked to be best man at his own father's wedding. Especially considering who the bride was. That was an unexpected twist.

Asking for help or acknowledging any kind of problem had never been Charles Sheridan's strong point. Maybe he should report back on what Lucas had told him.

Heath flipped open his phone when there was a polite cough and he looked up, blinking. The car had pulled to a halt and his driver was standing on the pavement, holding the door open for him while the rain soaked into the shoulders of his smart jacket.

Apologising profusely, Heath generously tipped the driver and stepped out of the executive car his father had sent to collect him from the airport. He stood long enough to take one quick glance up at the elegant stone building that was now the London office of Sheridan Press before the reporters realised who he was and ran out from the shelter of the arched entrance, cameras flashing.

Heath pulled his coat closer as protection against the heavy rain and smiled at the press.

Dealing with the media was all part of the job—as long as they produced column inches in the financial and trade press, then he was happy.

'Mr Sheridan. Over here, sir. Mr Sheridan, is it true that you are taking over Sheridan Press when your father retires, Mr Sheridan?'

'What can you tell us about rumours that the printing operation is going overseas, Mr Sheridan?'

'How do you feel about being the best man at your father's wedding? Is it third time lucky for Charles Sheridan?'

'Thanks for coming out in this typically English summer weather, everyone.' Heath smiled and waved at the cameras before turning to the female reporter who had asked the last question. 'Alice Jardine is a lovely lady who my father has known for many years as a close friend. I wish them every happiness together. Of course I was delighted when my father asked me to be the best man at his wedding this weekend—it isn't often that happens. As for the company? Business as usual, ladies and gentlemen. And no closures. Not while I am on the team. Thank you.'

And at that, by some unspoken signal, the main entrance doors slid open and Heath stepped inside with a quick smile and a wave.

But, just as he turned away from the press, a man's voice echoed from over his shoulder, 'Is it true that your late mother and Alice Jardine were good friends, Mr Sheridan? How do you feel about that?'

The doors slid shut and Heath carried on walking across

the pale marble floor of the hallway, apparently deaf to the question, and it was only in the solitary space of the elevator that he slowly unclenched his fingers.

One by one. Willing each breath he took to slow down as the words of that last question repeated over and over again inside his head.

Feel?

How did he feel about the fact that the woman who had been his mother's best friend was marrying his father?

How did he feel about the fact that Alice had been with his father while his mother lay dying in a hospice?

How did he feel?

Heath tugged hard at the double cuffs of his tailor-made shirt and fought back the temptation to hit something hard.

But that wouldn't fit into his carefully designed image.

Heath Sheridan did not get ruffled or upset or display outrageous bursts of emotion and temper. Oh, no. He played it cool. He was a Boston Sheridan and the Boston Sheridans kept their feelings buried deep enough to be icebergs.

Well, this ice man was not going to melt and let the rest of the world feel the heat of the raging temper that was burning inside him at that moment, threatening to spill out into some ill-judged outburst.

So what if his father's choice of bride hit one of his hot buttons?

He could deal with it. Was dealing with it. Would continue to deal with it.

Ironic that he should be asked that question outside the very house where his mother had spent the first twenty years of her life. The house had been built for his grandparents, who had been part of a group of aristocratic artist writers and intellectuals in the Arts and Crafts movement in the nineteen-thirties and the Art Deco features were original and stunning, especially in the library. Two storeys of hand-carved teak shelves were connected by a circular staircase which led onto an upper-level gallery, lit by a central domed roof.

Of course it had the wow factor for visitors to Sheridan Press, who were too much in awe to take notice of the fact that the recent catalogue of Sheridan books would fit neatly into one small part of the lower shelf.

Heath remembered playing hide-and-seek in the many stunning rooms, attics and cellars when he was a boy on rare visits to London with his parents, but now it was little more than a private meeting venue for his father and his circle of artist friends like Alice Jardine.

Closing his eyes, he could almost see his mother playing the piano in the drawing room below while he played with his grandparents in the patio garden outside the open French windows. The smell of lavender and beeswax. Old books and linseed oil. Because, above everything else, this house had always been filled with artists, the dinner table chatter was about art, the library full of books and exhibition catalogues about art and, of course, every available wall had been a living, constantly changing art gallery.

The thought of Alice walking these corridors where his mother had been so very happy was something that he was slowly coming to terms with. But he wasn't there yet. And he wasn't entirely sure that he ever would be.

That was something else he was going to have to work on.

In the meantime? He had a wedding to survive. A wedding where it was going to be crucial to pretend that all was rosy in the Sheridan family, and father and son were working together like the dream team they were pretending to be.

Heath strolled over to the lovely polished marquetry

desk and sat down heavily on an antique chair, which creaked alarmingly at the weight.

His father and his new fiancée had ordered a relaxed country house wedding—and that was precisely what they were going to get—with his help.

Heath opened up his laptop and was just about to dive into the checklist for the wedding arrangements when his cellphone rang and he flipped it open and answered without even checking to see who was calling him.

'Sheridan,' he said, and jammed the phone between his solid wide jaw and his shoulder blade so that he could scroll down the project plan and highlight the key activities while taking the call at the same time.

'Heath? Heath, is that you?' a female voice called down the worst phone line that he had ever heard. Loud crackling noises and what sounded like thunder screamed out at him.

Heath instantly focused on the call. 'Olivia, I was starting to get worried. Did you make your flight to London on time? Sorry about the British weather but the forecast is looking good for the next few days.'

The response was a loud clattering sound as though heavy objects were being dropped onto a metal floor, and Heath held the phone a few inches away from his ear until he heard his girlfriend's voice, which gradually became clearer. 'That's what I've been trying to tell you, but all the lines are down. I'm still in China. Heath?'

He closed his eyes and counted to ten before blinking. 'Olivia, tell me that you're joking.'

'The tropical storm that hit three days ago has just been declared a typhoon,' her echoing voice replied. 'A typhoon! Would you believe it? Even the helicopters have been grounded.'

Heath pinched the top of his nose, and then quickly typed in search details for the weather in Southern China.

Whirls of thick white cloud and misty shapes of land masses covered with warning symbols reflected back at him from the screen as he replied. 'This looks serious. Are you okay? I mean, do you have somewhere safe to go until the weather clears?'

'The valley has already flooded,' she yelled, 'so the whole team is being evacuated further up the mountain into the cave system.' Then she paused for a second. 'I have to be honest with you, Heath. Even if the weather had been good, I had already decided not to fly to London for your father's wedding.'

Tension creased his brow as Heath tabbed though the images and he slumped back in the hard chair. 'What do you mean? We talked about this a few weeks ago,' he replied and clasped the fingers of one hand around the back of his neck and rubbed it back and forth as a cold hollow feeling pooled in the pit of his stomach.

'No. You talked. And I tried to explain that I needed time away on my own to think about where our relationship was heading. It's been almost a year now, Heath, and you are just as cold and guarded as you were the day I first met you. Your work is more important than me. Than us. I'm sorry, Heath, but I can't keep this relationship alive on my own. I think it is better if we go our separate ways. I want something more. We both deserve a chance for happiness. And mine is not with you.'

She seemed about to say something when muffled voices and engine noise echoed down the phone. 'I have to go. Please send Charles and Alice my apologies and tell them I'll catch up the minute I get back. I'll be thinking of you this weekend and we'll talk more when I get back. And I am sorry, Heath, but this is goodbye. Have a great time at the wedding. Bye.'

And then the phone went dead.

Heath Sheridan stared at the completely innocent telephone for several seconds while he suppressed the urge to
throw it out of the stained-glass window.

This is goodbye? Have a great time at the wedding?

*What had just happened? Because, unless he had com-
pletely got it wrong...his girlfriend had just broken up with
him. On the telephone. From China.*

Okay. It was July and this would have been the first
time that they had spent more than a couple of days together since New Year. He had frantically completed a
major promotional tour for his bestselling thriller author
before moving to Boston to work for Sheridan Press. There
never seemed to be enough hours in the day, especially over
the past few months.

And what about her work?

Olivia's anthropology project with Beijing University
had turned into a major excavation into cave art which
would take years to complete. She had even had to send
the dressmaker her dimensions for her bridesmaid's dress
by email. He knew this because he was the one who had
taken the barrage of complaints from Kate Lovat about
making a bridesmaid's dress for a slim five-foot-three girl
who would have to wear the dress without a single fitting.

Heath's fingers froze on the keyboard.

Oh, no.

He was going to have to tell the bride that she was going
to have to walk down the aisle of the village church on her
family estate with three bridesmaids instead of four.

He dropped his head into his hands and groaned.

He was toast.

CHAPTER TWO

KATE STOOD IN the doorway to the library room and took a breath.

The last time that she had seen Heath Sheridan was at a high school dance and it had certainly been a memorable occasion. Just thinking about that moment when she had jumped on him to say goodnight made her feel so embarrassed and intimidated. And that was without the height difference, which meant that he towered over her without even trying.

Kate shrugged off her nerves. That was years ago. This time they were equal. Two professionals with their own businesses.

Unfortunately for her poor heart, Heath Sheridan had the nerve to have actually become even more handsome than the man she remembered and Amber talked about constantly.

The star student who had made his name turning around the popular fiction division of the family publishing company should be round-shouldered and wear cardigans with leather patches at the elbow.

He had no right to be so tall and clear-skinned. And that hair! Lush dark brown hair which curled into the base of his neck and seemed to have a mind of its own. He had never been vain—she knew that from talking to Amber—

but style and vanity were two very different matters and Heath Sheridan had style to spare.

Why shouldn't he?

Amber wore gowns by top fashion houses and his family were on the top level of Boston society. It made perfect sense for him to be wearing a tailored black suit and shirt which fitted him so perfectly she knew instinctively that they had been made to measure.

Those strong shoulders, slim waist and hips would be a gift to any tailor.

Oh, my. And how she would like to dress him.

Suddenly the room become stiflingly hot and it had nothing to do with the weather!

'Ah! There you are,' Kate called out through a tight throat. 'Special delivery for the man of the house, courtesy of Lovat courier services. Great to see you again, Heath.'

She waited for him to turn around and give her one of those fabulous grins that used to make her teenage knees wobble.

And she waited. And then she waited a little longer. But his gaze stayed totally locked onto whatever he was finding so fascinating on his computer screen. She could see that he was reading and typing so he was not asleep.

So she tried again.

'Hi, Heath. Your one-woman dressmaker and delivery service is here.'

Kate looked at Heath and then looked at the pretty dress box that she had slaved for hours to create and then carted across London in a downpour.

She might forgive him for not turning around to greet her but there was no way that he was going to ignore the fabulous work that she had done.

'Thank you, Kate. You were such a star to drop everything else that you were working on to create four amaz-

ing outfits at the very last minute as a personal favour,'
she murmured under her breath as she slung her shoulder
bag higher over her shoulder.

'Sorry I cannot find the time to even look at your work,'
she added with a mock lilt in her voice. *'Don't let the door
swing on your way out.'*

Heath did not even glance at her.

Right. Well, that answered that question. 'Bye, Heath.
See you around some time. Have a fabulous wedding. The
bill is in the post.'

Still no reply.

What had she been thinking?

The fashion design company she had created from
scratch and passion was in so much trouble. She should
be back in her studio working on ballet costumes for her
pal Leo, not spending what little free time she had stolen
from the day getting dressed up to deliver wedding clothes
as a favour for her friend's stepbrother.

Her friend's gorgeous, handsome, debonair and totally
oblivious to the fact that she existed brother.

She was delusional. And more than a little pathetic.

'Have a lovely wedding. I do hope everything goes well.
Why don't I just leave this last dress with you and call you
later? Bye!' she smiled and sang out in a sing-song voice.

Nothing. Not even a raised eyebrow.

Kate pressed a hand to each hip. *Well, now he was just
being rude.*

Kate tossed her bag onto a chair and stomped over to
the desk and, before Heath could do anything to stop her,
closed the lid down on his laptop and swivelled the chair
away from the desk.

And at that very moment he looked up and turned his
head.

His mouth twisted into a half smile that screamed out

that he had known that she was there the whole time. Eyes the colour of the burnt sugar coating on the top of a crème caramel dessert smiled at her, dazzling and driving any chance of sensible thought from her brain.

She half closed her eyes and scowled at him then rapped her knuckles twice on his forehead. Hard.

'Hello. Is anyone at home?' she said, ignoring his shouts of protest. 'Remember me? The girl who has just gone out of her way to hand-deliver the last bridesmaid's dress so that your new stepmum won't be followed down the aisle by a girl in cargo pants?'

'Kate. Yes. Of course. How long have you been waiting?' Heath replied with a groan as he rubbed life back into his forehead.

'Long enough to realise that you have not been listening to a word that I have said. In fact a person of delicate sensibilities might even call you rude and insulting.'

'Oh, no. Did I just zone out on you?'

She nodded slowly, up and down, her lips pushed forward. 'If that is what you call totally ignoring me for the past five minutes, then yes, you did.'

Then he did the smiley thing again and there was just enough of a twinkle in those eyes to drive away the clouds.

Wow, some men just ticked all the boxes. It was so unfair to the others.

'I apologise. It is one of my many flaws and I had no intention of being rude or ignoring you. I spend most of my time in an open-plan publishing office with a team who are never off the phone. Being able to disconnect is actually an advantage. But not always.'

She leant back and scowled at him, 'Really?'

'Really,' he whispered, and the corners of his mouth turned up into a small smile. 'I do that a lot when I'm stressed. And I am stressed. This wedding is driving me crazy. Am I forgiven?'

'I'm thinking about it,' she retorted. 'Well, that is such a pathetic excuse, but I suppose that it will have to do. But why is this wedding driving *you* crazy? Are you thinking of leaving the publishing world behind to retrain as a wedding planner?'

His eyes closed and he gave a pretend dramatic shudder. 'I don't know how they do it. This was supposed to be a small family wedding. Low-key. Intimate. You would think that it would be easy to manage. Think again.' He raked both hands back through his hair and her breathing rate went up a notch just at the sight of it.

'So why are you helping to organise this wedding?'

'Family, duty. And the fact that my dad asked me to be his best man just when he was supposed to be in the middle of launching a new publishing line in Britain. It was only when I started asking questions that it soon became apparent that the whole event was in need of serious organisation.'

He shook his head. 'Artists and writers are so talented, but their focus isn't usually on the minute details. The bride's cousin offered to make all of the arrangements as her—' and at this he made inverted commas with his fingers '—wedding present to the happy couple. I thought that my mum's family were bad enough but the Jardines have taken chaos to the next level.'

'Hey. I'm an artist. And we can be organised when we have to be!'

Heath Sheridan swivelled around in the heavy leather chair and gave his full attention to the pint-sized bundle of brightness and fun and energy who had burst into the hallowed library.

And then looked twice. Then looked again.

The girl standing looking at him in the elegant grey business suit had Kate's voice but she had certainly changed a lot from the fashion student with wild hair and wilder clothing who he vaguely remembered as one of Amber's school friends.

Her layered short brown hair framed delicate features and a pair of clear, determined and very green eyes. A sprinkle of summer freckles covered her nose but her eyes and lips had been expertly made up to make her features look magical in the diffuse light of the library.

Kate Lovat was a pixie in a skirt suit.

She seemed taller than he recalled from their last meeting but then he was sitting down and she was wearing... what was she wearing on her feet? Platform stiletto boots—but the front had been cut away so that her toes stuck out.

Why would anyone wear ankle boots—which were open-toed?

There had to be some logical explanation but at that moment he could not think of a single one, except that, oh yes—the quirky Kate was still there under the slick make-up and suit.

'Organised? I'm very pleased to hear it,' he coughed, quickly trying to drag his gaze away from her legs, 'because that would make two of us. My father wanted the wedding to go smoothly. So there was only one thing for me to do—take control of the arrangements as my gift to my dad. It's a different sort of wedding present, but at least it saves on wrapping paper.'

'Ah. Control.' She smiled and gave a small shoulder wiggle, which acted like a shot of warmth in the cool room. 'Now I'm getting the picture. Well, now you can relax because I have something special for you. The last of the bridesmaids' dresses. I finished it this morning and it is fabulous—' she paused and looked up from unwrapping a long thick card box and gave a small shrug '—of course—' then went back to untying the ribbons and lifting off the lid '—so you can relax and tick that off your list. They are all done. And, what's more, you have a chance to check the merchandise before the bride. Now that is an opportunity not to be missed. But clean hands only. No sticky paws.'

Sticky paws? What?

Heath closed the distance between them and leant down to peer inside the card box, which seemed to be filled with sheets of silky cream tissue paper.

Kate's tailored pale grey and white tweed jacket hung open at the front, revealing a coral-coloured stretchy-looking top which clung to her curves above a slim matching grey pencil skirt.

She might be wearing high-heeled shoes but she still only came up to his shoulder. A floral fragrance of roses, gardenias and jasmine filled his head. She smelt of summer on a wet and windy day and suddenly his world seemed a happier place. *How did she do that?*

'I have to admit,' she continued and slipped away from his touch, 'I am always happy to make personal deliveries to my customers, but you did cut it fine.'

He paused and glanced out of the window before strolling across to the fine wooden cabinet with a hidden refrigerator inside and picking out two bottles of water and two glasses. 'Last-minute decision. What do you give the bride who already has everything?'

'Um. Good point. A toaster wouldn't exactly cut it. I mean…' she turned her head from side to side as though to check that they were alone '…I take it that the bride is not some flighty gold-digger after your dad's loot.'

The water caught in his throat and went down the wrong way, making him cough and splutter over his computer.

Kate stood on tiptoe to thump him hard between the shoulder blades. Twice. Until he lifted his hand in submission and turned back to her. After a couple of deep breaths he blinked and wiped tears from the corners of his eyes, well aware that Kate's gaze was locked onto his face.

'Thank you,' he wheezed. 'And no. Alice is definitely not after my dad for his money. She was the one who wanted a family wedding at the Jardine country estate. She knows how my dad hates fuss. This suits him very well and I'm happy to help make it all go smoothly.'

'Are you in training for Amber's wedding?' She nodded. 'What? Why are you shaking your head like that?'

'Because there is no way that I ever want to do this again. Once is quite enough. You have no idea of the things I have had to deal with. And just wait until Alice and my dad get back from the airport with the last batch of guests. You do not want to be here when I break the news about Olivia.'

Kate reared back with a puzzled look on her face. 'Olivia? What news about Olivia?'

Heath pressed a finger and thumb into the bridge of his nose.

What news? How about the fact that my girlfriend has just decided to dump me days before my father's wedding? That's all. Because apparently I am cold and guarded. Nothing important. Nothing to worry about. Just one more relationship down the pan.

He closed his eyes for a second in a futile attempt to regain control. But Olivia's words kept echoing through his brain until they were all he could think about.

Cold and guarded.

This was pretty much the same thing the two girlfriends before Olivia had complained about. Was he cold? Guarded, yes. He did protect himself from becoming emotionally dependent on anyone, and especially a woman. Why shouldn't he? He had seen the massive damage that kind of relationship could have on the family and the man. There was no way that he could ever allow himself to love one person and one place so completely. Not when they could be snatched away from him at a moment's notice and he was powerless to prevent it. But cold?

Blinking his eyes open, Heath was about to reply to Kate's question with some casual throwaway comment, when his gaze fell on the open box.

Something sparkling and shiny nestled in the tissue paper.

In two steps he was standing, looking in disbelief at the confection of dusty pink lace and satin, scarcely able to believe his eyes.

'What's this?' he asked, pointing to the swirls of iridescent ivory-coloured pearls which had been sewn into the lacework across the bodice and sleeves.

'Embellishment, of course.' She grinned.

He should have known that things were going too smoothly. Embellishment!

Amber had trusted Kate, but then again Amber adored her friends and was obviously incapable of being objective about their abilities.

After today's little bombshell from Olivia, the last thing he wanted to do was deal with faulty bridesmaids' dresses.

Heath picked up his tablet computer and scanned through emails. 'Alice sent me very specific instructions about the bridesmaids' dresses that she required for her wedding. All four had to be the same design and made of the same fabric. Very plain. And no mention of the word embellishment.'

He looked up at her, eyebrows raised. 'Has she made any comments about the first three?'

Kate nodded. 'Alice has been travelling with your father for the past two weeks so I sent them over to the Manor yesterday. She texted me to say that they had arrived safe and sound but she wasn't going to open the boxes until her bridesmaids arrived.'

'So Alice hasn't checked the dresses yet.'

'What? And spoil the fun of opening the boxes with the gals? It will be like Christmas morning.'

'Right. All I asked you to do, Kate, was make four very plain dresses. That was simple enough, wasn't it?' His gaze focused on the beaded neckline. 'I didn't think that you would change the design into something more elaborate.'

'You're forgetting something very important.' She glared at him. 'People pay me to transform a simple idea into a beautiful design. Otherwise why bother having dresses made-to-measure? Alice could have gone to a department store for a plain dress. She expects me to do something creative with this idea. Don't you like the idea of being creative?'

Creative? He had grown up with an artist mother whose idea of responsibility was making sure there was always paint and canvas in the house. Everything else was unnecessary. Timetables were for other people to follow, not her. She was talented, celebrated, enchanting and, for a teenage boy desperate for some structure in his life, totally exasperating.

Kate Lovat was clearly cut from the same mould.

Not even an elegant grey and white pinstripe skirt suit could hide the fact that she was just as irresponsible and creative as the girl he remembered from the last time they'd met.

He should have guessed that Kate had not changed that much. Who else would choose to wear quirky red leather ankle boots with her toes sticking out the front on a wet July afternoon?

His gaze scanned her legs—and lingered a little too long on those shapely smooth legs before focusing on the footwear. Her toenails were painted in the exact same shade of red as her boots.

Fire engine red.

A flaming symbol of her attitude to life.

Well, it certainly fitted, because she had just managed to spark a match under the very last scrap of patience he had held on to for emergencies and burnt it to a crisp.

There was one thing he hated above anything else—and that was surprises.

'Are all four dresses like this one?' he asked with a rock-stiff jaw.

'Of course they are. You ordered matching outfits.'

A deep furrow appeared between Heath's brows and the air practically crackled with electricity as he exploded with a reply. 'Kate, Alice ordered plain. I don't know much about fashion, but this is not plain.'

Kate stepped forward so that her entire body was only inches away from his, and the fire in her eyes was the same colour as her toenails.

'And I know about fashion. Alice. *Will love*. These dresses. The bridesmaids *will love* these dresses. Your father *will love* these dresses. The entire clan gathered for this shindig will love these dresses. And the wedding will be a huge success, Heath. Job done.'

'Job done? I don't think so. Have you any idea how important this wedding is? This is the first time in ten years that my father's asked me to do anything for him. I'm not prepared to see their wedding day ruined by you taking creative licence. These dresses will have to be altered.'

Concern fuelled his anger but Kate's response threw petrol onto the flames.

Because she did not look away or back down. She stared him out, and the look in her eyes was something new, something he had not seen before.

This was not the same girl he remembered. Little Kate had certainly grown up.

'Change them? Do you have any idea what you are saying?' Her words came out in a staccato retort of crisp clear sounds as though she was struggling to contain herself. 'There is no way that I can alter even one of these dresses before the weekend. So, as far as I am concerned, this is it. No negotiation. No replacements.'

A surge of disbelief swept through him and he was about to launch into a tirade when his cellphone rang. His personal assistant was returning his call.

'Don't go anywhere,' he ordered, pointing the phone at her chest like a baton and turned back to the desk and the sales figures.

Kate desperately fought to find the words needed to frame some kind of response but was saved when he moved out of earshot.

With a twist of her heels she turned away from him and leapt back up the stairs and tugged open the glass cases that held the books and pretended to be fascinated in the first book she picked up.

Her eyes were too blurry to read the title on the spine or admire the fine end papers.

The one thing that she had been secretly dreading for years had finally happened.

She wasn't good enough for Heath.

And he had no idea whatsoever of how much pain and humiliation she felt at a few simple words of condemnation.

He was rejecting this dress that she had worked on for hour after hour of painstaking hand-sewing after a few seconds of his so very precious time. How could he not know that when he rejected her work he was rejecting her and everything she stood for and had worked for at the same time?

Time and time again she had come up against the same attitude, the same complaint, and the same demand. Keep it simple. Don't get clever. Conform to what everyone else is doing. That way we might like you and take you seriously.

Even her own parents thought that she should conform. Sacrifice her creativity and ideas on the altar of the bland and the stale and the conventional.

And just the thought of that made her heart shrink with pain and anguish.

She had always known that Heath would be different, but facing it head-on in a stark announcement like this was a lot harder than she had expected. The pain hit her just behind the knees and she casually flicked her skirt out and sat down on the step before she fell down and felt even more of a fool.

She had to get out of here.

That was it.

She had made her delivery. Her job was done.

The moment her legs started working again she could take off back to the studio and lock the door and laugh about what a silly teenage crush she had once upon a time on a man who turned out to be not worth it after all.

This was so totally crazy it was mad.

Heath had never looked on her as anything else than Amber's funny little school friend. Someone he had never taken seriously. Someone he humoured because he loved Amber and wanted to make her happy.

Part of her respected that.

Shame that the rest of her wanted to get home as fast as she could and cry her heart out over a bucket of ice cream.

This was not just futile but ridiculous and pathetic. She had finally had the rose-tinted spectacles whipped from her eyes so that she could see Heath for who he was and not the boy she had kissed on her doorstep all of those years ago.

Strange. She should be used to being disappointed with men, but she had always hoped that Heath would be different. That he would be the caring man that Amber adored.

She had dated fashion designers, artists and musicians who all claimed to be creative and experimental—but in the end they all turned out to be bland and conformist, too willing to change their ideas to fit in, and she had walked away from every one of them.

Hoping for something better. Hoping for someone who liked her exactly the way she was and loved what she did and did not want to change her or 'shape her talent' as one agent had called it.

No, thanks. She decided what she did. She set the standards and followed her dream and nobody, not even Heath, was going to stop her from keeping her fashion designs alive.

No. She would stay as she was. Amber's little friend. That way, Heath would never know how much effort it took for her to get back to her feet and look at him crossing the room through the raging sea of confused emotions and regret that were still roiling inside her.

'Fine,' she replied, and folded the tissue paper over the dress, closed down the lid on the box and popped it under her arm before staring up into his face with a clear serious expression. 'I'll take this dress. But you have to understand something. This might be your father's third marriage, Mr Sheridan. But this will be my fifteenth. Yes, that's right; so far fourteen brides have trusted me to be creative with their wedding garments and by the end of the season that will be twenty.'

She took a tight hold of the box, which seemed outrageously large compared to her tiny frame. 'You know where to find me if you change your mind. Good luck on the big day. You're going to need it. Because right now your precious girlfriend Olivia doesn't have a bridesmaid dress—and try explaining that to the bride. End of.'

And with that she turned on her heel and walked straight out of the door, her hips swaying, her high-heeled boots clicking on the hardwood floor and her seriously annoyed nose high in the air.

CHAPTER THREE

HEATH SHERIDAN STEPPED out from the back seat of the black London cab, tugged down his suit jacket, then turned and thanked the driver. The taxi slid away from the kerb, leaving him standing on the pavement outside Kate's studio feeling rather like a teenager watching his parents drive away from his boarding school on the first morning of the new term.

He knew that feeling only too well and it nagged at the deep well of disquiet before he rolled his shoulders back and strolled out into the bright July sunshine.

An imposing two-level stone warehouse stretched out the whole length of one side of the cobbled street. It reminded him very much of the Sheridan print works back in an old part of Boston which had not changed over the last one hundred years. Impressive buildings like these were created to intimidate visitors with the power and wealth of the owners in a time before press conferences and the kind of celebrity TV interviews he was accustomed to organizing for his bestselling fiction writers.

Well, he knew all about that. Sheridan Press had built up a reputation through years of hard work and quiet, understated excellence. Not flashy promotions or grand gestures. That was the world that his father had grown up in, which made it even more remarkable that he had swallowed his pride and asked Heath to help him.

In hindsight he should have guessed that there was more to the request than the business problems—but he had never expected it to be personal.

Just one more reason why Alice Jardine was going to have four bridesmaids walking behind her on Saturday, not three.

A passing delivery van snapped Heath awake and he straightened his back and strode towards the warehouse.

There was only one girl who would fit that bridesmaid's dress and that girl was Kate Lovat. So he had better gird himself to do some serious grovelling.

Attached to the wall was a modern nameplate with the words *Katherine Lovat Designs* in an elegant font.

It was classy but not stuffy or imposing. And it stopped Heath in his tracks.

Perhaps it'd been a mistake to underestimate Kate Lovat?

Kate had been an astonishing delight until he had opened his big mouth and put his foot in it. Surprising and intriguing and more than just attractive. She had a certain unique quality about her that Heath could not put his finger on and he was kicking himself for overreacting.

The breeze picked up some dry leaves and tossed them up towards Heath, bringing him back down to earth with a thump. He had to work fast. His father was already at Jardine Manor with Alice preparing the house for their wedding, which his son was organising so very brilliantly.

Heath slid his sunglasses into his hair and his smart black designer boots clattered up the well-worn stone stairs that led to the first floor.

He stretched out to press the doorbell just as he noticed

that a piece of pink fluorescent paper had been taped onto
the metal door. Someone had written in large letters:

> *Casting today 10 a.m. to 2 p.m. Gents to the left. La-*
> *dies to the right. All leotards and tutus must be col-*
> *lected before you leave. Any lingerie left behind will*
> *be recycled.*

Tutus? Casting? Heath quickly checked his watch. Nine-
thirty.

Amber had told him that Kate specialized in tailoring
for women, but nothing about running dance shows! Surely
designers used agencies for that sort of thing? Perhaps he
had come to the wrong address?

The door was slightly ajar and, with a small tap on the
frame, Heath opened the door and slipped inside the most
remarkable room he had ever been in.

The entire floor of the warehouse was one single space.
Large, heavy pillars supported the ceiling and no doubt
the floor above. A row of tall sash windows ran the entire
length of both sides of the room. Light flooded in and reflected back from the cream-painted brick walls, creating
an airy light space with the quality of light he had only
ever seen in an art gallery before.

He took a step further inside the room, the sound of his
hard heels beating out a tune on the hardwood floorboards
and echoing across the space. On each side of the door were
changing areas made from what looked like tents hanging
from the ceiling, and in front of the window was a very
professional photo set-up with camera and lighting stands
and lighting umbrellas and plain backdrops.

Someone had paid for the extras with this set-up.

But who? And where were they?

He strolled forward down the length of the room between two long white polymer worktables and a collection of ironing boards, tailors' models in various sizes, naked and partly dressed, and two draftsman desks covered with stacks of coloured paper.

Everywhere he looked were abandoned rolls of fabric, sewing machines and what looked like cutlery trays stuffed with scissors and all kinds of boxes and packets.

So, all in all—his worst nightmare. Clutter and chaos. No sense of order or control. If he ran his office like this they would be out of business in a month.

Blowing out hard, Heath shook his head and peeked behind an elaborate Japanese lacquered folding screen. And froze for a few seconds, scarcely believing what he was looking at before breaking out into a wide smile. It was the first time that he had smiled that day—but he had good reason.

Kate was sitting at a desk under the window, nodding her head from side to side as she sang along to a pop song in a very sweet voice.

Of course he could have interrupted her—but this was a totally self-indulgent pleasure he wanted to stretch out for as long as he could.

She was wearing a tiny lime-green strappy top, which was almost covered by a necklace which seemed to be made up of bright green and yellow baubles. Her short brown hair was tousled into rough curls with some kind of hair product that made it stand out from her head and yet still seem soft and appealing. *Touchable.*

As a tribute to the warm July sunshine which was streaming in from the window only a few yards away, she had chosen what looked like a tight stretchy tube to wear as a skirt, which covered her hips and upper legs but moved when she stretched across the table, revealing shapely tanned legs which ended in brown platform sandals. And those amazing painted toenails which had rendered him speechless the evening before.

It was strange how this colourful and totally unlikely ensemble only seemed to make her lovely figure even more attractive.

This version of Kate was startling. Entrancing, fresh and natural.

The elegant woman in the slick city suit, designer boots and smart make-up he had met the previous evening was gone, replaced by a slim girl in working clothes doing her admin early on a Tuesday morning. She did not need make-up or expensive clothing or accessories to look stunning— she was lovely just as she was.

The city girl in the suit he had met last night he could deal with, but this version of Kate Lovat with the tape measure around her neck was far more of a challenge.

Was this her workshop? Or was she an employee of some bigger company?

He should have asked Amber a lot more questions before he'd left the hotel—background information was always useful for negotiations, and suddenly he felt out of place. This was Amber and Kate's territory, not his. This pretty girl who looked absurdly cute might not be so generous when she remembered how he'd slighted her the night before.

Either way, he was standing here in a black business suit and crisp white shirt on a summer day, feeling completely overdressed, while she was comfortable and cool in her work clothes. He had rarely felt so out of his depth, or so attracted to a girl who was totally natural and comfortable in her own skin. And what skin!

That kind of combination would spell trouble if he stayed around long enough to get to know her better. She was dynamite with a slow-burning fuse. And the last thing he needed was another complication like Olivia to deal with.

Her right hand was tapping with a pencil on a pad of drawing paper while her left was holding up what looked to Heath like an invoice or delivery note. She was peering at it through pink-tinted spectacles with bright-red frames then scribbling something down on the pad. Then looking back at the printed sheet, and then back to the pad. And scowling.

'Why is this not adding up?' she asked with a long sigh, then reached out and rummaged through a large cardboard box which was overflowing with paperwork and ring binders and envelopes, pulling out individual sheets and tossing them onto the desk as she went until her fingers froze on what looked like a purple sticky note pushed inside an envelope. 'There you are,' she smiled, 'I knew that I had already paid you last week. Now stop hiding from me or I will never work out how to do these accounts properly.'

A self-satisfied smile flashed across her lips, which was so natural and unpractised that it made his heart melt just looking at her.

She looked so vulnerable and naïve.

And, judging by the accumulation of papers on her table, not the world's best bookkeeper. Her filing system could certainly use an overhaul and a simple spreadsheet would do all of the adding up she was struggling with. He could probably set it up in less than an hour, but somehow he didn't think that Kate would welcome another criticism of her working practices.

Not after yesterday. And certainly not from him.

Even if some part of him did yearn to dive in and sort out the mess she had clearly got herself into.

Heath was still working on some way of introducing himself without looking like a complete idiot when a voice behind him whispered, 'Hello, handsome. You're a little early for the casting, but if you want to take your clothes off over there, I'll be happy to take a look at what you can do.'

Heath spun around to find a tall, dark-skinned man in a slim-fit red-and-green windowpane check suit and narrow Italian shoes scanning his body from head to toe while tapping his chin with a forefinger.

'I have to break the bad news to you, handsome. You don't look like a dancer from here.'

Dancer? Remove his clothing?

A woman's voice laughed out loud and he glanced over his shoulder to see Kate grinning from ear to ear. She exchanged kisses on both cheeks with the man and wrapped one arm around his waist. 'Lovely to see you, as always, Leo. And as punctual as ever. As for our guest,' she said in a semi-serious voice, 'I can see what you mean. Not really the dancing physique at all. Good thing he's my client and not looking for stage work.'

'Your client? Oh, I see. Pity. *Ciao bella.*' Leo coughed and strolled away towards the entrance.

'Good morning, Kate,' Heath replied calmly, trying not to squirm in the suddenly overwhelming heat. 'I'm sorry to disturb your work but I was hoping that you could spare me a few minutes.'

She looked up at him wide-eyed, then turned away and rested her hand against the wide table. 'Why? Are you interested in being measured for a suit?' She gestured over his shoulder. 'I specialise in ladies' wear but, as you can see, I have a wide selection of fabric in an assortment of colours. I'm sure I could find something to match your complexion. A fetching shade of puce embarrassment tweed, perhaps?'

And then she looked up at him through her eyelashes

and their eyes met. And in that instant he knew that she was already two steps ahead of him.

Kate knew precisely why he was there and had absolutely no intention of letting him get away with anything.

She ignored the stack of papers on her desk and started pinning pieces of thin tissue paper to a tailor's model, smoothing each piece in turn to fit the curves of the shape below. Her fingertips moved in slow languorous strokes, sensually caressing each piece, one after another, with infinite care and such loving attention that Heath's blood pounded just a little hotter.

He paused and tapped his head with his forefinger. 'Touché. Actually, I have come to apologise for yesterday. Then I'm going to thank you nicely for making four charming bridesmaids' dresses at very short notice to help me out. Is that better?'

Kate twitched her lips but turned back to her model and kept on pinning and smoothing until the entire bodice was covered with what looked like a jacket. Only when she had arranged the pattern pieces to her satisfaction did she whirl around towards him with her back against the desk.

Heath inhaled slowly and braced himself for whatever was coming his way. Which was why when she did speak what she said knocked him more than he could have imagined.

'I am curious about one thing. Did you come to me as the last resort? Because you left it too late to ask anyone else to make the bridesmaids' dresses?'

He winced and gave her a brief nod. There was no point in denying it. 'Partly that,' he admitted. 'My father only announced that he was getting married a month ago. I had no idea that fashion houses need such a long lead time.'

And then he took a breath. 'But I also relied on Amber's judgement. She knows how important this wedding is, and would never have suggested Katherine Lovat Designs unless she was confident that you would do a good job.'

Kate sighed out loud through her nose and crossed her arms. She shook her head and clenched her small fingers into fists for a few seconds. 'And to think that I actually came all the way to your office yesterday, in the rain, to thank you for choosing me in preference to some big name couture fashion house.' Her knuckles wrapped on her forehead. 'Idiot.' Then she sniffed and started to stack the pile of papers on the table. 'Did you seriously hate the dress I showed you?'

'On the contrary. The colour is perfect for me but I suspect it would be a little snug across the chest.'

Her lips pressed together and she blinked several times but refused to look at him. 'Really? And what about the pearl embroidery on the bodice? All that embellishment that you have a deep aversion to.'

He took a step closer. 'It's lovely. Really lovely. Was it done by hand?'

Her head shot up and she stuck her neck out, openmouthed. 'No, the magic elves came in the night. Of course it was done by hand.' She lifted both hands and waved them at him. 'These hands, to be precise.'

He tried to take that information in, but words refused to form.

'You did all of that pearly embroidery?'

She nodded slowly up and down. Once.

'For all four dresses? On your own?'

Kate replied with a small shoulder shrug. 'This is a one-woman show. No assistants, no apprentices. And I had to get the pearls just right. Otherwise the design wouldn't match the pearl embroidery on Alice's wedding dress.'

Suddenly she winced in pain as though she had cut herself and launched herself at him and grabbed the sleeves of his suit jacket. 'Oh, no! Look what you made me do. I should not have said that. Should. Not. The wedding dress has to stay top secret until the big day. You have to promise not to say a word to your father. Seriously. Not a word. Okay. Promise?'

'What wedding dress is that? Never heard a thing. Was someone talking?' he replied in a calm voice and pretended to look around the room for a few seconds before gazing into her green eyes, which were sparkling with passion and sunlight. 'But why didn't you explain that last night?'

'Because you were far more interested in your phone call than listening to anything that I would have to say.'

Kate released her grip on his sleeve and smoothed down the fabric before looking up into his face with an expression which demanded his attention and held it there.

'Why weren't you listening? Was your pride hurt because I actually used my initiative and did not follow your specific instructions to the letter?'

Oh, Kate. If you only knew the kind of day I had yesterday you would understand why the dress was the last straw that burst the bubble of control I was clinging onto so badly.

Her gaze stayed locked on his, but as he stayed silent she slowly relaxed her grip and a frown creased her forehead. 'So, it had nothing to do with me. Did something happen yesterday? Before we met? Something which rattled you?' she asked in a low intense voice which seemed to echo around the space even though they were so close that he could feel her breath on his throat and see the way the sun brought out the highlights in her hair.

It was as though she had read his mind. *Intuitive.*

'Rattled? I don't get rattled,' he mocked.

'Yes, you do,' she whispered and shuffled back half a step so that she could look up into his face. 'Talk to me, Heath. Tell me what rattled you so very badly.'

He looked into those green eyes and knew instantly that she was not judging him or condemning him—she simply wanted to know what had happened. But there was something else in that gaze. Not pity. Concern. She was concerned about him.

And it shocked him to the core that he could not recall a single time that a girl had looked at him with concern in her eyes and meant it. Not Olivia. Their relationship had been based on mutual convenience and shared interests and a healthy appreciation of the benefits of an active social and sex life. But not concern. Not intimacy. Not sharing their hopes and fears.

The silence lengthened and she did not try to fill the silence with chatter but waited patiently to hear his response. Her light floral perfume and the sheer physical presence of this tiny woman who was within touching distance combined with the intensity of that one single look to reach inside him and knock on the locked door of his heart.

And for the first time in years he knew that he could trust another person with the truth. The real truth.

'A few minutes before you arrived, my girlfriend, Olivia, called from China to inform me that not only is she going to miss the wedding this weekend, but she had decided that our relationship is not working for her and it was time to go our separate ways.'

'She broke up with you? Over the phone?' Kate's jaw dropped in disbelief.

'Over the phone from China. So you see, as of yesterday I am officially single and without a wedding date.'

'Oh.' She sighed and blinked several times. 'Well, to use my good friend Amber's favourite expression—that sucks. Big time.'

Heath exhaled the breath he had not even realised he had been holding in and his shoulders seemed to drop several inches. 'It certainly does. And that is not the only problem. Alice had insisted that Olivia should be one of the four bridesmaids. And now she isn't coming.'

Kate's eyebrows went north and her mouth formed a perfect oval. 'Ouch. Does Alice know yet? It could be difficult to find another bridesmaid in less than a week.'

'Tell me about it. You already know that Olivia is petite and has tiny feet—you made her dress. There aren't many girls who would be able to fit into…' His voice faded away as his gaze scanned Kate from head to toe and back again. 'Miss Lovat, I have a question for you.'

Her chin lifted. 'Hello. Yes? What is it?'

'What shoe size do you wear?'

'It depends on the shoe but usually a size three or four British sizing. But why do you want to know that? Because Amber has told me all about your deep-seated dislike of anything that comes under the category of female fripperies. So if you are thinking of buying me footwear for some reason, thank you, but no.'

'Me? Ah. No. Not my thing. Now, Alice…' he sucked in a breath through his teeth like a whistle '…Alice insisted on buying all of the bridesmaids' shoes from some exclusive London designer. I know this because I paid the invoice. And guess what size Olivia takes? A three. How about that for a coincidence?'

He sighed out loud and crossed his arms, lips pressed firmly together. 'Shame that I shall have to return those gorgeous shoes now that Olivia cannot make it. And I know how much Alice wanted to have four bridesmaids. Not five or three. It had to be four. This is going to be such a blow. I'm worried that it might even ruin her big day.'

He cupped one elbow and started tapping on his lower lip.

'Of course, there is one other alternative,' he said in a lilting voice. *While staring directly into Kate's eyes.*

'Any idea where I might be able to find a replacement bridesmaid at short notice who would fit a slim petite dress and size three shoes? Um…?'

CHAPTER FOUR

KATE STARED AT HIM, open-mouthed, for all of two seconds before she got the message.

'Oh no, you don't. Not a chance, Sheridan,' Kate replied with a short sharp laugh and stepped back, both of her hands palm upwards.

'You would make a perfect bridesmaid, Kate,' he grinned, 'and I'm sure Alice would be delighted.'

'Are you mad?' She glared at him in disbelief. 'I might have spoken to Alice on the phone and by email but I have never even met your future stepmother in person and you may not be aware of this but usually the bride likes to have some say in who her bridesmaids are, not the best man. She is bound to have lovely friends and relatives who were furious to be missed the first time around. Or ring someone in your little black book.'

'No point—the dress has been made for Olivia—and is about your size. In fact, didn't Amber say that you modelled it because Olivia was overseas?'

Heath stepped back and then walked in a slow circle as he scanned her so slowly from shoes to head that she started to squirm. 'Although it might be a bit tight around the bodice, the length would work.'

Kate's head slowly came up and she crossed her arms over her chest.

'Ah, so that is the only selection criteria. I have to be short and flat-chested.'

'And pretty.' He shrugged.

'Short, flat-chested and with small feet,' came her choked reply. 'And not likely to crack the camera lens. My, you have a wonderful way of charming the ladies with your pick-up lines, Heath Sheridan. How could I possibly refuse when you hit me with that kind of flattery?'

Kate pressed her fingertip to her lips and laughed. 'Oh, wait. I do refuse. Sorry, Heath. Not this time, not any time. Not a chance. But don't panic. Alice is bound to know someone who would fit that dress.'

Heath crossed his arms and shook his head slowly from side to side. 'I researched every lady on the guest list last evening and not one of them is a match.'

'You have dossiers on the guests?'

'Of course. How else would I know how to engage the house party in idle conversation?'

Kate closed her mouth, inhaled deeply, lifted her chin, slipped the pin cushion back onto her wrist and gave Heath a finger wave. 'Well, I think that just about says it all. Best of luck with the bride. Have a lovely wedding.'

'Kate. Wait. You know I wouldn't ask you to do this unless I was desperate.'

'Yes, I am beginning to understand that very well.'

'Wait. This is important. I need this wedding to be a success,' he blurted out as she turned away from him.

And he just stopped himself in time before the words came tumbling out of his heart—but he pulled back.

This might be the only chance—the last chance—that I have to build bridges and get my father back into my life.

His true feelings were too personal and private to share with anyone. When it came to his parents, he was a closed book to the rest of the world and that was exactly how he intended to stay.

Kate lifted her chin and stood rock-still, her lips pressed together. Then she squinted at him and asked in a stubborn voice, 'Just give me one good reason why I should step in for your former girlfriend and be a bridesmaid when I haven't even met the bride and groom.'

Yes! A window of opportunity. And if there was one thing that Heath had picked up in ten years in publishing, it was that he had to make the most of each and every opportunity that came his way.

But what? What could he come up with? A reason?

His gaze dropped to the paperwork under her splayed-out fingers. The very messy paperwork which she was having trouble getting to add up. Which was hardly surprising if she was using sticky notes as receipts.

Yes. A bribe might just work.

'One?' Heath replied. 'I can give you several. But how about this for an idea?'

Heath took three steps towards Kate so that he was almost touching her and looked down into her startled face. 'I am prepared to offer you a trade, Miss Lovat. As a lady entrepreneur, you must be so incredibly busy with your creative designs that I suspect you could use some professional help to sort out all those pesky accounts and the mountain of business paperwork that comes with working for yourself.'

He stepped to one side, looked hard at the desk, then back into her face, and then back at the desk again.

He sniffed and waved one hand in the air. 'It just so happens that I am rather an expert in that particular area. I designed the office management system and helped to roll it out across the whole division. From what I have seen, I doubt that a company executive such as yourself would need more than a day or two to clear your backlog, bring your accounts up to date and put an easy but efficient system in place which could cope with any and all expansion plans. All I would need is some desk space right here in the studio. One business person to another. What do you say to that?'

He pressed the fingertips of both hands onto the surface of the table, trapping her within the arch of his body. And, to her credit, Kate did not shuffle away but locked her lovely green eyes onto his and refused to move. Only the longer he looked the more he wanted to look and it was an effort to blink, step back and focus on something other than her flawless skin and the amber and gold highlights mixed into the green of those eyes, which seemed to pop against the longest dark brown eyelashes that he had ever seen—and hers were real.

'Well, there you have it, Kate.' He laughed. 'One good reason why you should run away with me this weekend and be treated to full-on pampering—and all in exchange for wearing one of your lovely frocks. Say yes,' he murmured with his best molten-chocolate seductive voice. 'You know you want to.'

Kate inhaled deeply then blew out and wafted her hand in front of her face.

'Wow!' She laughed and waggled her fingers at him. 'Back off. Give a girl a minute here. I need some air if I'm going to think about it.'

Kate sat down heavily in her chair and dropped her head into her hands.

Decision time.

She could go back to her house and work on with some inventive ways to pay the rent and pretend that she did not care that Heath was one bridesmaid short of a wedding.

A wedding which might direct a lot of high-spending customers to Katherine Lovat Designs. She had even printed off some extra business cards.

Or. And she closed her eyes for a second and inhaled a breath of hot dusty air.

Or she could agree to go with Heath to his father's wedding, put on Olivia's bridesmaid dress, which she already knew was a perfect fit, and new shoes and walk down the aisle behind a bride she had never even met.

In front of Heath's fancy Boston family and friends.

She glanced up at Heath, who had taken out his smartphone and was already scanning his messages as he paced up and down her workspace.

Oh, Heath Sheridan. He is your dad and you love him and want him to love you!

If you only knew how similar we are, Heath. And how very different.

Taking a deep breath, Kate sat back in her pedestal chair and scrubbed at her temples with the fingertips of both hands. But when she opened her eyes the first thing she saw was the overflowing box of invoices and receipts which had built up over the past few weeks—okay, months—which she had promised Saskia that she would sort out the minute the bridesmaids' dresses were finished.

No excuses. She had to face them. This was supposed to be her business and there was no way that she could afford an accountant, so it was her or relying on Saskia again. If only she knew…a business professional who might be willing to do her accounts for her.

Heath's voice echoed across from the other side of the work table. She caught the words 'margins' and 'discounts' before he turned away.

Kate got to her feet and started pacing up and down in

front of her desk, glancing at the paperwork piled inches high around the boxes and then looking up at Heath.

Her steps slowed then speeded up again. Heath was a brilliant businessman—who was desperate for a replacement bridesmaid.

She was a hopeless businesswoman who was fairly desperate with her accounts.

Just looking at the boxes made her want to shove the whole lot back into the cupboard to join the others and get on with the exciting work on Leo's ballet costumes.

This could be the chance that she had been looking for to finally prove to her parents that she was able to make a living doing what she loved and she was not wasting her life on foolish nonsense. Taking her income to the next level would certainly come in useful too.

But a weekend wedding with the Sheridans? Ouchy ouch ouch.

It took five circuits before she stopped and braced her legs.

It might just work.

'Hey, handsome. Over here. I've had a thought.'

'Shall I alert the media?' he snorted and immediately coughed into his hand as she glared at him. 'Sorry. Carry on. You've had a thought. Does that mean yes?'

'Not so fast. I need to get a few things straight.' Kate's breath caught in her throat and she carried on pacing slowly up and down so that when she replied her words came out in one long stream.

'I would just be there as a stand-in bridesmaid, right? Not a wedding date. You'll fess up that Olivia is not simply delayed somewhere.'

'Absolutely,' Heath replied, the ice in his voice replaced by a warm edge and there was just the touch of a smile on his lips. 'And I promise that the speeches will be short and the champagne chilled.'

Kate relaxed her shoulders. She had done it now. Might as well go the full distance. 'How about dancing and frolics?' she asked.

Heath stopped frowning and his eyebrows lifted. 'As far as I know, there are no plans for dancing. Or frolics. This is my dad, remember. But Alice has friends in a symphony orchestra who are sending up some of the string section. It should be a very cultural event. And why are you groaning again?'

'Promise me that you will never move into sales because you are doing a terrible job at selling this to me, Heath Sheridan.' Kate jutted her chin out. 'A cultural event? This is a wedding. You know, romance, fun, happiness.'

Then she sniffed and gave a small shoulder shrug. 'Is it a church or civil service or both?'

'The local village church.'

Kate nodded slowly. 'Let me guess. The Jardines have lived in the village for generations and have their own pew in the ancient church and plaques on the wall. Am I right?'

'How did you know that?' he asked in a low voice. 'Do you know the village?'

'No. But I have been to a few like it. English tradition.' Her gaze locked onto his totally confused and bemused face and she burst out laughing. 'You really do not have a clue, do you? Oh dear.'

Heath replied by stepping closer so that their bodies were almost touching. She could practically hear his heart beating under the fine weave luxury cotton shirt. But for once she held her ground and looked up into his face rather than give way.

'Let me check that I understand the deal,' she whispered. 'One all expenses paid wedding, complete with bridesmaid duties, in exchange for two full days of your time as a business consultant. And you would be doing the actual number-crunching—not some minion. Okay?'

Heath took her hand and pressed his long slender fingers around hers and held them tight just long enough for her to inhale his intoxicating scent. Combined with the texture of his smooth skin against hers as he slowly raised her hand to his lips and kissed the back of her knuckles, sensible thought became a tad difficult for a few seconds.

Because the moment his lips touched her skin she was seventeen again and right back on her doorstep.

'Better than okay. It's a deal. Delighted to have you on my team—because I don't have minions,' he replied with a full-on, headlight-bright grin.

'Team,' she whimpered. 'Right. Now that is settled. What time do you need me to be there on Saturday?'

'Oh, didn't I tell you? I'm going to need you there on Friday morning so you're ready for the wedding rehearsal and dinner. I hope that isn't a problem.'

'Think musketeers. Think swagger and swords. Think Johnny Depp.' Saskia Elwood picked up a cake fork and pretended to have a mock sword fight with the china teapot on Kate's kitchen table.

'Okay, okay, I am thinking and drawing at the same time. Designing pirate gauntlets is not easy, you know.'

'Never said it was—that was why I came to the best. You are the only girl I know who spends most of her life in a fantasy world inside her head. You are a saviour, Kate Lovat.'

'*Flatterer.* You know my hidden weakness for pantomime,' Kate replied with a short salute. Then she looked at Saskia over the top of her spectacles. 'Why are you the person who always ends up running these projects when you have a business to run?'

Saskia shrugged then chuckled. 'I seem to have one of those faces that scream out—come and ask me to help and I will drop everything and do it for you. You would have thought that I would know by now, wouldn't you?'

'No—' Kate laughed and patted Saskia on the arm '—you have always been generous with your time and your heart. That's who you are. And I wouldn't want you to change a bit.' Then she gasped. 'Wait. I have had a brilliant idea. Why don't you go to this wedding in my place? The dress might be a tad short but you've got the legs to get away with it. Heath wouldn't mind a bit.'

'What? And deny you the vision of Heath Sheridan standing in a sunlit old church in his grey morning dress? All tall, dark and handsome. Oh, I couldn't do that…not after your little teenage *interlude*.'

Kate rolled her eyes and sighed in exasperation. 'I should know better than to call you and Amber. Two hopeless romantics who are determined to overlook a few rather important facts about the brown-eyed heir to the Sheridan empire.'

She coughed and counted them out on her fingers. 'Let's start with the fact that he lives in New York and works in Boston. Not London. Boston. Then move swiftly on to the fact that he thinks I am a loon. And thirdly—and most importantly—the one and only reason that he asked me to this wedding is because I fit the dress I made for the girl who dumped him over the telephone. Do you remember the last boy you dated who was on the rebound?'

Saskia gave a dramatic shiver. 'Hugo the horrible stalker. How could I forget—but you seem to have missed something out.'

'His dress sense. All black single-breasted suits. Purrleese.'

'Actually, I was referring to the fact that he is both lustalicious and you like him. You like him a lot and you always have.'

'That's two things. I liked the old Heath who I met when I was seventeen and he was young and free and his mum was still around. That was eleven years ago, Saskia. We've both changed more than we could ever have imagined.'

'Um. Something tells me that he hasn't changed that much—he's still the same charmer underneath those executive suits.'

'I'm not so sure,' Kate sniffed. 'You heard what Amber said last night. Heath has been through an awful lot in the past ten years. First his mum's death, then his dad's love life, not to mention taking on a complete part of the family business on his own. That's a lot of weight for anyone to carry.'

'This is a wedding, Kate, not a business conference. You're going to have a great time.'

Kate opened her mouth, ready to agree with what Saskia had said, but all she could see in her head was that tension behind his smile. He was hiding something.

'Maybe. Maybe not. I'll let you know more on Monday.'

'Your studio. Ten a.m.—I'll bring the chocolate cake.'

'You're on.' Kate smiled. 'But I really should get ready, because it has to be almost ten by now.'

'Ten? Make that half ten.'

'What!' Kate replied and leapt to her feet. 'Why didn't you warn me? You know that my nana's old watch runs slow. And Heath is bound to be punctual. Oh, no! I need to do something with my hair. And shoes. I need shoes. Saskia!'

'Slow down. You're all packed and lovely. I checked your case and you have clean underwear and "kiss me until I die" shoes. All ready and waiting in the hallway. *You are going to have a fantastic time!* Now, you go upstairs and get sorted and I'll guard the...'

She hadn't even finished speaking when the front doorbell sounded and the clock in the hall chimed the half hour.

Kate didn't wait to reply and shot past Saskia, who was on her feet and strolling to the door. As Kate pulled on white capri trousers, a white and navy blue striped sailor top and navy lace-up shoes, she could hear Saskia chatting to someone and she peeked out of the corner of her bedroom curtains.

Blood rushed to her head.

A long slick black limousine was parked half on the pavement and half on the street in her narrow side road, which had been designed for the width of two horses pulling carriages.

She couldn't travel in a limo! And what would the neighbours think?

Oh, no—too late. The antique dealer who had the shop next door was already outside and peering into the shaded windows. Any minute now some uniformed chauffeur with a peaked cap was going to step out from the driver's side and wave a sub-machine gun around.

Well, good luck with that. Because his shop was full of tat and had one customer a week. If he was lucky.

Still. It was going to be weird having a new neighbour after twelve years.

And he did order six pairs of cream fine suede gloves every Christmas.

Kate sniffed. She hated change. It was so unsettling. Why couldn't things stay the same? Steady. Calm. After the chaos of her day job, it was actually quite nice to come home to her version of stability every night.

'Kate!' Saskia hissed from over her shoulder. 'Stop gawping out of the window and get yourself down here pronto. Otherwise Heath is going to be sitting in your parlour. There isn't room for a hunk that size in your kitchen and I can't leave him standing at the door much longer.'

'Don't you dare, Elwood!' Kate cried out and jumped off the bed. 'That parlour is my sacred space. No boys or any other type of person allowed.'

'Then move.' Saskia grinned, then started fanning herself with one hand. 'You're keeping the hot millionaire publisher and his limo waiting.' Her laugh escaped with a loud snort and she ducked and grabbed Kate's huge shoulder bag and took off down to the hallway.

'Oh, thanks. That is just what I need to put me at ease,' Kate huffed and tugged on a cut-off navy cotton jacket with gold buttons and epaulets. A navy and white silk scarf. Mother-of-pearl sarong clip to keep it all in place. One liberal spray of the old-fashioned floral vanilla fragrance that her grandmother had worn all of her life and she was good to go.

Kate took one final glance in the dressing table mirror and turned sideways before grinning at her reflection and winking.

She couldn't think about Amber's warning about Heath. She had to push down the flicker of apprehension and make the best of this wedding, one way or another, for the sake of her business.

Limos. Manor houses. Hot millionaires. Oh, yes! *Bring it on.*

CHAPTER FIVE

HEATH KEPT LOSING his place in the financial report he had brought to read. Or maybe he was too distracted to make the effort to find it. Every time he started to work, he was interrupted by chatter, exclamations of excitement and questions from his travelling companion. But one thing had rapidly become only too clear.

He had never met anyone like Kate Lovat.

It was no doubt a lady's right to wear fragrance which filled the car with the smell of flower gardens in summer and not even the excellent air conditioning could cope with the way it seemed to linger on Kate's jacket and hair so that every time she moved a new waft came in his direction.

And she did move around. *A lot.*

Kate Lovat was an expert in the fine art of fidgeting.

The girl simply could not keep still.

She had explored every inch of the car in intimate detail before they had negotiated the narrow street where she lived. The drinks cabinet and mini refrigerator had been particularly fascinating but she had soon moved on to the personal control settings and pressed every button and toggled every switch in the car like a toddler high on fizzy drinks packed full of sugar and artificial colours.

It was a new experience for him to meet a girl who had

such an open and childlike enthusiasm for the new and was not afraid to express it.

The publishing professionals and booksellers he met in his work were focused on their careers and business plans. All working, heads down, all driven by a common passion for great books. *Eyes on the prize.*

Kate was like a squirrel. Leaping around on her seat as they passed one London landmark and then another, apparently only too happy to give him the complete tourist guide to the city he rarely visited these days and, when he did, it was only for business.

To Kate, London was a city of constant delight and amazement.

Heath tugged hard at the cuffs of his long-sleeved Sea Island cotton shirt, which had come from his favourite London tailor. His father had been the one who had decided almost a year earlier that he would open the London office and create a new marketing unit geared towards Europe and the Middle East.

Maybe it was simply coincidence that his father had started dating Alice Jardine again about a year ago?

Or maybe the London office was the excuse he needed to stay in England instead of working out of the Boston office where the company was based?

The team there rarely saw him these days and, for a private company in a challenging business environment, the one thing the employees needed was to see the company owner in his office or walking in the print room, talking to them and reassuring them that they had a future.

Not happenimg. Not yet at least.

But once this wedding was over…then they would have the talk.

Once the wedding was over.

Heath abandoned his report onto his seat table. Who was

he kidding? It was never going to be over. Alice would be in Boston, living in the family house where he had grown up. And his dad would be even more distracted than ever, trying to keep his new bride happy.

The cellphone in the inside pocket of his suit jacket beeped discreetly and Heath glanced at the caller display before answering it.

'Good morning, Lucas,' he said, picking up the call and looking out of the window at the motorway verges. 'Or should that be good afternoon in Hong Kong?'

There was a guffaw down the phone from the jovial Canadian with a passion for books and selling them. 'Hot and humid afternoon. How about you? All gathered for the big wedding?'

'On my way now.' Heath smiled. 'So you would make my day if you told me that the meeting with the distributor went well yesterday.' There was just enough of a pause for Heath to take a breath. 'Talk to me, Lucas. What are the customers telling you?'

'It's the same story I had last week. Our competitors are stealing the market with enhanced digital versions of the printed academic textbooks. You know how students love visuals and they are so loaded up with technology these days.' Lucas sighed down the phone. 'I have been promising our customers some news on the new lines for over a year now, Heath, and your dad won't budge. I know this might not be the best time to bring it up again, but seeing as he is going to be in such a good mood…it has to be worth a try.'

Heath pinched the bridge of his nose between his thumb and forefinger. 'Leave it with me, Lucas,' he replied in a low voice, trying to conceal his disappointment. 'I'll do what I can.'

'Great, that's great, Heath,' Lucas replied a little too quickly and with enough tension in his voice to make Heath sit up a little straighter in his seat. 'But...there is something else you should know about. It's only a rumour, and you know what terrible gossips publishers are, but I heard it twice at the trade fair yesterday. You might want to check it out with the team.'

Heath ran his tongue over his suddenly parched lips. 'Oh, I think I have heard just about every possible gloom-and-doom scenario these past few months. What's the latest?'

'Only this. Sheridan Press is planning to move the printing operation overseas to cut down on production costs. It would be a shame—the Boston print works is a great selling point. But, hey—you know how rumours spread—there is probably nothing to it. I'll call you next week with the updates from the Beijing Book Fair. Have a great wedding!'

'Bye, Lucas. Thanks.' Heath snapped down the lid on his phone and held it in the palm of his hand.

Move Sheridan Press. This was the *last* thing that he wanted to happen.

And if the rumour was true? *If.* Then his father had kept his plans for the company a secret from the one person he had brought in to help turn it around. All the work that Heath had done with Lucas and their team had been geared to promoting books which would be printed by the loyal employees who had given Sheridan Press the best years of their lives.

Suddenly it felt as though the air conditioning had been switched to Arctic ice and a shiver ran across his shoulders. His shirt felt damp with cold sweat in the hollow of his back and his collar was trying to strangle him. Breaking the habit of a lifetime, Heath loosened the Windsor knot in his silk tie and unfastened the top button on his shirt, desperate to get some air into his lungs.

Have a great wedding. Yeah. Right.

Suddenly all of the missed phone calls and unanswered emails made sense. Charles Sheridan was well known for being low-key but Heath knew better than most that beneath that quiet, introspective grey-suited executive was a sharp and scheming brain.

So much for working together.

He had been a fool to allow ridiculous sentimentality back into his life. Memories of a happy childhood were just that—memories. For children who had no control over what happened to them.

Stupid! He had left his own company in the hands of the management team—and for what? To help out the man who had cheated on his wife with Alice Jardine and then married Julia Swan within twelve months of his wife's funeral? The man who had barely spoken to him in over a decade and then suddenly wanted to be reconciled and play dad?

Well, maybe his son and heir wasn't ready to be made a fool of.

The fire that had been burning inside Heath's belly turned into a furnace. Molten lava flowed through his veins and he felt his teeth grind together in frustration.

The surprises still kept coming, no matter how hard he fought to control his world.

His gaze fixed on a spot on the road ahead of them as the car took the motorway exit and stopped at a roundabout for a few minutes in the busy traffic before heading down a country road.

For one full second he thought about telling the driver that he had changed his mind and to take him straight back to the airport. And there would be a bonus if he broke the speed limit to get there. Why not? He had his luggage and passport. He could do what he wanted and go wherever he pleased.

But he wouldn't. And he couldn't. He had given a commitment to the printers who had made Sheridan Press one of the most respected names in the world. *And Heath always, always kept his word.*

He could not go anywhere—until he found out whether there was any truth behind this rumour or not. By talking to his father. Man to man.

It took a not so gentle pat on the arm to bring him back to the reality of a car on a road and the fact that he was not travelling alone—which was very unusual.

'Erm…Heath? I think your tie surrendered five minutes ago. It would be kinder to say goodbye and put it out of its misery rather than see it suffer any longer.'

His tie? What?

His gaze followed hers. Onto what had been a burgundy Italian silk tie from a top designer in Milan, which Olivia had given him as a Christmas present last year when they had first started dating and the chance of a real relationship seemed tantalisingly close.

Now his fingers were wrapped tightly around a screwed-up piece of rag which been twisted and torn until the life had been squeezed out of it.

His teeth clenched shut to suppress the expletive that was forming at the back of his throat. *Unbelievable!*

Kate put both fingers into her ears and hummed a pop tune. 'Can't hear a thing. Just get it out of your system. You'll feel much better.'

Heath looked at Kate, who had turned away and was still humming to herself, looked at the tie and then slowly, slowly exhaled the breath that he had not even realised he had been holding in.

Kate was looking out of the window with a beaming grin of childlike wonder on her face, transforming her from pretty into the kind of woman worthy of more than only a second look. Or even a third?

In her warehouse studio he had not missed the fact that Kate was the kind of pretty girl who looked good without make-up, but in the morning sunlight her skin appeared pale and translucent, in contrast to the bright sparkling green of those amazing eyes. But it was her smile, her bright-eyed, rosy-cheeked smile that hit him hard in the bottom of his stomach.

This version of Kate Lovat was a stunner.

Something twisted inside Heath's gut and he swallowed hard.

When was the last time he had taken the time to meet a woman outside the publishing world? A real woman like Kate? A woman whose life was as different as it could be from his relentless working hours and the endless battering of information and words.

He would give a lot to spend time getting to know this girl and find out what it was like to have one of those smiles aimed in his direction.

Except he did not have the time. He only had a few days before he needed to get back to Boston to carry out some serious damage limitation.

Olivia was right. His work had always been more important than their relationship. Strange. He had never been ready to acknowledge that fact before today and now it seemed to be staring him in the face.

He had spent the last ten years fighting each and every day to take control over his life in every way possible. His work. The people he worked with and even the women he dated. The way he lived and dressed—all tightly controlled.

Until he'd made the decision to move out of that life and try and reconnect with his father.

He chose to make that change.

His choice. His problem. And if his father was trying to use his sentimental need to be a son against him? He would deal with it.

So instead of punching the air or causing even more damage to his teeth by grinding them to powder in frustration, he slowly and carefully undid his tie, pulled it out from under the shirt collar and folded it into a neat coil on the leather seat.

Heath lifted his chin and was about to thank Kate when a crystal tumbler of sparkling liquid was thrust into his hand.

'Tonic water on the rocks. Enjoy.'

His first reaction was to pass it back with a cutting comment about how he would ask for a drink if he needed one. Except that his throat felt as though he had inhaled half of the Sahara desert. He did need a drink. Rather urgently.

'Thank you,' he whispered in a rasp and took one long slug and then another until the tumbler was drained.

'Excellent. Because I have made you another one. And you are most welcome. It is not every day that I get to play barmaid in a limo. I rather like it. Even if the entertainment is a little more action-packed than I would have liked,' Kate quipped with a casual tone.

'Entertainment?' he replied in a much better voice and took a long sip of the cool drink and then another before turning slightly to look at her.

Kate was perched rather than sitting on the front edge of her seat, her hands folded neatly on top of a pad of drawing paper covered with markings. There was a pencil stuck behind her right ear and she was wearing spectacles. Rimless clear spectacles today, but spectacles all the same.

His gaze scanned her outfit, which he had been too distracted to notice properly before now. She was neat, beautifully groomed and as nicely dressed as any of Amber's friends. But different. Quirky. And there was definitely something in those eyes, which he suddenly realised were really quite a remarkable shade of green that told him that Amber's school friend was as observant and intelligent as any one of his team.

'Of course,' she replied. 'At least I found it entertaining.' Then her eyebrows lifted and she shook her head. 'I should make it clear that I don't usually listen to other people's telephone conversations but it is difficult not to eavesdrop when you are sitting a couple of inches away and bellowing about rumours about the company. I don't know what the rumours are all about—' she spread out one hand and waggled it from side to side '—but it sounded, well, dodgy to me.'

'Dodgy?' He choked on an ice chip and held up one hand when she moved forward to thump him. 'Not at all,' he coughed and spluttered. 'And I was not bellowing. I don't bellow. Bellowing is not my style.'

'How foolish of me. You were simply expressing your excitement and enthusiasm for the topic,' Kate said with a smile but one side of her mouth was turned up. She had a dimple in her cheek.

He had never seen a dimple up close and personal before, but on Kate? Somehow it fitted her perfectly. How odd.

So she had picked up on the rumour angle.

He was going to have to watch what he said from now on.

A flash of light caught his eye and he turned back to the window but at that exact same moment he saw the reflection of Kate in the glass.

She was holding her spectacles in one hand while in one smooth movement her head dropped back, her eyes closed and her fingers combed through a head of boy-short conker-brown glossy layers with a gentle toss of her head.

It was the most sensual thing he had seen in a long time, and the fact that it was natural and completely relaxed made it even more remarkable.

The dark brown hair contrasted with Kate's smooth clear skin and, in the July sunlight streaming through the car window onto her slim frame, she looked about twelve. She had been at school with Amber, so she had to be late twenties. Maybe it was because she was so petite. Or should that be concentrated?

And it was definitely time to change to subject.

'What are you drawing?' he asked, and pointed to her sketch pad.

'Oh, nothing,' she said, 'just doodling,' and tried to flip over the cover, but in an instant he had snatched the pad from her lap. She went for it but his long left arm held it high and firmly out of reach.

'Fine,' she sniffed and sat back in her seat with her arms crossed. 'Look at it if you want. I have nothing to hide. And no, I have not been taking notes about your so very important company information. Your trade secrets are safe with me.' And she gave him a quick salute.

Heath opened her pad and sat peering at the sketch for a few seconds before pointing to the page. 'What is it meant to be?'

'What do you mean?' she asked indignantly. 'What is it meant to be? They are gloves, of course. Gauntlets, to be precise. The local Christmas pantomime this year is Peter Pan and Saskia needs some swashbuckling specials for the auditions next month.'

'Pirates. Okay. And what about these?'

'Satin elbow-length prom-night specials. Very popular line. And not just white. Oh, no. The modern debutante likes violet and musk. I sell loads of those online.'

'Sell? Oh yes, of course. I hadn't realised that you made gloves as well. That must be a delightful hobby.'

A hobby?

Oh, Heath. Trust you to say precisely the wrong thing.

She could almost hear her father's dismissive voice. *'Oh, you'll soon get tired of that frivolous little hobby and start to do something serious with your life. But don't think we'll support you if you decide to throw your life away on worthless dreams.'*

A hobby. That was what they thought about her work. And now it looked as though Heath felt the same. Just when she was hoping that he was going to help her prove that her parents were wrong—by putting her business back on track.

Kate looked up into Heath's face as he flicked through the sketches she had slaved on for hours, evening after evening, day after day.

And part of her died.

He had no clue that his words had the power to cut her like a knife and leave her bleeding. How could he? He didn't know anything about her. All he saw was Amber's friend who sewed pieces of cloth into dresses and gloves. He probably didn't even remember coming to that high school party.

It would be so easy to pretend that the pages he was looking through so dismissively meant nothing and were only 'doodles'. That way he could go on believing that she was just another lowly dressmaker who was pretending to be a designer.

But that was only a tiny part of who she was. And what she was capable of achieving—with or without his help.

Kate dragged her gaze from Heath's long slender fingers as he stroked the pages and focused on the green fields and trees in the countryside at the side of the road. She pressed her lips together hard and swallowed down the burning sensation in her throat. She could use that cool drink she had just given away, but that would mean turning around and she wasn't ready to talk to Heath yet.

What was she doing here? In this limo with this gorgeous man who didn't know anything about her world and her life?

Kate pressed her right hand flat against her chest. Her heart was racing and she could feel the back of her neck burning scarlet as her mind raced.

Could she risk it?

Could she give him an insight into who she was and what she wanted in life? Show this man that she was her own woman with her own dreams and aspirations?

It would certainly make introductions to his family a little more interesting. And challenging.

Heath shuffled along the slippery leather seat next to her and she turned around inside her seat belt as he passed the sketchbook back to her with a nod. 'I'm afraid I am very traditional when it comes to gloves. Nothing like these.'

Kate stowed her precious sketches inside her tote. 'I will take that as a personal challenge. Leave it with me.'

Heath slid away but, before Kate could change her mind, she smiled across at him and added in a light voice, 'For once, Amber didn't give you an up-to-date resumé. I actually own a glove-making company in London. You have just been looking at some of my designs for next season's collection.'

He blinked. Twice. And she saw something new flash across his eyes.

Surprise. Astonishment. And intelligent awareness.

Almost as if he could hardly believe what he had just heard her say.

'You run two companies?' he asked and she heard just enough incredulity in his voice to make her hackles rise and she lifted her chin as she fought back the reply she would like to give.

Yes. Mr Smarty Pants publisher. I do run two compa-nies. The small fact that I don't make enough money from both of them put together to pay the rent is neither here nor there.

'Absolutely. I do have a day job in tailoring. But gloves are my passion. A girl can't have enough gloves.'

Heath's gaze scanned her face, his brown eyes slightly narrowed and blazing with intensity. The kind of inten-sity that warmed the already hot air between them on this sunny July day.

Fool! she told herself. *Now look what you have done.*

You have just given Heath a peek inside your world and he doesn't know how to handle it. See. This is why you should have kept quiet. This is why telling other peo-ple your dream opens you up to feeling exposed and vul-nerable.

Even if this person, this man, is the boy who you have lusted after for years. It still hurts when they cannot take you seriously.

She mentally braced herself for the cutting remark or put-down.

It had happened so many times before. Like at the high school ten-year reunion that May where she had met up with Amber and Saskia for the first time in years. Those old classmates of hers had been scathing in their total contempt for her. *You? Running a fashion design business single-handed? Purrleese.*

Kate sat upright on the fine leather seat, waiting for the put-down that would make it a lot easier for her to walk away in a few days.

'So, if I understand this correctly, you are running two different companies? Single-handed? Yes? That must make life complicated,' he said in a low voice.

Okay. So he was still reappraising her. She could deal with that in her usual fashion and laugh it off.

'Yes, I suppose it does. My choice. And they do say that variety is the spice of life. Don't you agree?'

Her heart rate increased to match the speed of her breathing.

Say the right thing, Heath. Please don't make me hate you. Please.

Heath replied with a smile that came from the heart and completely knocked her bravado out of the window.

'Not at all. I am singularly incapable of moving outside my area of expertise. Which makes your achievement even more impressive.'

He lifted his tumbler of melted ice and raised it in a toast. 'Congratulations, Kate. Running your own business takes a huge amount of work. Running two is extraordinary. All credit to you for taking that kind of risk. It seems that you have the better of me—I shall have to work extra-hard to keep my part of our deal.'

Then he shook his head before Kate could reply and chuckled. 'And now you have made me feel guilty about stealing you away from your work for a whole weekend.'

The tumbler slid back into its holder and Heath narrowed his eyes and tapped his finger against his full lips. 'This creates somewhat of a problem. How on earth am I going to make it up to you and give you a weekend to remember? Any suggestions?'

CHAPTER SIX

KATE GENTLY PUSHED at the heavy oak door and poked her head around to see if this room was the library.

It was the fourth door that she had tried since leaving her palatial bedroom and en suite bathroom, which was bigger than her entire apartment and workshop combined. It had to be here somewhere and it certainly wasn't on the ground floor—they were huge public rooms intended for people who liked to live in style!

Thank heavens for the lovely housekeeper who had apologised many times that Alice and Charles could not be there in person to welcome her but they were delayed at the airport waiting for a flight. But she had strict instructions to show Miss Olivia Scott and Mr Heath Sheridan to their rooms the moment they arrived.

Kate had blustered out an explanation that she was here instead of Olivia but it had caused such confusion that after a few minutes she had given up and decided to go with the flow.

She stood on the wide wood-panelled gallery with the oil paintings of the Jardine family through the ages and glanced from side to side in the echoing silence of this ancient space.

The wide double doors at the end of the corridor with the ornate carving over the archway had to be the library.

She strode down the red handmade carpet and stretched out her hand to push open the door a little further. Then pulled it back again.

The knot which had formed in the pit of her stomach since those last few minutes in the car before they'd arrived ballooned into a football of tangled nerves and feelings and expectations.

That peculiar anxious feeling had taken root the moment Amber had asked her to make the bridesmaids' dresses for Heath in the first place.

And now she was actually here. At Jardine Manor! This was so surreal that she didn't know whether to laugh with happiness that she had pulled it off or cry because she knew that this could be the one single event that proved to her parents that she was not some pathetic joke and butt of all their jokes.

She had Heath to thank for all of that. So maybe, just maybe, she could lighten his load in some way and bring back his smile again while she was here? It was supposed to be a happy family occasion after all and who knew? With a bit of luck she might see a glimpse or two of the real Heath underneath his smart black suits?

Swallowing down her apprehension, Kate took a deep breath, pushed her shoulders back, her chest out and her chin high.

Time to get the Heath and Kate show on the road.

The heavy door swung open with barely a creak and she strode inside.

Heath was sitting at a desk in front of a wide square window which flooded light into the dark wood-panelled library with its long floor-to-ceiling bookcases. Huge tomes, which had probably never been opened for years, filled the middle and upper shelves and, on the lower shelves, magazines and atlases and popular fiction.

All the books were behind glass to keep out the dust and she had to resist the urge to throw open every single one of those glass doors and let the air into the pages.

Didn't he know that paper and leather needed to breathe like humans?

But then, this wasn't his house. It was Alice Jardine's home and Heath would never do anything so impertinent as to try and rearrange her library.

'Ah. There you are,' she said with a smile. 'A girl can get lost in a place this big. Hello, handsome,' she said, trying to lighten his mood. He dragged his gaze from his laptop and turned towards her and his brown eyes locked onto hers and instantly the smile from his mouth reached those eyes and her heart leapt.

So what if she had to play the joker when he was around?

Every time she saw him, her reaction was exactly the same and the passage of time didn't seem to make a spot of difference.

He was still the best-looking man she had ever met. And the only one who could make her toes curl up inside her shoes.

And when he looked at her like he was now? As though he was actually pleased to see her? She was right back into crush mode. Heath Sheridan truly was the complete package.

She blinked a couple of times and covered up her embarrassment by peering at the books on the nearest shelf. She stepped back, waved her arms around and gave a half twirl. 'Have you seen this place? It's amazing.'

Heath crossed his arms and watched Kate skip up the circular staircase to peer at the leather-bound volumes which filled the lower levels of the heavy floor-to-ceiling bookcases.

'Cool.' Kate turned and looked at him over her shoulder. 'Would you mind if I brought a sleeping bag and moved in? I could have such fun here and you probably wouldn't notice in a house this big. Look at this library. I am drooling just at the sight of all of these books.'

She half twisted around towards him at the waist and pointed at her lower lip. 'See. Drool.'

He tutted. 'You look very fetching and there is no drool at all. Now please come down before you fall. Amber would never forgive me if you had an accident in those shoes.'

'This is true,' she replied, scrambling down from the step. She sat gracefully on the top rung, knees together, and tilted her head to one side before saying with a smile in her voice, 'You might have warned me that the Manor was actually a real, live Elizabethan manor house. I felt as though I should be paying an entrance fee for the guided tour. Does Alice actually live here? I didn't think people owned houses like this any more.'

'The Jardines bought the Manor several generations ago and yes, Alice definitely lives here.'

Heath paused then stood up and walked around the table so that he could look out at the garden and the gravel driveway beneath the library window. 'Speaking of which, I thought I heard a car pull up.' His voice dropped even lower and softer. 'And there is the lady herself.'

Kate strolled forward and stood shoulder to almost shoulder and followed his gaze. A tall man and a slim middle-aged woman were walking across the path from the flower beds towards the house. Her arm was around his waist and they were laughing and chatting away contentedly.

'Oh. Is that them?' Kate asked, peering over the stone window ledge. 'How sweet. They look like a lovely couple.'

The air between herself and Heath instantly dropped a

few degrees in temperature and she could actually see his body bristle, his breathing fast and heavy.

'Yes, indeed they do,' he whispered in a low voice that was so laden with sadness and regret that she thumped his arm with the flat of her hand.

'Hey. Cheer up. They are family. This reminds me. Amber says hello. And when are you going to come out to India to spend time with her and Sam?'

'India?' he replied and turned back to his desk, her distraction technique a complete success. 'I might be able to get away early next year when I complete this current assignment.'

She nodded. 'Amber and I both know what that means. Next year, as in never.' Then she sniffed. 'She would love you to go out and ride elephants and eat coconuts and try out some of those academic skills on the girls. It would be great! Unless, of course…' she ducked down below his chin level '…you are sulking and feeling a teensy bit redundant. A girl still needs her big older ex-stepbrother now and then, you know. That never gets old.'

His eyebrows lifted and his shoulders moved into a small shrug. 'Is it that obvious?' he replied. And the honesty and openness of those few words tugged at her heart strings and pulled her in even closer.

Kate stood back to full height. 'Only to people who know you and who notice these sorts of things.'

'Well, that cuts down the options. She is happy. And nothing could please me more. It's just that I suppose I got used to sorting things out for her. And now she has Sam Richards to do that.'

'Well, that's nonsense. You'll still be her favourite stepbrother. But if you have any spare time, perhaps you could hire yourself out. Stepbrother for hire. One careful owner. Reasonable condition. Could last for years if fed and watered.'

'Think I would get many takers?' He smiled and her little heart lifted at the same time as the corners of his mouth.

'Absolutely. In fact, you'll be able to meet her real dad's new family at Amber's wedding. All girls and all gorgeous. Won't that be fun?'

He snorted and started flicking through the papers on the table. 'I don't think that my idea of fun is quite the same as yours.'

'Fun? Now there's a thought. This house is gorgeous and perfect for a wedding, but so far I haven't heard any plans to have fun this weekend. Well, I am here and I am listening, so fire away. What does Heath Sheridan in his best man suit plan to do to kick off the proceedings with a bang?' Kate pressed the fingers of her right hand to the left side of her top, where she imagined her heart should be. 'And don't worry. Any naughty family secrets will be safe with me.'

Heath slumped back in his pedestal chair and whirled around to face her, open-mouthed.

'Naughty family secrets? Where did that come from?'

'Well,' Kate leant forward and fluttered her eyelashes at him, 'Amber did tell me about some off-the-wall expressionist paintings that you insisted on taking her to see at one time.'

'It was a passing phase. Like strawberries dipped in white chocolate. I moved on. Anything else?'

'Strawberries dipped in chocolate. Now you are talking my sort of language. That sounds delicious—and is now officially added to my must-try list. But you're avoiding the question. Out with it, Sheridan. What do you do for fun these days?'

'Sorry to disappoint you, Kate, but I spend most of my time chained to the computer. If I have a free weekend I might take in a gallery or the occasional theatre or a local restaurant. That is my idea of fun. So can we move on now so I can get back to organising this wedding? The remaining guests will be here in a few hours.'

'Not a chance, Sheridan,' Kate hissed and slipped into the gap between Heath and the desk so that she was blocking his view of the screen.

'You still owe me a dance from a high school party. Remember that?'

His fingers stilled on the paperwork and he glanced sideways at her, his gaze burning into her face as though looking for something, but when he spoke his voice was gentle and there was a spark in his eyes which illuminated his whole face with an inner glow.

Kate inhaled sharply through her nose.

There he was.

There was the real Heath. Saskia had been right. There was the man who she had fallen in crush with. He was still there. And still capable of making her melt with one look.

Heartbreaker Heath was back in town!

She would have collapsed with relief if she wasn't already sitting down.

'High school? I'm surprised that you still remember that.'

Remember? Forgetting was the problem.

He was watching her now, waiting for an answer. But to tell him the truth would reveal how important that dance had been to her and that would be bad news for both of them.

'Of course. In fact, Saskia, Amber and I would be prepared to give you excellent references. This could come in handy if you should ever choose to change direction and go into the male escort business. Now, don't look at me like that. You never know.'

'I think I shall keep that one for a last resort.' He coughed, his neck a lovely shade of red.

With that, she slipped down from the desk and rearranged her top and jacket.

'Righty. Time to go and meet my hosts. I suppose I had better get my story straight before I march in to say hello. What, exactly, did you tell Alice about me when you broke the bad news about Olivia?'

Heath started fiddling with the power cable on his laptop. 'Sorry, what was that?'

'*Heath,*' she whispered with a questioning lilt at the end of the word, and stood directly in front of him and peered into his face.

'Oh, no. I don't believe it,' she gasped and slapped the table. 'I can see it in your face. You haven't told them, have you?' She flung her arm out towards the door. 'They are still expecting your Olivia to turn up. Aren't they? No wonder the housekeeper kept calling me the wrong name.'

She half closed her eyes, planted a fist on each hip and stuck her chin out at him.

'Heath Sheridan, I could strangle you. You have had three days to call, text, email, fax and maybe even send a carrier pigeon. But, no. And don't you dare say that it slipped your mind—because I saw those spreadsheets just now and every tiny detail of this wedding is right there in black and white. And sometimes highlighted in red.'

She was shouting now, totally in his space and almost touching and did not care.

Her finger prodded Heath twice in the chest. 'Talk to me, Sheridan. Because you had better have a very, very good reason why I shouldn't pack my bags and head back to London this very minute. Because I will. I mean it.'

'Oh, I'm so sorry to hear that, Olivia,' a sweet musical voice said from behind her shoulder and Kate whipped around to see the same smiling middle-aged woman she had spied outside, strolling across the library floor to meet them. 'I was so looking forward to finally getting to meet you. Heath, darling, won't you introduce us?'

Heath darling seemed to stretch his back several inches taller, his jaw made of ice and stone. 'Good morning, Alice. How nice to see you again. Of course. I am sorry to say that Olivia couldn't make it so my friend Katherine Lovat has agreed to take her place. I believe that you two have already spoken. Kate was responsible for those superb bridesmaid dresses.'

He glanced down at Kate with a look of pure steel. 'So, if you will excuse me, I will go and catch up with my father. We have a few last-minute business matters to clear up before the fun starts. I'm sure that you ladies have a lot to talk about.'

'Of course it was Charles's idea to have the wedding at the Manor. I'm afraid that I embarrassed myself by crying for at least an hour after he proposed. We have waited so long for this moment, but I didn't dare hope that we could make it happen. I had already refused him twice, but somehow I just knew. This was the right moment.'

'Charles proposed before? Oh, how romantic. I have to know—why did you turn him down? Cold feet?'

Alice smiled and shook her head. '*Cold son.* Charles tried to reconnect with Heath so many times over the years and I didn't want to come between them, even if it meant being apart. Did Heath mention that we're having a dinner party after the wedding rehearsal this afternoon? I do hope that it will help to break down any awkwardness.'

Kate finished off a mouthful of the most delicious chocolate cake before taking a sip of tea and shaking her head. 'Not a word. You see, this is what happens when you leave boys in charge. They don't pass on the essential details. As for the proposal? Crying for an hour is nothing. I would cry for a week! It sounds very romantic.'

Alice grinned and loaded up her plate with another slice of cake. 'You're very sweet. Charles says the same thing, but after the past few weeks? I can see now why other people pay wedding planners.' She licked the icing from her cake fork. 'I thought it would be simple to hold it here with just a few family members and friends to help celebrate, but I had no idea how complicated the whole thing could be.'

'Complicated?' Kate repeated and shuffled forward to top up the teacups.

Alice hummed slightly and popped a large piece of cake into her mouth.

Kate took the hint. 'Ah. Heath. I know, but he does care. Amber adores him, and I've known him for years. It just takes a while for him to get used to things. Everything will be fine, and I'm sure that he'll give you a marvellous welcome into the Sheridan family.'

Alice put down her cup and smiled at Kate, then brought her knees up and curled up on the sofa. 'Heath hates me,' she whispered, and gave a small shoulder shrug when Kate tried to deny it.

'There's a lot of history which he hasn't told you about. You see, Heath's mother, Lee, was a very good friend of mine. We were at high school together and then at art college in London. Lee was lovely,' Alice said with a really warm smile, 'and I couldn't want for a better friend. We made the effort and stayed in touch over the years. I used to go to Boston several times a year teaching art classes, and Lee used to come to London for girlie weekends. It was great and we had the best fun.'

The smile faded. 'It broke my heart when she was di-
agnosed with an inoperable brain tumour. We had so little
time together at the end, so I put my life on hold and moved
to Boston for a few weeks. Does that sound crazy to you?'

Kate reached out and took Alice's hand in hers. 'Not
in the slightest. I have two wonderful friends, Amber and
Saskia. I would do anything for them. Anything. I understand completely. I'm so sorry for your loss. I'm sure that
she was grateful that you were there but it must have been
horrific. That was so brave of you.'

Alice brushed a finger under her eye. 'I wanted to be
there for Lee, but for Charles and Heath too. Those last
few weeks were an emotional turmoil for all of us and I
was alone in the city and Charles was there and grieving
and, well, when she died we comforted each other in the
only way we knew.'

Her tongue moistened her lower lip and Alice reached
out to the teacup in the silence that followed, but her hand
was shaking too much to pick it up.

'I'm not proud of what happened. But it was totally right
at the time. I had fallen in love with Charles Sheridan and
I knew that he loved me, but the timing?' She rolled her
eyes towards Kate and smiled. 'The timing stank. Don't
misunderstand, Kate, we both knew that these things happen in times of crisis and trauma. People need comfort and
support and sometimes words are not enough.' She looked
down at her hands. 'We both agreed to step away and work
out if these feelings were real or temporary before starting
a long-term relationship so soon after Charles had lost his
wife, who had been my friend. Our love didn't make me
feel less guilty, and I know Charles felt that he was almost
betraying her memory, but it was so hard to stay apart.'

'That must have been terrible for both of you,' Kate replied in a low voice, which was almost a whisper. 'Such conflicting emotions.'

Alice looked up at Kate and took her hand. 'It was terrible for all three of us. That's why I'm telling you all of this when we have only just met. Heath found us kissing one afternoon when he came home early from university.' She closed her eyes. 'I thought things were difficult, but then it became impossible. Heath was traumatised and he has never forgiven his father, or me, for betraying his mother's memory.'

Kate blew out long and hard. 'Alice, that was years ago. He's a grown man now.'

'It doesn't make any difference. Some things don't go away and nothing we do seems to help the situation.'

She pursed her lips. 'First of all Charles invited him to come in and help with the company, father and son, turning around the business side by side. And then I thought that asking Heath to be the best man would help him come to terms with the fact that I am in his father's life, which means I'm in his life too. Neither of those things has worked out so well. Frankly, Kate, I don't know what else to do to bring them closer together and make a family again.'

A single tear ran down Alice's cheek and Kate immediately shuffled over and put her arm around the shoulder of this woman who she had only just met.

Alice shook her head. 'You see what he does to me? I blurt out my whole life story when I'm sure that you would much rather be enjoying yourself back in London. I am so sorry.'

Kate turned around and faced Alice, passed her a tissue and smiled up at her.

'Don't be. Heath doesn't hate you. The only reason that I'm here today, at this minute, but talking to you and making a new friend, is because Heath was worried that your wedding to his father would not be perfect unless you had four bridesmaids. Not three. Four. He cares about you and his father and the business. That's why he wanted to help with the organisation. But he doesn't know how to tell you how much he cares. So he brought me along in place of Olivia because he didn't want you to worry. And I am very glad to be here.'

Alice gave a thin but warm smile, reached around and hugged Kate. And it was the warmest and most loving hug that Kate had enjoyed in a long time.

'Me too,' she said and blinked several times.

'Now, that's much better.' Kate grinned. 'Because you seem to be forgetting one very important thing. You—' and she pointed at Alice '—are the star of the show and we all have to bow and scrape before your goddess-ship. Okay? Okay. You leave Heath to me and focus on having the best weekend of your life. You are getting married to the man you love and who loves you back. Isn't that fantastic?'

'Do you know what? It is fantastic! And I *am* going to have the best weekend of my life.'

'Absolutely, and now we have that out of the way, may I see your engagement ring?'

Alice hesitated then stretched out her left hand to Kate, who grasped her fingers and almost choked on her cake when she took a look at the enormous heart-shaped diamond set in white gold.

'Wow,' she said breathlessly. 'That. Is some rock. That man is giving you some serious love here.'

Alice blushed and gave a small giggle, which reminded Kate so much of Saskia as she looked up and smiled at this woman who was still capable of being turned into a girl by a piece of jewellery. Alice pulled back her hand and bashfully replied, 'You might well be right. And I'm so embarrassed.'

'Why? Love can hit you any time of your life, there's no need to be ashamed of that.'

'Didn't you notice?' Alice said. 'My fingernails have been chewed to the quick over these past two weeks, building up to the wedding. I don't want Charles to be ashamed of me in front of all his important guests and at the social functions we're going to be attending. What do you think of acrylic nails? I've never used them before but it might be the right time to try.'

Kate shook her head very slowly from side to side. 'Don't go there,' she said. 'Trust me.' And then she smiled. 'You look lovely, Alice, and the last thing Charles will be thinking about tomorrow are your nails. He'll just want you to be happy. Right?'

'Yes, of course. How foolish of me. I just want to make it perfect for him. Charles is taking a terrible risk marrying me and I want to be the best I can.'

'Now, that I understand perfectly.' Kate paused and looked down at Alice's hands. 'You take about a size seven and five-eighths in gloves, don't you?'

Alice blinked. 'Yes, I have big hands and feet.' Then she looked at Kate in confusion. 'Does that matter?'

'It matters to the gloves.' Then Kate shuffled forward. 'You need gloves, girl. Classy, elegant and formal or informal as you want, but you need gloves until your nails have grown back the way you want them.'

'That is a fantastic idea.' Alice blinked. 'I don't know why I didn't think of that earlier. Of course, you are right. I love gloves.' And then she slumped. 'But where am I going to find gloves to fit my enormous paws in the next few hours?'

Kate grinned. 'You happen to be looking at the sole proprietor of Lovat Gloves of London. We specialise in making boutique gloves for private clients. I think I might be able to fit you in at short notice. What do you say? Lacy bracelet length? Or silk satin elbow? No, don't answer. I'll bring the lot.'

'Why, Katherine Lovat—' Alice smiled and lifted her teacup in a toast '—here's to you. You are certainly full of surprises. I shall expect you to dance at my wedding.'

Kate clinked her teacup very gently for fear of breaking the delicate porcelain. 'Alice, I fully intend to.'

Ten minutes later Kate stepped out of the front entrance and stood blinking in the warm July sunshine. She had only got lost twice this time. Heath had not gone back to the library and she scanned the grounds to see if she could track him down.

And immediately spotted him. Only this time he was not alone.

Heath was standing with a look on his face which matched the stone blocks in the old arbour, next to a tall man who looked so much like him that it was impossible to mistake. This had to be his father. And Lord, there must be a lot of tall genes in that bloodline because Charles Sheridan had to be at least six feet two inches in his shiny black lace-up shoes.

And Kate's heart sank. Every part of Heath's body was pointing forward, or to the side. Any direction away from his own dad. His gaze was locked onto his tablet computer and, as she watched, he passed it across to the older man, who was standing only inches away, their shoulders almost touching.

In silence.

Their jackets might almost be touching but the icy hostility was all there to see.

Not just the fact that they both thought it appropriate to wear suits with shirts and ties on what was forecast to be a warm, sunny July day. She could understand formality and their personal standards when it came to how to dress—she knew all about that.

No. It was because watching Heath and his father reminded her so much of the frosty relationship that she had with her father and mother that the sharp pain of unwelcome tears of regret and disappointment pricked the corners of her eyes.

She had tried so hard, time and time again, to help her parents to understand her passion for gloves and what they called the silly outfits that she made. Fashion shows, award ceremonies, even weddings. And it had all been in vain. They wouldn't change their minds.

It was almost as if she was watching her own failed relationship acted out in front of her on this sun-kissed lawn.

Neither of them willing to give way or compromise. Both of them stubborn and determined to win the argument—any argument.

Oh, Heath! You were supposed to be working with your dad to celebrate his wedding—not battling with him.

But he might need a little nudge from her to help him along the way.

Yes. She had promised Alice that this was going to be the best weekend of her life and Heath was not the only one around here who kept their promises.

She might have failed to win over her parents—but she could do something to help Heath.

Kate stepped back inside the hallway for a few seconds, desperately trying to think through some kind of plan, when a girl wearing a T-shirt with the name of a famous London catering company dodged past her carrying a stack of tablecloths. It was the same company that Saskia had used a couple of times. Maybe the chef was making a splendid cake that Heath could carry in on a silver tray?

And drop it on his father's head.

She whirled around and followed the girl through a set of highly decorated and clearly original wooden doors into the most stunning dining room.

Sunlight beamed in through a row of mullioned windows with small squares of glass, created in a time when glass was a luxury and hard to make. Larger panes had been painted with the coat of arms of the Jardine family. Glorious swirls and mythical creatures danced on a shield with proud swords and what looked like falcons.

The Jardines had certainly been flamboyant.

Unlike this room. Plain oak-timbered walls below a ceiling braced with heavy wooden beams broken only by the occasional carved boss. Polished oak floors and large sturdy tables and chairs.

No colour apart from a lot of brown.

Oh, dear. Not exactly a fun venue for a wedding rehearsal party.

Unless, of course, someone did something to change that.

It only took Kate a few minutes to confirm with the catering team that yes, this *was* where the rehearsal dinner party was going to be held, and no, as far as they knew, the only decorations were plain white table linens and some silver candelabras belonging to the house.

Kate strolled back into the hall and flipped open her cellphone. A plan was starting to form inside her brain and she had to rein it in before it ran away with her.

'Saskia, it's me. I'm here. And yes, it does look like something out of a Tudor history book. But that's not why I'm ringing. Do you remember all of those party decorations we got together for Amber's birthday in May? Yes? Do you still have them? You do? Excellent. Because I need to borrow everything you've got in time for a party this evening. Balloons too. Yes, I know it's cutting it fine.'

She quickly checked her watch and added ten minutes because it was always slow. 'I can be there in about two hours, if that's okay with you? Yeah. Great. Don't worry about the heavy lifting. I shall bring Heath with me. He needs some time out away from here. But I'll talk to you later. See you. Bye for now. And Saskia, get an invoice ready. Heath owes you. *Big time.*'

Kate looked up just as Heath took a step towards his father, his face rigid with tension and his right hand holding the blameless computer as though he was about to smash it into something hard. Like his dad's face.

Intervention time.

Kate lifted her chin and strode out of the entrance and onto the stone patio at the front of the house, squaring her shoulders and with her full-on charm offensive smile.

'Heath! There you are.'

The two men turned around to face her, and from the looks on their faces she wasn't entirely sure if they were shocked or pleased with any excuse for the interruption.

She zoned in on his father and stretched out her hand and grinned. 'Hello, you must be Charles. How lovely to meet you at long last. I'm Katherine Lovat, fashion designer to the stars, but do call me Kate. All of my friends do.'

To give him credit, Charles Sheridan recovered remarkably quickly and calmly accepted Kate's rather warm chocolate-cake sticky hand and, surprisingly, shook it with a genuine smile.

'Then it would be my pleasure to call you Kate. But only if you call me Charles.'

'Charles,' Kate repeated and cocked her head to one side. 'You don't look like a Charles to me, and I certainly don't think Charlie would be appropriate. Do you? No, I think that Chuck suits you much better. Much friendlier. Don't you agree, Chuck?'

There was a short cough from Heath but she smiled over her left shoulder at his stunned face for a flash of narrowed eyes before whirling around back to Chuck.

'Well, Kate, I haven't been called Chuck since I was at college.' Then he shrugged and snorted out a laugh which was so like the one she had heard from Heath in the library that it was astonishing. 'Why not? They were good times and I happen to be getting married tomorrow. You may address me as Chuck as many times as you wish.' He blinked, looking rather startled at the words coming out of his mouth.

'Excellent,' Kate replied and looped her arm through the crook of his elbow. She looked dramatically around in all directions before leaning closer and whispering, 'Now, down to the important stuff. Has Heath told you about his plan for the party this evening?'

A look of absolute astonishment crossed the older man's face and he raised his eyebrows at Heath, who was staring at her in disbelief.

'Not exactly, no. What precisely did he have in mind?' Chuck asked in a voice filled with dread.

'Oh, you boys are always talking business. Time for a break. Heath didn't want to spoil the surprise but we are going to decorate the dining room with party paraphernalia guaranteed to bring a bit more fun into the proceedings. As Heath says, a girl deserves to be spoilt for one evening. But don't worry,' Kate gushed. 'It will all be in very good taste. I am thinking balloons and bunting and banners. All the other guests can have fun helping to put it up and decorate the room.'

Then she stopped talking and drew back. 'I do hope that's okay with you, but it's meant to be a surprise. So you shall have to distract Alice from going in until the very last minute. Do you think you can do that?'

To his credit, Chuck only paused for a moment before nodding. 'Of course. Alice is very busy with the wedding arrangements. Hence the outside catering this evening. I'm sure that won't be a problem.'

'Did you hear that, Heath? We are good to go.'

His reply was the slightest shake of his head and his jaw stiffened.

Kate glared at him but he was not giving her any help at all. So she turned her winning smile onto his father and slid her hand onto his arm again.

'Only one small problem. I have foolishly left some of the party things back in London and I don't have transport. Would you mind if I borrowed a car for the next few hours? I am a very careful driver and Heath will be coming along for the heavy lifting.'

Chuck smiled to himself then fished a set of car keys out of his trouser pocket. 'I would pay money to see that. Have fun, little lady.'

And with a final flourish he dropped the keys into Kate's palm and closed her fingers around them. 'It has been a pleasure to meet you, Kate. A real pleasure.'

'Likewise. See you later, Chuck. I'll save you a dance.'

Charles Sheridan the Third paused in his stride for just long enough to shake his head before strolling into the Manor.

Kate lifted up the keys to a four-by-four and dangled them towards Heath but never got the chance to speak before he grabbed her by the arm and half dragged her towards the ornate gardens and did not let her go until they were hidden from the house by a tall hedge.

'Hey! You have to stop dragging me behind the bushes. People will talk and I have my reputation to consider.'

Heath replied by glaring at her and raking both fingers back through his hair.

'Your what? Kate Lovat, you are the most exasperating and impulsive woman that I have ever met. You seem to spend most of your time living in some fantastic fantasy world. Then just when I need you to be sensible and not embarrass yourself and me, you do something off the wall like this. Please explain before my head explodes.'

'Calm down! For some odd reason I actually want you to have some kind of relationship with your parents. And yes, as far as I am concerned, Alice is your new parent whether you like it or not. And don't look at me like that.'

She stabbed herself several times in the chest with her forefinger. 'It may have escaped your notice but I am a girl. Girls need to feel special. Especially when they are about to get married. Now—' she nodded slowly '—I am confident that you have an excellent checklist all ready for the wedding rehearsal this afternoon. I am expecting floor plans and timings, and I can see from your blushes that I'm not going to be disappointed, but here is your chance to do something remarkable. Something above and beyond the call of duty. Because you are going to start the celebrations with a fabulous rehearsal dinner party this evening.'

She sniffed and brushed imaginary crumbs from her fingers. 'Heath the hero. Job done.'

Heath stood back up and looked in silence towards the silent house, where two of Alice's younger cousins had just arrived, before replying in a tone of total disbelief, 'So you expect me to organise a party? For this evening? Without any advance notice?' And he shook his head slowly from side to side.

Kate held out the side of her jacket and gave a small curtsey. 'You are welcome. Leave the extras to me. In return I shall expect you to willingly volunteer to stand on a ladder and attach a range of bunting and balloons to the ceiling. And smile while you are doing it. Right? Of course right. The other guests will be dragooned and shanghaied into similar duties and you will all have a thoroughly enjoyable time. Now,' she said, checking her watch, 'we don't have much time. I need to get back to my place to pick up some gloves and then to Saskia's for the party stuff, then whizz back here pronto to put it all up…and where are you going?'

'This was your crazy plan and I have a mountain of work to do.'

Kate grabbed hold of his hand and held it with all of the strength that she could muster.

'Not a chance, Mister. I wasn't kidding just now. I need someone who can do the heavy lifting and that person is you. Joining in and doing something different just to please your old pater. Making it convincing. Right?'

'You cannot be serious.'

'I have never been more serious in my life. But relax.' She laughed as he groaned. 'You can work in the car if you must. How bad can it be?'

CHAPTER SEVEN

HOW BAD COULD IT BE?

Until that morning Heath had no idea how frustrating it was to be a passenger in a car, which smelt of his father, being driven by a girl who insisted on keeping below the speed limit on every single road, lane, highway and alley between the Manor and the quaint London street where she lived.

It had become very apparent, very quickly, that Kate had not owned a car since passing her driving test. Why should she when she lived in London and worked in London and enjoyed public transport in London?

So basically he was sitting next to a girl who had not driven a car for ten years. The concept of a global positioning system was a mystery to her and he had been obliged to use his smartphone to compensate for her total lack of a sense of direction after they had driven around the same roundabout three times looking for the exit back to London.

The real problem, of course, was that with the radio on and Kate chattering about the party extras which she wanted to pick up from Saskia's house, his mind was running on overtime and top speed about the conversation that he had just had with his father back at the Manor.

Just when he thought that he was starting to create some

form of working relationship with his father, Charles Sheridan had confirmed his worst suspicions.

The rumours were true.

He *had* been looking at contract printing overseas. No decisions, not yet, but to him it really was a viable option. Other companies and publishers were doing it, so why couldn't Sheridan Press?

But what really stung was that his father simply could not understand why Heath was so angry at not being informed when the market was already buzzing with rumours about the future of the Boston print works.

They had worked together for weeks on the new promotional campaign that Lucas was rolling out and not once, during all of those chatty business dinners and coffee breaks, had his father said one word about looking for other book printers.

Communication skills were clearly not a Sheridan strength.

Heath pressed his fingertips firmly into his forehead and tried to drill some insights and flashes of inspiration into his skull.

Perhaps he should be thanking Kate for providing him with a valid excuse to walk away from his father that morning and snatch the thinking time he desperately needed on his own.

The ramifications and pressure of what he needed to do and how fast he needed to work burned through his mind, so that by the time Kate bump parked the truck of a car onto the pavement outside her house, his nerves were shot, he felt exhausted and his shoulders ached with tension.

It was with huge relief that Heath could finally stretch out his long legs and he ran around to her side of the vehicle to open the driver's door for her.

'How very gallant.' She smiled and grabbed her bag

from the foot well of the car. 'I must say you have been an excellent passenger and not criticised my driving once, despite the small diversions now and again, and for that I thank you. In fact, you have been so splendid that if you want to come inside for a moment as a special treat I will let you peek inside my parlour.'

She turned on the pavement and leant closer towards him. 'I don't usually allow visitors to see where the magic happens, you understand, but in your case I'm prepared to make an exception.'

'How can I possibly refuse such an enticing invitation?' he said, smiling. Some of the exhaustion rolled off his shoulders as he waited for Kate to find her keys in the huge shoulder bag and open up the shop in the unbroken sunshine.

The quiet street was a mixture of private homes and small shops, no more than two storeys high. All of the buildings must have been homes at one time and some of them had been converted into shops at the bottom floor. It was really an enchanting area. Quiet but close to the hustle and bustle of the city.

The sort of place where a person could get to know their neighbours in the community and make a home. He almost envied Kate for having that privilege.

The only place he had ever truly called home was the tall stone-built house in Boston, where he had lived with his parents until he was seventeen. Since then home had been university accommodation, followed by a series of hotels, apartments and rented houses like the one he was living in now. Efficient, modern, clean. But not home.

Strange. He had never really thought about that until today.

Tiredness did that to people. Made them melancholy. And he was tired, so very tired.

Maybe next week he should make the effort to take some time out and relax more. The next few weeks were going to be tough. He needed to stay sharp. Even the keenest knife needed to be sharpened now and again.

Suddenly there was a rustle of papers and movement and he looked around just as Kate beckoned to him to follow her into the hallway of her terraced house.

When he'd come around to pick her up that morning, Saskia had chatted away merrily to him on the doorstep and handed him Kate's luggage, so this was the first time that he had actually stepped inside her home.

The hallway was narrow and long and seemed to extend towards a kitchen area past a steep staircase, which must go to the bedrooms.

Kate paused outside a door to his left, withdrew a small brass key from her purse and carefully turned it in the lock. He followed her inside, but immediately halted at the door with shock at what he was looking at.

It was one of the most depressing rooms he had ever seen.

Despite the bright July sunshine outside on the pavement, the room was dark and gloomy and lit only by an electric light bulb which hung from the ceiling on a twisted cord so that it looked more like a museum or a store room than a functional workspace.

The faint light only seemed to make the shadows darker and he could barely make out what the dark shapes on three large work tables could possibly be used for. Rows of hand tools hung from a rail along one wall opposite the door. Some he recognised from the print works in Boston but others were a complete mystery.

Large transparent plastic storage tubs with coloured lids were stacked three or four high across the floor so that he had to move slowly between the boxes to actually walk into the room.

As he did so clouds of dust rose up and he ran his finger across the nearest work table, leaving a trail in the dirt.

Kate could not possibly work under these conditions. And why was it so dark? The warehouse studio for Katherine Lovat Designs had been light and clean and modern and the exact opposite to what he was looking at now.

'I take it that housekeeping is not one of your strong points,' he murmured, trying to make an effort to be charitable. 'And what is that smell?'

She snorted a reply and pulled out yet another cardboard box from a wide shelf labelled with fading handwritten paper tags, which he tried to peer at but he couldn't make out the words.

'Not a priority,' she replied with a cough, as a thick layer of dust drifted off the lid of the box as she opened it and she tried to waft it away one-handed. 'As for the smell? That's from the leather which is laid out on those wide flat shelves at the back. I rather like it myself.'

'A suggestion,' he coughed. 'Perhaps you might see more clearly if I opened the curtains?' And with that he moved slowly towards the window, but he had only taken a couple of steps when Kate stepped back and placed one hand on his wrist and held it tight with a remarkably firm grip.

'The sunlight fades the leather and the paper patterns—' she shrugged '—and we will only need a few more minutes.' And then she sighed and her shoulders slumped dramatically. 'Ah. There you are. Sneaky little devil. What are you doing with the fuchsia satin bracelet-lengths?'

He folded his arms and stared at her in silence for a few seconds.

'Do you often talk to cartons?'

'Frequently,' Kate replied with a grin, and held up four slim cream-coloured boxes. 'Result!'

'Aren't you going to check what is inside? There might be moths or they might be damaged or something.'

Her eyebrows went north. 'Moths? Through three layers of cardboard? I will have you know that my French grandmother may not have had the finest command of the English language, but she was one of the neatest and most orderly people that I have ever met. Only pristine gloves were packed into Lovat boxes ready for the department stores. There are no moths here.'

'And how many years have they been on those shelves?'

Her hands stilled and she looked up at the stacks and stacks of bulging cartons with their fading labels and blinked as though she was working through the calculations.

'Nana died when I was about nine, so it has to be twenty years.' A faint whimpering sigh escaped her lips and her tongue flicked out and moistened her lower lip. 'Wow. I had forgotten it had been that long.' She looked up at the shelves and whispered, 'I really must do a stocktake one day soon.'

'But not today! I don't think we have enough time,' Heath said between his teeth.

She squeezed her eyes tight into slits and tutted. Loudly. 'Patience is a virtue, you know. But, if it will make you happy, you can take these into the hall and we can check them together before we leave.'

She shoved the slim boxes into his hands. 'I am expecting to see a size seven and five-eighths. White lace elbow gloves and please don't get them dirty. Now scoot. I have three more pairs to find and I don't want to be late for Saskia.'

'Heaven forfend.' He gave her a two finger to the fore-head salute. 'I shall be right outside.'

Heath wandered back into the hall and lowered the boxes onto an antique console table and wiped his fingers on a snowy white handkerchief. He was just about to open the lids when his gaze fell on a framed photograph on the wall to his left.

The sunlight streaming in through the coloured glass panel above the front door filled the narrow hallway with rainbow light and he could clearly make out the faces of the people in the photographs.

A young couple were standing in front of a shop front which looked familiar. He stepped closer and smiled. Little wonder—he was standing inside that same shop.

The woman was tiny, dark-haired and stunningly pretty and was smiling up into the face of a tall, slim, handsome man with curly dark hair. His arm was around her shoulders and he was grinning back at her with an expression of such love that it seemed to reach out and grab Heath and force him to look closer.

They looked so very happy.

'Ah, I see that you have found my grandparents,' Kate said behind him and he half turned back towards her as she staggered out with even more boxes. 'That photo was taken on the day they opened Lovat Gloves.' She grinned and shook her head. 'Look at them. Do you know the weird thing? He was still looking at her like that the day she died.'

'He was very handsome.'

'George Lovat was a remarkable man and I adored him. He taught me so much. They both did.'

Then Kate sucked in a breath and bit her lower lip. 'Come and see this,' she said, gesturing with her head back into the workroom.

Heath winced and looked at his watch. 'I don't think that we have the time to…'

She grabbed his hand and slipped her fingers between his. They were tiny and warm and without a moment of hesitation his fingers meshed with hers as though it was the most natural thing to do in the world.

It all happened so fast that his brain was still catching up as Kate marched through the door with her arm outstretched, tugging him behind her.

'That was where Nana sat—making gloves under the window. She said she needed the light for the fine stitching and her sewing machine but I think she just liked to see the garden she had planted. Now, Granddad, he was over here on the other side of the room, at his workbench with all of his leather work tools laid out on the bench. He pretended not to notice when Nana hummed to herself as she worked but we could all see the little smile on his face.'

Her forefinger touched the corner of her mouth. 'Just here. Then we used to giggle together until she realised that she was singing and rolled her eyes and laughed at us.'

Kate's gaze locked onto an old sewing machine. 'Singer, you see. She was singing while she was using her sewing machine, which was made by…'

He chuckled out loud. 'I get it.' His shoulders relaxed and they stood in easy comfort for the first time, her fingers completely enclosed in his paw. 'I'm not sure I could do that. Work with my wife in the same room day after day. Didn't they ever want to rent a workshop somewhere?'

'Nope. They loved being together, working side by side. Each had their own skill and craft but somehow the different types of creativity and different types of customer worked. Nana sold ladies' gloves to the big London department stores so she worked alone most of the time and that suited her very well. While Granddad?'

She gestured towards an old pedestal chair with a cracked leather seat.

'This was where he sat every day. I can see him now, hunched up in front of his work station, a bright lamp shining down on the leather, waiting for him to finish sharpening his scalpel blade and cut the intricate pattern on the lovely piece of leather that he had selected from the wide shelves behind him for this particular piece of work.'

She dragged her feet over to the work table and flicked on the light.

Kate's face broke out into a huge grin and she laughed up at Heath and swung his hand from side to side. 'He loved chatting with the customers who came to see him with their projects. And they came from everywhere. He specialised in gloves for theatres and film studios, so there were wardrobe experts from all over London—and beyond—knocking on the door day and sometimes night. Oh, they were such real characters—but they all had the same passion.'

She leant forwards and whispered, *'Gloves.'*

Then she stepped back. 'But you know all about passion, Mr Big Powerful Publisher.'

Heath peered at the handwritten labels and made out words like *feathers* and *diamanté*.

Tools were neatly laid out next to a modern sewing machine and glove templates hung from a teacup hook screwed into the shelf. Wooden hands stood upright on top of a cabinet with gloves on them. All different. All special. All…sad.

He felt Kate's fingers take a tighter grip around his, as though she had to hold on to something solid and real.

They stood in silence for a second and he inhaled the dust and heady atmosphere of a confined space, which seemed totally wrong somehow for this girl with so much verve and life and positive energy.

Why did she keep the door locked when all there was inside was a dark, lonely place?

'Do you live here alone?' Heath finally asked, desperate to break the gloomy silence of the space.

'Oh, no—I have the ghosts and memories of my grandparents to keep me company.'

He couldn't resist it. He had to chuckle out loud. 'Not so useful when you need someone to talk to—or do you talk to them anyway?'

'Wonderful inventions, telephones,' she said, smiling. 'I call upon my friends and amuse them with idle chatter about the silly things that have been happening in the world of tailoring or I go around to Saskia's place and help her with the house.'

'But they don't come here, do they?'

She half turned to face him in the tight, closed-in space and in the harsh light from the lamp he could see the dark shadows of her cheekbones.

'No, Heath. I rarely invite anyone into my parlour,' she said in a sad, low voice, which had the power to reach out and draw him in.

'Because of the ghosts?'

A faint smile flashed across her lips and she winked. 'Absolutely—they hate strangers barging into their home. And they refuse to talk to anyone except me so it would be terribly rude for guests.'

He glanced around before coming back to gaze into her sweet, lovely face. He was missing her smile suddenly and that flash of her green eyes when she irked him.

'You're quite right, I can't hear a thing. But what do they say to you?'

He could see a shiver run across her shoulders, and instinctively moved closer to give her some of his warmth.

It might be a hot July afternoon outside, but the ghosts of Kate's past walked in this room and called her name.

'What do they say? *Katherine, Katherine, why haven't you cleaned me? Why do you keep the door locked? You cannot seriously be still waiting for your parents to give up their scientific careers and make this a happy place like it used to be? That is not going to happen. That ship has sailed, sweet girl. They aren't coming back. They are not. Coming back.*'

The tears were running down her cheeks now and he reached up with his free hand and wiped them away.

Her eyes closed the second his fingertip touched her skin and he felt her gentle shudder ripple through her body and through her clasped hand into his own.

'Are they right?' he whispered, hardly daring to break their connection. 'These ghostly ancestors of yours?'

She nodded, her lips pressed firmly together, and it took a second before she blew out hard and answered in a shaky voice. 'My parents met when they were studying chemistry at university. Yes, I know. *Chemistry.* Apparently my grandmother came from a family of electrical engineers and scientists but the lure of the science lab skipped a generation because she couldn't change a light bulb without blowing power to the entire street.'

She choked on a deep sob which came from deep inside her body and shook her whole frame. 'But I'm a fool. I still cling onto the crazy notion that my parents will wake up one morning and realise that their work in the petrochemical industry is all a horrible mistake and I will fling open the door and they will be standing there on the doorstep with their suitcases.'

Then her eyes squeezed tight shut but Heath dared not speak. She had to tell him now or never say it at all. 'When my grandfather left this business to me, instead of his only

son—' she paused and sucked in a breath '—they tried
everything to make me sell the shop and move away and
retrain in a proper career where I wouldn't be wasting my
life on foolish dreams of being a fashion designer. They
are ashamed of me, Heath. Ashamed that their child wants
to spend her life refusing to conform to their ideas. Which
is more than just sad. It breaks my heart.'

Her fingertips moved of their own volition over a cut-
off scrap of pale grey suede which was still peach-soft.
'Leather was my grandfather's passion. Look at this piece
of suede. Isn't it lovely? Here it is, just waiting for the new
owner of Lovat Gloves to turn it into something beautiful.
Something to be treasured and kept in a special place by
a customer who appreciates fine things. He loved me for
who I am and believed in me. Only the new owner doesn't
know which way to turn.'

She collapsed on to the stool and Heath stepped forward,
their hands still locked together.

'I cannot stand the idea that I would let my grandparents down. It would kill me.'

Heath hunkered down so that his head was at the same
level as hers and, before he could rethink or stop himself,
he reached up and brushed a lock of Kate's hair back over
her ear and lifted up her chin.

'What do *you* want to do, clever, talented lady?'

His reward was a faint smile and the smallest of twin-
kles in her eyes. 'When I was studying art and fashion at
university I told everyone that one day this would be my
studio and I would find some way of combining fashion
design with the glove-making business that Isabelle and
George Lovat created from their passion for the work and
one another.'

'Fashion and gloves. In the same shop.' She sniffed and

jiggled her shoulders. 'Just thinking about it still makes my toes curl inside my shoes.'

'Then what's holding you back, Kate? What's stopping you from making that dream come true?'

Kate lifted her head and stared into his eyes, her green eyes brimming with tears. 'Life. Reality. I'm scared, Heath. I'm so scared that I'm going to lose all of this that it freezes me. That's why I agreed to come to the wedding this week-end, Heath. I need your help before I lose everything. Can you understand that? Can you?'

And before he could do anything to stop her, even if he wanted to, she slipped off her chair and fell into his wide-open arms so that he could enfold them around her tiny, slim, fragile body, crushing her to him and protecting her from harm with all of the strength that he had.

It had been such a long time since he had held a warm, beautiful girl in his arms, but the instant he felt Kate wrap her arms around his waist, he knew that this was differ-ent. Special.

He *wanted* to protect her and keep her safe.

Her hair tickled his chin and he breathed in the fragrance of the woman and the place and the moment, and was in-stantly drunk on it.

He could sense the pulse of her heartbeat against his chest and the heat of her breath on his shirt and he could have stayed there for ever. Words were not needed. This was the best and only form of communication he needed.

But, just as his treacherous hands moved higher up her back, drawing her closer to him, their silence was broken by a cellphone with a pop song ringtone.

Leave it, he willed. *Let the outside world get on with-out us for just a few precious minutes. Choose to stay here with me.*

Kate laughed into his chest and slid slowly, slowly out

of his arms until she was standing on her feet. Still sniffing and wiping her eyes, she flipped open her phone and checked the text message.

She laughed out loud and swallowed before looking sheepishly at Heath. 'Saskia. Do we want all pink or pink and white balloons? I say pink.'

He nodded, just once, and stood tall as she replied. And, just like that, her body moved out of reach and they were two separate people again.

Except they weren't.

Not any longer.

And he was going to have to add that to the list of things to deal with.

CHAPTER EIGHT

KATE PEERED AROUND the corner of the ornate stone pillar on the bride's side of the stunning village church. Heath was still standing at the front to one side of the altar, working down his checklist and trying to salvage what was left of his carefully worked out timetable.

The late afternoon sunshine was streaming in through the stained glass round window behind his head, creating a kaleidoscope of pastel colours on the old stone floor around him. The florist had come in with a posy of English sweet peas, roses and lilacs to show Alice, filling the space with stunning fragrance. It was going to be totally magical. For Alice.

Heath must have torn up his plan at least three times that afternoon.

He had been so confident when they'd got back to the Manor that they could grab a late lunch, run through the rehearsal super-quick and still have plenty of time to decorate the dining room before dinner.

Unfortunately those plans did not include herding a long line of very merry and alcohol-fuelled guests away from the dessert buffet and free bar and down the country lane to file into the church. He led the band as they staggered down the lane, with Kate and the other three bridesmaids following at the end.

She had no clue who started the singing but the rugby songs were not entirely appropriate for the occasion and Heath's dad and Alice's uncle had to dive in and try to hurry them along, much to the amusement of the friendly young vicar, who was clearly well used to having inebriated wedding parties in his church.

But eventually, with some cajoling from Alice, Charles and most of the ushers, all the guests were seated, Heath was standing next to Charles, Alice and the girls were all gathered at the open door and the organist played the opening few bars of the wedding march.

It was lovely to meet Alice's friends and they were so enthusiastic about being bridesmaids and wearing Kate's dresses that it was easy to get caught up in the excitement and put the morning's trip to London out of her mind.

But that was before she stepped in behind Alice and looked over her shoulder and saw Charles, smiling at Alice as she walked up the aisle towards him, carrying her pretend bunch of flowers at the regulation crotch level. The love and devotion shone out of his eyes like a tsunami which washed over everything else in the room.

This man and this woman. So much in love.

And something inside her had broken.

Was she ever going to have someone look at her with so much love in his eyes?

The closer they came to the altar, the more her heart wept.

Stupid girl!

She always got emotional at weddings, plus she was exhausted and frayed around the edges.

As for Heath? Heath simply rolled his eyes the minute she had sat down on the hard wooden pew with the other bridesmaids and laughed away her tears with some giggling joke about always crying at weddings.

But when the others leapt up and started streaming out and back to the Manor, she needed to sit in the cool church and gather her wits about her and she was still sitting there half an hour later, watching Heath wander down the aisle and collapse on the bench next to her.

'Well, that was different,' he said and his shoulders sagged.

'I told you that it was a mistake having wine and beer at the lunchtime barbecue. But there are lots of good dry cleaners in the area. They *might* be able to get the ketchup and mustard off your dad's nice jacket.'

'Hah. I would be pleased if that was the only thing to worry about,' Heath replied. 'Did you see the Jardine girls? They spent the whole time talking or texting. I could have been invisible.'

'Let's put it down to natural exuberance and being caught up in the emotion.'

Heath snorted and turned to look at her. He smiled and squeezed her hand. 'Are you okay?'

'Me? Oh, I always cry at weddings and shall probably disgrace myself completely tomorrow by weeping all over Alice before we even leave the Manor. No, I'm fine. Just catching my breath before we start our next exciting adventure—the decorating!'

He exhaled slowly, but then lifted his head and nodded towards his father, who was gesturing towards them.

'Ah. Be right there. But first I have to meet and greet the banking wing of the New York clan and try to keep them apart from the Jardine hedge-fund managers. Wish me luck!'

And he was gone, leaving her alone and bereft while he shook hands and chatted with men who made more money in a year than she would in a lifetime. Heath looked so at ease and confident at that moment. And it struck her hard just how very, very different their worlds truly were.

She had never minded working for a living. Far from it. She was doing something she loved every single day, creating marvellous things for other people to wear and enjoy, and that was special.

Not many people got to spend their lives doing what they were truly passionate about. She was a lucky girl.

A lucky girl who knew what it felt like to have Heath Sheridan's arms around her and to feel the warmth and strength of his embrace melt her resistance like ice in the sun.

The journey back from Saskia's house had been one of the toughest she had ever suffered. Heath had insisted on driving in the July heat and Kate had pretended to doze off now and again rather than face the difficult silence that always came when two people had cuddled who should not have done.

She was mortified at having revealed so much of her past and exposed the tender underbelly of her life. Heath had not said a word. He was too much of a gentleman to make a fuss of it, but the atmosphere between them was so tense that it was making her nervous.

What had she been thinking? Crying on his shoulder like that? Telling him about the pain of losing her grandparents? Stupid, reckless and totally pathetic. And, unless she stopped having these ridiculous feelings about him, it was all going to end in tears—her tears.

Heath was wealthy and handsome and used to the very best of things in life. Why should he put up with second-best like her?

Why should he want her as his girlfriend? Pretend or otherwise?

She was going to lose him all over again. He had his

life to go back to in New York and Boston, a lifestyle of wealth and luxury which was on a different planet from the one she inhabited. He was going to leave in a few days and they would both be back in their separate, lonely worlds.

Everyone she had truly loved had left her, one way or another. And setting herself up for even more loss was not just ridiculous but crushing.

She could do this. She was strong. She was going to get through this wedding with a smile on her face and then she was going to walk away from Heath and start living her life all over again.

Now all she had to do was convince her heart to stop dreaming about the impossible.

Heath stared into the mirror in his en suite bathroom at the Manor, adjusted the black bow tie below the wing collar on his dress shirt and smothered a yawn.

And he knew precisely who to blame for that!

The girl who had popped notes under the bedroom doors of every guest.

The girl who had cajoled and persuaded even the grump- iest and poshest of stuffy relatives and friends to join in with the decorating operation in the great hall. And not only had they had turned up but they had thoroughly en- joyed every second of it, just as she had predicted. Even the two great-aunts had been singing!

Singing. In tune.

And directed and conducted by the one and only Kate Lovat. Organiser. Indefatigable cheer-leader and mind- reader.

And gorgeous. Don't forget the gorgeous.

As if he could.

Heath wrapped his fingers around the cool ceramic washbasin and inhaled deeply.

He had let his guard down that afternoon and was paying the price.

There were a few rules that governed his life and one of them was written in tablets of stone and engraved on his heart.

He would never, ever allow himself to become emotionally dependent on any woman.

No matter how enchanting and remarkable she was.

No matter how much Kate had touched his heart when they were together in her tiny house. But seeing her tears in the church that afternoon and the gentle way that she had guided Alice into her role—that was something new. That was special.

Kate Lovat was a girl in a million. He could understand now why Amber adored her.

He was going to miss her.

In the car driving back from London that afternoon, Kate had fallen asleep in the passenger seat and he had been alone with his thoughts. Going over what she had told him when they had been alone in that dirty, cramped workshop, it had struck him with a powerful realisation that he had never once had the kind of conversation with his father or Olivia that he had shared with Kate in her tiny house. Not once.

Worse—he had no clue about what dreams and hopes Olivia had in her heart or what kind of life she had led until they'd met at a publishing conference.

Perhaps that was what Olivia had meant when she said that he was cold and guarded. And, if it was, then they were equally to blame for keeping their inner truths hidden.

Not everyone was as open as Kate Lovat.

A strange and tantalising thought whispered through his mind and he snatched at it.

His diary was already packed with meetings in Boston

and New York for the next few months so this would probably be the last time he saw Kate before Amber's wedding.

He looked into the mirror and a chuckle escaped from
the back of his throat and made its way to his lips.

She had asked him what he did for fun. Maybe, just for
this weekend, he could take that as a challenge and have
some fun, and show her that he could enjoy a party just
like everyone else.

Heath Sheridan had just changed his mind. He did need
a wedding date, and Kate Lovat was the girl.

He crossed the oak-panelled corridor in four strides and
knocked twice on Kate's bedroom door. The latch opened
on the other side of the door and Kate peeked out of a narrow gap.

'I'm not ready yet, you pest. Please go away and come
back in ten minutes.'

She tried to close the door on him. But he stuck his foot
in and then winced as she pushed harder against it.

'Kate! Stop that. You look very nice and we need to talk
before we meet the family.'

She pulled the door open, planted one hand at each hip,
stuck her chin out and glared at him. 'Are you crazy? How
can I look very nice dressed like this?'

Heath took one look at what she was wearing, or rather
not wearing, glanced up and down the corridor to check
that no one had seen, stepped inside her bedroom and shut
the door firmly behind him.

'Kate! Are you trying to give Uncle Harold a heart attack? Put some clothes on.'

Kate flung up her hands. 'What do you think I'm trying to do? Sit there and talk if you must while I get ready.'

Thankfully for his blood pressure and heart rate, Kate
strode into the bathroom and half closed the door behind her.

She was wearing a very short silk dressing gown which swung open as she walked. The last time he had seen a girl wearing a bra top, black French knickers, suspenders and stockings had been at a catwalk charity fashion show being held by one of Amber's model friends, who'd found his embarrassment very funny. And he had never, ever been this close to a girl's underwear up close and personal. Amber's modelling work and concert performances required beautiful ball gowns and some of them were a little revealing, but nothing compared to Kate Lovat in her underwear.

Even the girls who came to Amber's sleepover parties used to hide in the bathroom until they were fully clothed.

And Olivia... Well, he had seen a wide variety of designer and supermarket labels, depending on whether she was working on an archaeological dig that week or not.

He glanced around the room and was surprised to find that everything was neat and tidy and meticulously organised. After what he had seen in the workshop, he'd expected that Kate's room would be a mess of clothes scattered across the bed.

'Well, talk to me, Sheridan. What is so urgent that you need to talk to me now?'

As he glanced in the direction of her voice, he caught a glimpse of the delicious tight curve of her pantie-covered bottom reflected in the mirror and quickly turned away, palms sweaty. She had a waist so tiny that he could put both hands around and his fingers would touch.

He had felt every one of her ribs under the thin top she had been wearing in the workshop that afternoon and the heat of that sensation hit him hard all over again.

'We were so busy this afternoon I never had a chance to give you an insight into the family before we go down to dinner,' he replied after a quick cough, and flopped down on the corner of her bed. 'You've already met Alice's two great-aunts and the cousins. The New York Sheridans were the noisy ones who spent the time arguing about how to string the banners. They will probably rearrange my seating plan at the first chance they get.'

'Heath, you can stop now. I get it. You want me to say nice things and be charming and polite. But my world revolves around hemlines and shoes and gloves and hats with feathers in them and if they don't like it then they can look at my shoes instead.'

Kate stepped out of the bathroom with her hands still tugging on the back zip of her dress. And his heart stopped beating.

Shoes? He wasn't looking at her shoes.

His gaze was locked onto the short-sleeved black dress she was wriggling into. The shoulders were made up of two stiff collars of taffeta which showed her creamy neck and collarbone to perfection.

Apart from a slightly sparkly neckline, it was so totally different from anything else that he had seen Kate wear that he simply could not look away.

No flashy splashes of colour. No outrageous cutting-edge slashes held together with gold safety pins. She was elegance personified.

He had heard of the expression *drop dead gorgeous* but he had never experienced it before, not even when Amber had invited some of her model pals to a charity event in Boston.

Shame. It might have prepared him for the full-on sensory overload that was Kate Lovat in a black cocktail dress, cream satin evening gloves and a statement necklace which made her eyes sparkle with an even greater intensity than he thought possible.

'Well?' she asked, holding her arms out wide. 'Will this do? I thought about a hot-pink bandage dress but I thought it might scare the aunts and embarrass Alice. So. Black and jewels. Not original. But I think it works.'

'Oh, yes, it works just fine. Wow. I mean. Wow!'

She glanced down at her dress and sniffed. 'Oh. Last season's collection but it was popular. I'm glad that you like it.'

'Like it? I am overwhelmed by it.' And then he realised what he had just said and coughed away her smirk of delight.

'You look perfectly elegant and sophisticated, Miss Lovat. And it's not often I get to say that.' He smiled.

'Well, thank you, kind sir,' and she rolled her eyes. 'Although, I have to say, you clean up pretty well yourself. Dinner suit. Always a killer on a tall, slim man. Although your shoes are a little boring.'

He stared at his shiny black tassel shoes. Then stared at hers.

They seemed to consist of straps of magenta fabric which went up her legs in spirals. He knew this because she had stretched out one leg onto the dressing table stool and lifted her skirt a little so that she could tie the straps in a little bow at the top. Revealing a tantalising amount of thigh.

Aha—there was his Kate.

For a dazzling, bewildering moment he wondered what it would be like to be the one taking those shoes off, one ribbon at a time. It could be fun.

Except, of course, she would think that he had completely lost his mind.

'Did Olivia like shoes?' Kate asked. *As though she could read his mind.*

'No clue,' he replied, then laughed. 'But I have never seen her wear anything like that.'

'Good,' Kate replied. 'The trick is to make us as different as possible. Remember what I said in the car, or were you not listening again? I am Amber's friend from high school who works as a fashion designer and made the splendiferous bridesmaids' dresses. I don't want people thinking that you have been using me to cheat on your girlfriend when she is in China.'

An embarrassed silence filled the room but Kate carried on tidying away her things and organising the contents of a clutch bag, which seemed so small for everything that she was packing into it, completely oblivious to the fact that she had just dropped a bombshell.

'Good point,' he managed to reply. 'That wouldn't be fair on you.'

'On either of us,' Kate retorted and shook her head. 'There have to be people here tonight who know Olivia and would be happy to spread gossip if there is even a hint of scandal.'

'How stupid of me.' Heath blinked. 'I've just realised something rather important.'

'You're not wearing underpants?' Kate asked with her head tilted to one side.

'Sorry to disappoint, but I am wearing underpants,' he replied with narrowed eyes. 'It wasn't that. I have just realised that I didn't ask if you have a boyfriend at the moment. Apologies. I hope you haven't got any plans for this weekend and, of course, he would be welcome to join us for the wedding tomorrow.'

Heath glanced around the single bedroom. 'I could move out of the double and...'

'Relax.' She dropped her hand on his knee for just a second before going back to getting dressed. 'Stop getting so stressed. I'm between boyfriends at the moment,' she muttered, 'so this room is absolutely fine. And I can be a pretend bridesmaid. After all, you're not asking me to be your wedding date.'

Then she looked up and asked. 'Are you?'

Damn right he was.

'A wedding date? Um. Now, that's an idea. How about it, Miss Lovat? Want the job of fending off all of the lovely Jardine girls who are gathering downstairs planning their attack now that they know that I am a bachelor again?'

'It's a good thing you are so modest,' she replied far too quickly. 'But I forgot to pack my body armour. Sorry, Heath. I think that would go above and beyond brides-maid duties.'

Drat. Well, he had tried. But he wasn't giving up that easily—the evening was still young and there was always the wedding reception.

Kate gestured towards the gift bags dangling from Heath's hand.

'Is that your present for the bride? May I have a peek?' Kate asked and carefully lifted the lid from a lilac-co-loured card box.

He was so tempted to reach forward and maybe stroke her leg a little to test that her shoe was fitting nicely. *Bad idea. Bad Heath.*

Kate did her famous mind-reading act again and glanced up at him in surprise as she carefully opened up the tis-sue paper to reveal a heavily embossed burgundy picture album. She couldn't resist peeking inside and gasped out loud.

To his delight, she sat down on the bed next to him and gently lifted the pages. Each sheet was an original hand-painted watercolour with an interleaved protective gauze. 'These are stunning,' she gasped, and blinked up at Heath. 'Wow! This is certainly some present, and what an in-spired choice.'

She wrapped the book in tissue and held the box out towards Heath, who glanced at it just once and then nodded.

'Alice knew the artist and Sheridan Press employ some wonderful craftsmen who were happy to work over a weekend for a generous bonus.'

'What a wonderful idea. You have gone to a lot of trouble to come up with something very personal which she will love. Perfect. I am impressed.'

'And now for the bridesmaids,' he replied and swung the other bag from side to side. 'They are all different but I thought that you might enjoy this one. Don't hold back—dive in.'

Kate drew out a book bound in pale dove-grey super-soft suede from its tissue-lined box. The pages were ten love poems which had been hand-written in dark purple ink in a cursive font on lovely thick cream paper.

'Oh, Heath. This is beautiful. Any bridesmaid would treasure this for the rest of her life. I love it. Thank you,' Kate said and placed one hand on his shoulder, which startled him more than a little, but not as much as the gentle kiss she placed on his cheek.

His right hand moved automatically to her waist. She smelt heavenly and it took all of his willpower not to linger longer than he should and prolong the delight.

'Right, Mr Sheridan.' Kate grinned. 'I need to pop in to see Alice. And that's it! Time to get this party started. Leave those gift bags to me—you've done the hard work. Fun and frolics, here we come.'

Kate knocked twice on the white-painted door that the housekeeper had pointed out was Alice's bedroom. She had already spotted that Charles was escorting two older ladies down the corridor so she imagined it was safe to enter without interrupting anything.

'Alice, it's me, Kate. Can I come in?'

Alice opened the door wide within seconds and kissed Kate warmly on the cheek and invited her into the bedroom.

'I thought you might have escaped back to London after the mayhem at the rehearsal.' Alice laughed and patted the bed so that she could sit down. 'Thank you for coming back to keep me company.'

'As if I would miss a great party! Gorgeous dress.' Kate smiled and nodded at the pale lilac taffeta fabric wrapped around Alice's tall, slender frame. 'You look fantastic.'

'Thank you,' Alice sighed. 'This is the third one I have tried on this evening. I only hope it works.'

'Of course it will,' Kate replied with a wink. 'I have brought gloves.'

Alice whirled around and pounced on the now clean boxes of gloves Kate had brought from her workshop. She sat back and watched as Alice reacted with delight at the white, lilac and shoulder-length satin gloves.

'Please go ahead and try them on.' She smiled at Alice, who was sizing up the colours and shades. 'All yours to do with as you like.'

'Fantastic,' she replied. 'And I'm sure that I can find a fun evening bag to match. Be right back.'

Kate resisted the temptation to collapse back on the soft duvet cover and snatch five minutes, but that would be far too dangerous. Who knew that hanging balloons, laying tables with flowers, wedding treats and favours could be so exhausting? Thank heavens she wouldn't have to do that very often.

And then there was Heath.

Who had just asked her to be his wedding date.

Oh, Heath. If you only knew how desperately I wanted to say yes.

Kate looked around the pretty bedroom with its floral chintz curtains and matching wallpaper. Instantly her gaze settled on a large framed watercolour on the wall opposite the bed. It was a portrait of the Manor with the knot garden laid out in beautiful detail in front of the main entrance with its wonderful colouring and towers.

She shuffled off the bed and strode over so that she could look at it in more detail.

And the longer she looked the more she realised that it had been painted by the same artist who had created the watercolours in the book that Heath had chosen as a wedding present.

A smile creased her lips.

Somehow Heath had found out the name of the artist who Alice liked and had managed to track down some stunning miniatures and flower sketches.

It would be the perfect present and Alice would be delighted.

She was still staring at the picture when Alice came back into the room with an assortment of bags.

'Ah,' she said, and came to stand next to her. 'That's the last of her paintings but I simply couldn't bear to let it go. Lee was so talented and we had such fun that weekend. Charles understands why I hang on to it, but it's hard sometimes to admire the work without thinking back in pain and regret to the lovely friend who painted it just for me.'

Kate blinked twice and her mouth opened to reply but her mind was too busy working through the ramifications of what she had just heard.

It took a great deal of effort but she managed to keep her voice light and positive when she asked, 'Do you mean that this was painted by Heath's mother?'

Alice nodded. 'I know I should put it in another room, but I love this picture and it takes me back to happy times we spent together.' Then she gave a small shrug. 'Most of Lee Sheridan's work was sold in America to serious collectors and there is so little on the market. I'm lucky to have it. But do you know what Lee would say if she were here now?' She laughed. 'Where's the champagne? We have gloves, shoes, bags and the full works. How about we get this party off to a swinging start? I'll meet you downstairs in ten minutes and then you help me open some bottles.'

'I like the sound of that.' Kate laughed and turned towards the door, then paused and looked over her shoulder at Alice with a smile. 'I'll just be a few minutes. See you downstairs. There's something that I need to do.'

CHAPTER NINE

KATE PUSHED HER apprehension deep inside and switched on her happy face as she descended the majestic staircase that led to the stunning entrance hall where the drinks reception was being held.

And instantly spotted Heath.

He was looking out at the cluster of girls who were drinking champagne on the patio, the fading July sun casting a warm glow on his fair complexion and the white shirt. He was leaning against the fireplace, below a set of crossed swords.

A knight of the Manor.

To any of the other guests he would have seemed distant and remote. An elegant, tall, sophisticated and urbane publishing executive who should be on a poster for a classical city boy.

The girls looked like a flock of exotic birds compared to his sober look. But under that fine black dinner jacket Kate knew beat a heart that burned with sensitivity and passion for the things that mattered to him.

But there was something different about his expression. A certain sadness. As though he wanted to join in the fun but felt remote from it.

A hand grasped around her heart and twisted it a little.

She strolled a few steps closer and her eyes followed

what he was actually looking at. Not the girls, although any healthy male would be excused for enjoying the view, but Alice and Charles, who were walking hand in hand across the lawns towards them.

Alice looked amazing and the gloves Kate had given her suited her perfectly—which was wonderful. But it was Charles who Heath was really looking at.

The man who had been talking to Heath earlier that day, stony-faced and solemn, was transformed when he was with Alice into someone younger, brighter and happier.

That was it. Happier. Charles was laughing and joking and now waving to the party guests who were starting to gather in the hall.

Kate sighed softly. It must be hard for Heath to see his father with another woman, especially considering what Alice had told her about their past relationship so many years ago.

Her heart went out to him. There had to be some way of making this marriage easier for him to accept. Some way of easing the transition.

Perhaps she could be his wedding date—not for her, but *for him*.

She stopped at the foot of the stairs and slipped into the dining room. The decorations and balloons combined with the sparkling crystal and china and silver-wear to create a wonderful display—and she would be the first to congratulate Heath as being the chief bunting fixer-upper.

Kate walked slowly around to the head of the table and paused at Alice's name-plate, where several gifts were already stacked up on the tapestry-covered dining chair.

Suddenly indecisive.

Heath might not appreciate the little embellishment that she had made to his gift to Alice.

The gift bag swung from her right hand and she quickly

glanced inside, clutched it to her chest and carefully slid it to the bottom of the pile.

Exhaling slowly, she caught the sound of the famous string quartet that had started up in the hall.

Time to get some of that champagne Alice had talked about earlier.

It was party time!

An hour later, Kate had found the champagne, sampled two glasses, talked to several relatives from both sides and was now desperate for food and company.

That was one of the problems of being vertically challenged. Looking over the heads of the other guests for Heath was a tad tricky.

Just as she thought she spotted him, one of the Jardine girls bumped into her, almost spilling her drink, apologised and then peered at her for a few seconds before pointing at her chest with a wobbly finger.

'Wait a minute. I think I went to school with you,' the blonde rasped in a high squeaky voice. Her breath smelt of pink champagne and mushroom canapés and high school cliques.

'Crystal. How nice to see you again after all of these years. Fancy meeting you here.' Kate smiled sweetly. This was not the time or the place to rehash the bullying of arrogant posh girls like Crystal Jardine.

'Yes. I remember you now. You were the funny one.'

The funny one. Yes, that's me, the funny one. Class clown.

Be nice, Kate. You went through all of that at the ten-year reunion. And this is definitely not the place.

'Well, I did try and have some fun in class,' Kate replied and beckoned a waiter over for another glass of champagne.

'Of course. Christine, isn't it?'

Kate opened her mouth and was about to reply that she had changed her name to Gloriana Hephzibah Wilkes, just for fun, but she took one look at the vacant expression on the frozen Botoxed face grinning down at her with fluorescent white teeth and decided that this girl wouldn't understand the humour and abandoned the idea.

'Well, my mother still calls me Katherine on the telephone now and then when I have forgotten something important like her birthday present, but I prefer Kate. Kate works for me.'

'Kate.' She nodded. 'Of course. How stupid of me. And is the rest of the little band here tonight? You know, the gorgeous lanky one and the plain, quiet one whose dad got into trouble or something? What were their names? Oh, yes, Amber—she's the pianist, right? Everyone remembers Amber and we are all *so* jealous of that modelling gig she did. But the other girl's name completely slips my mind.'

'Do you mean Saskia Elwood?' Kate asked casually, over the rim of her champagne flute.

'Saskia. That's it.' Then Crystal narrowed her eyes.

'Wait a moment—didn't you used to date Amber's brother for a while when you were in the sixth form? Heath Sheridan. The groom's son.'

A knowing smile crossed the blonde's lips. 'Well, that would explain what you're doing here. Congratulations. You did well there.'

Well, she had got that right.

'How clever of you to remember that.' Kate smiled through gritted teeth. 'But I am here as a family friend.'

More is the pity.

'Well you must be regretting that. Our Heath is still just as handsome as ever, isn't he? So impressive. And quite the business guru. Perhaps you should have stuck with him, Kate? Or did he move on?'

'Our business interests are so different. I was in London, he was in Boston—it would never have worked out.'

'Really? And what are you up to these days?'

Scraping a living trying to be a successful designer.

'I have recently expanded my couture business to include Lovat Gloves,' she quipped, casually flicking off an imaginary speck of dust from her evening dress with her satin-gloved hand. 'Terribly exclusive, of course, but you would be surprised how many people adore having made-to-measure clothing and accessories. Amber DuBois is one of my favourite clients. Gloves,' she whispered, leaning in. 'So important to the modern concert pianist.'

The leggy blonde with the pneumatic breasts she had not been born with towered over Kate despite her four-inch heels and looked from side to side before leaning in to whisper in her ear. 'Is it true what they're saying about Amber DuBois? You know. That she had to retire from playing piano because of some unfortunate illness?'

What? Of all the...

'Absolutely rubbish,' Kate whispered, 'but on the other hand it's probably not a good idea to go around repeating gossip like that. You never know who might be listening. Heath adores Amber and is terribly protective. Lawyers are so expensive these days. Don't you find?' She smiled.

The blonde's lips twisted with disdain and she simpered. 'Ah. Well, I'll be sure to catch up with darling Heath later.'

'Did someone mention my name?'

A pair of long arms wrapped around her waist and Heath pressed his chin on Kate's shoulder. Kate whirled gracefully around in relief and clutched onto his arm with such force that he actually winced. 'Ah, there you are. Crystal and I were just catching up from high school. Such a small world, isn't it?'

'Absolutely. But I need to snatch Kate away from you,

Crystal. We're just about to go into dinner. But we must make time to chat later.'

Heath took hold of Kate's arm and linked it through his elbow so they could glide safely away and out onto the sunlit terrace where the orchestra was playing Viennese waltzes.

'You. Are my total saviour,' Kate hissed out of the corner of her mouth. 'Another minute with the lovely Crystal and I would have emptied the ice bucket over her head.'

'Heath to the rescue. Are you trying to lead me astray, Miss Lovat?'

Kate shrugged and linked her arm around the crook of Heath's elbow. 'I'm your pal. That's my job.'

'And you do it so well.'

'Awww. Thanks, handsome. That's the nicest thing anyone has said to me all day.'

'Seriously?'

'Seriously.'

'Speaking of nice things… I think we are ready for the great unveiling.'

Heath nodded towards the dining room.

Charles had one hand up in front of Alice's closed eyes, then, as the family and guests looked on, he whipped them away. Alice took one look at the decorations, glanced at Charles, who nodded, then looked again in disbelief. And burst into tears.

'She loves it.' Kate nodded. 'We do good work.' Then she hooked her arm a little tighter against Heath, grinned and cuddled closer. 'And I seem to recall that you promised me a dance, young man.'

'Absolutely.' Heath grinned back and extended both hands palm upwards. 'May I have the honour of this dance, Miss Lovat?'

Kate bathed in the heat of Heath's gaze as he smiled

down at her, clearly determined to make her dance. He looked sexier and even more handsome than ever and any resolve *she* might have had to stay frosty and cool seemed to melt like ice.

In seconds they were on the patio and mingling with the other guests, who were finishing their drinks and drifting back in for dinner.

Her senses were so alive when he was close like this. The garden suddenly seemed full of the sound of birdsong and insects. Bees from the roses and lavender were the soundtrack to the beat of her heart and the soft music playing in the house. It was magical. Tonight they sang for her. And for Heath. And only for them.

She simply could not resist him. And it had absolutely nothing to do with the fact that he looked every inch the executive in his superb dinner jacket. No. This was the man under the suit.

Oops. She had a vision of Heath minus his clothes. Big oops.

Kate willed down the intense blush she could feel on her cheeks as she felt Heath clasp hold of her fingers and draw her to him.

'Thank you, sir. How kind of you to think of us poor wallflowers. All alone and overlooked.'

'Um. Right. You have never been a wallflower in your life. You look amazing. That dress…' He exaggerated a shiver then hissed, 'Amazing,' bringing Kate's blush even hotter. And with one swift tug on her hands she was in his arms. One hand slid strategically onto her waist, the other clasped firmly around her palm. And her body…her body pressed tightly against his chest.

'Exactly what kind of dance is this?' she dared to ask, her nose about two inches away from Heath's shirt. He smelt of expensive cologne and man sweat combined with something musky, spicy and arousing. Something which was uniquely Heath. A flash of something horribly close to desire ran through her body, startling her with its intensity.

Her back straightened and her head lifted away as she tried to regain her self-control, only to become suddenly aware that the string quartet had a neat collection of waltzes.

Instantly Heath drew her even closer, so that his hips moved against hers, swaying from side to side. Taking her with him. She had no choice but to follow his actions, his broad chest and strong legs pressed so close to the thin fabric of her silk dress that she felt glued to him along the whole length of his body.

'Time to channel your inner ballroom dancing lessons,' he replied, his voice close to her ear and muffled by her hair. And rough, urgent. She was clearly not the only one who was starting to become rather warm. 'Lots of shuffling and gliding and sliding together. Leaning backwards, skipping and dipping come later…although…'

He stopped talking and Kate took a deep breath and asked, 'Although?'

His hand moved sinuously up her back as the pace increased and his legs started moving faster. 'Perhaps not in that dress. It is—' and he sighed, the implications only too obvious as his fingers splayed on the bare skin of her back and his grip tightened '—far, far too tempting.' And without warning he leant forward from the waist, so that she moved backwards chest to chest, both of his hands taking her weight with effortless ease and agility. Except that she had been so captivated by his words that she had not seen the move coming and her arms clenched hard around his neck to stop herself from falling backwards and she cried out in alarm.

With a gentle movement and a firm hand on her back,

Heath slowly brought her back to a standing position, his hands drawing her closer and holding her against him as she dragged in ragged breaths of air in a feeble attempt to calm her heart rate.

'Sorry,' she eventually managed to squeak out, feeling like a complete idiot. She knew that Heath would never let her fall. She had overreacted, her body once more letting her down.

Heath paused and released her long enough so that they could look into each other's eyes as his fingers spread wide so that they could caress her skin in delicious soft circles.

His forehead pressed against hers so that his voice reverberated through her skull. Hot, concerned, tender and understanding.

'You have to trust me and let me lead, Kate. Just this once, let someone else take control. Can you try?'

Kate closed her eyes and tried to calm her heartbeat and failed. Her mind was spinning as his words hit home, while all the while Heath's body was pressed close to her, filling her senses with his masculine scent and the sheer physicality of him.

She knew that he was talking about more than placing her faith in a dance partner. And part of her shrank back from the edge. She had never truly allowed anyone to lead her. Not deep down. In fact the more she thought about it, the more she knew that she had always danced to her own beat.

His breath was hot on her face as he patiently waited for the answer which would decide where they went from here. And not just for the evening. He was asking her to trust him with nothing less than her heart. Was he also asking her to trust him with her future and her dreams?

'I...don't know,' she whispered, her heart thumping so

hard that she was sure that he must be able to hear it, but not daring to open her eyes. It would be too much.

'Then perhaps I can persuade you?'

Gentle pressure lifted her chin and, although her eyes were still clamped tight shut, she felt every tiny movement of his body as his nose pressed against her cheek, his breath hot and fast in time with the heart beating against her dress.

A soft mouth nuzzled against her upper lip and she sighed in pleasure as one of his hands slid back to caress the base of her skull, holding her firm against him. The fine hairs on his chin and neck rasped against her skin as he pressed gentle kisses down her temple to the hollow below her ear. Each kiss drove her wild with the delicious languorous sensation of skin on skin.

He was totally intoxicating.

The tenderness and exquisite delicacy of each kiss was more than she could have imagined possible from Heath. More caring. More loving… Loving. Yes. They were the kisses of a lover. *Her* lover. And it felt so very right.

Which was why she did something she had believed until a few short days ago would never happen again. She brought her arms even tighter around Heath's neck and notched her head up towards him. And with eyes still closed.

Kate kissed him on the mouth.

Only this was not the kiss of a teenage girl on her doorstep. This was the kiss of a woman who recognised a kindred spirit and wanted, just this once, to let him know how she felt before she lost him for ever.

His hands stilled for a moment and she paused to suck in a terrified breath, trembling that she had made the most almighty mistake.

This would change everything. What if she'd totally

misunderstood what he had told her? And he only wanted to lead? Not share.

She felt him shift beneath her and, daring to open her eyes, she stared into a smile as wide as it was welcome, but then his mouth pressed hotter and deeper onto hers, blowing away any hint of doubt that he wanted her just as much as she needed him with the depth of his passion and delight.

A shuddering sigh of relief ran through her and she grinned back in return and buried her face deep into the corner of his neck. His hands ran up and down her back, thrilling her with the heat of their touch as his lips kissed her brow and her hair.

Kisses so natural and tender it felt as though she had been waiting for them all of her life.

Every sensation seemed heightened. The warmth of the fading sun on her arms, the touch of his fingertips on her skin, the softness of his shirt under her cheek and the fast beat of the heart below the fine fabric.

It was Heath who broke the silence. 'Now will you trust me?' He was trying to keep his voice light and playful but she knew him too well now, and revelled in the fact that she was the source of his hoarse, low whisper, intense with something more fundamental and earthy.

The fingers of one of his hands were playing with her hair, but she could feel his heartbeat slow just a little when she chuckled into his shirt. 'Well, I just might. We are talking about dancing. Aren't we?'

His warm laughter filled her heart to bursting. 'Absolutely.' He brushed his lips against the tip of her nose. 'Time to join the others, I think, before we're missed.'

'Missed?' Kate repeated and looked over Heath's shoulder just in time to see Crystal's shocked face staring out from the other side of the patio, open-mouthed. 'Somehow I don't think that they have missed a thing.'

* * *

Two hours later, Kate had come to the conclusion that this was one of the best parties that she had been to. *Ever.*

The delicious meal, wine and fantastic birthday cake were followed by more champagne, excellent speeches and thanks from Charles and Alice. Kate and Heath were required to stand up and give short bows for all their work on the decoration. In general, everybody had a fantastic time. Even the snooty cousins behaved themselves. Crystal Jardine actually grinned and meant it and no one started a food fight.

Just as Charles announced that coffee and chocolates would be served on the terrace, Alice tugged at his sleeve and pointed to the presents, which had been stacked on the table behind a chair.

Kate smiled warmly at Heath and nudged his arm as she nodded towards Alice.

But then her smile faded. Because when the gifts were moved, her gift bag was now on the top of the pile and the first present which Alice was going to open.

Kate sat back in her chair and took very tight hold of the napkin on her lap. She scarcely dared to watch as Alice stood up, presented the bag to the whole party and then carefully, slowly, drew out the box, smiling as she went, and then opened the lid and lifted out the book which Kate had first seen only a few hours earlier.

Kate's heart leapt into her throat.

This was it. Triumph or disaster.

Alice looked at the book cover with total delight and astonishment and clearly didn't know what to expect, but then she opened the cover; her right hand went to her throat as tears streamed down her cheeks.

Charles looked up in alarm, then Alice smiled and laughed away his concern and, smiling directly at Heath with a quivering voice, she read the inscription at the front of the book to the whole party. *'"To the future Mrs Sheridan. Your love is a beacon in our darkness. Welcome to the family. Heath."'*

'Oh, Heath,' Alice cried out and, to Kate's astonishment, she put down the book and ran around the table and, to Heath's horror, she threw her arms around him and hugged him and kissed his cheek in a display of open love and affection.

In front of all of the Sheridan and Jardine relatives and friends, who gave a rousing cheer.

Heath was mortified. Kate could see that, and she instantly rushed around and hugged Alice to take the attention away from Heath.

Charles strolled up behind her and man-slapped Heath hard on the back before gesturing for the rest of the party to join them on the terrace for coffee.

It took a moment for Kate to disengage herself from Alice and her relatives, who were gathered around Heath's gift, turning each page in obvious delight.

With total relief, Kate skipped back up to her bedroom to collect her wrap before venturing out into the cool evening air. She couldn't be happier.

She was standing outside her room and was just reaching out to turn the door handle, when Heath stepped out behind her, grabbed her arm and pulled her into his bedroom.

CHAPTER TEN

'Why?' HE ASKED in a voice that was burning with fire to match the fierce intensity in his eyes.

He turned away from her and started pacing, two steps back and forward, then three on the fine carpet. His right hand was pressed hard against the back of his neck as though he was holding it in place and fighting to gain control.

'Tell me why you thought that you had the right to change my gift and make me look like a pathetic fool. Tell me, Kate. Because I really want to know why you decided to humiliate me and I want to know right now.'

Kate lifted her chin and tried to control her breathing. She had never seen anyone with so much suppressed anguish in his face as the man she was looking at right now. She wasn't frightened for herself. But she was for him.

She waited for a second until she could speak clearly, but her words still emerged shaking and trembling in the intensity of his stare. He was glaring at her, his hands clutching onto the back of the solid chair in front of him.

'You knew that Alice would treasure those paintings for ever,' she replied. 'But you forgot something important. Tomorrow is Alice's *wedding day*—the one day in her life when she wants to be beautiful and loved and treasured and admired. But those paintings aren't about Alice, they are all about her lovely friend, Lee Sheridan, your mum. The woman her fiancé loved. And I couldn't let you ruin her happiness by bringing the past crashing into her future. That's not fair, Heath.'

Heath's face twisted as her words hit home.

'Fair? Did she tell you? Did Alice actually tell you how she betrayed her friend with my father when the woman she was supposed to care about was dying in a hospice bed?'

He took a step closer until his nose was only inches from hers, and she could feel the heat of his breath on her cheeks. He was trembling with emotion, so that when he spoke his words exploded into her face. 'Did she tell you that she was sleeping with my father while my mother was dying, Kate? Did she?'

She couldn't speak. It was impossible. Any sort of answer would only make him more angry and upset.

'Oh. For once you don't have anything to say.' He nodded. 'Apparently my future stepmother thinks it is acceptable to share my family's personal secrets and sordid past with strangers.'

Stranger? That wasn't right.

'I'm not a stranger any longer, Heath. I'm—' she interjected, but was cut off instantly with a single finger pressed against her lips.

'No. You *are* a stranger. You don't know how hard this is for me. I trusted you. I told you how important it was that my mother's memory was not forgotten. Alice knew her. Can you understand that? She went to art college with my mother and was as close to her as you are to Amber and Saskia. Would you cheat on either of those girls with her husband? No, I didn't think so. And tomorrow afternoon I have to stand next to my father while he marries the woman who is taking over from my mother in his life. That is hard. I'm used to hard; I'll do it. I will survive, but if I have any chance to rebuild a relationship with Alice I have to do it at my own pace.'

His hands thumped again and again onto the back of the chair until she was sure that they must be bruised. She dared to reach out and try to take one of them and calm him and comfort him, but he instantly swiped it away dismissively.

'Did you really think that I would give them to Alice out of bitterness or as a stunt to ruin her wedding day with some constant reminder of what happened when my mother was dying? I hope that I am better than that. No. That album is very rare and special and Alice is one of the few people who would truly appreciate my mother's work. I wanted her to have them. I want my father to have a chance of happiness, but not by playing games where each of us is scoring points from the other.'

'I only wanted to help,' Kate whispered, her voice trembling.

'There is a fine line between helping a friend and interfering in other people's lives, and you crossed it tonight,' he hissed through clenched teeth. 'You think that you know all my family after meeting them for a few hours? You haven't the faintest idea.'

'Then tell me. Tell me why you feel so strongly about one inscription on a book?'

'I don't like surprises and I particularly don't like being ambushed. I never have. And it isn't the first time.'

He collapsed down on the bed with his back against the headboard and dropped his head back and blinked up at the ceiling. 'You want to know about the Sheridan family?' he said in a low voice as though he was trying to control his emotions and failing. 'Okay, I'll tell you about the high-and-mighty Sheridans.'

He looked across at her, his chest lifting and falling with

every word. 'Do you remember Amber's mother? Julia Swan?'

Kate sighed out loud and sat down on the bottom corner of the bed. 'Remember? I was summoned to take tea at Saskia's place last month. She still hasn't forgiven Amber for getting engaged to Sam Richards instead of the Crown Prince of some large European country, hell, any country.'

Heath nodded. 'Well, then you will understand how I felt when my dad informed me out of the blue that he was marrying Julia not twelve months after my mother died from cancer. I came home from university to find the staff taking down my mother's photographs and clearing the house of every sign that she had ever lived there so that Julia and Amber could move in.'

Heath inhaled deeply and rolled his shoulders back. 'I was very angry and extremely disappointed with him for doing that.' He meshed his hands around the back of his head, his gaze locked onto the ornate plaster work ceiling rose. 'As far as I was concerned he had betrayed my mother and I told him that very clearly before walking out and going to stay with my grandparents. I didn't go to the wedding. He couldn't make me and I had absolutely no intention of giving Julia Swan the time of day. And the marriage was even more of a disaster than I could have predicted which, believe me, was quite an achievement.'

'I don't understand,' Kate replied in a small low voice. 'Amber told me that you were a terrific stepbrother.'

He snorted and replied with a small shoulder shrug, 'Amber was a victim just as much as I was. We got to know each other when Julia and my father went on a very long European honeymoon, leaving Amber in a strange house with only a nanny and the staff to keep her company. I went back to pick up some things and found her crying in the music room. I never blamed Amber for her mother's faults. When Julia got bored with Boston and took off for a new lover in London I kept in touch. I think my dad had even less of a clue what to do with a daughter than he had with a son.'

'But your dad has just asked you to be his best man. What has changed?'

Heath hesitated and his gaze locked onto a silk dressing gown that had been left on the bed cover, which he casually picked up and set down again.

'To the rest of the world, my father is a brilliantly successful businessman who inherited one of the oldest and most respected publishing houses on the East Coast of America. Quiet. Intellectual. The kind of man who doesn't make a fuss and likes to keep a low profile, despite all of that power and wealth that Sheridan Press provided.'

She nodded. 'Business profile. Done. Now answer my question.'

'Are you always this bossy?'

'No. Only with you.' She narrowed her eyes and made a point of glancing at a very old wristwatch. 'What changed?'

'I remember the father I used to know as a boy.' Heath took a breath and this time he slid forward on the silk cover, reached out and picked up Kate's hand and turned it over. She tried to snatch it back but he examined each finger as he talked, as though it was the most wonderful thing that he had ever seen.

'My summer holidays were filled with laughter, fun, football games, tennis and swimming. We had the most fantastic Christmas parties where my mother would decorate the entire dining room of our Boston house with fabrics and paint and dad would light a huge fire, make hot chocolate and read stories by candlelight. My birthday parties came with real ponies and trips to the circus.'

'Has Disney bought the film rights for this?'

'Just be patient. I haven't finished yet. But yes, it was a magical childhood that I thought would never end. And, like a fool, I took it all for granted.'

Heath slowly, slowly curled Kate's fingers back around his and held them firm. 'And then my mother was taken ill and it only took six weeks for that world to implode. Six weeks to make the first sixteen years of my life seem like a happy dream where I had two parents who loved me and a happy home I could always come back to.'

He shook his head and blinked. 'I don't know about your parents, but to me they were the one solid rock in my world that made me believe that I could be and do whatever I wanted, safe in the knowledge that they would always be there for me and for one another.'

A small ironic laugh escaped his lips. 'Wrong. Wrong. Wrong.'

He sucked in a breath and his gaze shifted to Kate's eyes.

Those wonderful brown eyes were so full of emotion and pain that she instantly felt guilty.

He was right. She had no right to barge in and try and take control—not when Heath was still suffering so badly. She didn't know the first thing about his family.

Only hers.

What a fool she had been.

As though trying to rebuild Heath's relationship with his father would bring her family back together again somehow. Stupid!

'How did you get past that?' Kate asked.

'We didn't,' Heath replied in a sad but matter-of-fact voice. 'It took me months—no, years, to rebuild my life after my mother's death. But my father was not part of that life. Not any more. Not after his betrayal. Oh, he tried. Many times. But, as far as I was concerned, I had to mourn the loss of two parents, even though only one had actually died.'

A shiver ran across his back and Heath shuddered. 'But he did teach me a lesson. Relying on people for your happiness is doomed to failure. People let you down. People leave and your world collapses. People take away any hope of control you ever had over your life. And I would be a fool to open up my heart and let that happen again. My relationship with my dad has never been the same since.'

'Until now,' she interrupted.

With a gentle smile he stroked the back of her hand with his thumb. 'Three months ago he flew down to New York out of the blue and asked me to come back to Boston to inject some new life into Sheridan Press. I was totally surprised, but he had made the first move. It hasn't been easy to work in the same office but over the weeks we made some progress until he found the right moment to tell me that he was getting married to Alice and to ask me to be his best man.'

'He wants your forgiveness,' Kate murmured as her gaze flicked across his face.

Heath opened his mouth to answer, closed it again and then gave a long sigh. 'He wants me to drag Sheridan Press into profitability, but yes, it did give me one final chance to rebuild some sort of relationship with the only real family I still had left, my father, before it is too late for either of us. And now I don't know where we are.'

He closed his eyes and curved his hands into fists. 'You're impulsive and irresponsible. Exasperating. Never thinking about the effects of your actions. In your world it is okay to ambush other people and expose their feelings.'

'Wrong,' she whispered. 'I know exactly what I've done. I saved you from making the biggest mistake of your life, Heath Sheridan.'

He looked at her for a second in silence, his gaze darting across her face, but, just as she thought she had his acceptance, Heath got to his feet and started to walk away from her.

She snatched at the sleeve of his jacket and held it firm.

'Alice loves your father and he loves her. But did you know that she was the one who suggested that you be the best man and then agreed to let you help organise the wedding? She did that because you are more important to both of them than you could possibly imagine. Do you understand what I'm saying? She was determined to find some way of bringing you closer to your father instead of driving you further away. And she couldn't bear that.'

'Why didn't you talk to me first?' he asked in a low voice, his gaze locked onto the surface of the table. 'It took me a long time to decide on that wedding gift and I'm fighting to stay positive—and so far all that you've done is take over and snatch any chance of control out of my hands and throw it to the winds.'

Those last few words echoed around the room, penetrated her heart and pierced her soul. He meant them.

'Probably. But you know us creative types, as you call them,' she choked, trying not to cry. 'Total romantic. For some reason I want people who love each other to be together. Call me crazy, but there you are. And, by the way, I know that you love your father. And don't turn away from me like that. You love him and you wanted him to be with you when your mother died. I understand. Truly, I do. But that was then. They have been apart long enough. It's time for you all to go home.'

She reached out towards him and tried to touch his face and comfort him, but the cold shutters had come down and the happy man she'd spent a wonderful afternoon with went back behind the barriers.

'This wasn't a good idea, Heath. I'm going back to London tonight. But know this. I am going to come back here tomorrow to help Alice and Charles celebrate their love, whether you want me to be here or not.'

'What?' He laughed. 'You're leaving?'

'I need to get back to my work and my life without having to worry about upsetting any more of your carefully controlled plans.'

'Your life? And what kind of life are you going back to, Kate? Tell me that—what do you have waiting for you back in London? You're going back to that museum you call a home. Is that it?'

She whirled around and gasped, 'What did you just say?'

'Your house is not a home. It is a museum to a lost world and the people you loved and lost. Maybe it's time to step out of the museum and start living in the real world.'

'Look who's talking.' She swung her arms around. 'This is one of the most beautiful houses that I have stayed in, with a stunning library. But every book is locked away out of touch behind a glass case. Well, I have news for you—books need to breathe, just like humans. In fact, why don't you start here and now? It will keep you occupied until the wedding.'

He tugged both of her hands close to his chest, so tightly that it would be impossible for her to escape.

'I do have a life. A life of my own,' she gasped. 'A life where I decide what to do.'

'Do you? Do you really?' He shook his head slowly from side to side. 'Not from what I saw.'

Kate stopped struggling and tried to calm her breathing. 'Then you don't know me at all, do you?'

She took a breath. 'Charles and Alice love one another and have finally found the courage to declare their love out loud and to hell with the rest of the world, and that includes you. And, unless you want to lose them for ever, I suggest you change your attitude. And fast. Because you need them a lot more than they need you. Talk to them, Heath. Even if you are the one who has to make the first move—you have to talk to them and become the man I fell in love with.'

The words were out of her mouth before she could snatch them back.

Stupid!

She was too upset to control her emotions. And now she had told him the one thing she knew that would drive him away. She'd told him that she loved him.

But, instead of pushing her away, Heath whirled around and in one smooth movement he pressed the palm of his left hand flat against the door frame so that the cuff of his fine dinner jacket was flush against her upper arm. Kate was aware that his right arm was high above her head, bracing his whole body on the two hands. Trapping her inside the circle of his arms and his body.

In her heels and his flat shiny black dress shoes, her eyes were on the same level at his nose.

It would be easy to slip under the wide arch of his arm and escape into the sanctuary of her bedroom, but she couldn't. She wouldn't.

His gaze locked onto her eyes, shocking in their intensity. Mesmerising and totally, totally captivating so that it was impossible for her to look away.

And what she saw in those eyes took her breath away.

This was the man she had fallen in love with. This was the man who she had glimpsed that one time before. A man burning with passion and love and power.

This was not the workaholic, cool and introspective man the rest of the world saw.

This was the real man. The real Heath. And she revelled

in it. Her heart soared as she looked into those dark brown eyes. Words would not be able to describe how she felt.

She thought that the pressures and struggles of the world had crushed that spark out of Heath and that he had lost that inner spark of true passion.

That long, hard body that was leaning closer and closer until she could feel the heat of his hot, hard, fast breath on her cheeks. He was not touching her. Anywhere. And yet it felt as though every inch of skin on her entire body was burning up in the fire of the intensity of that gaze.

Her skin screamed at her to move forward just one more inch so that her leg could slide alongside his trouser.

He was the golden apple hanging on the tree of pleasure and heady delight. She knew that just one small bite would destroy her—no, destroy them both for ever.

Temptation had never looked so good.

She had never been the kind of girl who could resist the last doughnut on the plate, or the last inch of double-chocolate ice cream calling out to her from the bottom of the carton.

But they were nothing compared to the temptation that was Heath Sheridan at that moment.

He was wounded, hurt, exposed and raw, and in that moment he was truly himself.

She had never wanted anything so badly in her life—not the business, not even her parents' acceptance—came close to the fire that was scorching her whole body and setting it alight.

The hot July sunshine might burn her pale skin and freckled nose, but this fire came from deep inside her, in that locked room where she kept her secrets and her desire and passion.

And then cold reality hit home.

The only reason she was here was to act as a stand-in for the girl who had dumped him.

A temporary replacement. That was all she could ever be to Heath.

Instinctively she stepped backwards to increase the space between them, until her bottom pressed against the hard wooden door. But if anything that extra space made it worse, because now she could see the veins in his neck pulse faster as his breathing speeded.

Kate pressed her head back and bent her knee so that the heel of her sandal was braced against the door. Without shifting his gaze, Heath slid his right leg closer so that the fine fabric of his suit trouser pressed against her thigh.

The sensation of texture on texture was so heavenly that a small half sigh escaped her lips and her eyelids fluttered in a ridiculously girlie act she would never admit to. A tender smile reached his eyes and his gaze released just long enough to shamelessly scan her face and neck and give a lightning-fast glance down her cleavage.

If he was waiting for her to slap him with her clutch bag he was going to be disappointed.

She wanted to hold that face in her hands and tell him how much she had missed him over all of these long years that they had been apart, and how he had filled the emptiness of her long lonely nights.

Who was she kidding? She wanted to drag this sexy, hot, rich, heavy-breathing man she loved by his lapels into her bedroom and find out what his skin tasted like. Her imagination filled in the gaps. His stubble on the sensitive skin on the inside of her thigh. Her throat. What it would feel like to wake up with him in the morning, his body next to hers.

She wanted to know what heaven felt like. Even if it was for just one night.

She slowly raised her lace-gloved right hand and ran a

fingertip down his cheek. He swallowed and sighed low and deep, his eyelids flashing closed for just a second.

And in that instant she knew that he wanted her. Almost as much as she wanted him.

Thrilling excitement surged through her. This changed everything.

Torment raged inside her and her brain whirled faster and faster.

Sleeping with Heath would destroy both of them. He might want her now. But in the morning? They didn't have a future together. They never could. They lived in different worlds.

She lowered her hand onto the front of his pristine white shirt and instantly felt a connection to the warm beating heart of the man she loved. She had to be the strong one. Even if it did break her heart all over again.

Tears pricked the corners of her eyes and she opened her mouth to speak but words were impossible. His brows came together as a tear rolled down her cheek.

Kate dragged her hand from his chest, lingering as long as she possibly could, lifted her gloved fingertips to her lips, kissed her fingers then pressed them against Heath's lips. And held them there.

A look of surprise, alarm, delight and confusion swept across his face and his eyes were bright.

Her shoulders slumped in distress. But she did what she had to do.

Kate released her hand from his warm soft lips, shook her head very slowly and deliberately from side to side. And then she pushed him away from her.

As she struggled and failed to stop the silent tears and gentle sobbing intake of breath, Heath leant back and lifted one hand from the door so that he could wipe a tear from her cheek with his forefinger.

The sensation was so delicious that she gave a half sob and rubbed her cheek against his hand.

He looked bewildered and through her blurry vision she saw the passion and fire fade in his eyes. And she already missed it so much that she could hardly speak.

Heath instantly released his hands from the door and almost staggered back upright.

They had not spoken one word in the last ten minutes. And yet she felt as though she had just had one of the most intense conversations of her life. Only with Heath. It had always, only been Heath.

She was the one who turned away, opened the door and stepped outside into the corridor and her own bedroom, bracing the door behind her, knowing that beyond the turmoil and chaos which she had created in his room was a man who wanted her. Body and soul.

Which probably made her the biggest fool on the planet.

CHAPTER ELEVEN

KATE BIT DOWN so hard on her lower lip as she pushed her front door key into the lock that she could already taste the metallic tang of blood as she pushed open the door and half collapsed over the threshold.

It took all of what little strength she had left to push the door tight shut behind her and draw the bolts across. Only then did she let her legs collapse slowly under her as she slid down the door and sat down in a heap among the letters and junk mail on the carpet.

She was safe now.

Safe back in her own home.

Safe behind locked doors and windows.

Safe.

Her head fell back against the solid wooden panels and she closed her eyes and tried to breathe again. But it was no good. All she got was the complex aroma of leather and glue and old machine oil that filled the air in the enclosed space between the hallway and the parlour.

The day had become hotter and hotter and the air inside the hallway was heated by the south-facing window above her head. There was no movement of fresh air in the tightly locked house and suddenly she felt oppressed by the stifling heat.

Her eyes flickered open.

She should wash and get changed and have a cool drink. Then everything would be fine and back to normal again.

Wouldn't it?

Kate looked around the hall. There were cobwebs under the console table where the telephone and key tray sat and the carpet she was sitting on was pale with a thick layer of dust and fraying at the edges where they were not hidden under the deep wooden skirting boards. The paint was peeling off the woodwork and the lovely Edwardian light fitting hanging from the ceiling was thick with dust and dead flies.

She blinked and peered down the hall towards the kitchen and the mismatched china and faded painted cabinets.

Tears pricked the corners of her eyes.

Whenever Amber or Saskia of any of her fashionista pals came around she would laugh off the state of the house by calling it 'shabby chic'. But, seeing it now, from floor height, it wasn't chic. It was just shabby. Shabby and worn and tired and dusty. Just as her grandfather had left it on the day he'd died.

Was that it? Was that why she hadn't changed anything in five years? Because she wanted to hold on to anything connected to the man who had loved her so unconditionally?

The tears trickled down her cheeks.

This was how Heath had seen it.

A museum, that was what Heath had called it. And he was right.

It *was* a museum and she had made herself into the curator. As if freezing the house the way her grandfather had left it would somehow bring back the love and laughter and positive encouragement that he had taken with him when he'd died.

She was a fool. The only thing her grandparents ever wanted was for her to be happy, and she had let them down.

Because she wasn't happy.

She was so miserable she could barely breathe.

Her sobs turned into a torrent of self-pity, and she scrabbled about in her bag until she found a tissue.

And then another. Then another, until her sobbing faded away and she sucked in breath after breath of hot dusty air.

She loved Heath. And she couldn't have him.

Their worlds were planets apart and staying with Heath would mean giving up her creativity and conforming to what went for the standards of life in his world. Become acceptable. And it would destroy her. Destroy their chance of happiness. Destroy her dreams.

And she couldn't do it.

She couldn't live like that, even if it meant giving up the man she loved.

He had given her so much. She would never forget him.

Whatever happened, going forward there was only one pledge that she had made on the slow, horrible drive from the Manor at dawn that morning after a sleepless night knowing that the man she loved was only a few steps away across the corridor.

She was going to change. She was going to make her terrible sacrifice worth the pain. She was going to claim her passion—her work—and make it shine by working harder and smarter than ever before.

And that started right here. And right now.

Kate gritted her teeth and pushed hard enough on the rough rug to get back onto her feet. In a second her bag was stowed under the table and she was striding forward through the crates of goodness knew what over to the window above her grandmother's sewing machine.

She didn't need a warehouse she couldn't afford when

she had a perfectly good work space right in her own home. *If she could find the courage to clear the space and make it her own.*

Her hand quivered for a fraction of a second but Kate pressed her lips tight together and grabbed hold of the centre edge of the heavy curtain and pulled it sharply across with all of her strength.

She hadn't expected the curtain rail to fall down with a clatter, knocking most of the sewing kit all over the cluttered floor and bringing down what was left of the now ripped curtain with it.

Bright white sunlight blinded Kate with its brilliance. And for the first time in so many years she looked out through the grimy windows at the patio garden, as her grandmother had done. But this time it was different. Because the cloud of dust that had been trapped on the curtain started to settle in the still air and, as Kate coughed and flapped it away, she half turned and saw the truth in the clutter. This was not the proud, happy place it had once been. How could it be?

They were gone.

And she was here.

A vision flickered through her mind of what she could do with the long wide space and she caught hold of it and held it firm before it floated away like the dust.

Kate pushed hard on the window latch. It fought her for a few seconds but gave way with a jolt and she opened it wide. Fresh air and birdsong replaced the dark gloom and she collapsed down on the work chair with a slump.

It took a couple of deep breaths to take in what she was looking at. Shelves and shelves of boxes and bags of dirt-faded fabric and tired, useless trimmings and hand models mocked her great plan.

Reaching into her pocket, Kate flicked open her cellphone. It was answered in three rings. 'Hi, Saskia. It's me. Any chance you could pop around? It looks like I have some gloves to sort out.'

Heath sat behind the library table and picked up the best man's speech he was supposed to be memorising. He stared at the first card, tapping his pen on the desk, but he couldn't concentrate.

Rubbing his eyes, he blinked and shook his head, trying to clear away the fog that came with a sleepless night.

This was it. His father's wedding day. A happy occasion with plenty to celebrate.

And he had never felt so lonely or miserable in his life.

Perhaps that was why he had worked so feverishly most of the night to block out any thoughts except the business. Trying every trick he knew to hold on to control with his fingertips.

But it was useless.

Because all he could think about was Kate.

Heath lifted his head and stared out of the window at the sun-kissed gardens, which were bright with colour and life from the wedding party guests who wandered amongst the flower beds and knot garden after their early morning coffee. The party had gone late into the night but a few early risers were already enjoying the day.

Their happy laughter echoed up to his first-floor window and he smiled back, envious of their easy, relaxed manner. He glanced down at the cards and tried to make some sense of the words he had written weeks earlier in his Boston apartment.

Strange how the lists and charts he had prepared only a week ago seemed petty and ridiculous at that moment.

He turned to the next card, and instantly did a retake.

Because, handwritten in the purple ink that Kate liked

to use, was a smiley face and a few lines of a good joke which was so perfect for the audience, and yet he would never have thought of it. He flicked through the cards and, time and time again, she had marked in some witty remark or funny comment which he already knew would make his father smile and Alice laugh out loud.

This was the girl he had accused of being a stranger. And yet she understood his father and Alice better after two days than he did. How did that happen?

Was it Kate? Or was she right? He was trapped in the past even more than she was.

It was almost as if Kate was standing here, teasing him, making him step outside the carefully drawn lines that he had drawn for himself.

They might have started in very different places but in the end they were so similar. Both longing for reconnection with people they had loved and lost, and both struggling to find a way forward and make a life for themselves.

Perhaps that was why Kate understood exactly what he was going through?

He had never felt this connection with any girl before. Amber had been too young to really understand how he was feeling when her mother had moved into his home. And Olivia?

He had never once talked to Olivia about his past, the way he had talked to Kate last night after the dinner party.

He had been with Olivia for over six months and yet he had never told her the truth about what had happened between his father and Alice.

Why was that?

Heath raised his head at the sound of a familiar voice and watched in silence as Charles and Alice walked across the garden. His father popped a flower he had just plucked from a shrub behind Alice's ear and then pretended to be taking her photo with a four-finger camera until she waved him away. But she kept the flower.

His father, the romantic. Well, that was a revelation.

Like so much of this past week.

He would never have believed it possible that a few days in the company of Kate Lovat would make him rethink everything he'd used to hold sacred.

From the second she'd walked into the London office carrying her box with a bridesmaid's dress in it, with her cute suit and fire-engine-red toenails, his life had been one roller coaster of shocks and delights, one after the other. With him hanging on for dear life.

Last night they had crashed into the barriers.

Kate Lovat had robbed him of a tranquillity and inner calm that perhaps had never been there in the first place, but it certainly wasn't there now.

She had already left when he'd eventually headed down for breakfast. There had been a note for Alice, asking his father not to report that his car had been stolen because she would be coming back for their wedding.

No note for him. *Not that he blamed her.*

When she'd told him that she had fallen in love with him, he had not even tried to tell her how much he had come to care about her. But she knew that he needed her, but wasn't ready to say the words which would open up his heart for pain.

So much for his rule of not becoming emotionally dependent on any one woman!

In the course of one week his comfortable life had been turned over and his outer shell of cool disdain swept away and destroyed for good.

She was the most annoying and frustrating and irresponsible and enchanting woman that he had ever met.

He was cool and she was as fiery and temperamental as the weather.

Which was probably why he adored her.

It had not taken him long during the night to realise that he had been kidding himself. He *had* given Alice those paintings to show her that he was prepared to accept her.

Just so that he could stay in control of his life, and keep the people he loved close by and safe and protected. People like his father and Kate.

His fingers froze.

Love? Was that what he was feeling?

The breath caught in the back of his throat and he had to cough out loud as the sudden realisation of what he had done hit him hard.

He was in love with Kate Lovat.

Just when he'd thought that his life couldn't be more exciting and terrifying and amazing. And he had never even told her how much he truly cared about her and how very special and remarkable she was.

Kate was his Alice.

And God, he loved her for that.

And he had just let her go. No—not let her go. He had driven her away.

So what did he do now?

If only there was someone he could talk to about the whole mess. Amber was Kate's friend and he had no other close friends.

But he did have his family.

Inhaling a deep breath, he picked up his cellphone and dialled.

Down below in the garden, he watched his father flick open his cellphone as he watched Alice chat with some of the guests.

'Dad? Spare a minute?'

'Heath? Sure. What is it?'

'Something I should have said a long time ago. When Mum died we should have talked it through together like we used to. But instead I pushed you away. I couldn't deal with the pain so we left everything unspoken.'

'I know. It is one of the things I have always regretted.'

'You shouldn't,' Heath replied. 'I'm beginning to understand how love can creep up and surprise you out of the blue. Alice is the only woman who can make you happy and you have waited long enough to be with the one you love. Go for it.'

Charles looked up at the library window and smiled. 'Heath, that sounded positively romantic. What has gotten into you? Or should I say, *who* has gotten into you?'

'Sorry, Dad. Can't talk now. I have to go and persuade Kate Lovat to give me a second chance. You're in charge. But we'll be back in time for the wedding.'

'Not so fast, son. This calls for team work. We'll be right up.'

CHAPTER TWELVE

FOR THE FIRST time in years, Kate threw caution to the wind and turned the water heater to maximum, never mind the cost, and filled her bathtub full of steaming hot water and the scented bubbles that Amber had given her for Christmas.

It was divine and just what she needed to help calm her aching muscles, fevered brain and painful wounded heart.

Saskia had been amazing and, with the help of Charles Sheridan's huge car, every box of gloves in the workshop and all of the plastic crates of materials and tools had been moved out, loaded up and transported over to Saskia's cavernous cellar storeroom. It had been dirty work and, by the end of it, both of them were filthy, exhausted and in serious need of a change of clothes and tea.

Of course Saskia had invited her to stay at her place and be cosseted and cared for and the offer had been so tempting that it shocked Kate with how needy and fragile and vulnerable she had become.

But it was no good, she had explained. She *had* to do this on her own. She had to change her life and make her fashion designs the most important thing in her life.

She loved making gloves. That would never go away. But Heath Sheridan had shown her just how many compromises she had made in trying to hold on to the past. And she couldn't live like that any longer.

It was time to take the risk and make her dream come true or live the rest of her life with regret about what could have been.

The problem was, as she smoothed the bubbles over her now very wrinkly skin, her kind treacherous heart was reliving over and over again those moments she had shared with Heath.

Her skin ached to feel his touch.

Her heart ached with his loss.

Compared to that, her aching muscles were nothing.

An hour later she struggled out of the bath, literally glowing with hot water and bubbles and threw on the first clothing she found in the top drawer, little caring who saw her in her scraggy old shorts and tiny string top.

Kate strolled downstairs, glancing only briefly into what had been her parlour and was now a large, mostly empty space which was aching to be cleaned and reclaimed. There was still a huge amount of work to do, but a smile creased her face as she walked out through her kitchen door onto the patio garden.

Totally drained, she slumped down on the old silver-grey wooden bench with her hands wrapped around a glass of cool water out of the tap, because there was nothing else in the fridge except some date-expired orange juice, and pushed her legs out in front of her to cool off in the shade, a pile of mail and paperwork by her side.

This was her space now. This patio was full of weeds, the once pristine grass and flower beds a jungle of overgrown plants and straggly neglected roses and shrubs. But it was hers. And she was reclaiming this garden, just as she was reclaiming her house and her dream.

All they needed was someone to love them.

This was it. This was her life.

She loved this place so much and she had let it go to ruin.

Frightened to take on such an enormous task.

Frightened to do it alone.

Frightened to do the work and fail.

Kidding herself that she wanted to live this way and would get around to it when she found the time and energy.

Balderdash and piffle.

Strange how this garden was so much like her life. She had deliberately chosen to leave the garden pretty much as her grandparents had loved it.

Just like the workshop.

What had Heath said? That she was going back to a museum?

Full marks to the man in the suit.

Zero marks to the woman who had created the museum in the first place out of a world that had once been so full of life and laughter and happiness. As if keeping the physical things unchanged would bring back the people who had loved her and made her feel special and wanted.

So much for the great, brave Kate Lovat.

Katherine Lovat wasn't brave at all. She was just very good at being in denial.

Shame on her. Shame on her cowardice.

She didn't deserve Heath.

But she was going to.

Kate blinked her eyes and sat up straight on the bench.

She needed Heath. She wanted Heath. And if that meant fighting for him then so be it. He had filled her dreams and thoughts from the moment she'd driven away from Jardine Manor but it was not nearly enough.

She had a wedding to go to. Pity that she would be spending her time ogling the best man rather than the bride and groom. But one thing was certain.

The last few hours had shown her what she could do when she put her mind to a task.

No more compromises. No more excuses.

Kate dropped her head back and grinned as the July sunshine warmed her skin.

Watch out, Heath Sheridan, I'm coming to get you!

'Well, that looks comfy,' came a man's voice from her neighbour's garden.

Kate shot upright and looked around, froze and looked again.

Heath Sheridan was leaning on the fence which divided the garden from the antique dealer's. His arms were stretched out in front of him and a sweet smile played across his face.

She stared at him in stunned silence, her heart racing with the shock of seeing his face. It was almost like a dream come true.

'Heath?' she gasped. 'What on earth are you doing here? You're supposed to be at the wedding!'

'I slipped away for a few hours,' he quipped with a grin, 'to chat up one of the bridesmaids. They have things pretty much under control so I thought that I would leave somebody else in charge for once. I thought that I might surprise you.'

She closed her eyes and dropped her head down with a groan. The next thing she knew, there was a creaking sound and she blinked up just as Heath vaulted over the fence with his long legs as though it was nothing and strolled casually the few steps towards her.

'You weren't answering your phone or your front door. So I decided to take direct action. Don't you think that was rather bold of me?'

'Bold. *Bold?* Oh, Heath.'

Kate looked up into his smiling face and they grinned at one another.

But she couldn't say the words she needed, so she blustered instead.

'You have had a terrible influence on me, Sheridan,' she said and picked up the top sheet of invoices which she had brought back from her studio.

'Look at this. I am going to have to learn about spreadsheets and how to do calculations and costings and don't get me started about the Internet auction sites. Why did nobody warn me that they are so addictive? And I only went on them to sell gloves.'

'Sold many?' he asked and perched on the edge of the bench next to her.

Too close. *Too, too close.*

'Lots. Even the pink cotton elbow-length with the seed-pearl trim. Prom-night specials. Amber has been coming up with the marketing slogans for costumiers and fashionistas but Saskia has taken over the actual posting. Apparently I am not to be trusted with combining a customer's address with a glove box with the correct glove in the size they ordered. And she might be right there.'

Kate pressed her lips together tight as she stood up and gathered together her things, suddenly needing to create some distance between them where the truth would not be so hard to express. 'No more locked doors. That ship has sailed, and I realise now that I was only keeping it on because of my granddad. But I am keeping the tools,' she gushed. 'I won't stop making gloves.'

'I expected nothing less,' Heath replied as he followed her into the kitchen, slipped off his smart tailored jacket and leant back against the cooker with his arms folded.

'You're the girl who gave her best gloves to a perfect stranger. Alice says hello, by the way and… What? What is it…?' He looked around to see what Kate was staring at, open-mouthed. 'Is something the matter?'

'My eyes! You're wearing…a polo shirt.'

'Ah,' Heath replied and ran his hand down the front of the pale blue short-sleeved top. 'Yes. Apparently my new step-uncle enjoys golfing.' He looked down at her through his eyelashes. 'What do you think?'

'Think? I am too stunned to think and…what is that? Sticking out from under your sleeve?'

She slapped her hand over her mouth. 'I don't believe it. Of all things. *You.* Heath Sheridan, of the Boston Sheridans. Has a tattoo.'

Heath replied by unfolding his arms, reaching down and tugging the polo shirt over his head.

He ignored the gasp from the lady sitting at the table in the tiny kitchen and turned and flexed his biceps at her.

'The artist was a little inexperienced and we weren't quite sure how to spell Katharine but I think it works.'

The silence in the room was so thick Heath could almost touch it, until Kate exhaled long and slow.

'It does work. Very well, indeed.'

'That's my girl.' Heath nodded and strolled over to the table, reached out and hoisted her onto the table so that she was sitting with her legs hanging over the edge.

In a second she was in his arms with her head pressed sideways on his bare chest. This time there was no struggle or bluster, just the feeling of the girl he wanted against his skin. And nothing he had done had ever felt so right.

'I have some bad news.' Her voice was muffled and she lifted her chin so that she could smile coquettishly at him.

'Hit me with it.'

'Katherine is spelt with a middle letter e. No *a*. Can you stand the pain to have it changed?'

He grinned and revelled in the simple pleasure of pushing her hair back from her forehead with his fingertips as his gaze locked onto her face as though it was the most fascinating thing that he had ever seen. 'Sorry. Did you say something? I was otherwise occupied,' Heath replied with a low growl at the back of his throat, then casually glanced down at his tattoo.

'Oh. The body art. No problem.'

He released one arm, licked his fingertip and rubbed it against the letter, which instantly melted and blurred.

'Alice sacrificed some of her best watercolour pens. I hope you like the flowers and hearts—that was my idea. Dad was responsible for the actual drawing because Alice was laughing too much and...'

She pressed one finger against his lips.

'You tattooed my name on your arm. And you asked your parents to help. I'm not sure if I can take any more surprises.' She sucked in a breath and pressed both of her hands flat against his chest. 'I have to ask. I'm scared to ask...but it must be done.' Then she sighed out her question in one complete breath. 'Does Alice hate me for running away?'

'Alice does not hate you. Far from it. We had a long talk this morning and it turns out that she is actually willing to put up with me to make my father happy.'

'Really? I knew that I liked her straight away. Smart girl.'

'The smartest. And I like her too. But you know what that means, don't you?'

'Lots of family dinners?'

'I was thinking of something more important I have to decide on first. You see, I want to stop being your pretend boyfriend and start being the man who is good enough to be called your real boyfriend. Do you think I can do it?'

'What do you mean, you want to be my real boyfriend?'

Kate asked with a lilt in her voice, her heart thumping. Her blood racing.

'As in stand up and shout it out to everyone in the street and in front of the family at my dad's wedding and for the entire world to hear kind of boyfriend.'

'Ah. That kind. Is that all you want?' she asked in a low soft voice.

Heath lowered his head so that his forehead was pressed against hers and gently, gently brushed his warm full lips against hers.

'I want to be your friend,' he whispered and started to nibble on her lower lip before tilting her head back so that he was taking the complete weight of her body in his arms, and she was helpless to resist the delicious pleasure of a deep, sensual, tender kiss which left them both breathless at the end of it.

'Your lover,' he added and ran the fingertips of both hands down the centre of her back from neck to hips. 'And the man whose smiling face you wake up to every morning.'

'Me?' she whispered as her head tried to catch up with the surge of emotions and sensation that were sweeping through her. 'I am still impulsive and irresponsible. That is not going to change.'

'Good,' he murmured as his mouth found the sensitive hollow beneath her ear. 'And now it's my turn to talk, because you missed out a few things. Such as the fact that you are sexy beyond belief, and I can be swept away by the way you light up a room.'

He stepped back and she instantly missed his touch but he pressed one finger to her lips and, as she watched, the deep caramel of his eyes melted into warm butterscotch.

'I want you,' he whispered. 'For the first time in my life I know what I want and I am not going to question it or overanalyse it. I simply know that I am never going to look at another woman and feel the way I feel about you. You take my breath away.'

His smile spread into a grin so infectious and warm that it penetrated the last remaining barriers around her heart and blew away any lingering doubt.

'I am in love with you, Kate. You are the girl who rocks my world and fills my dreams at night.' He squeezed her hand and looked deep into her eyes. 'I even wrote you a love letter, which I understand is the romantic thing to do. I realise that I shall have to work on my bookbinding but I did have to improvise.'

Heath dived into his trouser pocket and pulled out a piece of white typing paper which had been folded in half and stapled down the spine. A red stick-on gift ribbon had been added to the top and the glue was starting to lift, but Kate stared at it in wonder.

'That is the most beautiful booklet that I have ever seen. But tell me the message. I want to hear you say the words out loud.'

Heath put down the paper, cupped her head in both of his hands and gazed into her face. 'I struggled with the exact phrase but I know how you like people to say how they feel and not waffle on for ages.'

'Heath. Tell me now. What does the letter say?'

He smiled and kissed the end of her nose. 'I wrote— *Stop talking and kiss me.*'

'I couldn't have put it better myself.'

CHAPTER THIRTEEN

KATE SNATCHED A calming breath and took a minute to cool down as Alice fidgeted on the back seat of the vintage Rolls Royce and checked for the third time in five minutes that the stunning diamond tiara Charles had presented to her as his wedding gift was not in danger of tumbling from her head, bringing the vintage lace veil down with it.

Little chance of that, Kate thought. Alice's hair had been gelled, sprayed and pinned into glossy sleek submission by a team of expert hairdressers who had already been hard at work by the time Heath had pulled up outside the Manor in his dad's car.

Of course she had protested about turning up to an elegant wedding wearing shorts and a strappy top, but he had insisted. She was perfect as she was. He didn't want her to change a thing. And the people who mattered would not care a jot. And those who would care didn't matter. Not to him. Not any more.

It had taken four attempts before he'd stopped cuddling her long enough so that she could pack a bag, *again,* with what she needed from her bedroom. Not that she was complaining. Far from it. She had dreamt of lying in Heath's arms for so long. And the reality was even better than she could have imagined. This was really saying something.

In the end, it had been a mad dash to make it back to

the Manor in time to get changed, phone calls flying back and forward every minute of the way. But, even so, she had barely time to hug Alice before slipping on the bridesmaid's dress and matching gloves. The dress fitted perfectly.

As for the shoes?

Alice had chosen the shoes and they were magical. Ivory-and-beige lace, low-heel courts. With a big satin bow on the heel. No stilettos or platforms today. Not when she was carrying the train of Alice's absolutely stunning designer crystal and pearl-embellished strapless oyster silk taffeta extravaganza. She had seen the dress in a Paris wedding shop almost eleven years earlier when she had fallen in love with Charles for the first time and kept it hidden safely away in her hope chest until today.

This truly was her dream come true, and every girl in the room, including the two cousins, Alice's elderly aunt, and even the Dowager Sheridan great-aunt, had simply melted when they saw her in it for the first time. Alice was breathtaking.

Then Heath had popped his head around the bedroom door, which caused much screaming from the cousins, to give a five-minute warning that the boys were just about to leave. He was wearing morning dress, which fitted him to perfection, and her foolish teenage girl's heart just about leapt out of her chest at the sight of him, especially when he gave her a toe to head scan followed by a very personal saucy wink.

That was when the panic started. Four bridesmaids and a lovely bride. All frantic. It wasn't pretty.

Someone slid a fascinator made of feathers and cream rosebuds into her hair, but in all of the rush she had no idea who.

But now here they were. Gliding to a halt outside the tiny stone church where Alice's ancestors had gathered for baptisms, weddings and funerals for generations. Her uncle and a cluster of photographers and guests were gathered in the warm sunshine, all waiting for the bride.

One minute ahead of schedule. Heath would be delighted.

Alice reached out and held Kate's hand for a fraction of a second before she took a couple of deep calming breaths and slowly exhaled.

This was it. Kate gave her new friend a tiny hug and a grin, and then practically leapt out the second the driver opened the door so that she was ready to hand Alice her wonderful, perfect bouquet.

Kate and the other guests sighed out loud as Alice stepped out of the car. She looked so stunningly beautiful and happy that every second of the work of the last few days seemed worth it a thousand times over.

It only took a minute to adjust the short, heavy silk taffeta train before Alice glanced back to Kate over her shoulder and beamed the glorious smile of a happy bride before taking the arm of her handsome, debonair uncle.

Above them the church bells rang out an old tune and, by some hidden signal, the ancient church doors swung open and the opening bars of the Wedding March drifted out of the high arched stone entrance.

With a single nod from Alice, Kate picked up the train, the other three bridesmaids stepped into line and, with a rustle of the heavy silk taffeta gown on the stone paving, Alice and her uncle stepped into the narrow aisle and began their stately way down the church filled with their friends and family, who had turned out en masse with smiling faces to share their happiness.

Bright July sunlight beamed through the stained-glass window above the altar so that the air was tinted with subtle pinks, lilacs and blue tones, contrasting with the garlands of cream lilies, bright ivy and roses decorating the ends of the pews. The sweet heady perfume of the flowers lifted with their every step.

Kate walked slowly behind Alice and her uncle, trying to concentrate on not stepping on the train or letting it snag but the whole time her eyes instantly searched out and fixed on the tall man standing to the right of Charles Sheridan, who was waiting so patiently to finally claim his bride after so many years apart.

Heath looked so handsome as he grinned at her that it took her breath away to know that his smile was not just for his new stepmother—but for her.

Every step down the aisle was taking her closer to this remarkable man who she had loved for so long. And who loved her in return.

He was her new family. He was where her heart was.

In those strong arms she knew she'd found a home and love for the rest of her life.

It was amazing what you could achieve in a weekend if you stepped out into the rain.

EPILOGUE

'KATE, YOU HAVE to stop whatever you are doing,' Saskia squealed. 'I mean it. Right now. Put that sewing down! I don't want you to stab yourself somewhere important. Because I have *news*.'

Kate laughed down the phone at Saskia. 'Hey, calm down, lovely. What's going on?'

'I have just had a call from Amber, that's what's going on. And do you know what that mad woman wants to do now? She's not content with causing uproar in Kerala. Oh, no. Now Amber wants to hold her wedding at—wait for it—Elwood House. My house! On New Year's Day. Kate! This is going to be my first wedding and it is only months away…and I think I'm hyperventilating.'

'Take a deep breath, then another.' Kate chuckled. 'Well, our girl certainly knows how to choose the best. It's a fantastic idea! In fact, I don't know why we didn't suggest it in the first place. A winter wedding at Elwood House. Oh, Saskia, it is going to be fantastic.'

'I know. I've already been thinking through so many ideas my head is buzzing. But there's more. She wants us both to be bridesmaids so I'm relying on you for the frocks. And, oh, Lord,' she gasped, 'I have just thought of something. The mother of the bride. Julia Swan. Help! I don't know if I'm ready for this.'

'Of course you are. And don't worry about the frocks or Amber's mother. We can handle those little challenges. No problem. We are goddesses, remember?'

'Goddesses. Right. Well, this goddess is going to have a little lie-down now before she gets ready to host a business seminar for some accountants. Amber will call you and Heath later! Bye, gorgeous.'

Kate pressed the handset to her chest, closed her eyes and sniffed away a wave of emotion. The first of their little band was getting married.

On New Year's Day.

Then she blinked and shook her head. Saskia was right. That was only a few months away. Ah, well, she would just have to fit in two winter bridesmaids' dresses and a wedding dress which was out of this world. *No problem.*

The sound of laughter broke through Kate's concentration and she looked up to see her two apprentice fashion students comparing designs for embroidered evening gloves for an Edwardian costume drama. Katherine Lovat Designs had taken off at the perfect time and an international TV company had commissioned her to create the gowns and gloves for all twenty episodes.

There was enough work for Kate and her two apprentices and more to last for months and the best thing was—it was wonderful work. Creative, luxurious and challenging. She had spent the morning in London museums exploring the original designs worn by the characters in that period.

She was one lucky girl.

Kate sat back in her office chair and looked around the room that had been transformed in only a few months from the cramped space that her grandparents had used into a bright, clean and airy open plan studio. Wide, glass double doors had replaced the tiny windows, and it had been Heath's idea to extend the workshop into a long conservatory room which was filled with flowering plants, bringing energy and life into the long late summer evenings.

Of course, Heath had every right to develop the house as he wanted. He did own it.

Heath had bought the building from her, after all. And the house next door. But they had worked together, side-by-side, all during the summer to clean and renovate the rooms, see its potential and fall in love with the house all over again as they fell in love deeper and deeper with each other.

It was amazing what you could achieve in a few weeks with the help of the right architect and a dream team of craftsmen.

The whole of the first floor of the two houses had been combined into one single large apartment with wonderful woodwork and artisan bookcases created by craftsmen.

Best of all, the antique dealer's cluttered shop and storeroom next door was now the spacious London office of Sheridan Press. Heath had created a modern technical marvel of an office with a meeting room which extended into the garden. The whole atmosphere of his office was unfussy, friendly and efficient and the two professional e-book designers who worked there cheerfully admitted that it was one of the best working environments they could ever want.

Of course, it helped that Heath and his father had worked solidly for weeks to come up with an innovative design for the newly launched Sheridan Press which combined a wonderful hand-bound book with an enhanced e-book digital content which was totally interactive. The awards had come flooding in with orders from around the world.

Alice had made a wonderful new home for Charles in a different part of Boston from the house he had shared with his first wife and they were frequent visitors. But London belonged to Heath. This was his domain, his speciality and his delight. He had made Sheridan Press the success it was and she couldn't have been more proud of him.

Time to share her news with the man who truly was her best friend.

The beeper on her waistband flashed out a very private code in reply, which made Kate blush and she slid from her chair and strolled over into the garden room.

Heath Sheridan was leaning on the small white-painted wooden gate, which separated the two houses, with a big cheesy grin on his face.

Kate slid open the glass doors and stepped out into the early September air.

She reached up with both hands to take his face, tilted her head and kissed him with all the warmth and tenderness in her body. His reply was to kiss her back hard enough to make her toes tingle and her knees melt.

'Hi, handsome,' she said, getting her breath back. 'What's new?'

'Oh, the usual.' He smiled and, in a pretend serious voice, said, 'More awards, more orders, more news from Boston.' Then he grinned. 'How about you?'

'Amber is coming home for New Year and has decided to get married at Elwood House. Many new frocks and gloves will be needed. But I wonder who she could possibly ask to help organise the event. Any ideas?'

His reply was to press his lips against hers. 'None at all,' he whispered. 'Because I am fully booked, and I am going to stay booked for a very, very long time.'

* * * * *

BLAME IT ON THE CHAMPAGNE

BY
NINA HARRINGTON

CHAPTER ONE

Elwood House: Must-Do list—Monday
- *Meet up with Kate and Amber to finalise Amber's wedding—do NOT let Kate talk you into fuchsia or satin—walk away from the satin.*
- *Decide on classical music pieces for the bathrooms.*
- *Be ready to fend off that very persistent new wine merchant.*
- *Stay in for the garden centre delivery of the spiral box trees for the front porch.*

'Snow. I AM going to need lots of snow. And tiny white fairy lights sparkling in the trees and over the pergola. Can you do fairy lights?' Amber's voice tailed off into a dreamy whisper. 'It would be so magical and romantic.'

Saskia Elwood rolled her eyes and grinned at her best friend Amber, then clicked in the box next to the garden lighting option on her wedding planner spreadsheet.

'Of course I can do white fairy lights. As for the snow? That shouldn't be too difficult for New Year's Day in London. But, you know me, if you want it to snow on your wedding day, then snow you shall have, even if I have to track down a snow gun machine and make you some. Although… Won't it be a bit cold? From the designs I have seen, that dress Kate is making for you would be perfect for a tropical beach wedding—but London in January? Brr...'

Amber giggled and flicked her long straight blonde hair over one shoulder in a move she had perfected in fashion shoots and as years performing as a concert pianist. 'I know,' she replied, wrinkling up her nose in delight. 'It is so perfect. Sam is going to love it.' Then she sighed out loud and strolled out past Saskia and through the conservatory into the garden with a faraway expression on her face. 'Just love it.'

'She's off again,' a cheery voice sounded from behind Saskia's shoulder as Kate Lovat bounced into the room with a bundle of wedding magazines in her arms. 'Dreaming of the fabulous Sam. If I wasn't so smitten with my Heath I would find it a bit sickening. In fact, sometimes I'm surprised you put up with the two of us. Always talking about the lucky men who we have agreed to marry one day.'

'Right now,' Saskia replied with a snort, 'I am more worried about Amber getting frostbite in that skimpy, mostly backless dress you are planning for a winter wedding. Any chance of a jacket? Thermal vest? The poor girl is going to be blue, which is not a good look for any bride.'

Kate replied by playfully hitting Saskia on the head with a rolled up bridal magazine and sat down next to her at the conservatory table. 'Blue? With that fabulous suntan? No chance.' Then she relaxed and rested her elbows on the table. 'Relax. There is a beautiful full-length quilted ivory coat to go on top of that slinky dress for any outdoor photos. Fear not. The girl shall not freeze. When the dancing starts she will be glad of that layered silk gown, even if the beads will be flying everywhere.'

Kate arched her eyebrows and peered at Saskia's computer screen, her green eyes bright with amusement. 'Does that say dinner and reception for twenty-six? I thought this was just going to be a small family wedding. As in no professional musicians, fashion models or anybody else in Amber's world who will make us feel totally inadequate as human beings.'

Saskia laughed out loud and started counting out on her fingers. 'How could you forget Amber's first dad and his huge new stepfamily, her second dad Charles Sheridan—' she pointed towards Kate, who waved a magazine in the air '—with Heath and his new family. Her third dad might bring his new wife but she is having some "freshening up" surgery post-Christmas and might not have the stitches out in time. Oh, and her mum, of course. Julia is bringing the latest beau plus entourage, including her aunt and three American cousins and...' the air whooshed out of Saskia's lungs '...twenty-six hungry, cold people are going to celebrate the best wedding they have ever been to. Amber's friend Parvita and her husband are looking after the music and I booked the waiting staff last week. All I have to do is enjoy myself.'

'Um. Yeah. Right,' Kate replied and looked over the top of her spectacles at her. 'And exhaust yourself in the process of getting everything ready up front so it looks easy on the day. Who is kidding who here? We know you far too well, girl.' Kate smiled and gave her a one-armed hug. 'Now, let me see that list again. Aha. Thought so. You have missed out a crucial item. Tut tut.'

'What?' Saskia glanced at the screen in disbelief and then back to Kate. 'I spent most of my Sunday double-checking the plan. Out with it. What have I missed?'

Kate slid out of her chair and came around to stand in front of Saskia. 'Wedding date for a very picky hostess to be provided by her pals. Tall, dark and handsome. Danc-

ing skills an advantage but will settle for extra hot. And
you're not typing that in.'

Saskia sat back in her chair and lifted both hands into
the air. 'Trust you to find me a date? Oh no. I still remember that graphic designer who offered to paint my portrait
if I stripped down to earrings and a cheeky grin.'

Kate fluttered her eyelashes and tugged down the hem
of her perfectly fitted jacket over her petite curves. 'We
do such good work.'

Saskia snorted and turned back to the laptop. 'Thank
you for the offer but the last thing I want is a boyfriend.
You do know that this is the first wedding that Elwood
House has ever seen, so no pressure at all.'

Kate waved her arms around and then cocked her head
on one side and pushed out her lips. 'This house is gorgeous and that curvy staircase was made for a bride to
walk down on her father's arm. *It is going to be fabulous,*
even if we do feel guilty about leaving you to do most of
the work.'

Saskia took a breath then shrugged off the lingering
disquiet by tapping her wristwatch with her home-mani-
cured fingertip.

'And I feel bad that I am making you late for your sexy
lingerie fitting appointment. You know, the one that you
booked three weeks ago.' She waggled her fingertips at
Kate. 'Go. A new wine merchant and his sales team will
be here soon and the last thing they want to see are you
two drooling over wedding brochures. Scoot. And have
a great time!'

Kate gasped, whooped, flung the magazines onto the
table and ran out to grab hold of Amber's arm. Two minutes later all that was left of Amber and Kate were empty
coffee cups and plates, a whiff of couture perfume, lipstick on her cheek and a smile on Saskia's face that only

spending breakfast with her two best friends in the world could bring.

They had known each other since high school. Totally different in every way and yet she could not want better pals. They might only have reconnected at a high school reunion that May, but now it felt as though they had never been apart.

Had it only been May? Wow. So much had happened in the past few months. Amber was engaged to Sam and spending most of her time living the dream in India, while Kate was sharing her home with Amber's stepbrother Heath only a few streets away. They were both so happy... and off to be fitted with sexy lingerie by the most famous bra shop in London.

Suddenly the wedding planning spreadsheet lost its appeal and Saskia sniffed and sat back in her chair. She envied them the luxury of having time to spend comparing fine lingerie, while she was sitting here trying to decide on whether to have background music in the bathrooms. Or not.

Ah. The joys of running your home as a private meeting venue.

A whisper of self-pity flitted into her mind but she instantly pushed it to the back of her brain in disgust.

She had so much to be grateful for. Her friends Kate and Amber were the perfect pretend family who knew her a lot better than her absent parents. And then she had her home, Elwood House the architectural masterpiece which she had shared with her Aunt Margot until last year.

A gentle breeze wafted in from the garden outside the conservatory room and Saskia smiled out at the hardwood planters overflowing with autumn blossoms.

She had spent so many summer evenings with her aunt in this very room, talking and talking about their grand plan to transform Elwood House into a fabulous private dining venue. Her aunt had been the acclaimed wine expert with superb taste in interior design who was happy to leave Saskia to work on the details and business plans. Together they had been a genius team who had started the project together.

It was so sad that her aunt had never seen those plans come to fruition.

Shuffling to her feet, Saskia gathered up the breakfast dishes and loaded the dishwasher. Clasping hold of the marble worktop, she let her arms take the weight and closed her eyes for a second and took a couple of breaths.

The past six months had been harder than she had expected.

A lot harder and much more expensive. But she could not think like that. She had to make her home into a successful business because the alternative was too terrible to think about. A day job in the city would not come close to meeting the running expenses of a house this size.

Elwood House had been the home of the most famous wine merchants in London for over one hundred and fifty years. It was strange to think that she was the last in the line and responsible for preserving the heritage of the house the first of the Elwood clan had built in this smart part of London.

It was her safety net. Her home. Her sanctuary. And her security.

Saskia inhaled deeply and waggled her shoulders to release the tension.

No matter what it took or how many hours she had to work, Elwood House was going to pay for itself.

Patience. That was what she needed. Patience and a lot of new bookings.

She had only been going a few months and it took time

to get a private meeting venue like hers off the ground. Reputation spread by word of mouth and she was already attracting repeat clients, but it was a mightily slow process and she had a big gap to fill before the Christmas party season started. Maybe Amber's wedding would turn things around and she could start the New Year with hope and excitement burning in her heart?

And as for a date for Amber's wedding? That was so not going to happen. She had served meals and coffee to an awful lot of businessmen over the past few months but she had not the slightest interest in dating any of them. Just the opposite. She had learnt the hard way the cost of giving up your independence and she had no intention of repeating her mother's mistake any time soon.

Her gaze fell onto one of the wedding magazines that Kate had brought for Amber to look at and a headline on the cover leapt out at her.

Read all about the huge rise in Civil weddings at home. Celebrate your wedding in the intimate and private venue of your own home.

A spark of an idea flashed bright. *Civil weddings.* Now that was a thought. Amber's wedding might be the first wedding reception that Elwood House had seen. But it need not be the last… Um… Perhaps there was a market for small private house weddings in a city this size. Not everyone wanted an extravaganza of a huge hotel banqueting suite.

The idea was still rattling around inside her head a few minutes later when the telephone rang. Saskia barely had a chance to pick up the handset and say the words 'Elwood House,' before a transatlantic female voice belted out down the line at such a rapid-fire pace that she had to hold the phone away from her ear for a second.

'Oh, good morning, Angela. Yes, I am still available

to talk to Mr Burgess and his team today. Not a problem at all. And there has been a change to the agenda. Right. Have you got the details? Tell me everything.'

Rick Burgess leant his elbows on the solid white railings of Waterloo Bridge and watched the water taxis mooring at the jetty below. The River Thames flowed beneath his feet and wound in wide lazy curves eastwards towards the sea. Stretched out across the horizon in front of him, high-rise marvels of modern architecture reached tall into the sky against the backdrop of landmark ancient cathedrals and majestic stone buildings that made up the city of London.

A fresh breeze wafted up the river and Rick inhaled deeply, his chest rising under his white open-necked shirt and soft black leather biker jacket.

Fresh air.

Just what he needed to clear his head after being cooped up inside an aircraft and then underground trains for the past four hours.

He ran his fingers back through his tousled dark brown hair.

Yesterday he had spent the afternoon talking wine over a plate of antipasti in a sunlit garden on a Tuscan estate with a young Italian couple who had sold everything they had to buy a tiny prestigious vineyard that he knew would be taking the world by storm in time. And today he was in London under a cloudy sky with only patches of blue peeking through to lighten the grey stone buildings.

He knew exactly where he preferred to be and it certainly was not here!

It was on mornings like this that it hit more powerfully than ever that it should be his older brother Tom who should be getting ready to go into a crucial sales meeting with one of the most prestigious private dining venues in London. *Not him.*

Tom had been the businessman. The IT genius who had transformed a small chain of family wine shops into Burgess Wine, the largest online wine merchant on the West Coast of America.

Rick shook his head and chuckled. He had a pretty good idea of what Tom would've said about the crazy enterprise he was just about to launch in this city and the language would not be fit for his parents to hear.

Tom had been a conservative businessman to the core. He would never have taken a risk with a group of independent young winemakers making tiny amounts of wine on family estates across Europe.

Not all of the wine was remarkable yet. But some of it was amazing.

It was going to have to be if he had any chance at all of redeeming himself in the eyes of the media. As far as the wine trade press were concerned, Rick had certainly never earned his place on the board of directors of Burgess Wine. *Far from it.*

To them, Rick Burgess would always be every bit the renegade who had walked away from a job with the family wine business to become a professional extreme sports personality. What did he know about the modern wine trade?

And they were right.

If Tom was still alive his business ambitions would have stayed in the world he knew—professional sports and adventure tourism. They had always been his passion and still were.

But Tom was dead. And there was nothing he could do to bring him back.

Just like he couldn't change that fact that his parents

were both in their sixties and needed him to take Tom's place and work for Burgess Wine.

It had never been his decision or his choice. But as they said, there was nobody else. Burgess Wine was a family business and he had just been promoted to the son and heir whether he wanted the job or not.

Mostly not.

He didn't like it. They didn't like it. And they still didn't completely trust him not to mess things up or run back to his old life.

Emotional blackmail only went so far.

This was probably why they'd set up this sales meeting with an important client he had never met. Of course they would deny it if he questioned them, but he had been long enough in the sports world to recognise a challenge when he was presented with one.

This sales pitch was just one more way they were asking him to prove that he could pull off his crazy idea to open a flagship wine store for Burgess Wine in London.

Which in his book was even more of a reason why he had to make the wine world take him seriously. *And fast.* Even if he did detest every second of these types of business meetings.

The upbeat rhythm of a popular dance track sang out from the breast pocket of his jacket and Rick flipped open his smartphone.

'Finally! Were you actually planning to check your emails some time this morning, Rick?'

'Angie, sweetheart.' Rick chuckled. 'How delightful to hear your welcoming voice. I have just got off the plane and getting used to being back in London. Turns out I miss my chalet in France almost as much as I miss you.'

'Sweet talker! Sometimes I don't know why I put up with you. Oh. I remember now—you pay me to sort out the boring stuff in your life. But forget sightseeing for the moment—I'll take you on a tour later. Right now I need you to take your head out of the latest extreme sports magazine and flip over to the message which I am sending… now. I have some news about the sales meeting this morning, but don't worry, it's all under control.'

Rick straightened his back and turned away from the river, suddenly very wide awake.

'Good news or bad news? Talk to me, Angie. I thought we locked down this meeting weeks ago.'

His personal assistant knew him well enough to immediately gush out, 'We did. But do you remember those two TV wine experts who we approached to help promote the new store in the build-up to the launch? The ones who were so terribly busy appearing on cookery shows to get involved with yet another wine merchant? Well, guess who emailed me late last night. Apparently they heard a rumour that Elwood House might be investing in the new generation wines and suddenly they might be interested after all.'

Angie laughed down the cellphone. 'Turns out your mother was right. The Elwood Brothers connection has paid off.'

Rick exhaled slowly, pushed back his stiff shoulders and flicked through the research information on the people he was going to have to convince to take him seriously.

'Got it. I should be there in about ten minutes. And thanks for sorting out things at the London end, Angie.'

'No problem. We have an hour before the presentation. Catch up with you soon.'

Rick closed down the phone and stared at it for a few seconds before popping back into his pocket with a snort.

So that was how the game was played.

The top wine experts he needed were only prepared to turn up and listen to what he had to say if he had the credibility of a famous name in the wine trade like Elwood Brothers behind him.

Yet another example of exactly the kind of old world narrow-minded network he detested. Instead of asking what he could bring to the business, all they were looking for was the validation of the old and worthy established family of wine merchants.

Rick exhaled slowly.

Was this how it was going to be from now on?

This was not his life! His life was base jumping and pushing his body to the limit under blue skies and cold air. Not walking into a conference room and selling the idea for Rick Burgess Wines to closed minded traditional hotel owners who had already made up their minds before they heard that he said.

He was about to take the biggest leap in his life and launch a flagship wine store in the centre of London. His name above the door. His future on the line.

Only this time it was not about him or his reputation as a daredevil sportsman. This time it was about passion. A passion for life, a passion for wine, and a new passion for championing small businesses.

Rick Burgess the mountaineer. Rick Burgess the champion paraglider. And now Rick Burgess the wine merchant. Same passion. Same determination to prove that he was up to the challenge he had set himself, even if it had been foisted onto him.

Frustration burned through his veins.

He inhaled slowly, pushed off from the railing and strode away over the bridge.

He needed this to work for the employees and winemakers who relied on him and for his parents who were still locked inside their grief.

He had the presentation in his head. He had time to

spare to calm down and clear his head before facing one of the greatest challenges in his life. Bring it on.

Ten minutes later Rick turned the corner towards the address that Angie had given him, his hands in the trouser pockets of his designer denims and the breeze at his back.

A flock of pigeons swooped down in front of him into the tall oak and London plane trees which filled the small residential square. Families and dog walkers flittered between ornamental flower beds and wooden benches in the broken sunshine. On the face of it, just another quiet city square.

But one thing was certain, in the crazy world that was his life—you never knew what to expect.

Like now, for example.

It wasn't every day that you saw an executive secretary having a row with a delivery driver in the middle of a prestigious London street, but it certainly made a change from dodging tiny dogs on glittery leads. Even if the pretty girls on the other end of those leads had been trying to catch his eye.

Rick slowed his steps.

He needed to take some time out before facing an incredulous wine buyer around a conference table in some soulless, stuffy meeting room. Or the first person to mention the words 'dead man's shoes' would end up being decked, which would be a seriously bad move in more ways than one.

This was a far more entertaining option.

His girl was standing with her pretty hands splayed out on both hips and she was definitely a secretary but an executive one.

She was wearing a slim-fitting skirt suit in that strange shade of grey which his mother liked, but had never clinched a tiny waist with a cream coloured sash. He could just make out the tiny band of cream fabric at the cuffs of the jacket. Her long, sleek sandy coloured hair was gathered into a low ponytail at the nape of her neck.

Her very lovely long, smooth neck.

Now that was a neck he could look at all day.

As he watched, the shorter older man in the overalls who she was talking to in a low, patient, but very assertive voice, which reminded him of his junior school headmistress, suddenly shrugged, gave her a 'nothing to do with me' flick of both hands, jumped into a white delivery van and drove off, leaving the city girl standing on the pavement, watching the tail lights of the van disappear around the corner.

She stood frozen to the spot for a few seconds, her mouth slightly open, and then turned to glare at a pair of large shiny navy blue ceramic pots which were standing next to her on the pavement.

A five feet tall cone of what looked to Rick like a green cypress tree spilled out over the top of each planter then whirled upwards in some deformed mutant spiral shape which had nothing to do with nature and everything to do with so-called style.

Rick looked at the two plants and then back to the girl, who had started to pace up and down the pavement in platform high heeled slingback shoes, which most of the girls at his mother's office back in California seemed to wear.

Not exactly the best footwear for moving heavy pots.

But they certainly did the trick when it came the highlighting a pair of gorgeous legs with shapely ankles.

So what if he was a leg man and proud? And she had brightened up his morning.

He could make time for some excellent distraction activity.

'Good morning,' he said in a bright casual voice. 'Do you need some help with those?'

Her feet kept walking up and down. 'Do you have a trolley handy?'

He patted his pockets. 'I'm afraid not.'

'Then thank you but no.' She nodded, then stopped and stared at the huge plants, with the fingers of one hand pressed against her forehead as though she was trying to come up with a solution.

'Good thing it's not raining.' He smiled. 'In fact it is turning out to be a lovely September morning.'

Her head slowly turned towards him and Rick was punched straight in the jaw by a pair of the most stunning pale blue eyes that he had ever seen. The colour of the sky over Mont Blanc at dawn. Wild cornflowers in an alpine meadow.

Dark eyelashes clashed against the creamy clear complexion and high elegant cheekbones. Full-blown lips were outlined in a delicious shade of blush lipstick, and as she gawped at him a faint white smile caught him by surprise.

'Yes, I suppose it is.' She blinked. 'But, if you'll excuse me, I really do need to find some way of moving these plants—' she flung the flat edge of her hand towards the nearest plant and almost knocked it flying '—from the pavement into my porch and some time in the next ten minutes would be good.'

'The delivery driver?' he asked casually.

She sniffed and closed her eyes, teeth gritted tight together, then lifted her chin and smiled. 'Bad back. Not part of his job description. Just delivery to the kerbside.' Her voice lifted into a slightly hysterical giggle. 'Apparently he was expecting a team of porters to be all ready and waiting. Porters! As if I could afford porters. Unbelievable.'

'Ah. I understand completely,' Rick replied, nodding

slowly and scratching his chin, which seemed rather stubblier than he had expected. 'May I make a suggestion?'

She glanced up at him through her eyelashes as she pulled out a cellphone, and sighed out loud. 'Thank you again, but I can manage very well on my own and I am sure that you have some urgent business to attend to. Somewhere else. In the meantime, I need to call a burly bloke moving company. So good morning and have a nice day.'

Rick chuckled under his breath. It was not often that pretty girls gave him the brush-off and maybe a city girl had reasons to be cautious.

'Did your mother tell you not to talk to strangers? Relax. I can spare five minutes to help a lady in distress.'

Her fingers paused and she glared up at him, her eyebrows lifted in disbelief. 'Distress?' There was just enough amusement in her voice to make him take one step forward, but she instantly held up a hand. 'You are mistaken. I am not in distress. I don't do distress. I have never done distress, and I have no intention of starting now. Look.' She popped her phone in her jacket pocket and gingerly wrapped her fingertips around the edge of a pot. And tried to lift it an inch closer.

The pot did not move and she threw a single glance up at him, daring him to say something, but he simply smiled, which seemed to infuriate her even more.

This time she squared her shoulders, gritted her teeth and bent slightly at the knees to go at it again. The pot wobbled slightly then shuddered back to the ground as she hissed in disbelief and stood back with a look on her face as though she wanted to kick the pot hard.

Rick had seen enough. He stepped forward and gently took her arm. 'No need for that. You have all the lifting power you need right here. It's a simple matter of leverage.'

'Leverage!' She laughed and nodded. 'In these shoes? I don't think so.'

'I could move those pots for you. No problem.'

Biting down on her lower lip, the suit looked up at him and he could feel her gaze take in his new Italian boots, denims and leather biker jacket, slowly inching its way up his body until their eyes locked.

And stayed locked.

He watched her expression change as she mentally jostled between necessity and asking for help, which was clearly something she didn't like to do.

Necessity won.

Her tongue flicked out and moistened her lips before she lifted her chin and asked, 'What exactly did you have in mind?'

CHAPTER TWO

Must-Do list
- *Make sure that the new spiral box trees are arranged very elegantly either side of the main entrance. This is bound to impress the clients and set the right tone.*
- *Try and forget how much these two trees cost and watch out for dogs!*
- *Come up with a brilliant plan to shamelessly but unobtrusively use these wine folks to bring in more business.*

IT WAS THE long green twirly plants on sticks that were the problem.

Rick had worked out a way of lifting up the edge of the heavy planter using a wooden door wedge then tipping it forward just enough to use the pot as a lever, but the moment he started to roll the bottom rim of the china pot along on one edge, the plant started waving out of control in all directions across the pavement like some demented flagpole, causing mayhem with the pedestrians.

It was amazing how the street seemed to fill up with girls pushing baby buggies, dog walkers and children in the space of ten minutes, but after two narrow escapes where his secretary had to dodge out of the way or risk getting a tree branch in her eye, Rick had managed to roll one planter all the way from the pavement to the patio without causing serious injury to people or the china base.

'Brilliant,' she gushed, trying to catch her breath after waving away a dog with a full bladder. 'One small step and we're there!'

Rick scratched his chin. 'Tip and shuffle. I tip the pot back and then roll it slightly forward until the edge is on the step. But someone has to hold the greenery out of the way when it swings onto the step. Two man job. Are you up for it?'

He looked up into her face and his breath caught. Close up, he could see that her flawless creamy skin was not a product of pristine grooming and clever make-up but natural beauty which went beyond pretty without being in-your-face gorgeous. The splash of cream at her neck was a perfect contrast to her brown hair and eyebrows and seemed to make her pale blue eyes even more startling.

He had never seen eyes that colour on a girl before but everything about her screamed out that he was talking to a real English rose.

'Absolutely,' she replied with a quick nod and reached for the bottom of the tree. 'Let's do it. Ready? Yes? Go! Oh, ouch. It got me. Almost there. Done!'

Rick stood back, peered at the pot from several angles then leant forward and shifted it to the left slightly.

'That's better.'

'Better! It's fantastic. I don't know what I would have done if you hadn't come along. Thank you so much… Oh, I'm sorry, how rude of me. I don't even know your name…'

'Just call me Rick,' he replied with a wave of one hand. 'And it was my pleasure, Miss…'

'Rick! You found it.'

He half turned as Angie bounded up the pavement towards them, her huge shoulder bag bouncing over one shoulder and a bulging document folder stuffed under her arm and stretched out her hand towards his secretary.

'Miss Elwood, lovely to meet you. Angie Roberts—we talked on the phone earlier. Thanks again for fitting us in at such short notice. What a fabulous house. And I can see that you have already met my boss.'

'Thank you, Angie, and welcome to Elwood House. If you would like to come inside and…' She paused, opened her mouth, closed it again, inhaled slowly and turned back to face him. 'Your boss?'

Rick pushed his shoulders back and glanced sideways at the high gloss painted door of the house whose porch he was standing in. The words 'Elwood House' were engraved in a curvy elegant font on a small brass plaque attached to the stone portico.

It would appear that he had arrived at his destination.

And his English rose was one of the Elwood dynasty.

A low chuckle rumbled in his chest. So this was the hardened old wine merchant he was going to be making his sales pitch to! Well, that showed him. How wrong could he be?

'Rick Burgess.' He grinned into his secretary's stunned face. 'Apparently you are expecting us.'

Rick braced his shoulder on the ornate white marble fireplace in what had been the elegant, huge formal dining room of Elwood House and held the colour brochure for Rick Burgess Wines in one hand as he watched Saskia Elwood glide effortlessly around the sunlit room.

The back split in her slender, elegant pencil skirt fanned open just enough to give him a tantalising glimpse of a pair of very long slender legs above shapely ankles. Not immodest. Oh no. Demure and classy, but tantalising all the same. Just enough to fire up his imagination.

She was impressive.

Every one of his sales team she spoke to looked away from the press release and winemaker portfolios that Angie had passed around to smile up at Saskia and spend a few minutes chatting before going back to their work with that smile still on their lips.

The men and women in the room knew talent when they saw it. Not everyone was able to put a guest instantly at ease. They had expected Saskia to treat them as sales people who were worthy of a cup of instant coffee and a plain biscuit. Well, she had confounded their expectations by treating every one of his four-person team as a guest and potential client in her private meeting venue. Their coffee and tea had been served from silverware with the most delicious homemade pastries and canapés.

Very clever. *He liked clever.* Even if it was obvious to him what she was doing.

His sales people were going to be working with clients from the finest hotels and private homes around London, and Saskia had already worked that out. She might be hosting a sales meeting, but there was no reason why *she* could not sell them the benefits of Elwood House at the same time.

Their hostess was elegant, warm, unpretentious and genuinely interested in her clients. Attentive to their needs, but not intrusive or overfamiliar.

It was precisely what the hospitality industry was all about. And Saskia Elwood had it in spades. He loved watching experts at work. He always had. And the lovely lady of the house was at that moment giving him a master class in exactly the type of customer service he was going to expect in the flagship London face of Burgess Wine.

He glanced back down at his phone. Ten more emails. All from his mother. All wanting urgent updates.

Rick exhaled slowly. A well buried part of his brain knew that she was concerned about him, while the upfront and only too blatant part screamed out a message loud and clear: *They don't think you can pull this off. After two years of hard work you are still the black sheep who is never going to be taken seriously. So you might as well give up now and go back to the sports where you are the best!*

No. Not going to happen. He had made a commitment and he was going to see it through, no matter what it took. Rick Burgess had not risen to the top of his sport by being a quitter.

Strange how his gaze shifted automatically up from the screen towards the slim woman in the pale grey suit, refilling an elegant coffee pot.

Her light brown straight hair was tied loosely back in a shell clip at the base of her neck, which on any other woman would look too casual, but somehow looked exactly right. She knew exactly what she looked like and had taken time to perfect her appearance. Subtle day time make-up, but with skin that clear she didn't need anything but a slick of colour on her lips. This woman knew that her eyes were her best feature and made the best of them. Her eyes were totally riveting. Those eyes captured your attention and held it tight.

Just as they were doing right now as she looked across and flashed him a glance.

Rick slid into a comfortable dining chair and instantly refocused on the business proposal, making notes on the points still to be resolved as he scanned down the snag list. But all the while his left hand tapped out a beat on the fine table and curiosity pricked his skin.

Maybe that was her secret? That hot body that every

man in the room had probably already visualised, which lay under that surface layer of clothing. Tempting the men and impressing the women. She could turn on the heat for the men and the friendly girl power for the ladies.

A clever girl with a hot body wrapped in a teasing and intriguing package.

A frisson of excitement and anticipation sparked across Rick's mind.

It would be quite a coup if he could sign up Margot Elwood's niece to stock his wines and serve them to her guests before the store even opened.

Perhaps that would be the proof he needed to convince his parents that their reckless and, in their eyes, feckless second son would not let them down after all?

Now all he had to do was talk her into it.

Rick glanced around the table. Everyone was seated. They had their promotional material and Saskia was already scanning each page.

The game was on!

'I have just spent the last two years tracking down the finest wine from the new wave of young winemakers all over Europe and persuading them to supply it exclusively to my new flagship wine store right here in central London. Every wine on our list has been personally chosen and vetted.'

'You can say the same thing about every family run wine shop in London, Mr Burgess,' the girl he now knew as Saskia Elwood replied in a light soft voice as her pen tapped onto the cover of his glossy brochure. 'Standards are high.'

'Yes, I know. You heard it all before. But this is new. This is a direct personal connection between the winemaker and the consumer.'

'How confident are you that these new cellars will deliver?' she asked. 'A new prestigious wine store in the centre of London is one thing, but what assurances can you give me that these winemakers will come back to you year after year? I need to know that I can rely on a guaranteed supply of any wine I add to my list.'

Rick caught her sideways sigh and downward glance but, instead of stomping on her, he grinned and saluted. Her question had not been asked in an angry or accusatory tone. Far from it. She genuinely wanted to hear his answer.

'Great point. What can I give you? My energy and my commitment. I took the time to travel to the vineyards and meet these winemakers. It was not always easy to persuade them to work exclusively with Burgess Wine, but there's one thing I know from my work as a sportsman. Passion recognises passion. These young winemakers have invested everything they have because they are obsessive about creating the most amazing wines using modern and traditional techniques. I see that in them. That's why I want to champion these ten small family estates because that is the only way I can guarantee that there will never be such a thing as a boring wine ever again.'

He walked around the table slowly, gesturing to the impressive brochure his parents' marketing team had spent weeks perfecting.

'Right now there's a team of marketing experts back in the Californian headquarters for Burgess Wine working on websites for each of the individual growers. When you buy a bottle from this store you will have access to everything you need to know about the wine and the passion of the person who made it. I think that's special.'

'Sometimes passion is not enough, Mr Burgess. You need to have the experience and expertise to create a remarkable wine. And these new winemakers are still learning the trade. Not everybody is as…adventurous as you are.'

Rick wrapped his hands around the back of the solid antique dining chair and nodded down the table, making sure that he could capture the attention of Saskia and the three new members of his sales team.

'They don't have to be. The ten growers I've chosen are all part of a mentoring scheme I've created with well-established major winemakers who have been supplying Burgess Wine customers for years. My parents are happy to invest in the wines we select.'

'Don't you mean the wines you select?' Saskia asked with a touch of surprise in her voice. From where he was standing, Rick could see that her gaze was locked onto the back cover of the brochure, which carried an impressive colour photograph of Rick in full climbing gear on a snowy mountain. 'If I am reading this correctly,' she whispered, 'you already have a career as a professional sportsman, Mr Burgess. Does this new store mean that you have turned your back on adventure sports?'

And there it was. Just when he thought he might leave his past behind for a couple of hours and be taken seriously.

Rick pressed the fingers of one hand tight into his palm and fought back his anger. He had to stay frosty.

'Let's just say that I'm focusing on the less hazardous aspects. I haven't broken anything important in years and I have every intention of staying around for a lot longer. So much wine, so little time!'

A ripple of laughter ran around the room but he could almost hear the unspoken question in the air which even his sales team were not prepared to ask out loud but were obviously thinking.

What would happen to this store if Rick Burgess jumped

*off some mountain with a parachute strapped to his back
and the wind caught him and sent him crashing against
the rocks before he could regain control?*

It could happen. In fact it had already happened. One
accident only a few months after Tom died.

How could he forget that day? It had been his first trip
to the mountains since the funeral and he'd needed it as
badly as any other addict needed that cigarette or fix of
their choice.

The oppressive atmosphere of the family home and the
overwhelming grief had finally become too much to bear
and there was only one way he knew to try and get some
balance and peace back into his life. Not trapped in a house
all day staring at the four walls until he wanted to hit a
wall. And go on hitting it until the pain subsided.

He needed to climb a high mountain with a specialised
parachute strapped to his back. He needed to feel the rush
of adrenalin as the wind caught in the parachute and he
felt the power of the air lift him into the sky.

Free. Soaring like a bird. Released from the pain and
trauma and grief of Tom's death.

This was what he did. This was what had taken him to
the awards podium of the European paragliding championships for three years in a row.

And for ten minutes of glorious tranquil flying in long
winding curves he had been precisely where he wanted to
be. Doing what he loved best.

Until one simple gust of wind in the wrong direction
had ruined an otherwise perfect day.

But that was all it had taken to leave him with a broken
collarbone and a badly sprained ankle.

His parents had been shocked and traumatised and full
of complaints about how reckless and uncaring he had

been. How very selfish and irresponsible. But that was nothing compared to the fall in the company credibility in the press.

The media loved to see a reclusive, obsessive sportsman with the golden touch take a fall. And this accident had given them the ammunition they needed to focus on one thing—his lifestyle.

Tom Burgess had been a strategic genius. But his brother Rick? What was he going to bring to the business? He might have taken Tom's seat on the board but maybe the company was taking too much of a risk by bringing in their untrained and reckless second son.

Suddenly major wine producers who had supplied Burgess Wine for years were sucking in their cheeks and wincing about the management team at Burgess Wine.

Never mind the fact that he'd worked tirelessly to be a world-class paraglider and reach the top of this field. Never mind that he was prepared to give the same energy and determination to Burgess Wine and the family business that his brother Tom had transformed into an international company.

Never mind that he had spent the last two years since Tom's death coming up to speed with the business to the point where his family were prepared to even listen to his ideas, despite their misgivings.

Time to make this deal swing his way. Time to take one of those risks he had become famous for. He needed buyers like Saskia Elwood to be interested and excited in this idea, not for himself but for his parents, who had taken a leap of faith. And for every one of the ten small businesses who trusted him with their future.

Rick strolled around the dining table in the sumptuous room towards the head of the table and caught Angie's eye with a quick nod. She instantly slipped out of the room and returned a few minutes later with two silver ice buckets and gently placed them onto silver platters on the fine polished wood table.

'Why don't I let the wine do the talking for me?' Rick smiled and nodded towards the slim wine bottles poking their heads out of the ice buckets. 'Angie tells me that the sample cases are on their way here now, Saskia, but I thought you might like to try something special. A late harvest dessert wine from a single estate in Alsace which is turning out to be one of my favourite discoveries. Are you willing to give it a try?'

'Of course,' Saskia replied, slightly irritated that he thought it appropriate to choose the wine for her. But, as Angie went round the table, pouring the golden liquid into tiny green-tinted glasses, the genuine smiles of appreciation from the men and women in the Burgess sales team as they inhaled the aroma of the wine knocked her sideways.

They might be young but everyone around her table had one thing in common; a real and genuine passion for wine. But did that include the man himself? Her rescuer in denims and the leader of this merry band. Rick Burgess?

Rick sat back down and smiled in encouragement as Angie started a conversation about the Burgundy harvest at the other end of the table while they enjoyed the wine.

Saskia raised the glass of dessert wine to her nose, twirled the glass and inhaled the aroma, which made her eyes flutter in delight and astonishment. Then she sipped the wine ever so slowly.

It was rose petals, musk, vanilla and deep, warm spice. And on the tongue? An explosion of flavour and tingling acidity.

Saskia instantly put down her glass and reached for

the bottle to read the label on the wine bottle. Twenty years old. Rare, exclusive and made by a tiny vineyard she had never heard of in Alsace. It was absolutely delicious. Unique. Expensive. But amazing.

It was so good that this wine could easily have come from the cellars of Elwood Brothers. Her mother and aunt's family had been one of the oldest and most respected wine merchants in Britain, with traditions that went back hundreds of years. The Elwoods were famous around the world for having the finest collection of prestige wines and for employing the leading experts in their field.

Their reputation for quality and excellence had been built up over centuries. It had seemed like the end of a familiar institution when Elwood Brothers finally closed their doors a couple of years ago when the last of the brothers had decided to retire.

It was a shame that she couldn't borrow some of that reputation for excellence to attract more clients to use Elwood House for their board meetings and private dining, combined, of course, with modern technology. The old and the new. The traditional and the modern.

But that was impossible now… Wasn't it?

Saskia felt that familiar prickle of the hairs on the back of her neck as an outrageous and exciting idea gathered shape. Elwood House already had the kudos that came with the name. It would need a lot of investment, but what if she could build up the wine list into one of the finest in London? The best of the old wines and the best of the new.

Perhaps Rick Burgess did have something to offer her after all?

'I am interested to hear your opinion about the wine,' Rick said as he raised his glass towards her. Those grey eyes seemed to almost twinkle as he turned his charm offensive to maximum power. 'I would be a happy man if I

can persuade Saskia Elwood to serve my wines to her dis-
criminating and expert guests here in Elwood House. So,
tell me. Do I leave here a happy man? Or not?'

CHAPTER THREE

Must-Do list
- *Thank the wine merchant for any free wine they bring. Kate and Amber will be very grateful for the bottles. No promises to buy any, of course.*
- *Canapés. People in the wine trade can eat! Use the sales team as guinea pigs for a couple of new savouries which might work for the Christmas parties. Let them come up with the wine to match— could be interesting.*
- *Do not let this new wine merchant leave without a few of the lovely brochures that Sam worked on. Who knows? Word of mouth recommendation is always the best. They might have some flash customers in need of a private meeting venue.*

BY THE TIME the Burgess Wine sales meeting finally closed, the grey September morning had turned into a bright sunny day. In the light breeze it was still warm enough for the conservatory doors to stay open, and Saskia looked out towards the sales team, who she had invited to finish their coffee on the patio.

The golden coloured flagstones had absorbed the sun and warmed the terrace, creating a welcoming enclosed private garden. Brightly painted Mediterranean-style flow-

erpots created a soft barrier between the hard stone floor
and the exuberant English flower borders and old stone
wall covered with fragrant climbing roses and honey-
suckle.

This was exactly how she had imagined it would look
that cold January when her Aunt Margot had died suddenly, just when she seemed to be recovering from the
strokes which had made her life so difficult. Little wonder that these experts in the wine trade were in no hurry
to dash out into the rush-hour traffic and fight their way
home in this busy part of London.

Saskia glanced quickly over her shoulder towards the
table where Rick Burgess and his personal assistant Angie
were huddled around a laptop computer.

The strength in Rick's shoulders and back contrasted
so fiercely with his long slender fingers. His neck was a
twisted rope of sinew as though he was barely holding in
a volcano of suppressed energy and power.

This was the man who had effortlessly lifted a planter
that morning as though it was weightless.

She had felt such an idiot when Angie had arrived and
her knight in denim and a leather jacket had turned out to
be the client that she had been waiting for.

It had so totally floored her that she had felt off balance
for most of the morning. Not that she would ever let him
know that, of course.

The company directors she met did not usually turn
up to meetings wearing clothes more suited to a motor-
cycle rally. In fact she wouldn't be surprised in the least
if there was some huge, hulking two-wheeled machine
parked around the corner at that minute, waiting for him
to leap on and roar away.

Combine that with tousled dark curly hair and designer
stubble.

Rick Burgess was certainly a company director with a difference.

She watched him stand and share a laugh with Angie as they gathered up their papers and, just for a fraction of a second, she wondered what it would be like to be on the receiving end of the full-on charm of that power smile that beamed out of a rugged, handsome face.

She knew that she had never been the pretty one, or super-creative or musically talented like her best friends Kate and Amber. But it would be nice now and again to have a handsome man really look at her as a woman and like what he saw. Instead of asking where the toilets were and could he have more coffee.

Her beautiful mother Chantal had often said that Saskia had skipped a generation and would be much happier back in rural France on the vineyard where her own mother had been brought up, instead of living the high life of a city girl.

And she was right in so many ways.

Her mother could never understand why the teenage Saskia had begged to spend the school holidays working at the *auberge* with her extended French family instead of sitting on some tropical beach with her mother and her friends, while her father stayed in his room and worked on some financial deal or other.

Of course that was when her grandparents were alive and her parents were still together. When her father left them everything changed.

Suddenly her practical skills were useful and Saskia became the girl who made sure that there was food in the refrigerator and the bills were paid as her mother struggled to come to terms with what had happened and failed. Saskia had never once missed school or turned up without a clean uniform and brushed hair. When her mother's world imploded she had become the dependable one who made sure things happened.

The girl who would always help you out at the last minute.

Not done your homework? Ask Saskia to help. All you had to do was pretend to be her friend, just long enough to get what you wanted.

It had been a long apprenticeship forged from hard times, but, like it or not, fifteen years of training and hard work in the hotel and food trade had brought her to this point. She should be happy, ecstatic really, but all this was hers and she had made the business feasible on her own.

Not that there was any choice. Without Elwood House, she would be working for someone else. She couldn't go back to that. Not ever.

Not after she had promised her aunt that she would take care of the house and make all of their great plans a reality.

It was worth the exhaustion and never-ending strive for excellence.

As the Burgess sales team moved into the hall, Saskia pressed her fingertips hard against the fine marble surface of the console table and took a deep breath before lifting her chin and personally thanking each of them in turn as they left the building, discreetly counting to make sure that no one had got locked in the washroom or had decided to take an unsupervised tour of the bedrooms upstairs.

She sensed rather than heard someone coming up to speak to her and she spun around. 'Miss Elwood. Could you spare a moment?'

Up close and personal, Rick Burgess was just as physically impressive standing in her hallway as he had been on the pavement that morning. Even after two hours of what had been sometimes intense discussions, back and forth across the table, the intelligence in his grey eyes sparkled

with life and vigour against a tanned face which had never
seen a tanning salon.

'Of course,' she replied. 'How can I help, Mr Burgess?'

'Oh, please call me Rick,' he replied and stretched out
his hand to shake Saskia's. 'I just wanted to say a huge
thank you for agreeing to see us today. We appreciate your
time and your warm welcome into your lovely home.'

'I am delighted that you enjoyed it.' She sucked in a
breath when he released his grip, which was a lot firmer
than she was used to. As in finger-crushing firmer. 'If you
should ever need a venue for a business meeting, I do hope
that you will consider Elwood House.'

'A business meeting?' His eyebrows rose and, as he returned her smile, the deep tan lines at the corners of his
mouth and eyes creased into sharp falls. 'Sure. My project team will need to get together every few weeks during
pre-launch. Angie will get in contact. Although I do have
one request before I take off.'

His hands pushed into the pockets of his denims. 'Prepare to be shocked. I am about to declare a terrible failing.'

'A failing?' Saskia replied, trying not to smile. 'Surely
not.'

Rick sighed out loud and raised both hands in the air.
'I can understand that such a thing is hard to believe but
here it is.' He paused for dramatic effect and stepped just a
little closer than she was comfortable with. 'I'm not known
for my patience. There were a couple of times during the
presentation that I picked up some sense that you might
be interested in buying from me. Am I right?'

'Ah. Well, now it is my turn for confession,' Saskia replied, her gazed locked onto his face. 'I try not to make
snap decisions when it comes to spending my money. My
late aunt, Margot Elwood, taught me that loyalty to a sup-
plier means a very great deal. I am therefore rather cautious

about who I give my loyalty to, and one bottle of wine is no guarantee that the others will be of the same quality.'

'Loyalty. I like that idea.'

Rick glanced over Saskia's shoulder. 'How about I give my future loyal customer a hand and carry that box of sample bottles down to her wine cellar? Who knows? I might pick up a few tips from an Elwood.'

'My wine cellar?' Saskia repeated. 'I'm very flattered—' she smiled '—thank you, but I am sure it would be boring compared to the wonderful wines you have in your stockrooms. And I am quite capable of carrying a few bottles down a corridor.'

Saskia straightened and kept her smile firmly fixed as she gazed past Rick Burgess towards the front door. 'I wouldn't want to keep your team waiting.'

Rick replied by tilting his head. 'They're already heading back to the office. So you see, Miss Elwood, I'm all yours. Now. Where do you want me to put this box?'

'I store the specialist wine and ports in the basement. Oh, and please mind your head. These old cellars were built for shorter people.'

Rick followed Saskia down the narrow stone steps that led from her modern stainless steel kitchen down into the brick and stone storeroom and cellar that ran almost the full length of the house. He carefully lowered the large cardboard box of wine onto a sturdy old wooden table before following her into the cellar.

Saskia flicked on the lighting system and started her tour with the classic red wines she had bought for the coming autumn and winter season before moving on to the older and more prestigious wines. Racks and racks of bottles were laid out on their sides in purpose-built curved trays, label up, creating a superb display.

Rick peered politely at each of the winemakers and vintages with only a quick nod to indicate that he was only vaguely interested in what he was looking at.

It was not just annoying, it was unsettling!

She was just about to turn back when Rick pointed towards the cabinet where she stored her most precious white wines, most of which she had inherited from her aunt.

'I recognise that wine, it's one of my father's favourites.'

'Then we have something in common.' She smiled. 'It's one of my favourites too. It also happens to be made at the vineyard once owned by my Elwood grandparents. Yes, that's right. This is my family wine.'

'Ah—' Rick chuckled '—you see. I was right—I have learnt something new. Although it does make me wonder why you don't promote your connection to the famous Elwood family more on your website. That is a remarkable heritage to be proud of.'

She replied by smiling and shaking her head. 'There is a very good reason for that. I might be an Elwood but I have never been a wine merchant and I wouldn't want anyone coming here under false pretences.'

Rick strolled up, pressed his shoulder snugly against hers and dropped his gaze onto a copy of a wine label that she was holding in her hand. His long wide mouth curved up into a smile that raised the temperature of the air in the cellar by several degrees. 'I know about that.' He chuckled. 'Here I am, with a new career as a wine merchant and about to open a new wine store. Everything I know about the business I picked up from a lifetime living with a family who is obsessed with everything to do with wine.'

'Aunt Margot may have been the last of the Elwood family but there was nothing that you could tell that lady about wine. I only wish I had her experience and knowledge.'

'Exactly!' Rick said in a voice bubbling with enthusiasm. 'This is why I need to be totally honest with you about the real reason that I am here today.'

'Real reason? What do you mean?'

His reply was to move closer, stretch out one long muscular arm to the stone wall behind her shoulder and lean forward so that their faces were only inches apart. Trapping her in the space between his body and the wine racks, which were pressing into her back.

Any closer and she would be on intimate terms with his shirt buttons.

She could hunch down and dive under his armpit if she had a mind to but this was her cellar, not his. And, damn him, but she was not the one who was going to have to move first. Even if he did smell of soft leather and fine wine underpinned by a faint citrus tang of some no doubt very expensive male grooming product designed to act as instant girl attractor.

And Lord, it was worth every penny he had spent.

His gaze scanned her face for several too long seconds before he whispered and stepped so close that she could almost feel the heat of his breath on her brow. 'I think you are being far too modest, Saskia. From what I've seen today, the clients who come to Elwood House are lucky enough to have the very best and the excellent taste of the *mistress* of this fine house.'

The way Rick lingered on that last word sent shivers up her spine which she blinked away. Was he trying to flirt with her?

As for modest? What choice did she have? Her mother might have fled to Los Angeles, leaving her with her aunt, but it was her father who had truly ripped her heart out. She never mentioned him to anyone, not even Kate or Amber. She had even changed her surname the same week her mother had finally agreed to a divorce and went back to being Chantal Elwood again. But he was always there at the back of her mind. A constant itch that could never be scratched away. Reminding her to be careful and not take risks, no matter how tantalising they might appear.

Saskia lifted her chin slightly. She had to stay professional. Even if he was totally inside her comfort zone and oozing enough testosterone to make her forget her own name.

'Just this.' He breathed low and hoarse, his head tilted slightly to one side. 'What would you say if I was prepared to sign a contract committing Rick Burgess Wines to hold a lunch meeting at least every week right here in Elwood House for the next two years?'

He paused and let the silence create the anticipation he was looking for.

'What would I say?' Saskia repeated, lifting her chin slightly sideways so that she could smile up into his face without straining her back. 'I would say thank you very much and here is a piece of paper and a pen.'

'I thought that you might. But there is a catch.'

'Am I going to like it?'

'Like it? I hope so. You see, my company specialises in exciting wine made by a whole new wave of brilliant new winemakers from right across Europe. I need customers like you to take a risk and invest in these wines. But one short presentation is not nearly long enough. So...' his hips shifted slightly, just in case she had not noticed how tight his jeans were, stretched over his muscular thighs '...I was hoping that you might be available to have dinner with me this evening. It would give me a chance to tell you more about what I had to offer. If you were free.'

Free? She was free for dinner every evening.

Rick was smiling at now, but she could see the muscles in his lower arm move slightly as they adjusted to a shift in his position. Dark brown hair curled onto broad muscular shoulders. Sinewy neck and jaw. Beyond rugged, physical and potent.

Butterflies fluttered in the pit of her stomach under the intensity of that gaze and she had the sudden urge to toss her hair back, stick her chest out and flirt with him outrageously. His dark blue-grey eyes shone bright in the low light she used in the cellars to protect the wine. There was a certain slight unease around his lips as though he wanted to say something, reveal something, but thought better of it and held back.

What he had to offer? Oh, she had a pretty good idea. *Dangerous.*

Buying wine from him? *Oh no.* Fingers. Hot. Burnt.

Suddenly she felt a desperate urge to fill the silence with chatter.

'Building a reputation for excellence takes time. I only opened up the house to guests a few months ago and I cannot afford to risk my reputation by serving any else but the best.'

'Absolutely.' He nodded. 'This is why I think my business proposition might just solve both of our problems rather neatly. My wonderful wines. Your fine reputation. Perfect fit.'

She paused and licked her lips. 'I don't want to seem rude, but my clients expect the very best and it's my job to make sure that they are not disappointed. But don't worry, Angie has given me her contact details and has promised to be in touch about any future business meetings. I look forward to seeing you again at Elwood House.'

Saskia stretched out her hand towards Rick and he glanced at it for a second before moving back, chuckling and wrapping his fingers around hers.

'People don't usually turn me down,' he whispered,

stepping forward under the spotlight until he was far enough away for Saskia to see the fine white scar lines that ran up one side of his face. 'I'm curious. Are you always so sceptical? What do you want to know? Ask me anything during our dinner this evening and I'll promise that I will tell you the truth.'

Saskia was still reeling from his reply when Rick's cellphone blared out a top ten music track and he glanced quickly at the caller ID, breaking the intensity of the moment.

'You seem very confident that you have something that I might be interested in, Mr Burgess. Perhaps you could ask Angie to make an appointment for later in the week.'

'Nope. Has to be tonight. I'll pick you up at seven.'

Pick her up. Oh no. This was not a date. She had to take some control back!

'I sometimes walk along the South Bank around half seven,' she gushed before her brain had time to engage.

'Got it. Later.'

Two fingers to the forehead in a quick salute and he turned on his heel and strolled away to the stairs as if he owned the place, leaving a Rick-sized space in her cellar.

He hadn't waited for her answer.

The strange thing was; she couldn't remember saying no.

Saskia peered at her reflection in the screen of her smartphone, wiggled her head from side to side several times and pushed several stands of hair behind her ear. Large ornate drop earrings in the shape of a leaf swung freely in the late sunshine, reflecting back the light from the finely worked Indian silver.

'Thanks, Amber. Those earrings are just perfect. I love them. You are a genius when it comes to style. What's that?

Takes one to know one. Well, thank you, kind lady. And don't forget to thank Kate for the loan of her jacket. The colours work so well together.'

She glanced quickly around the busy pavement to check that her quiet smirk had gone unseen. 'Amber! Stop that. You are making me blush. Those earrings are staying on. This is not a hot date. I keep telling you. Business meeting. Stop laughing. Business! And no, I don't want you to wait up for me. Cheek! Now go and be creative with the wedding plan. Talk to you later if you must. Later. Yes. Okay. I promise that I will have a nice time. Thank you. Yes.'

Saskia chuckled out loud and flipped her phone closed. Kate and Amber had just spent over an hour helping her come up with the perfect outfit but, she had to admit, her style consultants had pulled together a smart but casual look which created just the right impression.

Neat wraparound plain navy dress, smart designer jacket, which Kate had run back to her studio to collect at the last minute, discreet jewellery and medium heels which she knew that she could walk in, just in case Rick turned up in his boots again and took off across London on foot.

She was determined to show Rick that she was a professional to the core and not just another girl who he could order around on a whim.

This was meeting a client for drinks away from Elwood House.

Not a date or meeting a friend. This was a business meeting with a potentially large booking in the balance.

Just because she had agreed to go out for drinks did not mean that she was saying yes. It was simply playing fair and giving him a chance to discuss this mysterious business proposal.

Wasn't it?

Of course she was intrigued—how could she not be?

What did he think he could offer that the wonderful London wine merchants could not?

Nothing to do with that molten chocolate voice and dark blue-grey eyes. Oh no. She was not going down that road.

The man was a maniac. A riveting, passionate, handsome charmer of a maniac.

Who was clever enough to dangle something he knew that she might be interested in, but hold it just beyond her reach.

How did he expect professionals to take him seriously if he turned up in denims and leather and barely shaven? Did he really not care what he looked like? Or was he simply playing a trick and acting out a persona created by the company PR department?

Squaring her shoulders, Saskia pushed back from the railing and glanced along the Thames Embankment in the fading September sunshine.

And froze. Because strolling towards her on the wide pavement was Rick Burgess. No entourage, no team, just Rick. Wearing exactly the same clothes that she had last seen him in.

His hips swung out with each stride, purposefully and in line with the rock-solid body under those tight denims.

Every inch of his body screamed out confidence and self-belief. He could fit in anywhere he went and, judging by the backwards glances from the ladies he passed with each purposeful and determined step, it was a look which guaranteed him an audience.

And, just like that, she got it.

Rick truly did not care one bit what other people thought about his appearance.

He dressed to please himself and if the rest of the world did not like it—that was not his problem.

This was no act designed to provoke a reaction or a

cheap media gimmick to attract some extra press coverage because he was so deliberately different from other wine merchants in the city.

He was Rick.

Take it or leave it. That was him.

No artifice, no pretence, no insincere gestures to placate his audience.

He knew who he was and was totally happy inside his skin.

He was the real deal.

It blew her away. And terrified her so much that it was not even vaguely funny.

Rick Burgess was exactly the kind of sex on legs man that she had been avoiding since the day her dad was arrested. She knew the type and she had tasted what it felt like to be consumed by the fire on the altar of their all-powerful ego. And she never wanted to be burnt alive again.

The problem was, back in Elwood House she'd been surrounded by the familiar rooms and furniture and high-tech presentation equipment and other people.

They were her security screen.

But at that minute in this public street she felt as though they might as well have been the only two people on the Embankment that evening, with not even Aunt Margot's dining table between them.

Her gaze simply could not move away from that powerful dark face as he strode towards her. It was as though he had a huge magnet which was pulling them closer and closer together, making it impossible for her to break the connection.

All of the carefully worded and highly professional refusals and excuses she had planned in the kitchen when she was clearing away vanished from her brain, wiped out by the stunningly relaxed and sexy-as-hell smile he was giving her. The corner of one side of his mouth lifted as he strolled closer, creating crease lines in his cheeks and the corners of his eyes.

Perhaps she should have looked Rick Burgess up on the Internet instead of cleaning the house and polishing it back to perfection. It might have given her some ammunition to fire at him and scare him away.

Which was what she wanted…wasn't it?

To politely turn him down while still keeping the bookings.

What other reason could there possibly be?

So why did she find it so difficult to lift her chin and take the few steps to close the distance between them?

'Nice earrings.'

'Nice boots.'

He smiled and replied with a small shoulder shrug. 'My mother told me that I should smarten myself up before the meeting today. And, like the good boy that I am, I always do what my mother tells me.'

She replied by raising her eyebrows. A good boy? She doubted that very much.

Her silent gesture must have hit home because he strolled forward and startled her by nudging her ever so gently along one side of her arm.

It was the touch of a friend, not someone she had just met.

How much more outrageous could he get?

Then that amazing wide mouth broadened into a smirk of a smile and his grey eyes focused on the river.

'Yeah, I concede that one. Maybe not a good boy all of the time. But hey. It's nice to have something to aim for. As you know. But let's not talk about business. Not yet, anyway. This is way too nice an evening.'

He sniffed and looked around. 'You know, it's been years since I was on the South Bank. But, as it happens, I know a family-run Tuscan restaurant right on the river you might enjoy. Willing to risk it?'

Risk it? No, thank you. She gave up on risk a long time ago. Not when she had experienced first-hand the fallout from other people taking risks they should not have.

On the other hand, there was no point arguing in public with a company director who could put Elwood House into profit with one contract.

She could risk his choice of restaurant for a few hours, even if it did turn out to be a kebab shop.

'That sounds perfect. Do you need a map?'

'Maps? Maps are for people who don't know where they are going. Where is the fun in that? Oh no,' he said and, without asking permission, he took hold of her hand and looped it over the crook of his arm, capturing her and holding her tight. 'Let's rock.'

CHAPTER FOUR

Must-Do list
- *This is NOT a date—simply drinks and dinner with a prospective client. Stay charming and professional at all times. Do NOT flirt with the handsome man who wants you to buy his wine. He probably has a lovely wife and family back home. Ignore any advice from Kate and Amber on dating techniques.*
- *Do not panic or blurt out your life story if the conversation flags.*
- *Keep your taxi money handy—you will be going home alone.*

TWENTY MINUTES LATER Saskia strolled out of the ladies' room at a wonderful Italian restaurant she hadn't known existed until that evening, just in time to see Rick being back-slapped by the rotund father of the family while Rick chatted away in fluent Italian to the two sons who took care of the bar and waiter service on a Monday evening.

He might have been part of their family.

How had he done that?

The other diners in the packed restaurant were certainly enjoying whatever story he was regaling them with.

In fact they were almost disappointed when Rick broke

off mid-anecdote to go back to their window table and pull out a chair for her.

It was strange how the most delicious-smelling piping-hot rosemary and olive foccacia suddenly appeared on the table with a bottle of the best wine on the list, which the owner himself insisted on opening and checking before pouring Saskia a generous glass and then he turned to Rick, who joined in the joke. He swirled the glass with an over the top swagger, inhaled and then guffawed with appreciation—which led to even more waving of arms and laughter from the kitchen area.

Rick turned back to Saskia and raised his glass. 'Your health, lovely lady. This food smells good. Mind if I go first?'

'Dive in. Okay, I am impressed. You speak excellent Italian for an American wine merchant.'

'Born in Scotland, moved to Napa aged twelve, but spend most of my time in the French Alps close to the Italian border,' Rick replied between bites of foccacia. 'I might have picked up a few words. And this is great. Try some.'

'Thank you, I will,' she replied and sat back and looked around the restaurant for a few seconds. The stress of the day, the week and the month seemed to ease away in this cosy atmosphere. She felt her shoulders drop as she relaxed and enjoyed the moment.

'That must have been difficult,' she whispered.

'Difficult?' Rick looked up.

'Moving to another country when you were twelve must have meant leaving your friends and relatives behind. Not easy for a young person.'

He opened his mouth, paused and then closed it again, his gaze scanning her face. 'No—' he shrugged after several minutes '—it wasn't easy at all. But my parents and older brother helped me settle into a new life. Of course, once I saw what the sports facilities were like I had a great time.'

'Modest too. Well, it seems that you are full of surprises, Mr Burgess.'

He chuckled and shook his head. 'Mr Burgess is my dad. I only answer to Rick. Okay? And I'm pleased that you like it.'

She waved one hand daintily in the air and tore off a piece of bread and popped it into her mouth.

And the explosion of flavour hit her hard.

Wow.

She looked over Rick's shoulder at the patron, who winked at her from the bar.

Winked.

'Do you know,' she managed, between more bites, 'I have been eating in Italian restaurants all over London with my aunt since I was ten years old and this is the best foccacia that I have eaten, and the wine…' she picked up the bottle and peered at the label '…is from a tiny estate just north of Florence. I have been trying to persuade them to supply me for months. It's fantastic.'

'Wait until you taste the fresh pasta with anchovy and tomato sauce. Mario's mother is in there making it herself, just for us.'

'How? Why? Or do you normally have this effect on complete strangers?'

He smiled and rested his elbows on the table so that he could lean forward into her space.

'The recommendation came from Mario's nephew and his new young wife. Yesterday morning I was putting together a business plan for their fledgling winemaking operation a few miles closer to the sea from where this wine was made. It's going to mean a lot of hard work but the vines are old and run deep in the poor soil. They are going to go places. And the family are right behind them.'

Then he leant back. 'They are just one of ten young winemakers who will have their work showcased by RB Wines. They're excited, I'm excited. You see, I am buying all of their wine. Every last bottle. I am their only customer and I have signed a contract to say that their wine will only be available from one shop. The flagship store I am opening in the spring.'

'But Burgess Wine is a huge online operation. Doesn't it make more sense to sell their wine around the world?'

'You're right.' Rick shrugged. 'My family have worked hard to expand the online wine business to cover most of the West Coast of America. But not Europe. Plus these growers are only making a few hundred cases every year at most, which is not nearly enough for the online trade. Different style. Different market. Different customers. They are taking a risk, of course. If I can't sell their wine in London...' He flipped his hands into the air in a very Mediterranean style.

'You go broke and so do they.' Saskia sighed out loud and took another long sip of wine. 'You are asking prospective customers like me to spend money on an unknown winemaker based solely on your recommendation and hoping we are happy with the results. That is one brave marketing plan.'

'I suppose that is what it comes down to in the end, yes.'

'I see,' she whispered and focused her complete attention on the crumbs left in the bread basket, her lips pressed tight together.

A roar of laughter rang out from the man across the table and she sprang back and looked up into Rick's face. His whole body was shaking and he had to wipe away the tears from his eyes before shaking his head and grinning at her.

'Please promise me that you will never take up a career as a poker player. Oh dear, the look on your face was priceless.'

'I am delighted to have provided you with such amusement,' she sniffed.

His response was to reach across the table, pick up her hand and kiss her knuckles before lowering it back to the table.

'I'm not laughing at you—' he smiled '—just your reaction. It was the perfect confirmation of what I already suspected. Did you really think that I picked these winemakers out of the phone book by closing my eyes and sticking a pin at random on the pages?'

He narrowed his eyes and shook his head slowly from side to side. 'It has taken me two years of tracking down a shortlist of growers based on word of mouth recommendation from people I trust in the business. Then I spent my time and money sending in a team of experts who can pull together a complex combination of geology and climate and do all of the background checks before we went to the vineyard and met them in person. These are not ten random growers. They are the future stars of the winemaking world. And I got there first.'

He tilted his head to one side. 'But you don't see that when you look at me. Do you? You don't see the work and the long hours that go on behind the scenes. You see Rick the maverick sportsman.'

He held up his hands as she tried to bluster a response. 'Well, do you know what? A few years ago you would have been right. I didn't come into the wine trade by choice. But once I make a commitment to do something, I stick to it.'

Rick tipped his head towards her. 'I do things my way.

I don't stick to the rules and dance to someone else's tune. I know who I am and I know what I want. And sometimes people have a hard time coming to terms with that.'

He switched on that killer smile that left no doubt at all in her mind that he was used to getting precisely what he wanted, from any female of any age in a hundred yard radius.

'Now, I am talking too much about myself. It took me a few minutes to make the connection between Elwood House and the Elwood Brothers wine merchants. I only went there once—' Rick saluted with his bread '—and it was an education. Shame it closed. Professional curiosity. Where do you buy the wine for those cellars you showed me today? Not from Burgess Wine—I checked.'

'From the growers, mostly. Aunt Margot was quite a character and there was a time when Elwood House was a sort of unofficial bed and breakfast hotel for any passing winemaker who was in town. She had an address book other wine merchants could only dream of.'

'Add me to that list. That must have been an amazing experience.'

'Oh, it was—I was sent to bed early on many occasions when things were getting a little too jolly in the kitchen, if you know what I mean. There are some real eccentrics in the wine business. Luckily for me, they kept in touch after she passed and they're still willing to ship me their best vintages at market prices. The clients certainly appreciate the quality.'

'I can vouch for that. Do you still talk to the Elwood side of your family?'

'I am sorry to say that I am the last of the line and my mother has her own life.' Saskia looked up from her glass. 'What about your parents? Burgess Wine is based in California now, isn't it?'

'Aha. So I am not the only one who hit the Internet today. No need to blush. You already know the office is in the Napa Valley. A long way from central Scotland where they started, but it's where the wine producers are based so it makes perfect sense. And the climate is slightly better.'

'Just a bit,' Saskia replied, feeling a lot more relaxed when he was talking about his family and not hers. 'Oh, my goodness. Look at that!'

Rick sat back in his chair opposite Saskia and watched her inhale the aroma of the huge bowl of the most delicious pasta, then turn to the chef with a grin and chatter away in perfect Italian, much to Mama's delight, who couldn't wait to share the recipe.

Apparently, adding a ladle of the pasta water to the sauce made all the difference!

It was worth letting his cheese melt just to look at her.

He had half expected Saskia to wear her business suit and a body armour type of corset, but instead he was enjoying dinner with a girl who could have been poured into a wrap dress which clung to all of the right places and gave a man just enough of a tantalising glimpse of what lay beneath to click the right buttons.

Combine that with a brain and an attitude which made him stay awake and pay attention and he was more than interested in Saskia Elwood the woman as well as the heir to the Elwood name.

At Elwood House she was the body in a suit which he couldn't resist. But here? Here, she was a knockout.

Not that he would ever admit it, of course, but it had thrown him when Saskia had asked about his move to California as a boy.

How could he possibly explain to this girl just how tough it had been? Anger at the injustice of being dragged away from everything he knew and having no say at all in the decision was the one common emotion he remembered only too well from those terrible first few years. It hadn't helped that his elder brother Tom had been the seventeen-year-old genius who'd excelled in every academic subject he'd turned to at their new high school in California.

Not that he blamed Tom for being the academic son in the family. That was who he was. But the brighter Tom's star had shone, the more the young Rick Burgess had become a damp firework. And the more the teachers and other pupils had compared him to Tom, the angrier he had become at the injustice and ridicule he had to endure.

Pity that his parents had been too busy working every hour of the day to build a new online wine business to notice that their second son was desperately unhappy.

But he had been honest with Saskia about the sports. Without a physical outlet for his suppressed anger and resentment, he could have turned that energy into something far more damaging.

Saskia waved at Mario and Rick joined in the laughter for a moment before tucking into his food.

Perhaps it was not so surprising that Saskia had picked up on that part of his life?

Angie had come up with so much background material on the Elwood family that he had barely had time to skim-read the essentials when they'd got back to the London office. But one thing was clear. Saskia Elwood Mortimer had become Saskia Elwood for a very good reason. *Her father.*

It had taken him all of five minutes to work out that Hugo Mortimer would not be winning any prizes as a father and a husband and as a property developer he was a disaster. Dropping the Mortimer name made sense for a teenage girl who was the daughter of a man whose embezzlement scandal hit the headlines around the world. Worse, it was an investment scam that had finally taken him to the law courts and a long prison sentence in an American jail.

Saskia Elwood had every reason to be cautious around men with big ideas and bigger promises.

He got that. Better than she might imagine. He was not Tom. But he shared Tom's drive and determination to do what he had to in order to achieve his goals. He always had.

It was time to get creative and do something nobody expected him to do.

He had spent most of his life pushing the boundaries and asking forgiveness later; much to his parents' despair.

Life was not for hanging around waiting for other people to give him permission.

And he had absolutely no intention of changing that philosophy any time soon, even if that meant cutting corners a little when it came to making his store a triumph of innovation and excitement.

Direct action. No more talking and a lot more walking.

He was going to show Saskia Elwood that he meant business and she could trust him to deliver on his promises in the only way he knew how, up front and personal.

All he had to do was find some way of persuading her to leave her cosy little nest and jump on the morning flight back to France.

Persuading women to agree to his every whim was usually not a problem for him. Shame that Saskia was not the type of woman he normally met. He liked girls who could stand up for themselves and make their own way. Running a private meeting venue on your own was not a trivial thing. He admired her for that.

But, from what he had seen today, there was something she wanted. Something that he could give her. Something she might find too irresistible to turn down.

'It's good to see a girl enjoying her food,' he quipped as

Saskia liberally tossed cheese and black pepper over the generous portion of pasta that she had piled into her bowl.

Her hand froze, then relaxed as he chuckled quietly under his breath and loaded his bowl with twice her portion.

'Guilty as charged. I love my food and drink. Always have.'

'Well, here is a thought. How you would like to travel to France with me tomorrow? It shouldn't take more than three or four days to visit each of the vineyards, but I guarantee that you will be back here for Monday morning.'

'France? Why would I want to go to France with you?'

Rick waggled his eyebrows a couple of times up and down and then grinned when she groaned and turned back to her food with a shake of her head.

'I fell into that one.' She waved. 'Please. Carry on.'

'Apart from the pleasure of your delightful company, I thought that you might be persuaded to buy wine from me if you met some of the producers in person.'

'Ah. Emotional blackmail. Once I meet the growers you know that I will not be able to say no to them. Now that is a low trick.'

He paused and took a sip of wine before looking up at Saskia. He knew all about emotional blackmail. His parents were experts.

'Not at all. Creating my own business means that I have the freedom to create my own list of premium customers. Customers like you.'

Her head came slowly up and she continued chewing for a moment before replying, 'Me? I don't think so.'

'But I do. I want you to be part of that first wave of special buyers in London, Saskia. No. More than that. I need you to support my launch. In return, I am offering you an amazing discount on the wine and I will promote Elwood House along the way. That is special.'

'Why do you want to sell to a one-woman operation like me?' she replied with a short cough of disbelief. 'Why not focus on the big five-star hotels where you can be guaranteed large orders?'

Rick swallowed down his pasta and waved the fingers of one hand towards her chest. 'Because of who your family are, of course. I want the Elwood name to be attached to my store. It's as simple as that.'

She stared at him in shocked silence as though she could hardly believe what she had heard. So he continued to twirl his linguini and talk at the same time. 'My parents sign contracts with bulk producers over slick boardroom tables without even visiting the vineyard. I cannot work like that. No. I refuse to work like that.'

Risk shook his head. 'I deal with people one to one. When they sign a contract they are signing it with me, not some faceless organisation who will drop them at the first sign of trouble. I am the person who commits to making their dream come true and in return they make the best wine that they are capable of. And that is something very special. Something you can be part of.'

He scanned the table for a second then pounced on the bowl of Parmesan, deliberately ignoring the fact that Saskia was glaring at him with a look that could freeze ice.

He brushed his hands off and pushed the bowl across the table to her abandoned dinner. 'More Parmesan? No? It is quite simple really. I meant what I said earlier. You want to serve the best. And I believe that I have the best. Come to France with me tomorrow and I'll show you why I'm sticking my neck out. No glossy brochures, no fancy advertising agencies. Just a hands-on demonstration of the quality RB Wines is going to become world famous for. That way we both win!'

Saskia slid back in her chair and folded her arms. 'So let me get this straight. You want me to buy wine from you so that you can use the Elwood name as some sort of seal of approval for your producers. You don't need me at all. You just need the name to bring some credibility to a risky business venture. Isn't that more like the truth?'

'Oh, I want a lot more than that,' he replied as he lowered his wine glass. 'I want to buy credibility and respectability with a huge dollop of tradition and heritage on the side.'

His fingers traced out a sign in the air between them. 'RB Wines. Suppliers to Elwood House, London. It would give me just the kudos to bring customers in the door, and, once inside the shop, we can create the most tantalising selection of prestige wines in the city. Which you get to see first. The best for the best.'

'*We* can create the selection of wines? I'm not sure I believe that. Not when the mighty Richard Burgess ego is part of the decision making process. It's almost as if you want to become the new Elwood Brothers but all on your own.'

He paused then slowly nodded his head. 'Yes, I suppose I do.' A strange look crossed Rick's face and he chuckled at the back of his throat. 'Now that is one hell of a crazy thought. Yeah. Actually that is amazing. Thank you.'

'In fact, you have a brother, don't you?'

He looked up at her as though he had temporarily forgotten that she was there.

'Not any longer. But that doesn't matter. RB Wines is going to be spectacular.'

She unfolded her arms and leant forward and stared at him in the eyes. He didn't even blink or look away.

'This is a vanity project, Richard Burgess. And I'm not interested in pandering to your ego by selling out my family name. Not for any money.'

'Selling out your name? Oh no, that's not what I'm offering. I haven't got to the good bit yet.'

'Oh, there's a good bit? Well, please carry on. This should be most entertaining.'

He put down his fork and bent from the waist so that their noses were almost touching. 'I don't want to buy your name, Saskia. I'm offering you the chance to take the inside track on the best new producers in Europe and, as a bonus, my company will commit to using Elwood House for the next two years. Now that's what I call a partnership made in heaven.'

Of all the arrogance!

Saskia glared at Rick and decided that she must be hearing things.

Otherwise, this casually dressed hotshot had just demanded that she drop everything and take off to France with him for a few days. With the promise of a long-term meeting contract—if she agreed to buy and, more importantly to her, serve his wine to her clients, who expected her to give them the best.

RB Wines would be sitting on her shelves next to a handful of growers who had been supplying the Elwood family for decades and, in the case of some chateaux, for over a century.

As if flashing his money around would open the doors to the cellars. Hah!

She had grown up surrounded by people who thought that arrogance and bravado could get them where they wanted to go. Charming, attractive people like her father, who believed that they could do what they liked and tell people what to do and get away with it.

Her father was not so different from Rick.

Handsome, tall, dark, with wonderful eyes and a smile that could disarm a woman the minute she laid eyes on him and persuade even the hardest businessmen into handing over their money and investing in commercial property in cities all over the world.

And they had.

Shame that her father thought that using other people's money to pay for his high risk building projects was a perfectly acceptable thing to do. He was arrogant enough to believe that he couldn't fail and his plans for office buildings designed by cutting-edge architects had become risky and riskier. *Blame the property market,* he used to say, *not me. Just wait until the economy picks up. Companies will be desperate to use my office space and everyone will get a great return on their money.*

It had come as quite a shock when the courts disagreed.

Saskia remembered only too clearly what it was like for her mother on the day he'd been arrested for embezzlement and fraud. She'd believed in him, trusted him and had faith in all his excuses and rational explanations for why they were losing money day after day.

They had both loved him so badly that the truth was hard to accept. He was a fool. An arrogant and delusional man who thought that money could buy him status and class and power. That was why he'd married her mother. Chantal Elwood was the only daughter of one of the famous Elwood brothers, the most respected wine merchant in Britain. And the oldest. The Elwood family had given him access to clients he would never have otherwise met.

Little wonder that they'd trusted Hugo Mortimer when he came to them with an idea for a thirty-storey office block in a mid-west American city. *Trust me,* he'd said. *These buildings are going to be safe havens for your money in the current financial climate.* And they had trusted him.

And he had abused the power and influence and robbed them and cheated them.

She yearned to tell Rick exactly what he could do with his proposal but she couldn't.

'A partnership made in heaven?' She gulped. 'Well, your idea of heaven is apparently a lot different from mine. What are you thinking?'

She put down her fork and looked around the dining room. 'You don't know anything about me apart from what you have picked up through a few Internet searches.'

'That can be changed. And yes, I do know you.'

'Really? You might think you do. Well, I certainly do not know you.'

'Then come to France with me tomorrow and find out for yourself.'

'Thank you, but I have a business to run. What makes you think that I can just take off when I please? Life is not like that.'

'It can be. Let's decide this here and now.'

He grabbed a paper napkin and scribbled something on it and slid it across the table in front of her.

'This is the consultancy fee for your expenses. If, for some crazy reason, you still feel the same way at the end of the week, then Angie will set up the bookings at Elwood House regardless. But if you do decide to buy from me? We will be in the right place at the right time to create something amazing.'

Saskia glared at him for a second and then glanced down at the napkin. And then picked it up and blinked at it in disbelief at a number with lots of zeroes on the end of it.

'You can't be serious,' she gasped.

'You said yourself. Your time is valuable. One week of your time. Seven days. I have a generous marketing budget and every time you serve RB Wines to your prestigious guests at Elwood House you are promoting my company. Your excellent taste. My producers. Take a risk, Saskia. You have nothing to lose. Tempted?'

And, almost casually, he picked up his fork and went back to his pasta.

While she had suddenly lost her appetite.

Unbelievable!

Her gaze landed on the delicious bottle of hugely expensive Italian red wine she was enjoying and she took a long sip to cool her dry throat, taking the time to savour every drop.

Of course she was tempted!

She was running on credit and the nest egg Aunt Margot had left was not going to last much longer. She needed to make Elwood House work. She needed the bookings and she needed them now.

What was she going to do? Ruin her credibility and family reputation for the sake of a few bottles of dodgy wine? Her fingers stilled.

The very last thing she wanted was to get involved with yet another conman who could talk the talk but not deliver the goods and, most importantly, keep his side of the bargain when it came to the push.

Her fingers pressed hard into her forehead as she tried to process everything that Rick had said. And failed.

Oh he was good.

Okay, her father had been a city boy born and bred. Perhaps the similarity ended there. But one thing was abundantly clear. Rick Burgess was every bit the same type of hustler, with the power to make every single woman, and even those not so single, swoon with one look.

Been there. Done that. Still trying to put out the flames.

She was still human, and a girl, but that didn't change a thing.

There was no way she could take this man, who she had only met a few hours earlier, and introduce him as a serious wine merchant to her guests.

How could she even think about putting them through what they had suffered at the hands of her father? He had been credible and his clients adored him.

Hugo Mortimer the man was a delight, the life and soul of any party. Charismatic and charming.

Hugo Mortimer the property developer was a disaster who had destroyed her life and certainly ruined the lives of more than one family around the world who'd trusted their savings to his ridiculous arrogance and high risk schemes.

She just couldn't do it. She couldn't take the risk. Not where Elwood House was concerned.

'I'm not going to France with you, Rick. Don't take it personally. I decided years ago that I wanted to stay independent. That way, there are no compromises or surprises. And I certainly don't want to take orders from someone else once I sign a contract.'

'I understand that.' His smile widened to the point where she thought that she might fall into it and be swallowed up. 'But then I didn't expect you to run Elwood House on your own. The hotel owners I know are notoriously male, egotistical and stubborn. Or at least… That record stood until today. You opened my eyes to what I have been missing.'

His gaze wrapped around her shoulders and neck and slowly, slowly made its way up her face and into her hair, until she had to fight not to squirm under the heat so she frowned at him instead. 'On the other hand, maybe the stubborn bit still applies.'

She leant forwards across the table until her nose was only inches from his.

'I would hate to thwart your expectations. You might never recover from the shock.'

'I think I can handle anything you throw at me,' he replied, his upper lip twitching.

'Really?' Saskia picked up her glass of excellent Italian red and swirled it under her nose before taking a long sip. 'Then come up with a proposal that doesn't involve me selling out my reputation for excellence.'

'Okay. Final offer. If you don't like the wine I offer you then you don't have to buy it. And I still pay your consultancy fee and use Elwood House. Is that any better?'

Saskia tilted her glass until the last drop touched her lips. 'Move your company office into Elwood House. Long-term contract.'

'Done.'

'I can't guarantee that I will buy anything from you. You know that, don't you?'

'Of course. Buy hey, with what I am going to show you, how could you possibly resist? And can I order the Prosecco now?'

She inhaled slowly and then gave a small sharp nod.

And instantly regretted it because he immediately leapt out of his chair, pulled her to her feet by grabbing both shoulders and kissed her hard on the lips. Then he dropped her back down like a sack and rubbed the palms of his hands together.

'Brilliant. What time can you be ready in the morning?'

CHAPTER FIVE

Must-Do list
- *Be sure to pack the spare chargers for phone, camera and notebook computer.*
- *Deliberately leave behind the list of chat-up lines that Kate emailed. Way too dangerous and some of them would crash the car.*
- *Remember your CDs—just in case Rick is a fan of heavy metal.*
- *Stay focused, stay frosty. No getting sidetracked by the lovely view etc. I have a fine view right here in London, thank you.*
- *Try not to worry about the house more than every few minutes. Amber and Kate have things under control. EEP.*

'No, KATE. No more gloves. *Seriously.* I do not need eight pairs of gloves for a week in the French countryside, so please take at least some of them out of my case,' Saskia protested.

'Spoilsport,' Kate hissed and held up a plum-coloured satin slip. 'Amber? What do you think of the seduction power of this one?'

'Not bad, actually,' Amber laughed and sidled over to

Saskia, who was sitting on the bed with her head in her hands.

'Why did I ask you two to help me pack?' Saskia whimpered as Amber gave her a shove. 'I keep telling you. It's a business trip to three vineyards in France—that's all. The Champagne region. Then the Alps and north to Alsace. I am talking muddy fields and icy-cold cellars, not salons fit for satin.'

'A business trip. Yes.' Kate nodded wisely. 'Of course it is.' Then rolled her eyes. 'One week on the road and all alone with the hunk of the year. Believe me, that boy will see you in your lingerie one way or another before the week is out. And you might as well get used to the idea, even if you don't plan to show him your knickers.'

Saskia clutched the edges of her practical thick towelling bath robe tighter across her chest. 'Katherine Lovat!'

Then she sniffed and peered into her suitcase and gave a small shoulder shrug. 'Good thing I only have huge cotton granny pants. They should work as instant boy repellent in case he gets any ideas.'

'That may not be entirely true.' Amber smiled and pulled out a bag from under the bed with the name of an exclusive lingerie shop on the side. 'Kate and I decided that we were being extremely selfish going shopping for fripperies today while you worked, so we splashed out on a little something to brighten your top drawer. I hope you like it.'

'Of course we would have bought a lot more if we had known that you were being wooed by Rick the Reckless, but hey, this should keep him interested and no, you are not allowed to open up your present until the occasion calls for it.'

Saskia smiled and gathered Amber and Kate for a hug on her bed. 'Thanks. I am not going to need it, whatever it is, but you are so kind to me and I promise to wear whatever pretty frilly you have chosen, even if it is to walk up and down freezing-cold wine cellars. I shall feel very special.'

'Of course you will,' Kate snorted. 'But don't forget to book Rick as your date for Amber's wedding. New Year is a busy time for boys and he ticks all the boxes for tall, dark and handsome.'

'My date? This is Rick Burgess you are talking about. He never takes anything seriously. It's as though life is a great joke to be enjoyed at someone else's expense. He's obviously coasting and filling in time before he can slip off to the nearest ski slope or some yacht. Well, I know his type only too well. My dad was exactly the same. Well-off, handsome and super-confident. And a complete disaster when it came to managing his finances and relationships. As far as I'm concerned Rick might as well be standing there waving a red warning sign with the words "Danger. Keep away" written in large black letters.'

Saskia shivered in dramatic horror and then paused and narrowed her eyes as she whizzed around to face Kate. 'Wait a minute. How did you know what he looks like? Oh no. You looked him up on the Internet, didn't you?'

'That was me.' Amber giggled. 'Your Richard is quite the professional sportsman. Very fit. You are a lucky girl.'

'I give up,' Saskia groaned. 'You two are quite incorrigible.'

'That's why you need us,' Kate replied, fluttering her eyelashes. 'And don't worry for a second about this place. Amber is house-sitting and answering the phone and I promise to pop over every evening and gobble up all of the treats in your freezer and drink your wine.'

She paused and waved both arms in the air with a flourish. 'We've got it covered. All you have to do is smile and charm your way through the week with your usual flair. Piece of cake!'

Saskia stood silently on the golden stone patio of the Chateau Morel in the September sunshine and looked out over the rows and rows of neatly trained vines that were destined to create the greatest sparkling wine in the world; champagne.

And thought seriously about dumping Rick and catching the first train back to London.

Piece of cake, Kate had said.

Well, there was nothing sweet about how Saskia would describe the past few hours.

Rick had changed his mind and decided that it would be easier to drive them to the first of the three independent vineyards himself. Which meant that she had been strapped into the passenger seat of the macho four-by-four that Rick had borrowed from one of his team for what had seemed like an eternity.

All the while trapped within arm-touching distance of Rick Burgess on the drive down through the flat countryside of northern France, which she'd thought would never end.

Rick had an incredibly annoying ability to look completely calm and unstressed no matter what delay hit them on the way. The traffic jams on the motorway to the coast—no problem. Dodging in and out of the traffic chaos of the French road works madness as a lorry veered in front of them? It only made him smile that certain smile which turned the corners of his mouth a little higher.

While she was clutching onto the roof straps of the car with both hands in terror.

It was totally infuriating.

The problem was, the more unruffled and calm Rick appeared, the more she wanted to take hold of his shoulders and give him a violent shake and scream out that it was time to wake up and get to work. He could be laid-back any time he wanted, but not now. Not when she had work to do back in London.

Take now, for example. They had been right on schedule arriving in Reims and she was all ready to get started on the details when Rick decided that he needed to take a look at the vines. Leaving her behind in the cellar.

That was two hours ago.

The heels of her high-heeled designer shoes dug into the loose gravel chippings as she tried to walk calmly across the patio and back towards the chateau. She refused to look down and check the damage. Rick would get far too much satisfaction from that. He had taken one look at her footwear that morning and snorted with a dismissive shake of his head. His smart flat leather boots were, of course, perfect for strolling down between the rows of vines and across the rough stone flagstones.

To make matters worse, her cellphone had never stopped ringing from the moment she'd got into Rick's car that morning and, after two hours of terrible mobile reception and her increasing frustration, he had barely given her time to research a few new suppliers of kitchenware before declaring that his car was an Internet-free zone and laptops were not allowed.

She needed to confirm these new bookings for the spring, not make conversation about soil type and climate and all the things that came together to make this small estate unique in over three hundred of the champagne houses in the Reims area of France.

The cheek of the man. She was supposed to be helping

him out! What did he expect her to do? Just forget about Elwood House and treat this trip as some sort of holiday?

Not going to happen.

Even if he was paying her and the setting was absolutely glorious.

The Chateau Morel looked like a white fairy tale castle which had been dropped gently from the sky into the fields of vines.

While the wine? Okay, she had to confess that the champagne that these grapes produced was special. Rare and expensive. In fact, it was precisely the kind of wine that Rick needed to boost the status of his flagship store, after all, there was not a wine shop in the world which did not stock champagne. Elwood Brothers had been famous for their range and quality for decades.

What was even more infuriating was that Rick kept reminding her that she should be excited to see the grapes before harvest! But the truth was she felt too preoccupied and anxious about her work to enjoy the moment.

Saskia rolled her shoulders back with the warm sun on her face as she watched Rick and their host, the Comte de Morel, stroll towards the chateau between the vines, pausing only now and then to taste the grapes. The sound of their gentle chatter rolled towards her.

Just when she thought that he couldn't spring any more surprises on her, Rick had turned the tables. The man she was looking at now was asking exactly the type of intelligent and knowledgeable questions that any grower would expect from another professional.

That was it—professional. Right down to the smart jacket and expensive wristwatch and cufflinks. The denim and boots were just the same. The designer stubble and tousled hair hadn't changed, but his whole attitude and mood had transformed once they'd hit the open road.

If this was Rick trying to impress her and convince her to buy the wine, he was making a fine effort. And, so far, he had not embarrassed her once.

This was not the Rick she had met in London. This was Rick Burgess, the working wine merchant and negotiating charmer. His laughter rang out and suddenly her confidence faltered and she felt out of her depth.

This was so ridiculous.

She was Saskia the calm. Saskia the girl who was always in control. Saskia the girl who knew exactly what she was doing at all times.

It was just that it had been such a long time since she had stepped away from Elwood House and given herself over to someone else to make decisions and take the lead that she was finding it hard to adjust to Rick being in the driving seat.

Excitement combined with anxiety meant that she had barely slept the night before, after the girls had left, with promises to keep them informed on how a little trip with Rick the Reckless, as Kate called him, was going.

If she had come here alone, or with Aunt Margot, she would be able to relax and take the time to learn from the best. Building her knowledge and experience.

But she was way too much on edge to relax for even a second.

Plus, Rick was expecting her to pay attention and make a decision whether to buy this wine, not take time out on holiday. And there was one thing she had learned and promised herself over the years. Once she made a commitment to do something then she would see it through. No false promises. No tricks.

She had promised Rick that she would visit the vineyard and she had. Now came the hard part. Making sure that the Elwood connection was not pulled into whatever Rick was trying to prove here. For better or for worse!

Time to get to work. Because here he was, casually walking towards her as though they had all the time in the world.

'You are looking a bit fierce standing there with your conference folder and pen,' he quipped. 'All ready to stomp into a business meeting and start taking notes.' Then he gestured towards the house. 'I think you scared Pierre off.'

'That is what we are here for, after all. Business. And does the Comte de Morel normally answer to the name Pierre?'

His gaze slid onto her face. By way of her cleavage and neck. Which, of course, made her neck flare up, adding to the embarrassment.

'Why not? That is his name. And I keep telling you, this is the new generation. Pierre prefers guests to be informal.'

Saskia lifted her chin and tugged down on the hem of her smart suit jacket. 'Not sure I can do that. Too many years of training.'

Rick's cellphone rang out with the first beats of a popular dance track and he glanced at a few screens and winced before replying. 'You can put your folder away. Don't worry about the production figures.' He tapped his smartphone with two fingers. 'Pierre has just copied me with the latest costings and projections so we can talk them through when we're back on the road. Now, don't look so surprised. I can do business planning when needed.'

'Surprised?' Saskia cleared her throat, hating that she had been so obvious. 'Not at all, Mr Burgess.'

'It's Rick,' he groaned. 'We are trying to keep things informal. Remember?'

'Is that why you decided to drive yourself?' she asked, teasing him. 'I'm sure that a big company like Burgess

Wine could afford to provide a limo with a driver. Your parents must be pleased that you are taking such interest in the wine business. Quite the entrepreneur, in fact,' she chuckled, looking out over the fields of vines.

'There are okay with it,' he replied, hooking her arm around his elbow and stepping closer so that their bodies were side by side and it was impossible for her to move away. 'Results shout louder than promises. Or something.'

'Okay.' She hesitated, and her feet slowed a little even in the gravel. 'Do they know that we are here today, talking to growers? I don't want to get involved in some family dispute.'

Rick came to a dead stop and whirled around to face Saskia. His gaze locked onto her face. And those grey eyes were suddenly not so warm in the September sunshine, but more like granite. Fierce, commanding but intelligent. For the first time Saskia had a glimpse of some of that inner steel that drove men like Rick to become professional sportsmen. It was the kind of look that had no place in a nice, safe office job.

'Family dispute? What gave you that idea?'

Saskia tensed and licked her lips before replying. 'What I meant to say was that I thought the Burgess Wine empire is based in California. Opening a London branch is a complete departure. It makes me wonder if the company is splitting into separate divisions. That's quite a challenge.'

Rick exhaled slowly then sniffed, as though weighing up what to make of her question.

'Challenge?' Rick's eyebrows crushed together and he frowned. 'Is that what you think?'

But before Saskia could create some sort of answer he tilted his head to one side and gave a small shoulder shrug. 'A challenge,' he repeated, nodding slowly. 'Yeah. When I pitched the idea to my parents last Christmas, they used a few more colourful expressions to describe the notion. A challenge just about sums up the general response.'

'I see,' she replied. 'Wait. Did you say last Christmas? Surely you have seen your parents since then?'

Rick took tighter hold of her hand and started walking towards the house. 'No need. Modern communications. I can work anywhere. They run the business out of Napa and right now the biggest wine festival in the world is about to kick off. They don't want to be involved in the new enterprise in London. Small beer.'

Saskia glanced back at him. She recognised that tiny change in his voice that was so familiar to her it seemed like an old friend. She knew what it was like to defend her parents and their decisions and their over the top lifestyle choices. Especially when those choices did not include her.

What was surprising was that Rick had the same problems she had. Real problems. Problems she recognised only too well. He was trying to keep the tone of his voice light and smiling but below that effortless charm was a well of sorrow.

'You've reminded me that I need to arrange my mother's Christmas present. She's staying in New York with her latest beau this year and I'll be working in London, as always. Thank heavens for telephones.'

He chuckled somewhere deep down in his chest. 'It seems that we have a few parental issues in common.'

'Oh?' she replied in a calm, low voice. 'Is your father in prison too?'

Rick burst out laughing at that and released her hand as he held open the door.

'Touché. You win that one. Why don't we drink champagne and leave our families where they belong? Out of sight and out of our lives. Deal? Deal.'

* * *

'More cheese, Rick? I tried to save you the last slice of the walnut bread but I was too late, Pierre got to it first.'

Anna gestured with the cheese knife towards her husband, Pierre Morel, the tenth generation owner of the Chateau Morel, who threw his hands up into the air in protest. 'Can I help it if I have a healthy appetite? Anyway, you are one to talk. I only turned my back for two minutes to load the dishwasher and what was left of those excellent handmade chocolates Rick brought with him had done a magic disappearing act.'

Anna kissed the top of Pierre's head. 'It's quite true,' she laughed and pressed one very dainty hand to her chest. 'Sweet tooth and a total chocaholic. Now, that is a pretty deadly combination. And I feel totally guilty.'

Rick chuckled and sat back on the wide kitchen chair and patted his stomach. Things had certainly changed an awful lot since he had visited the estate with his parents and Tom as a teenager. The old *comte* and *comtesse* of the Chateau Morel had insisted on serving canapés and coffee in the huge echoing great hall with waiting staff glaring at every crumb which fell onto the thread-bare hand-woven and embroidered carpet. Before the *comte* haughtily declared that he did not sell his prestigious wine to anyone less than premium outlets. He had made it only too clear that the list did not include an online wine retailer who specialised in affordable wine for barbecues and sharing over a plate of pizza.

Now their grandson Pierre and his charming Dutch-born wife Anna were wearing casual trousers and shirts and seemed genuinely delighted to welcome them into their warm, cosy kitchen and a delicious, simple family meal.

'Please don't feel guilty.' Rick smiled. 'It was incredibly kind of you to offer us lunch at such short notice, and I couldn't eat another thing.'

'I could.' Saskia laughed. 'This cheese is amazing.'

'A local goat farmer makes it for us to a traditional recipe. It was one of the first things we stocked in our farm shop and it is always a best seller. I am glad you like it.'

'Delicious,' Saskia replied and cut another wedge. 'And thank you again for the tour. Especially just before harvest. Such an exciting time of year.'

'We have been very lucky with the weather.' Pierre nodded. 'But you're right; this is going to be an excellent vintage.'

'You know, my Aunt Margot always adored Chateau Morel dry champagnes and refused to serve anything else. Although…I do seem to recall that your grandfather persuaded her to try a few magnums of pink champagne for special occasions now and then. It was her special treat on hot summer evenings. Are you planning to continue that tradition?'

Anna shrugged and looked across at Pierre before pouring the coffee. 'We're not sure that there is enough demand to make it worth our while, but it is definitely something we will continue for the next couple of years at least.'

'That's wonderful. I love it so much.'

Pierre nodded and then smiled gently across at Saskia as he rolled his coffee can between his fingers, but when he spoke there was some hesitancy in his voice. 'I remember meeting your Aunt Margot. It must have been about fifteen years or so ago and I was a young apprentice winemaker. I can still remember walking through the doors of Elwood Brothers. Your aunt ran the best wine merchant in London and yet she took the trouble to welcome us as old family friends. She was a remarkable woman and a very loyal customer. I am only sorry that she never had an opportunity to visit us.'

Anna sat quietly sipping her coffee with her head down as Pierre squeezed her hand.

'I am sorry too,' Saskia whispered. 'I still miss her very much. Margot would have adored coming here.'

Saskia pressed the forefingers of her left hand to her mouth and sucked in a breath and just for a moment looked as though she was about to start crying.

Rick hadn't expected that!

A trembling flicker of connection started deep in his stomach. From what Saskia had told him, she was not close to her mother and he knew that her father was serving time for embezzlement. Her aunt must have been the only family she could rely on.

Saskia had come here with no clue that she was going to be emotionally ambushed by a stranger who had known the aunt she'd so clearly adored.

And now Margot Elwood was gone and she still hadn't got over it.

Well, he knew what that felt like.

Worse, Saskia was sitting in this kitchen because he had changed his mind overnight and picked her up in one of the team's cars and driven them here instead of flying to Strasbourg and going directly to the *auberge* in Alsace.

His decision. Flying by the seat of his pants. Changing the rules at the last minute. Stirring things up.

Well, that hadn't worked out so well. He had brought her here to this place where she was forced to relive her grief, just when she thought it was all behind her.

Only it was all over her face. Her beautiful, wrecked, tragic face.

She was feeling that grief and loss all over again.

A familiar pain hit Rick deep inside his heart but he

shoved it down the way he always did when the memory of Tom came flooding back into his consciousness out of the blue. Perhaps it was this chateau? He had such clear memories of that day they had come here as a family.

Now Tom was gone. And he was left to pick up the pieces, just as Saskia was trying to do. *Life wasn't fair. On either of them.*

He shuffled in his chair and picked up another slice of cheese and bread and casually looked up with a wave of his cheese knife.

Rick chuckled out loud, instantly cutting through the tense atmosphere.

'That's why I'm working so hard to bring your champagne to customers like Saskia. The girl right here today has inherited the best qualities of the Elwood family and her clients expect the very best. Which is precisely what we are going to give them. Saskia and I are looking forward. Not backward. Aren't you?'

A faint glimmer of a smile flickered across Pierre's face and Anna's expression lightened.

'I could not have put it better myself, Rick. Of course, that was a different generation and that is exactly what we want to do; move forward.'

'Why else am I here?' Rick smiled and relaxed back in his chair. 'And thank you for being so honest and generous, and for your time today so close to the harvest. Don't forget, next time you're in London I'll be delighted to return your hospitality and show you around our new showroom. In the meantime?' He raised his coffee cup. 'I think a toast is required. To a successful harvest and many of them!'

'Well,' Rick said with a low sigh, 'that went well. Nice lunch. What did you think of the extra dry champagne? That is a winner in my book.'

'A winner? Yes, the champagne was lovely and I will definitely order some. Out of guilt if nothing else,' Saskia said in a voice that was trembling with emotion. 'That lovely couple gave us such a warm welcome and all I could do was fall apart. They must think that I am a complete idiot.'

She half turned towards him in the passenger seat and grabbed hold of the dashboard to give her strength. 'I cannot believe that I embarrassed myself like that. I had no idea that Pierre had met Aunt Margot and admired her, but I certainly don't normally react that way. I suppose it hit me out of the blue, but it was still so humiliating.'

'Who for? Me?' Rick glanced once at Saskia before concentrating on driving down the narrow farm road. 'Not at all. What is there to be embarrassed about? You cared for your aunt and she was clearly admired.'

His fingers tapped out a rhythm on the steering wheel. 'How long has it been?'

'Just over a year.' Saskia exhaled slowly and when she spoke her words were very calm and measured. 'But it feels a lot longer.'

Rick said nothing but slowed the car on the narrow country road and pulled into the next tourist viewpoint on the brow of a hill.

Before Saskia knew what was happening, he was out of the car and had opened the passenger door for her.

'Come on,' he said, and held out his hand towards her. 'Let's get some air.'

'Air?' she repeated disbelievingly. 'I have had more than enough air at the Chateau, thank you. I can be just as miserable right here.'

'Then have some more. I'm not driving another mile until we have this out.'

He stood there, looking at her with a smile on his face

which reached his eyes and was impossible to resist. His fingers twitched, gesturing her to reach out and take his hand.

Resigned to the inevitable and too exhausted to complain further, Saskia slowly and carefully unclipped her seat belt, took his hand and stepped down onto the grass in her smart heels.

But, instead of releasing her hand, Rick wrapped his fingers firmly around hers and drew her away from the car and onto the brow of the hill, where they stood in silence looking out onto the golden leaves and autumn colours of the neat rows of grapevines. Side by side. So that when he broke the silence it was as if he was talking to the vines.

Rick rolled his shoulders. 'I know what it is like to lose someone you love. And believe me when I say that a year is not nearly long enough to get over wanting to burst into tears just at the sound of that person's name. But nobody in the world will think less of you if you miss your aunt. Nobody.'

Then he sniffed and gazed out at the golden autumn colours.

'Do you know what I'm thinking?' For several long minutes all Saskia could hear was the *tink, tink, tink* from the car as it cooled and birdsong from the fields stretched out in front of them.

'That inside my business suit I'm a fraud?' she whispered.

He whipped around towards her and his blue-grey eyes turned into the colour of steel as they glared at her. Hard, demanding and not prepared to take any argument.

'Wrong. And don't you ever let anyone make you feel that way. Ever. You are not a fraud. Okay, so you get emotional and blub over your silk blouse. Only to be expected. Just think how hard it is for us guys! We have to play the macho game and wait until we get home to let rip. So get that out of your head right now, gorgeous. Not a fraud. Are we clear?'

'Okay.' She blinked and drew back a little. 'Quite clear.'

'Good. I don't want to hear it again. You are, however, the worst mind-reader I've ever met. Because actually—' and his voice lowered and seemed to warm in the sunshine '—I was thinking about how very lucky we are.'

He flung his right hand out towards the hills and his left hand clung on to Saskia even more tightly as though he was afraid she might run away.

'Look at this view. The birds are singing and the sun is shining. No traffic noise. No buses, taxis, or email or a clamour of people demanding our attention. For the next few minutes this is all ours. And I happen to think it's special.'

He turned back to her with a smile, reached out and stroked her cheek with one finger so tenderly and gently, and she felt like crying for real. 'Change of plan. I was thinking of staying overnight at this great hotel some friends of mine own, but you know what? It's time to go home. No. Not London, the chalet in the French Alps that I call home. I've done enough talking. Time for action. That way, we can take time out to enjoy ourselves tomorrow morning before the wedding.'

'Wedding? What wedding?' Saskia asked.

'You'll see.' Rick laughed and tapped the end of her nose with his finger. 'You'll see.'

CHAPTER SIX

Must-Do list
- *Be sure to buy Alpine red and white fabric to make Christmas soft furnishings and decorations. Take photos of the window displays for ideas.*
- *The wine and cuisine from this part of France is very interesting and delicious. Pick up some recipe books and ideas.*
- *Never forget that Rick is a salesman and try not to weaken in this gorgeous chalet with its amazing views.*

'I CAN'T BEGIN to describe how gorgeous this chalet is,' Saskia whispered with a long sigh. 'Think tourist postcards of the Alps. All golden wood and snow-capped mountain views with ancient wooden skis stacked in the hall. And window boxes. Rick has window boxes with real red balcony geraniums hanging out of them. I didn't expect that.'

Just like I didn't expect him to back me up yesterday after the Chateau Morel.

'The fiend,' Kate sniffed, and Saskia could tell that her friend had the phone jammed in the corner between her chin and her shoulder. 'Log cabins and mountain views? I think you should call the authorities immediately. The next thing you know, he will be opening doors for you and helping you on with your coat. I can see it now. All part of his ruthless plan to lower your resistance and make you like him!'

'Well, it's working. Coat. Tick. Doors. Tick. He even brought my suitcase inside and insisted on taking me out to dinner last night. Which was amazing. I had no idea that Savoyard food was so delicious. And of course he knows everyone. So they immediately thought that I was, and I quote—"his new squeeze". Hah! As if.'

'You tell them,' Kate replied. 'Your standards are much higher. Sort of. Well, they would be if you ever actually dated, but you know what I mean. Higher. Who wants a tall, dark and handsome hunk on her arm anyhow? Oh no. Or should that be yes?'

'Well, thanks. You are a lot of help.'

'You don't need help. You have never needed help,' Kate laughed. 'So, just for once, go with the flow and see where it takes you! How about that for an idea? Oh—must go. My client has arrived and this jacket is still missing a pocket. Bye!'

'Bye,' Saskia replied, but Kate had already gone. Busy as always. Which was great. Kate had worked hard to make her fashion design business a success. But it didn't stop her from worrying about Elwood House, no matter how wonderful the diversion.

Saskia sat back in her comfy bedroom chair and stared out of the square wooden window at the stunning view of Mont Blanc set against a bright blue sky. It was so perfect that it could have been a framed photograph instead of a real, huge, snow-covered mountain.

When they'd driven into Chamonix the previous evening the sun was starting to set behind Mont Blanc and the whole peak and the glacier that streamed down into their valley had been touched with a strange pink glow which she had never seen before. It was almost as if the mountains were blushing.

Well, she knew all about that. She hadn't been joking about the good-natured teasing Rick had received from the locals and restaurant staff about his new lady friend—her! Introducing her as a business colleague had made them laugh even louder. If she picked up the accent correctly, it was very rare for Rick to bring anyone but fellow professional sportsmen to his chalet, and never a woman, so she was a definite first.

In Chamonix, Rick was very much a man's man.

Perhaps that was why he was so keen to say goodnight as soon as they'd got back to the chalet?

Not that she was complaining. Far from it. She had been treated to a delicious meal with local wine and was feeling a lot mellower when she walked through the door into the warm and cosy log cabin.

It simply would have been nice to talk about his plans for his programme of vineyard visits without an audience within earshot of everything that they were saying. She had so many questions. And so few answers.

Starting with the wedding she had been invited to today.

It was a lovely idea, but they didn't have time to go to his friends' wedding. She needed to get back to work on her plans for Elwood House and go through the vineyard production forecasts Rick had promised he would provide, rather than wedding plans. But he had refused to take no for an answer.

All Rick would say was that it was one of the ten couples whose wine they would be selling, and that was it! No details at all.

Rick Burgess seriously needed to work on his communication skills.

Time to help him with that. Starting right now!

Saskia stood up and checked her side and front view in the mirror. The wedding was not until that afternoon so she could be smart casual for a few hours. Fitted three-quarter length black trousers and black medium heels. High-neck ivory silk shirt. Hair sleeked back. Discreet make-up. Simple jewellery. Yes. That would do for any impromptu business meetings he might have set up to surprise her.

Because, one way or another, she needed to get this business trip back on track and focused on the work. Even if she was enjoying herself far more than she was prepared to admit.

She lifted her chin and saluted her reflection with a grin. All present and correct. Ready to face the world.

She marched over and flung open the bedroom door. And stood there. Frozen.

Because Rick was standing next to the dining room table, surrounded by what looked to her like the entire contents of a camping store. With extras. He was wearing black ski wear which clung to the bands of muscles across his chest and abdomen. And hot did not come close to describing how fit he looked.

'Dare I ask?' she muttered.

He looked up and smiled in a totally casual and relaxed fashion. 'Morning. Hope you slept well.'

'Very well, thank you. And please explain.'

He gestured with his head towards the table. 'Help yourself to breakfast and I'll do my best. We're setting off in about an hour.'

Saskia made her way carefully across the floor by standing on tiptoe to avoid treading on the equipment. Laid on the table was a wonderful platter of continental cooked meats, cheese and Danish pastries and croissants. Fresh butter and jams. Fruit. 'You must have been up early.

But why are you dressed like that? I thought we had a business meeting today and an hour doesn't seem long enough.'

Rick nodded and adjusted something which had the word 'Altimeter' on the side before setting it down next to his plate. 'Small town. Baker and supermarket are right next to each other. Makes it easy.'

He pointed with the end of a hand-held radio to a ceramic pot covered with a red and white checked fabric circle. 'Try the wild blueberry jam. My neighbour collected the berries this week high on the mountain; it's pretty good. And relax, I haven't forgotten what we are here for.'

Saskia sat down and broke up a croissant and piled it with the jam. He was right, it was amazing. Almost as good as the view of her host, who was standing right in front of a large glass-panelled door which led out onto a wooden veranda. There was a perfect backdrop of green forest, blue sky and the snow-white mountain Mont Blanc behind his head and a professional stylist could not have created a better composition in a million years.

And, just like that, something flipped deep inside Saskia's stomach and she slowed down to appreciate every mouthful of her breakfast, and every eyeful.

Rick really was spectacular.

Also a mind-reader because, just as she was ogling his chest, Rick glanced around at her and caught her in the act and grinned that knowing kind of grin which made it ten times worse. Saskia knew that her neck was flaming red as she blushed, especially wearing a pale shirt, but there was nothing she could do about it. So she loaded up her plate from the platter instead.

'You were about to tell me where we are off to,' she said in a calm, controlled voice, knowing all the while that it wasn't fooling him in the slightest.

'A treat for you.' He smiled and strolled over with a pot

of the most delicious-smelling coffee and poured her a cup. 'After weeks on the road, I needed to step away from the business and get back to my life. But today? Today, I think it's time for you to meet one of our ten growers.'

'Good idea.' She nodded. 'Is the vineyard very far? I need ten minutes to charge my laptop and camera and I'll be ready to take minutes.'

'Just in the next valley, but that's not where we're going. Oh no. Jean Baptiste has a passion for flying as well as grapes. Time to show you just how much fun you can have if you team up with me.'

The buttered slice of baguette halted halfway to her lips. 'Flying?' she whimpered.

'Of course. We. Are going paragliding. Saskia? Are you okay? You are looking a little pale.'

She just managed to put her breakfast down without dropping it.

'*Paragliding,*' she whispered, feeling that her throat was full of breadcrumbs.

'Sure,' Rick replied, stuffing all kinds of helmets and equipment into a huge backpack. 'Burgess Wine sponsors the local paragliding club and I won a few championships a couple of years ago and like to keep up the practice. Have you ever tried it yourself?'

Saskia blinked at him and tried to form a sensible reply but gave up. 'Is that where you tie a parachute to your back and jump off a cliff and hope the chute slows you down before you hit the ground?'

'Not quite, but you have the general idea about controlling the descent with a canopy.'

She inhaled slowly and decided to break the bad news all at once.

'I am really sorry, especially since you stuck your neck out for me yesterday, but I have vertigo on a stepladder and have to pay people to climb up and clean my bedroom windows because I can't lean out and do it myself.'

She shook her head slowly from side to side. 'I don't do heights.'

His hands stilled and he looked at her, eyebrows high. 'Seriously?'

'Seriously.' She nodded very slowly, up and down. Twice.

'Oh—' he sniffed '—not a problem. You can jump onto my harness and I can fly you down in tandem. I do it all the time and you don't weigh a thing. Wait and see, you'll enjoy it. But er…' His gaze scanned her from head to toe and then back up again and there was just enough of a cheeky grin on his face to make her want to cover her chest with a cushion. 'You might want to change your clothes. Have you brought any ski wear?'

She narrowed her eyes and tilted her head slightly to one side before replying. 'Strange. As a matter of fact, I have not. You see, I packed for a business trip. Fancy that!'

An hour later, Saskia had changed into cold weather layers, survived being driven by Rick to a ski lift at breakneck speed and then a hair-raising trip trapped inside a glass-sided gondola which took twenty minutes to climb up the side of the valley wall.

The good news was that Rick had kept her talking and focused on him for the whole journey and she had not lost her breakfast as the gondola slid up the loose cable, juddering along every pole before coming to a gentle swaying halt at the top.

It was almost worth it for the views. Stepping out from the ski station, Saskia was hit square between the eyes by a panorama of the snow-covered mountains on each side of the valley that was so breathtakingly lovely that she forgot that she was supposed to be scared for all of five minutes—before she turned around and saw Rick talking to another man carrying another huge backpack.

'Saskia, come and meet Jean Baptiste Fayel. Jean is one of my winemakers I was telling you about who we are going to showcase in the London store.'

A handsome fair-haired young man stepped forward. If Saskia thought that Rick had a firm handshake then Jean Baptiste was trying to do a fine job of shaking her arm out of its socket.

'Great to meet you, Miss Elwood.' He grinned, still shaking her hand. 'Rick has told us all about the fantastic plans you have to serve our wine. We're really excited.'

'Leave the poor girl alone.' Rick laughed and shook Jean by the shoulders before turning to Saskia. 'Jean is getting married this afternoon so we thought that it would do us good to escape away from the mayhem back at his house and get into the air for a few hours.'

This was the bridegroom?

Saskia turned back to Jean with a smile. 'Congratulations. How wonderful.'

He blushed slightly, which was very charming. 'Thank you, and of course you're invited to the wedding. Nicole and I would love to see you there. Rick has given us a lifeline to a great opportunity. And that is something to celebrate.'

Saskia flashed a glance at Rick, who nodded slowly.

She had been ambushed! Any chance of doing work was now completely out of the window!

'I'm looking forward to it,' Saskia replied with a smile. 'Thank you.'

'Excellent,' he replied and then nodded towards the cliff and checked his chronometer. 'If you'll excuse me, my future bride has a house full of guests who cannot start the eating and drinking until I get back. See you at the landing strip. But you go first. I'll follow on.'

Rick came up and stood next to Saskia and they watched Jean Baptiste stroll casually over to the edge of the cliff, sit down as though there was not a huge drop only feet in front of him and unpack the same type of huge sack that Rick had brought.

It was like a magical toy box with an invisible bottom. Helmets, ropes, gloves and clothing, instruments like the ones she had seen in the kitchen that morning and then finally a tightly folded huge blue and red piece of canopy fabric emerged from one single bag. It was unbelievable! And scary.

She was still watching him slip into a harness when Rick slid closer and whispered into her ear. 'You've just been talking to one of the most promising members of the French paragliding team. Jean Baptiste is a star. All I can do is help him with a few pointers now and then when he thinks he needs coaching. But he knows what he is doing.'

'Good,' Saskia gasped. 'Because I am terrified just watching him walk over the edge onto that slope. I have no idea how he can do that.'

Rick burst out laughing and she scowled at him.

'It's not funny. We all have our weaknesses and this happens to be mine,' she whispered through clenched teeth. 'And you really should warn me about these little adventures in advance. You knew that I wouldn't be able to refuse Jean Baptiste and I have so much work to do I'm never going to catch up.'

'Where would be the fun in that? So you're not tempted to take up my offer and jump into the harness with me?' he asked, waggling his eyebrows up and down several times, and then reared back. 'Oh, now that is a fierce look. I'll take it as a no.'

Rick pressed a hand to the small of her back and guided her just a little closer to the edge, then opened her hand, splayed out her fingers and flashed her one of his killer smiles. For just one second Saskia thought that he might kiss her fingers, but instead he dropped a large bunch of keys onto her palm and closed her fingers over them.

'I'm flying down. But I could really use a pickup from the landing site. You can work out where it is. Please try not to crash my truck, and have some fun! I'm going to.'

Fun! Crash!

Saskia glared at the keys but when she looked up Rick was already sitting just below Jean Baptiste on the slope, on the steep curvature of the mountain with his backpack open, splaying out the ropes of his parachute and equipment.

Risking vertigo, Saskia edged closer to the cliff so that she could see what he was doing. 'Do be careful,' she called out. He must've heard her because he replied with a quick salute to his helmet and then untangled one of the ropes which ran between his harness and the bright orange curve of a fluted canopy which extended behind his head.

Then, as she watched with her hand pressed over her mouth, her hair whipping in front of her face in the breeze, Rick got to his feet. He took a couple of steps forward and the canopy seemed to inflate all on its own behind him, making the rope lines go straight.

And then Rick Burgess ran off the edge of the mountain.

Her heart leapt into her throat. She could not move. Dared not move. But, by leaning one more inch closer to the edge, she could see that his parachute had formed a perfect rippling rainbow arc in the sky just below her. She couldn't move her gaze from the tiny figure suspended by the ropes below.

He was sitting in some form of fabric seat made from

his harness, with his legs dangling over… Nothing but air. Hundreds of feet, possibly thousands of feet, of air.

Saskia sucked in a breath as the orange canopy fluttered slightly as he turned it towards the forest of pine trees they had passed over on the way up from the safety of the gondola ski lift.

He was spinning out of control and was going to crash into the forest! Saskia's hand pressed firmly into her mouth. But he didn't. The parachute made a slow, gentle spiral away from the rocky mountainside and forests below and turned back across the valley, spiralling in slow wide circles ever downward.

Her hands were clutching the keys so hard as she watched him descend that the points were pressing painfully into her flesh, but she could not look away. She had to keep watching Rick as he circled down, down, moving towards the mountain and then back towards the Chamonix valley. Their landing field was so far below the viewpoint that for a fraction of a second she lost sight of Rick behind some trees on the ground.

Had his harness come undone? Had he fallen out? No. She was able to breathe again. There he was. Moving in tighter and tighter circles towards the other parachute. And just when she thought he was on the same height as the first trees next to the white flowing river, he was down. On the ground. Safe.

Saskia's legs gave way and she sat down heavily on the rough path of gravel and Alpine grasses.

Collapsed down would be a better description.

Now she could breathe again. *If she remembered how. Because Jean Baptiste was getting ready to do exactly the same thing! And he was getting married today!*

Her chest had only risen and fallen a few times when the familiar ringtone of her cellphone sang out and she flicked it open to read a text message: *Down safe and well. Great flight. See you soon. R.*

Her fingers clumsily stabbed at the keypad. *Terrifying. Heading back now. S.*

Her shoulders slumped. And she flicked her phone closed.

Rick had been impressive. Watching his flight had been terrifying, horrific, awe-inspiring—and totally exhilarating at the same time.

Rick clearly did know what he was doing and Jean Baptiste respected him as a friend and a mentor and as a coach. That meant a lot.

The two men were friends and sportsmen working together to make something remarkable happen. A tiny bubble of pride in what Rick had achieved rose up from her admiration and popped into her brain before her logic could burst it.

How many more sides to Rick Burgess were there?

She had seen Rick in full-on salesman mode at Elwood House back in London.

Rick the wine merchant was a different man at the Chateau Morel and now Rick the friend and paraglider was taking the lead at home in the Alps.

She had never met anyone who was so capable of astonishing her on a daily basis.

His life seemed to be one series of constant personal challenges, all fuelled by a burning sense of life and energy and passion and drive.

No doubt about it. He was an achiever and he worked hard for those achievements.

Kate had been wrong about him.

He was not Rick the Reckless. He knew the risks and made the judgement call based on skills and talent and experience rather than some arrogant sense of his own self-importance.

Perhaps she was wrong about the wine store? Perhaps this was not a vanity project, but a real business initiative created by someone with genuine entrepreneurial zeal and passion for what they believed in.

Saskia stood up and brushed the dirt from the seat of her pants, then looked over the cliff for the landing site far below, where a blue canopy was now stretched out next to an orange one and she instantly felt sick and dizzy.

She might have been wrong about Rick, but there was one thing she was definitely clear about. There was no way she would ever, *ever,* jump off a cliff with a fabric bag above her head to break her fall. Even if she was strapped to Rick at the time.

She liked her feet to stay firmly on solid ground. Safe.

She stepped back from the edge and started strolling down to the ski station to catch the gondola back to the valley.

A cold hollow feeling swelled up in the pit of her stomach and it had nothing to do with the icy-cold wind that was blowing in from the snowy peaks around her.

She recognised that feeling only too well. It was a present from her old friends, fear and anxiety.

What was she doing here?

There was only one way this trip was going to end and it was in disappointment and regret for both of them.

She was too afraid to make the leap.

Whether that was running off a mountain strapped to Rick, or taking such risks in her life.

She dared not risk that precious security that she had worked so hard to create by giving her time and energy to RB Wines, and it would be a lot of her time, she could see that now.

Now all she had to do was work out how to tell Rick that she could not accept what he had to offer; and mean it.

CHAPTER SEVEN

Must-Do list
- *You are going to a wedding—the worst kind of emotional blackmail. Rick should be ashamed.*
- *It is okay to admit that you are not keen on heights. This is not a weakness at all. Simply a statement of fact.*
- *It is okay to admire men who jump off mountains with a grin on their face—just for fun. But that does not mean that you have to buy wine from them. Oh no.*
- *It is okay to let people surprise you on a daily basis.*

'What a lovely dress. That colour is amazing on you.'

'Thank you, kind sir,' Saskia replied and turned around to face Rick. 'My friends tell me that coral is very fashionable this season and…' But then the words stuck in her throat.

Rick Burgess was wearing a suit. And not just any suit. This was a silk and cashmere blend that Kate would have slobbered over. Midnight-blue with a tiny paler blue stripe, which fitted his broad shoulders and narrow waist to perfection.

Matched with a pale blue shirt which highlighted his tan and a pink and blue tie.

He looked like a male model who had just walked off a fashion display. Tall, dark, clean-shaven, swept back hair and so handsome it was a joke. There were movie actors who did not look that good.

'My, this is quite a transformation, Mr Burgess.'

Rick glanced down at his suit and smiled. 'Oh this little old thing? I like to wear it now and again to keep the moths away.'

'Moths? Um. So you wear a gorgeous made-to-measure suit, and yes, I know that to be a fact because my very good friend Kate is a fashion designer, for a local wedding in rural France, but choose a leather jacket for a business meeting in London? How curious. You really do like to play with people's expectations, don't you?'

'Play? Are you implying that this is some sort of a game, Miss Elwood?'

Saskia strolled forward on her high heeled sandals and reached up and straightened out the yellow rosebud on his lapel and then stepped back, gave his jacket one final pat and nodded.

'Maybe. But you are quite an expert player. I have tried so many times over the past few days to switch to work or our business and so far you have succeeded in diverting me to a fabulous champagne chateau, a paragliding flight and now a wedding party. I can squeeze in two hours tops but that is it! Seriously! Should I expect fireworks and a grand finale before we actually get around to doing the work?'

He snorted out loud and strolled over to the fireplace, which was crackling with resin from the pine wood logs, and picked up a set of cufflinks from the mantelpiece.

'You're starting to understand. I do things my way. We'll get the work done. You wait and see.'

Saskia sighed and picked up a silver-framed photograph from the bookshelf next to the fireplace. In the photograph, Rick was standing on what looked like a podium, dressed in black ski shirt and trousers and mirror shades, with his arm around a taller man who was squinting at the camera as the sun reflected back from the snow. The taller man was wearing smart beige trousers with a crisp front pleat and a formal check shirt and tie. In contrast to Rick, his body language was stiff and he looked very uncomfortable standing on the snow.

She sensed rather than heard that Rick had strolled closer and looked over her shoulder at him.

'Is this your brother? Tom, isn't it?'

Rick glanced at the photograph in her hands, then coughed out loud. 'That's Tom all right. *Not* one of life's natural sportsmen. He turned up out of the blue just in time to see me take the championship for jumping from the top of Mont Blanc. Typical. Right place and right time. I think it was the first time he had ever been on a mountain in the snow and I seem to remember that he had a problem with the ski lift.'

Rick glanced at Saskia and smiled. 'In those days it was a wooden bench attached to a chain bar at the front to stop you from falling out, but your legs dangled over the huge drop.' He shook his head. 'We came down off the mountain in a snow plough. Can you believe that?'

'That sounds perfectly sensible. I understand completely.' She laughed and replaced the picture on the shelf. 'I would have done exactly the same thing. What is Tom doing now? Is he still in the wine trade?'

Rick's eyebrows came together and he turned away from her and slowly walked over to the fireplace and rested one hand on the mantelpiece as he raked over the burning logs with a heavy metal poker.

Rick?

His gaze was locked onto the burning embers, but when he replied his voice was ice-cold. 'I thought that you already knew. Tom died, Saskia. He died two years ago.'

She gasped and crossed the gap between them and laid her hand gently on his arm.

He looked around and their eyes locked for a few seconds before a silent smile clicked back on.

And in that instant her heart melted.

Because, for the first time since they'd met, she knew that she had finally seen the real Richard Burgess beneath the tough man shell.

He had lost the brother he adored and it still hurt. It hurt so badly that he was incapable of expressing it. Two years was not nearly long enough to recover from that kind of loss.

Two years. Why did that stick in her mind?

Of course. Rick had been working for Burgess Wine for two years.

She should have known. She should have done her research.

Saskia broke the silence, her voice low, to disguise her thumping heart. 'I am so sorry. I didn't mean to pry. It was really none of my business and I feel awful to have brought back such painful memories.'

Rick answered by reaching out and taking Saskia's hand in his, startling her. He slowly splayed out each finger as she tried to clench her hand into a fist and stared down at her palm.

She couldn't breathe. Could hardly dare to speak at the sadness and regret in the man's voice; a sadness that almost overwhelmed her, a sadness that made her want to wrap her arms around him and hold him.

'Long life line.' He looked up into her eyes. 'Most people take a little longer to make the connection, but you've worked it out already, haven't you?'

He lifted one hand and pushed his hair back from his forehead. 'No regrets. Once an adrenalin junkie, always an adrenalin junkie. But you know what? We were not so different. Tom used to get exactly the same rush from solving some complex IT problem. He loved his work. Couldn't get enough.'

Saskia looked up and raised her eyebrows, and let him continue.

Rick stopped and physically turned Saskia around and gestured towards the window, which was dominated by the towering mountain that was Mont Blanc.

'I remember when that photograph was taken as though it was yesterday. The biting cold. The brilliant sunshine. The exhilaration that comes from jumping from the top of the mountain with only a parachute and a pair of skis!'

He looked at Saskia and grinned. 'Those sorts of memories have to be earned. You can't buy them or trade them. You just have to be there, at that moment in time and space. That's special. And Tom understood that. He really did. He had built up Burgess Wine from nothing by risking the business on an Internet system for selling wine which he didn't know would work or not. We were both risk-takers, just in different fields. We had so many great ideas about working together on some grandiose project or other, but not once did he ever try and make me walk away from life as a sportsman. That was always going to have to be my choice.'

Saskia turned her back on Rick, then whipped around, her voice trembling. 'I've never understood it. Never. People in London who knew my parents think that I have somehow come to terms with the terrible risks my dad took with other people's money for years before it all collapsed, but they are so wrong. You heard it with your own ears at Chateau Morel. People have long memories. They remember your brother for the best reasons and my dad for the worst. And, like it or not, we are both suffering from the fallout.'

She stretched out her hand towards Rick as he started to speak, but she turned back to face him so quickly that he caught her off balance, and he had to grab her around the waist and pull her towards him to steady her.

Saskia pushed down on his shoulders to steady herself, and made the mistake of looking into his face. And was lost, drowning in the deep pools of his eyes, which seemed to magically bind her so tight that resistance was futile. She tried to focus on the tanned, creased forehead above a mouth that was soft and wide.

Lush.

He was wearing an aftershave that smelt of warm spice, his head and throat were only inches from her face, her bosom pressed against the fine fabric. In a fraction of a second, Saskia was conscious that his hand had taken a firmer grip around her waist, moving over her thin silk dress as though it was the finest lingerie, so that she could sense the heat of his fingertips on her warm skin beneath.

She felt something connect in her gut, took a deep breath and watched words form in that amazing mouth.

'I think we make our own destiny...' Rick whispered, his gaze locked onto her eyes, and slowly closed the gap between their bodies, drawing her towards him by invisible ropes of steel.

'Destiny...?' she whispered.

'Who dares wins. Don't you take chances, Saskia?'

'Only with you...' Saskia replied, but the words were driven from her mind as Rick's fingers wound up into her hair and, drawing her closer, he slanted his head so that his warm, soft lips gently glided over hers, then firmer, hotter.

The sensation blew away any vague idea that might have been forming in her head that she could resist this man for one second longer. Her eyes closed as heat rushed from her toes to the tips of her ears and everything else in the world was lost in the giddy sensation.

She wanted the earth to stop spinning so that this moment could last for ever.

Before she could change her mind, Saskia Elwood closed her eyes and kissed Rick Burgess back, tasting the heat of his mouth, a heady smell of coffee, chocolate crumbs and aftershave, sensing his resistance melt as he moved deeper into the kiss, her own arms lifting to wrap around his neck.

She let the pressure of his lips and the scent and sensation of his body warm every cell in her body before she finally pulled her head back.

Rick looked up at her with those blue-grey eyes, his chest responding to his faster breathing, and whispered, 'Here's to taking chances,' before sliding his hand down the whole length of her back and onto her waist, the pressure drawing her forward as he moved his head into her neck and throat, kissing her on the collarbone, then up behind her ears, his fingers moving in wide circles over her back.

'Hey Rick, just to let you know that I dropped that champagne off at Nicole's place... Oops. Later...'

Saskia opened her eyes in time to see the back of a man's coat jog out of the door and in one single movement she pulled back and smoothed down the ruffled fabric of her dress with one hand as she gathered up her hair, which had mysteriously become untied.

'I...er...need to get my bag,' Saskia just about managed

to stammer out and waved her hand towards the bedroom. 'Handbag. For the wedding. And do something with my hair. Ten minutes.'

Rick coughed. 'Great idea. Ten minutes. Right.'

Rick stood at the table and flicked through his notes on the speech that he planned to give at the wedding party, but the words refused to sink in.

All he could think about was Saskia.

He hadn't planned to kiss her or touch her but one touch was all it needed for him to give in to the magnetic attraction he'd felt for Saskia since that first time he'd seen her standing on the pavement only a few days earlier.

His eyes squeezed tight with frustration.

When had he become such an idiot? And just when he'd thought that she was close to agreeing to work with him, trying to achieve something. Together. As his business partner and best customer, not his lover.

He had tried that before with a girl he'd thought he knew and been burnt.

Saskia had been honest with him from day one.

She was scared about stepping outside her world and working with him, he could see that. And now he might just have blown their fledgling relationship out of the water.

In a few short days Saskia had become a friend, the person he wanted to talk to and spend time with.

But what happened now?

Because one thing was clear. He would only make a commitment to Saskia Elwood that he was prepared to deliver. His life could change at a moment's notice. He was the last kind of man who could give her what she needed.

Last night in the restaurant his neighbours had teased him mercilessly with their gentle ribbing about him bringing a girl home for once. Even the waitress had whispered sweet words about his pretty *'amour'* in his ear on the way out. And now he was off to Nicole and Jean's wedding with an unexpected lady guest.

Little wonder that his friend had seen him with Saskia and thought they were more than work colleagues.

Well, they were wrong. *In so many ways.* He was not the kind of man who wanted a long-term relationship and Saskia must have worked that out for herself. She was a clever girl.

Except…when he'd kissed her face? Everything had changed.

No going back. But maybe, just maybe, he could rescue their friendship and build on it. Create a bond that was more than physical. A bond that linked them through a common passion for the one thing they both knew about. Family.

She would know not to expect anything more from him, wouldn't she?

CHAPTER EIGHT

Must-Do list
* *Be sure to take lots of photos of the outdoor wedding theme. Would it work in a walled garden and patio in London?*
* *Focus on the cake and the food and lighting. Take notes and cadge a few recipes if you can from the locals.*
* *Remember to take tissues in case you embarrass yourself at the wedding.*
* *Do NOT let Rick talk you into buying their entire wine production as a wedding present, no matter how much you would like to. BAD idea. Taste it first and check the numbers. Heart. Head. Frosty*

'HEY. THIS IS A wedding. You are not supposed to be in the kitchen,' Rick whispered into her ear as he sauntered up to her and grabbed her around the middle. 'Although I suppose it is an improvement on taking notes on your smartphone during your tour of the cellars.'

'Who, me?' Saskia answered, both of her hands too occupied at that moment to fend him off or scold him. 'I have officially given up all hope of doing anything work-wise for the next few hours so I am forced to enjoy myself. And the bride needs to be with her family, not plating up choux buns. I am happy to help out since they were kind enough to invite me.'

'Agreed. It's been years since I've seen a proper champagne sword being put to such excellent use in demolishing a toffee profiterole tower. And they say chivalry is dead.'

'It was the highlight of the cake-cutting ceremony.' Saskia nodded. 'Nicole's mother made the croquembouche fresh this morning, with lots of help from her two nephews. They are the eight and six-year-olds who are running around on the table right now, high on fat and sugar. Apparently they gobbled up any odd-looking profiteroles so they wouldn't spoil the display. It was very generous of them.'

'Family loyalty. And you can't beat a proper profiterole tower for impact.'

'Quite right. In fact, this gives me an idea for the perfect wedding cake for my friend Amber, who's getting married at Elwood House at New Year. I'm thinking golden profiteroles, crème patissèrie, toffee sauce and a cloud of caramel veil, but with fresh mango and raspberry. Delicious! Orchids on the side.'

Rick picked up one of the choux buns with his fingers and bit into it. Saskia simply shook her head and carried on plating out the delicate pastries, using two spoons to break up the crystal caramel and dividing the profiteroles into groups of four on lovely china plates.

'Pretty good,' he murmured and popped the other half into his mouth. 'And I don't have a sweet tooth.'

'Excellent. More for the rest of us.' She laughed and slid the plates onto the dessert table, where they were whisked away, with the platters of mini macaroons and tiny light-as-a-feather fairy cakes topped with fresh berries, to the round tables which filled the patio around the central fountain outside the main stone house where the wedding had been held. 'Because I do have a sweet tooth and this is heaven.'

Rick wiped his hands down and peered at what was left of the tower as she cracked through the crisp caramel and divided out the buns. 'I would say at a guess that you've done that before.'

Saskia stood back and admired the table. 'I now declare that this croquembouche is officially demolished. And yes, I have broken up caramel shards and clouds before.'

'Well, in that case—' Rick nodded '—let's grab our plates and join the party. I want to hear all about your previous career as a pastry chef.'

'Career? I could hardly call it that. My Elwood grandparents used to run an old *auberge* in Alsace. Yes. In the vineyard where they produce that dessert wine you enjoy so much. I might have picked up a few catering tips during my visits as a girl. And I do recall lots of family birthdays and weddings.'

Images of wonderful afternoons spent baking with her family flooded Saskia's memory and she chuckled out loud in delight for a second before her smile faded. Now she cooked and baked alone and she hadn't realised just how much she missed the companionship until that moment. How odd.

She blinked across at Rick and smiled. 'But that's very boring. Unlike your little speech to the guests just now, singing the praises of the bride and groom. I was impressed, Mr Burgess. And all in the most excellent French.'

'Why, thank you. I meant it. They have a great future ahead of them and the passion to go with it. All praise to that.'

Saskia stopped at the entrance to the stone courtyard, then turned away and strolled out to the edge of the garden and looked out over to the low hills covered in neat rows of grapevines, which she could just make out in the fading light. The ambers, golds and reds of the autumn trees and leaves contrasted against the green foliage of the conifers to create a lovely autumn scene. It was tranquil and serene and everything that she remembered about Alsace.

'It is so lovely. Are you planning to come back for the harvest?' she asked.

'Nope. I would only get in the way and I have appointments in Argentina with some amazing new wine estates. Nicole will let me know about yields and her first impressions when she's ready. I only hope they can relax on honeymoon for a week before coming back to the harvest. The weather forecast is looking mixed for the rest of the month but it should be a good vintage.'

'My goodness, Mr Burgess—' she smiled '—for a moment there, you sounded like a wine merchant.'

He burst out laughing and spun her around by twirling her waist. Then, before she could complain, he pressed his warm lips against hers and held them there for just a fraction of a second too long to be a friendly kiss between colleagues.

She might blame it on the atmosphere of the wedding and the beautiful setting, but it was probably one of the most romantic and lovely moments she'd ever had and it was so, so tempting to lean into that kiss and turn it into something else.

But that would mean giving into the sensation and letting him take over her life.

The Rick she had seen at this wedding and earlier at the chalet was so tempting. He was so charming, so handsome and so beguiling that her poor girlish heart yearned to see where that kiss might take them and not care about the consequences.

She had known all along that he was dangerous. From

the very start. But this was different. This time she wanted to be dangerous.

'You really must stop doing that!' Saskia protested and pushed him away. 'What if I kissed you in public?' she asked, pressing her hands on the front of his beautiful suit. 'How would you like it?'

'Like it,' he growled. 'I would write song lyrics and put posters up all over town with photographs to prove it.'

'You really are completely shameless. Do you know that?'

'It has been said. But it is a burden I have come to live with over the years.'

She rolled her eyes and shook her head. 'I give up. I relax and enjoy myself just this once and take a few hours away from work and I get pounced on. You see. This is what happens when I try to live in the moment or whatever it is you do.'

'Weddings. Happens all the time. Hey, you're a girl. What is it about weddings that makes every woman in the room turned back into a giggly schoolgirl and then go all weepy? And don't think I didn't notice you passing around the tissues during the service.'

'Do you really want to know or are you trying to come up with an excuse for kissing me?'

'I really want to know. And I don't need an excuse.'

'Okay then, I will tell you. Because, as you correctly point out, I'm a girl, and you are potentially going to become one of my wine merchants. Which, in my book, means that we should be open and honest at all times. And you can stop looking at me like that. I'm quite serious. Honest and open.'

'Right. If you say so. Should I be taking notes?' He patted his pockets as though looking for pen and paper.

'Right. That's it. I'm off to join the ladies and scoff desserts and chocolates. You are on your own.'

'I apologise. Please. I'm genuinely interested in your answer.'

Saskia looked into those grey-blue eyes, which were gazing at her at that moment with such an innocent expression that it was impossible to stay angry at him. Perhaps that was it? Perhaps he just beguiled ladies into submission?

'Very well,' she replied in a low voice. 'Weddings. A to Z. Key points.'

She gestured with her head towards the long kitchen table, where the wedding guests were laughing and singing and passing around desserts and wine. It was dusk now and the crystal glassware reflected back candlelight and the warm glow from lanterns hanging from the branches of the plane tree above their heads.

'I see this as a celebration. Look at this wonderful setting. Friends and family all gathered together having a wonderful time celebrating love and happiness.'

He shrugged. 'Great people. Food was good. Wine was amazing. Sounds like a pretty good combination for any party to me.'

'The food was better than good. It was splendid and I have several recipes tucked away in my trusty clutch bag. The wine was outstanding—as you predicted. Including the pink champagne from Chateau Morel, which was an inspired choice. And you're missing the point. This is not a dinner party or Christmas lunch or a birthday celebration or some other family meal. No. We're all here today to celebrate the love Jean Baptiste and Nicole have for one another.'

Almost as the words left her lips, the bride and groom slipped from their chairs and kissed lovingly under the lanterns to a great cheer before strolling down the table chatting to their guests.

'They are a lovely couple with such great hopes for the future. The future you…' she prodded him in the chest to get her point across '…are a big part of. You promised these two people an awful lot, Mr Bigshot. You had better deliver.'

'Don't you mean *we*—' he prodded her in the arm right back '—had better deliver? My best customer. Remember that?'

'How could I forget? I keep telling you that I'm still thinking about it, and yet you have reminded everybody several times of the fact that the heir to the Elwood name is on the case. I was starting to get nervous about my big build-up until I tasted the wine.' She sniffed. 'Not nervous now at all. It's a great choice. Brilliant. I wouldn't be ashamed to serve that wine to any of my guests; I'll give you that. But that still doesn't mean that I'll sign up with you. Not yet.'

Rick straightened his back and flicked off a small dry leaf from the jacket of his suit. 'Am I good? Or am I good?' he asked with a smile.

'If the other nine new generation winemakers are like this couple…then you're good.'

Rick responded by cupping one hand around his ear and leaning closer. 'Would you mind saying that again? I couldn't quite make it out.'

'I said that your scouting team have identified a suitable wine for the shelves of RB Wines. Congratulations.'

'Ah. Was that it? Thank you, kind lady.'

Then he snorted and pushed both hands deep into his trouser pockets. 'They're a great couple who have actually taken time to get to know each other. Which means that they are going into this marriage with their eyes wide open. Good luck to them.'

'Aha. I see,' she replied, her gaze still enjoying the happy scene on the patio. 'Things are beginning to become a little clearer. Do I detect a hint of personal experience there, Mr Burgess?' She laughed. Then looked back over her shoulder into Rick's face, and her smile was wiped away as a flash of regret and pain flicked across his eyes before he realised that she was watching him.

'My one and only engagement. Las Vegas. Four years ago. I'd been with Amy for six months and there wasn't an inch of that woman's body that I didn't know on a daily basis.'

Saskia groaned and lifted her hands to cover her ears. 'Oh, please stop. No details. I've just eaten.'

'Honest and open, right?' he replied and tugged her hands away. 'As I was saying. Six months. I thought I knew Amy. She was a sports journalist. Smart, funny, we both knew the same people and moved in the same crowd. Best of all, Amy was a total adrenalin junkie and loved going for the rush in extreme sports just as much as I did. Brilliant skier.'

'I'm waiting for the *but*.'

'We'd been to an Elvis wedding chapel ceremony with two Canyon climbers and in the spirit of the occasion and after several bottles of actually quite good champagne, I had a moment of weakness and decided that maybe getting married was not such a bad idea after all. It was a brave decision. The *but* came the day after our happy engagement when she cancelled a white water rafting trip because her parents had just sent her the latest property lists for her home town in the Midwest. Apparently they couldn't wait for us to relocate so they could be close to their future unborn grandchildren.'

Saskia stopped breathing and tried to speak, but ended up opening her mouth and closing it several times.

'Yeah—' he laughed '—that's right. I was engaged for a grand total of three days. Apparently my lovely Amy forgot to mention that in her opinion life as an adrenalin junkie was fine for single girls but the moment we walked down the aisle after the wedding, that was it. Forget the sports. Forget the old life. Forget all the reasons why we fell for one another in the first place.'

'I take it that this town was not close to any mountain regions.'

'Oh, Amy had that all sorted out. There was a climbing wall in the local school gym and cycling. Lots of cycling in this truly flat part of the Midwest. Great schools for the kids, though! And so close to Mom and Dad.'

Saskia exhaled slowly and whispered, 'Oh dear.'

'It got worse. I was crazy enough to agree to go and visit my future in-laws the day after we got engaged and, within half an hour of arriving at their mansion, it became pretty obvious that my lovely Amy had no clue about who I was and where my spirit lay. The crunch came when her dad offered me a nice secure nine-to-five job in his office supplies company over dinner that evening. I politely declined and made it clear that Amy and I would be moving very soon to California for my new career in the Burgess family wine trade.'

'How did that little bombshell go down?'

'Amy started crying and screaming about how selfish I was. The sisters started crying. Her mother started crying. And the father looked as though he was about to cry. I left when her aunt and uncle started to cry. Eighteen months later, Amy married a great bloke who was truly excited about a career in office supplies. In fact, I got a Christmas card from them last year, with a delightful photograph of the happy family and their two chubby toddlers.'

'She didn't know you,' Saskia whispered with her eyes downcast.

'And I didn't know her. She told me that she wanted to share my life as a professional sportsman but, when it came down to it, Amy wanted what her parents had. A quiet, steady life in a quiet town, with me working a steady day job. And I couldn't give that to her. We both dodged a bullet that would have killed us one way or another.'

Rick sighed long and low. 'Engaged for three days. That has to be a record.'

A peal of laughter rang out from the patio and Rick smiled and gestured towards the dining table. 'But these two? They've grown up together in the same small town since junior school. They know how the other person ticks and are building a life together and a future based on what they both want in their hearts. I believe in them and think they'll stick it out. Otherwise, I wouldn't have invested in a tiny vineyard like this.'

'This is their home. They love it.'

He blinked and shook his head. 'I couldn't do it. Stay in one place every day of every year and be content doing so. Not for me.'

'Why? What is so wrong with staying in one place and learning to love it? I love London and I love my home. I couldn't think of living anywhere else.'

Her voice tailed away. She thought wistfully of her old garden and all the work waiting for her when she got back. Even in this stunningly pretty vineyard, surrounded by people she would love to get to know better, she couldn't wait to get back and start in her settled life with her friends.

Rick turned round so that his whole body was facing her when he replied, those blue-grey eyes sparkling with excitement and passion with every word he spoke. In the light from the kitchen, the sun-bleached front of his hair contrasted with his tan to give him the air of a man who spent his days in the fresh air and sunshine.

'Have you never wanted to travel, Saskia? To see the world in all its glory? To watch the dawn come up over the Andes or climb up to Everest base camp and sleep on the glacier? You can hear the ice creaking underneath your tent as it slips away further down the mountain day by day. You can't replace that. The excitement. The buzz I get from paragliding or mountaineering. There's nothing like it. Nothing. I need that in my life, even if I have to break the rules here and there to make it happen.'

Saskia could see the pulse in his neck race as he talked about the life he led and just the way he spoke was enthralling.

He meant it. He would never settle down in one place. And in some ways she felt sorry for him. But envious at the same. She had never known that feeling of being free to do whatever she wanted and take off at a moment's notice.

She yearned to tell him about the exotic places her parents had dragged her to as a child, then leaving her in a hotel room with some stranger while they went out to a nightclub or beach party. That her mother had made sunbathing next to a pool into an art form while her academic daughter was left in the shade alone to read books. Neither of her parents ever had the slightest interest in the culture of the country they were visiting. Just the opposite. They went out of their way to keep things as English as possible.

She had learnt the hard way what being a tourist was like.

That was not her life—but it was his.

'You're not a great fan of staying in one place and making a stable home, are you, Rick?'

'Sure I am. I love my chalet. Let's just say that rules have their place but I have learned from personal experience that people who follow the rules often don't have a clue what they're missing out on in life until it is too late. I don't intend to let the rules get in the way of what I want to achieve.'

'And what about promises?'

'Ah. Now that, Gorgeous, is a very different matter. I make a promise. I keep it. No negotiation. No compromise. Done deal.'

'As simple as that? No second thoughts?' She smiled.

'No. Never. I have learnt to trust my instincts and go with my gut, no matter how risky it might look. If I make a mistake like I did with the lovely Amy, then I accept it with a good heart and move on.'

Saskia took a sharp breath before asking, 'Does that apply to the London wine store? Is that one of your risky ventures?'

'Not at all. I only take risks with my own skin and my own money. Not other people's. Promises, remember?'

Then Rick froze and his gaze scanned her face, his eyebrows crushed together, and Saskia felt that the air between them seemed to crackle with electricity before he tipped her chin up and looked at her straight in the eyes.

'Wait a minute. You said that this was a vanity project back in London. Is that what is holding you back? You think that I have spent two years making false promises to families like this one because of some arrogant whim to show that I can pull this off until the next tantalising opportunity turns up? Oh, Saskia. Just when I thought we were starting to work like a team. Sorry to burst your little bubble, but I have never been so determined to see something through in my life. I will create that store with you or without you. And I am in it for the long-term. Does that answer your question? Excellent. Because now it's over to you. The waiting time is over, Saskia. What is it going to be? Are you in or are you out? I am not having this discussion again.'

And before she could even think about an answer, he raised one hand and smiled across at the groom, who was gesturing for them to join them, and without a single glance he strode off.

She watched him back-slapping the young men gathered around the drinks table in the warm dusky glow as the women fluttered around like butterflies in their pretty summer dresses and heels.

He wanted her decision. No. He had demanded it.

Rick was a risk-taker. That was not going to change. It was what made him who he was and she had to respect that. Entrepreneurial. Adventurous and driven. Those traits were a fundamental part of his nature, which he had put to good use with his mentoring scheme and it was obvious to her that it would attract exciting new winemakers.

Rick knew what he wanted and was not going to change for anyone.

And she admired him for that, more than she could say. How many times had she gone the extra mile and had to change her plans to accommodate a so called pal or client and they had not shown the slightest gratitude? She had always been the one other people expected to change. Not the other way around. Anything to avoid upsetting people or letting them down.

If she agreed to buy wine from him then she would have to accommodate his attitude to taking risky decisions, which frankly bewildered her.

And maybe that would not be such a bad thing? She had been independent for so long. Perhaps it was time to shake things up?

Saskia was still thinking through Rick's question when Nicole strolled up to her in her long white lace wedding dress. She wound her arm around Saskia's shoulder and gave her such a loving hug that Saskia felt like crying all over again.

'Come and join the rest of us,' Nicole said with a smile. 'I'm so pleased that Rick brought you here today. It's so exciting to meet one of the buyers who will help us bring our wine to the world.'

'I've had a wonderful time and you have made me feel very welcome. Thank you, Nicole.'

'I'm glad. You know, twelve months ago we were unsure whether we would be able to invest in the new cellar equipment we needed. Then Rick came along out of the blue and suddenly everything seems possible. The mentoring programme, technology and the best advice we could ever want; it seems like a miracle.'

'It's a miracle to me how Jean Baptiste and Rick can jump off a cliff with a parachute strapped to their back. I was terrified this morning. Are you not scared?'

'Yes.' Nicole shrugged. 'But that's who he is. And I love him for having that strength and courage to live his dream. We are so different, but together we seem to balance each other out. We make a good team.'

Then Nicole tilted her head to one side with slightly raised eyebrows. 'I think you might know what that feels like.'

Saskia exhaled slowly and they both turned and looked towards Rick, who was on his hands and knees in his lovely suit playing hide and seek with the children under the table. 'I'm beginning to,' she replied in a low voice. 'But it might take me a while to get used to him.'

'Stick with it,' Nicole said and hugged Saskia one last time before stepping back. 'It has taken me six months to persuade Jean Baptiste to take one week away just before the harvest so we can have a honeymoon.'

'Congratulations. Where you going?'

Nicole blinked. 'We fly to Napa Valley tomorrow morning for a week-long international wine festival on the beach. All courtesy of Burgess Wine. Didn't Rick tell you?'

'No,' Saskia replied with a gentle smile. 'He never said a word.'

CHAPTER NINE

Must-Do list
- *Be sure to catch up with Kate about any new phone calls about bookings. Only had a few texts today—most unlike her. Probably out having too much fun.*
- *Email Amber about the new idea for the wedding arch—it could look gorgeous in January with the right flowers.*
- *Type up all of my notes on the outdoor wedding and place settings. Floral china is so pretty. But has to be top quality.*

'OF COURSE AMBER was delighted about my brilliant idea for the new wedding arch on my patio. Nicole and Jean Baptiste's wedding was so wonderful today—thanks to Rick for persuading me to go in the first place. Not that I would admit that, of course. I had to pretend that it was a networking meeting with two of his producers, but their wine is amazing.'

Saskia wiggled her shoulders back and forth and giggled like a five-year-old. 'It's been years since I have been so excited about changing my wine list and adapting my recipes to match. Oh, Kate, I really think that this could be the boost I needed to take Elwood House to the next level. It is going to be so magical that I can hardly wait to get started. Even if it does mean taking the risk and buying wine from Rick.'

'Magical. Oh yes. Absolutely,' Kate murmured.

'Do you remember that chocolate cake I made for your engagement party? The one you made me promise to make for your wedding? I might have found the perfect dessert wine to match it. We're off to visit the vineyard tomorrow in Alsace so I will be sure to bring a few bottles back for you to try.'

'Oh, great cake. Lovely.'

'You sound very absent-minded tonight.' Saskia laughed. 'Is work getting you stressed out again? Because, if it is, I can recommend some fabulous hotels in the Chamonix area.'

'Work. Oh no. No…' Kate replied as though she was finding the words hard to find.

Saskia paused. She knew Kate Lovat far too well—something was clearly bothering her but she wasn't talking. And that was not like Kate at all. Shutting her up was more the usual problem.

'Did I mention that Rick Burgess is prancing up and down on my bedroom carpet right at this very minute wearing nothing but a smile and that wonderful silk dressing gown you gave me as a surprise present? He looks quite charming in it. And that shade of cerise goes so well with his tattoos.'

'That's lovely… What? He's doing what? And where are these tattoos?'

'Um…I thought that would wake you up. Come on. What's going on? Tell me and get it over with. You know that I won't let you put the phone down until you do. Out with it, Lovat. What's bothering you?'

There was a loud sigh at the other end of the phone.

'Bully. I told Amber that you would want to know but we didn't want you to worry and spoil your trip.'

Saskia sat up straight against her bed head. *Worry? Spoil her trip?* Alarm bells started sounding loud and clear inside her head.

'Well, that is very reassuring. Come on, don't keep me in suspense. You know that I have a vivid imagination. Oh no. There isn't some bad news about Sheridan Press or your building permits for the new extension to your studio, is there?'

'No. Nothing to do with Amber or me.' Kate paused. 'You know we had a big storm last night in London? Lots of wind, gales, that sort of storm. And you know those really tall lime trees that are outside your bedroom window? Well, one of the branches might have crashed into your house and cracked an upstairs window and I am really sorry not to have told you earlier, but Heath organised a glazier and it's all fixed and as good as new. All done. That's it. That's the news. And I can breathe now.'

Saskia exhaled very slowly before speaking. 'The branch broke a window?'

'Cracked. Just cracked. No broken glass. All repaired. Nothing to worry about. Really. Heath organised the men who are working at our place to change the glass super-quick. And it wasn't raining…much. Sorry.'

Saskia closed her eyes and swallowed down hard. Then pressed her thumb and forefinger tight onto the bridge of her nose.

'There is nothing for you to feel sorry about. From the sound of it, you and Heath saved the day and were total heroes and I owe you one wonderful wedding in exchange. Thanks for being there, Kate. And thank Amber too. I am so grateful that you were there to help me out.'

'No problem. Have to scoot. My boy is back with the take-out dinner. Bye, angel. Have a wonderful trip and see you soon. Bye.'

Rick heard Saskia's footsteps stomp up and down the wooden floorboards in the other room and frowned.

He wasn't used to having overnight guests in his chalet, even pretty ones. This had always been the one place on earth that he called his private home.

One small spare bedroom. One kitchen diner and a cosy living room with a huge fireplace. Perfect for a young couple or a bachelor.

And, handily, not so perfect for his parents and their entourage, who preferred to stay at the local five-star hotel in Chamonix with its award-winning restaurant and spa facilities.

Of course Tom had just laughed and called it 'Rick's garden shed' and organised a high-tech Internet connection to be fitted at huge expense while he was away for a couple of days.

Chuckling to himself, Rick hunkered down and poked at the log fire which was burning brightly in the grate.

Saskia Elwood was a definite one-off. In more ways than one!

It had been quite a day and definitely time to relax with a glass of something special.

He settled down with his feet up on his comfortable fireside sofa, the music system playing a classical piano concerto, and was just reaching for his glass of Merlot when the door to Saskia's bedroom was flung open and she marched across the living room and stood in front of him, blocking his view of the fire.

Not that he was complaining because his new view was equally delightful.

Saskia was wearing a long silky dressing gown tied at the waist with a sash which begged to be tugged away. Her hair was down and messed up around her shoulders and her bare legs ended in toenails painted in the most interesting shade of coral, which probably matched her dress but he had not noticed before now.

But there was only one place which pulled his gaze and held it there in a fierce magnetic attraction he had rarely felt before.

His mother used to tell him that the eyes were the window of the soul.

Damn right. And right now Saskia's pale blue eyes were telling him that this soul was heading towards a very non-celestial place. Fire. Ice. Cool iceberg-blue. All wrapped in turmoil and anxiety.

In fact he was not astonished in the least when she lifted her chin and said in a quivering whisper of a voice, 'I can't do it, Rick. I just. Cannot. Do it.'

And then she burst into tears.

Sitting up straight on the sofa with Saskia's legs over his lap, Rick rubbed some warmth into her frozen bare toes by rubbing them gently between his palms. He had tried blowing on them but it turned out that the girl was a lot more ticklish than she pretended and she had almost wriggled off the sofa.

'How does that feel?' he asked, smiling across at Saskia, who was cocooned inside a warm fleecy blanket, sipping Rick's glass of wine. 'Any better?'

She replied with a small closed mouth smile. 'I want you to know that I am not usually such a mess.'

'Noted.' He nodded with a pretend serious look. 'Miss Saskia Elwood. London-based entrepreneur and expert dessert disher upper. Not a mess. Got it.'

He waited for her low chuckle to die down before raising his eyebrows and turning to face her. 'It was a broken window, Saskia.'

She groaned and covered her face with a sofa pillow. 'I know, I know. This is why I feel so totally pathetic at overreacting the way I did. And I really am sorry about blubbing all over you and your sweater. It was most unprofessional behaviour in front of my new wine merchant.'

Rick froze and then slowly turned his gaze to her feet, carried on rubbing her toes and gave a wide-mouthed grin. 'As my very first buyer, I am prepared to offer you this kind of customer service whenever needed. Good to have you on board. So you can stop groaning. If it makes you feel any better, I would like to think that we were friends before anything else. That works for me.'

She took a long sip of wine and flashed him a shy smile before whispering, 'Me too.'

'Excellent,' he replied with a twisted smile and covered her feet with the blanket. 'And now that is settled, you can tell me why one broken window is such a big deal and upsets you so badly. Between friends.'

Her head dropped back and the warm glow from the table lamps and the flickering firelight reflected back from the crystal tumbler in her hand before she slowly lowered it onto the coffee table.

Then, just as she was about to answer, Saskia gasped, grabbed onto his sleeve with one hand and pointed towards the window on the other side of the room with her other. 'Rick, look. It's snowing!'

Saskia threw off the blanket, wrapped it around her shoulders, slipped her feet into a pair of Rick's shoes and stepped out onto a long wooden terrace that ran outside the back of the chalet. And what she saw in front of her took her breath away.

The sunshine and dry crisp weather they had enjoyed at the vineyard had been replaced by heavy clouds in the cool night sky, creating a dark ceiling without moon or stars. And, stretched out along the long valley down below the chalet, was the picture postcard Alpine village that Rick called home.

The smell of wood smoke and pine resin filled her head with their musky, heady scents. Warm golden squares of light shone out from the chalet homes on either side of the river, interspersed with the occasional street light so that it looked like a long winding ribbon of Chinese lanterns which twisted away into the distance and the next valley.

And, falling straight down from the sky like a net curtain, were light flurries of large, fluffy flakes of snow.

It was like something from a movie or a wonderful painting. A moment so special that Saskia knew instinctively that she would never forget it.

And suddenly she understood why Rick had made this place his home. Of course. It was his refuge, just as Elwood House was hers.

She loved London, she always had. Elwood House was in a popular part of the city with a constant stream of traffic and pedestrians no matter what time of day or night. The contrast to where she was standing could not be greater. The village was quiet, tranquil and serene while her life seemed to be in constant turmoil.

She grasped hold of the polished wooden railing and looked out over the garden towards the mountains, her heart soaring, and she felt the anxiety of the phone call with Kate slip away in the exuberant joy of the view.

Up above them was snow and ice, while she felt safe and sheltered on this simple wooden terrace. It was icy-cold, snowing and her feet were turning blue but she did not want to move from the spot. It was truly magical.

It was almost a shock to feel a strong arm wrap her fleecy blanket around her shoulders and tuck it in and she turned sideways to face Rick with a grin and clutched onto the sleeve of his sweater.

'Have you seen this? It is astonishing. I thought the view from the top of the cable car station was spectacular, but this is wonderful. I love it.'

'I can see that on your face.'

Then he turned forward and came to stand next to her on the balcony, his left hand just touching the outstretched fingers of her right.

'You probably don't realise it, but there are very few people who I would invite to share this chalet. But you are one of them. You have a special gift, Saskia Elwood. I can tell from the way you describe your two friends that you care about those girls and then do something about it. I don't think that there is a selfish bone in your body. I admire that.'

'You admire me? What do you mean?' Saskia asked, taken aback by the tone in his voice. For the first time since they'd met, Rick sounded hesitant and unsure, in total contrast to the man who had been joking with his friends at the wedding.

Rick looked down at Saskia's fingers and his gaze seemed to lock onto how his fingers could mesh with hers so completely. 'These past two years have taught me that you don't know what life is going to throw at you, Saskia. You can't. I've learnt to take the opportunities that come along and enjoy them while I can, even if it does mean being totally single-minded. Selfish even. Always on the move. Filling the day with life and activity. That's the way I chose to live.'

Saskia looked into his face and remembered to breathe again.

'And how is that working for you?' She smiled.

Rick sighed low and long and shook his head briefly from side to side. 'My parents are still strangers trying to come to terms with losing Tom and I am not exactly helping by spending more time on the road than back at base. Chamonix is a long way from Napa.'

'That must be so hard, for all of you.'

He turned back and instantly switched on his smiley face.

But it was too late. She had taken a glimpse of who the real man was beneath the mask he wore in public. And the shock was, she liked them both.

'Oh, there are some benefits,' he replied, eyebrows high. 'It means that instead of freezing my important bits off climbing some mountain in Pakistan I am here in France enjoying time out with a lovely lady who might have a different take on life.'

He lifted one of Saskia's hands and kissed the back of the knuckles. 'I have even found the time to enjoy a vineyard wedding and a parapent jump on the same day. Imagine that.'

'Yes. Imagine. I was terrified this morning just watching you jump off that cliff top! I was almost too scared to watch you land. All your scars are testament to the adventures.'

Saskia turned back to the railing and gave a small shoulder shrug. 'I don't have that kind of courage, Rick, and I never will have. Yes, I am probably too generous with my time and my energy when it comes to my friends. But just the thought that there is a problem with my house makes me shake in my boots.'

She held both of her arms straight out at him. 'See.

Shaking. But it's all I have and I can't risk anything happening to it. That's why I totally panicked when I heard that it was damaged in the storm.'

'Why? Oh it's a lovely house and I was mega-impressed. But there are plenty of people who would have sold the place and used the cash to do what they wanted. Like go to university and study things that they are passionate about, or travel and find out firsthand what the world has to offer. Crazy things like that.'

Then he smiled. 'Don't give me that look. You have a good brain behind those pretty eyes and look hot in everything you wear. You could go anywhere you want. Do anything you want. So what made you decide to stay and rent out dining rooms in your house? What's keeping you in London?'

Saskia sniffed and dropped her head. 'Thank you but I think you already know the answer to that question, Rick. Let me give you a hint. Does the infamous Hugo Mortimer investment scam ring any bells?'

'Your dad made some really bad decisions and stole a lot of money from a lot of people. But they were adults and nobody forced them to put their money into bricks and cement. You were a child.'

'Nice idea in theory.' She cleared her throat. 'Shame it doesn't work like that. He was impulsive and arrogant and delusional and the rest of his family were simply supposed to go along with everything he wanted without question.'

She slapped her hand down hard on the wooden rail in anger and frustration. 'Do you know the worst part? I still have nightmares about the day he was arrested. The police came to our huge expensive house in three cars, lights flashing and sirens blaring like some TV cop show, and literally dragged my dad out of my mother's arms. I was about fourteen at the time and had no clue what was going on or why they threw him to the floor and were putting handcuffs on him…and I was screaming for them to stop. To leave my dad alone…'

Words became impossible because of the stinging in her throat and the blinding tears which blocked out her vision.

All she could feel was Rick's strong arms, which wrapped around her and held her tight against his chest with her head nestling into his shoulder.

He didn't say a word but she could feel his strength seep out from below his fine sweater and reach into her heart and quell her pain until she could suck in deep breaths between her sobs. She tried to slip her arms out but his grip only tightened in response.

'Hey, you can stay right where you are,' he whispered into her hair and snuggled in closer, his hands splayed out on her back. 'Take five minutes. Hell. Take as long as you like. No scars? You have plenty of scars, gorgeous.'

He slid one arm up her side and pressed two fingers flat onto her chest so they rested above her heart and she could feel the warm pressure of his fingertips through the wool throw. 'But they are not on the surface like mine are. They are all in here. And they hurt just as bad. Because I think other people pushed you beyond the limit of what you were ready to handle. But here is the thing. From what I've seen, the only perfect and constant objects in this world of ours are the sky, the oceans and the mountains. Everything else needs work and is likely to change at a moment's notice. And that goes for every single one of us.'

'Then how do we cope with all of that chaos?' Saskia blinked. 'My dad took everything my mother and I had, and more besides. We lost everything. Savings. Home. Everything that could be sold was sold. Don't you see? That's why I am struggling to make the leap into taking a risk on your new business. All I have left is my credibility and reputation. If I lose that by serving my guests anything but the best then I lose everything I have worked so hard to build up. I am alone, Rick, and I have to take the decisions alone. It is a huge gamble for me and I have learned the hard way that taking risks is a fool's game.'

'How do we cope?' he asked, his lips pressed against her temple. 'We do what our heart yearns to do or go to our graves full of regret and pain and loss for all of the things we didn't get to do and the words we did not say.'

'I'm not sure that I am capable of doing that.'

He responded by slipping back just far enough so that he could tip up her chin and tap her on the end of her nose.

'I've been watching you, Saskia Elwood. You are going to be astounded at what you are capable of. And if you don't succeed you learn from your mistakes and do what you have to do to get back up and try again until you can prove to yourself that you can do it. And then you keep on doing that over and over again.'

'No matter how many times you fall down and hurt yourself?'

'You've got it. Your Aunt Margot would be proud if she could see you now.'

Saskia turned her face and rested her cheek on his chest and looked out towards the horizon, suddenly needing to get some distance, some air between them. What he was describing was so hard, so difficult and so familiar. He could never know how many times she had forced herself to smile after someone let her down, or walked away without even thanking her after she had worked so very hard to please them.

Saskia blinked back tears and shrugged deeper into the fleece blanket while she fought to gain control of her voice. 'Some of us lesser mortals have been knocked down so many times that it is hard to bounce back up again, Rick. Very hard.'

Tears pricked her eyes and she swallowed down the pain to get the words out. 'I loved working in my aunt's wine shop after school and at weekends when my mother was away with her rich pals. But after my dad was arrested I couldn't...' She took a few short breaths before going on. 'I couldn't work there a minute longer. They knew it was nothing to do with me, and I was family, but...I just couldn't embarrass them like that. Do you understand?'

Rick replied by wrapping his long arms around her body in a warm embrace so tender that Saskia surrendered to a moment of joy and pressed her head against his chest, inhaling his delicious scent as her body shared his warmth.

His hands made lazy circles on her back in silence for a few minutes until he spoke, the words reverberating inside his chest into her head. 'Better than you can imagine. What did you do then?'

Saskia raised her head, laughed in a choked voice and then pressed both hands against his chest as she replied with a broken smile. 'I went to school every day and kept my head down and stayed in the background with my pals and made a life for myself with my Aunt Margot in Elwood House. What else could I do? My mother had run away to kind friends in Los Angeles to escape the press scrum and my aunt was the only one holding us all together. And I never left.'

'That was a long time ago, Saskia. What's holding you back now? Today? This minute?'

He tilted his head sideways to look at Saskia as she moistened her lips, her mouth a straight line.

'Isn't it obvious?' she whispered after several long seconds. 'Losing Aunt Margot hit me hard and I still haven't recovered from the shock. I'm scared.'

'Scared of what? Failure? Hell, girl, I've made so many mistakes these past two years I must have been the laughing stock of the wine business. Good thing I am able to laugh at myself and enjoy the journey.'

'How did you do that? How did you pick yourself up after losing your brother? Your parents must be so proud of what you have achieved.'

'Oh, girl. If only that were true. My mum and dad have never understood this compulsion I have to push my body and my mind through challenges which need high mountains and ridiculous adventures. I don't blame them for that. Far from it. Tom was always the academically gifted crown prince. The quiet, hard-working golden boy who could do no wrong. But me?'

A long shuddering sigh echoed out from deep in his chest and Saskia felt the wave of sad regret wash over her. 'I was a mystery to them as a teenager and I am still a mystery to them now. They know that I still resent being called back into the family business. Once a black sheep, always a black sheep. The problem is, I am the only black sheep they have left so they have to give me a chance and put up with me doing things my way.'

Saskia gasped. 'But you have worked so hard.'

'I am slowly persuading them that there is more than one way to get the job done.' Rick smiled, his face suddenly energised, the laughter lines hard in the warm light flooding out from the living room. 'And that includes trusting my gut reaction to choose who I work with.'

Then he shrugged and tilted his head slightly to one side. 'Here is an outrageous idea. I have already committed to moving my London office into Elwood House. Let me take that further. You need financial backing with someone you can trust. I need someone who can help promote the wine store. Why don't we combine the two? Let me invest in your business the same way that you are taking a risk and investing in mine.'

Rick pointed two fingers at her chest, folded his thumb into his palm and fired off a single shot. 'I choose you, Saskia Elwood. You are the woman I want to work with in London and nobody else will do.'

CHAPTER TEN

Must-Do list
- *Damn, but Rick is a good salesman and apparently does know a few things about his customers after all. The wine I tried today would be perfect for Amber's new wedding menu. Buy some before it is all snapped up by other customers.*
- *Last night in Chamonix and in the chalet. Perhaps take the rest of the night off. Need to be fresh and alert for journey back north tomorrow. Shame. I will miss this chalet.*

RICK STOOD IN silence, his gaze locked onto Saskia's shocked pale blue eyes as she took in a few breaths of the cool night air.

What had he just done? So much for playing it cool.

Rick inhaled very slowly and watched Saskia struggle with her thoughts, her dilemma played out in the tension on her face.

She was as proud as anyone he had ever met. Including himself. This was quite something.

And just like that, the connection he had sensed between them from the moment he had laid eyes on her standing outside Elwood House kicked up a couple of notches. And the longer he watched her, the stronger that connection became until he almost felt that it was a practical thing. A wire. Pulling them closer together.

And every warning bell in his body starting screaming *Danger* so loudly that in the end he could not ignore it any longer. And this time he was the one who snapped the wire binding them together and stepped back, away from her.

She shivered in the cool air, fracturing the moment, and he stepped back and opened the patio doors and guided her back into the luxurious warmth of the log fire and the living room.

'Say that again,' Saskia stuttered. 'I thought that you simply wanted me to buy your wine?'

'I do. This is extra.'

Saskia sucked in air, her shoulders heaving as her brain struggled to catch up. Then she flung her head back and glared at him though narrowed eyes.

'Extra? Wait a minute. When did you come up with this brainwave? Because the last thing I want is your pity just because I told my sad little tale. No, Rick. I am independent for a reason. I make my own decisions. Remember?'

His reply was to wrap both arms around her back and pull her to him in a warm hug before sliding his arms out and smiling into her face.

'I don't do pity. We have just been talking about taking risks and going for business opportunities when we see them. And I see one in you. It is as simple as that. I want to invest in you.'

'Me? Right. I think I need to sit down now.'

'We can do this,' Rick murmured as he stood behind her with his arms wrapped tight around her waist. 'And you know how much I like a challenge.'

'Is that what I am?' she asked and he could hear the smile in her voice. 'Another one of your challenges?'

'Absolutely. I might have to use every bit of technical

know-how I have to pull it off and get back to ground in one piece, but you're the girl I want to jump off the cliff with. Even if I have to strap you into that harness myself. No more watching from the sidelines. Not any more.'

'What?' She whirled around and looked him straight in the eyes and gasped, until she saw his smile. Then she thumped him hard on the chest. 'Oh, just for a second I thought you might be serious about the jump.'

'It might happen,' he said, blinking.

'No chance. I promised Amber and Kate when I left London that I would take care of myself and not do anything dangerous.'

She pushed her lips out and shrugged. 'Sometimes a girl has to keep her promises.'

Rick took one step forward and, before Saskia realised what was happening, he had wrapped his hand around the back of her neck, his fingers working into her hair as he pressed his mouth against hers, pushing open her full lips, moving back and forth, his breath fast and heavy on her face.

His mouth was tender, gentle but firm, as though he was holding back the floodgates of a passion which was on the verge of breaking through and overwhelming them both.

She felt that potential, she trembled at the thought of it, and at that moment she knew that she wanted it as much as he did.

Her eyes closed as she wrapped her arms around his back and leaned into the kiss, kissing him back, revelling in the sensual heat of Rick's body as it pressed against hers. Closer, closer, until his arms were taking the weight of her body, enclosing her in his loving, sweet embrace. The pure physicality of the man was almost overpowering. The scent of his muscular body pressed ever so gently against her combined with the heavenly scent that she knew now was unique to him alone.

It filled her senses with an intensity that she had never felt in the embrace of any other man in her life. He was totally overwhelming. Intoxicating. And totally, totally delicious.

And just when Saskia thought that there could be nothing more pleasurable in this world, his kiss deepened. It was as though he wanted to take everything that she was able to give him and without a second of doubt she surrendered to the hot spice of the taste of his mouth and tongue. Wine and coffee. And Rick.

This was the kind of kiss she had never known. The connection between them was part of it, but this went beyond friendship and common interests. This was a kiss to signal the start of something new. The kind of kiss where each of them were opening up their most intimate secrets and deepest feelings for the other person to see.

The heat, the intensity, the desire of this man was all there, exposed for her to see when she eventually opened her eyes and broke the connection. Shuddering. Trembling. Grateful that he was holding her up on her wobbly legs.

Then he pulled away, the faint stubble on his chin grazing across her mouth as he lifted his face to kiss her eyes, brow and temple.

It took a second for her to catch her breath before she felt able to open her eyes, only to find Rick was still looking at her, his forehead still pressed against hers. A smile warmed his face as he moved his hand down to stroke her cheek.

He knew. He knew the effect that his kiss was having on her body. Had to. Her face burned with the heat coming from the point of contact between them. His heart was racing, just as hers was.

Saskia slowly, slowly slid out of his embrace and almost

slithered off the sofa. And by the time she was on her unsteady legs she was already missing the warmth of those
arms and the heat of the fire on her face.

'I think I've talked and been on my feet far too much
for one day. Now we really should get some sleep. Vineyard number three is expecting us tomorrow and with the
weather turning snowy it would probably be best to make
an early start and put snow chains on and…'

She knew that she was babbling but she had to do something to fight the intensity of the magnetic attraction that
she felt for Rick at that moment. Logic screamed at her
from the back of her mind. They were both single, unat-
tached, they were alone in the most romantic chalet that
she had ever seen in her life, and they wanted one another.

She had never had a one-night stand in her life. And if
she was going to do it, this was as good a place as any…
except, of course, it would never be casual sex. Not for
her. And, she suspected, not for Rick either.

Working together would be impossible if they spent
the night together.

Wouldn't it?

Rick stood up in one smooth movement from the hips
and instantly stepped forward so that his hands encircled
her waist. He gently drew her back towards him so that
their faces were only inches apart at the same height.

His hand moved to her cheek, pushing her hair back
over her left ear, his thumb on her jaw as his eyes scanned
her face, back and forth.

'The snow chains are already on. Don't lock me out.
Please.'

His voice was low, steady. And, before she could answer, his hand moved to cup her chin, lifting it so that
she looked into his eyes as he slowly, slowly moved his

warm thumb over her soft lips. Side to side. No pressure. Just heat.

She felt his breathing grow heavier, hotter and her eyes started to close as she luxuriated in his touch.

'Take a risk on me, Saskia. Can you do that? Trust me not to let you down?'

Risk? He was asking her to take a risk?

Her eyes opened wide and she drank him in; all of him. The way his hair curled dark and heavy around his ears and neck. The suntanned crease lines on the sides of his mouth and eyes. And those eyes—those amazing grey eyes which reflected back the flickering light from the log fire and burned bright as they smiled at her.

She could look at that face all day and not get tired of it. In fact, it was turning out to be her favourite occupation.

Rick the man was temptation personified. And all she had to do was reach out and taste just how delicious that temptation truly was.

Did he know what effect he was having on her? How much he was driving her wild?

Probably.

Shame that he had to go and ruin it all by asking the one question she had feared. The one question which would decide which path she would take in her life.

'Are we talking about the car journey to Alsace?' she whispered.

'Maybe. Maybe not.' He smiled as his gaze found something fascinating to focus on in her hair. 'What do you think?' He winked.

Saskia was about to retort with a polite refusal when she made the fatal mistake of looking into those eyes and was lost.

'Is that the way you usually interview business partners?' Saskia asked, trying to keep her voice casual and light. And failing.

He simply smiled a little wider in reply, one side of his mouth turning up more than the other, before he answered in a low whisper. 'I save it for cold weather emergencies. And for when I need to know the answer to an important question.'

'Hmm?' He was nuzzling the side of her head now, his lips moving over her brow and into her hair as she spoke. 'Important question?'

Rick pulled back and looked at her, eye to eye. 'I had to find out if you were seeing anybody at the moment. And now I know the answer, I can do something about it. So. Are you going to take the risk and jump into my car for a drive to Alsace tomorrow?'

Saskia leant back against the sofa and took another breath before grinning back at Rick. 'Well, I might. If you smarten yourself up a little.'

He bowed in her direction. 'Any time.' He dropped his hand and pushed it deep into the pocket of his denims. 'Would you care to join me for breakfast later this morning, Miss Elwood? No strings. Or do I have to use my emergency procedure again?'

'I might just risk your croissants.' She nodded. Then a warm sweet smile lit up her face. 'But, in the meantime, you can call your parents and tell them the good news. Elwood House has agreed to be your first paying customer. That should put a smile on their faces. Deal? Deal. Goodnight, Rick. Goodnight.'

Rick leant against the wood-panelled wall at the front of the dining room with a glass in his hand and enjoyed the view.

Saskia Elwood was on her third piece of Kugelhopf cake

and sweet dessert wine and savouring every mouthful, much to the delight of the elderly great-grandmother of the Alsace winemaking family who had made both of them.

They had spent a great day celebrating the grape harvest, which had been collected in perfect weather just before the frost, ending in a family party at the local *auberge*. And Saskia had been the star of the show every step of the way, from the very first moment she'd started chatting to the family in a perfect Alsace accent right through to her donning an apron to help out in the kitchen when there was an unfortunate incident involving their Labrador puppy, Coco, and some wild boar sausages.

They had eaten to bursting, danced until they couldn't stand and laughed. Really laughed. Saskia had made herself part of the extended family and dragged him along with her.

It had been a long time since Rick had felt so mellow and connected to a group of people who shared a common bond through the love of life and family.

Family. In the end, it all came down to that one common bond.

And one person was at the centre of it all. Saskia. His Saskia.

On the car journey from Chamonix to Alsace they had talked and laughed for hours. Sharing tales about their favourite music, food, friends, silly stories about their school days and people they had known. And yet they still kept coming back to the families who loved and exasperated them in equal measure.

Somehow Saskia had helped him to open up and talk about all of those memories from the happy times he had spent with Tom and his parents in Scotland and then California. Christmas parties and family weddings with all of the aunts and uncles, cousins and neighbours he had not thought about for years. Good times. Better times.

It was as though she had opened a window on another way of looking at the turmoil of the past two years and put it into some sort of perspective. This amazing woman he was looking at now had a father in prison and her mother was a stranger living her own life in another city, while he had two wonderful parents who were still grieving as much as he was.

Parents he was trying so hard to impress while all the time perhaps they simply needed him to talk to them.

Rick flicked open his cellphone, licked his lips and scrolled down to the number he had not called for days.

Now was as good a time as any.

'Dad? Rick. How is the weather in Napa today? That's great. Did Mum get those photos I emailed about Nicole and Jean Baptiste's wedding? Oh, of course. Too busy getting ready for the wine festival. Yeah. Just calling with two pieces of news. First—Chamonix has snow. I know, in September! But there's more. Do you remember me telling you that I was meeting with Margot Elwood's niece in London? Well, guess who is going to be my first serious customer for the new store? I know. I'm pleased too. Saskia Elwood is someone I can work with, I'm sure of it. Okay, I'm talking too much. Tell me about the festival. I want to hear all about it.'

Saskia stood in the front porch of the *auberge* where they were staying and waved goodnight to the last of the family of local winemakers who were still singing as they wound their way down the narrow lane to their homes in the village.

Most of the inhabitants of the Alsace village had gathered together to celebrate bringing in the wine harvest in the dining room of the *auberge,* and quite a few of the children too.

There were going to be a lot of hangovers and bleary eyes tomorrow morning. She checked her watch. Make that later *this* morning!

Thank goodness they all lived within walking distance. Or should that be staggering distance? It'd been a brilliant celebration and the winemakers had welcomed Rick with open arms. And when he'd announced from the front of the room that she was going to be their very first buyer of the new wine in London? She might as well have been an honorary member of the family.

Her feet had never left the ground since.

The food was spectacular, the wine amazing and the atmosphere? Oh, the people and the atmosphere had reminded her more than any words could say of the tiny vineyard her Elwood grandparents had made their home. Working and living with people whose lives revolved around tending the grapevines they had inherited from generations of family winemakers before them.

Rick had been right. She did need to spend more time away from London and all the pressures that came with Elwood House. She used to love coming to Alsace as a girl to be with her family and yet somehow she never found the time to take a real holiday.

But what could she do? Her life was in London and her grandparents were long gone. How could she steal away for weekends and holidays and spend more time here?

A shiver ran across Saskia's shoulders. The crisp night air was cold enough for a light frost on the lawn and stars shone brightly in the inky-dark pollution-free sky.

Breathing in deeply, she was just about to turn away when she sensed Rick's presence behind her in the hallway, even before she had seen him. A feather-light duvet coat fell onto her shoulders and she wriggled deeper inside it.

Rick came up and stood beside her and she felt one arm wrap around her waist and snuggle her to him for warmth.

She sighed and tutted out loud. 'Aren't you cold?' she asked in a joking voice as she took in his shirt sleeves.

'Not a bit.' He smiled. 'This is nothing. And, besides, I've got a girl to keep me warm.'

'Have you indeed?' She play thumped him on the arm, which only hurt her hand and did nothing to him at all. 'Well, in that case, Mr Cool, thank you for the coat. It is too gorgeous an evening to say goodnight quite yet. Look at the stars!'

His reply was to pull her closer.

Saskia gazed up into his face. In the warm golden light from the porch she could make out the stubble on his tanned chin and upper lip and the way his hair curled around his ears and onto the pristine white shirt. It was so, so tempting to raise one hand and stroke that chin and find out if her memory of his kisses matched the reality of the man she was holding now.

Almost as if he could read her mind, Rick glanced at her and his dark eyelashes fluttered slightly in hesitation before he pressed his lips, those warm, full lips, against her forehead and held them there until her eyes closed with the sheer pleasure of his touch. It was almost a physical loss when he slid his chin onto the top of her head and exhaled slowly. She could feel his heart race to match hers.

Saskia closed her eyes and revelled in the sheer sensation of being held in Rick's arms. She wanted this moment to last as long as possible. To hold on to the glorious feeling that came with knowing that she was in the right place at the right time with the right person.

Especially if that person had a stubbly face and spectacular broad shoulders.

Rick Burgess made her heart sing just at the sight of him and her knees wobble at his touch.

How had that happened?

No. She was not going to overanalyse it. She was going to allow herself, for once, to relax and live in this moment. Not thinking about all of the things that she should be doing or planning for the next event.

Just living in the moment. And enjoying that moment to its full potential.

She had never truly done that before. Ever.

Ever since she could remember, her life had been one long series of lists of things that she should do or should not do, when to speak, what to say and how to act. To be released from that pressure felt magical.

And she knew just who to thank for showing her what her life could be like, given the chance.

The man who was holding her now. Rick the Reckless— who was not so very reckless after all. He was just…Rick.

This man had pressed buttons she did not know that she even had. And a few which surprised her. Shown her what being in love could be truly like.

She tilted her head so that she could look more closely at the pulse in his neck, his chest rising and falling.

She was willing to take that risk with this man.

Watching him now, his face relaxed, warm, handsome, it would be so easy to be seduced into the sweet and tender kisses of the man she had come to care so very much about.

Tonight had swept away any lingering, unspoken doubts she could have had.

This was what she had truly been frightened of, what she had always feared would happen when she gave her heart.

And she had truly given her heart, no doubt about it.

They had become attached with bonds you could not cut with a sharp tongue or kitchen knife.

She was doomed.

No. She would never forget him. His laughter. His teasing. His touch on her skin.

How could she walk away from this man? When she wanted him. Knowing that she was setting herself up for loneliness and pain if she walked down that road.

Rick stirred slightly and she grinned up at him. 'It was a wonderful evening. Thank you for making it possible for me to be here.'

Rick chuckled for a moment before answering. 'You are most welcome. I only hope that I can still dance like our host's grandfather when I get to his age.'

She slowly twisted her body around so that there were only inches between them, so close she could feel the warmth of his breath on her face as it condensed into a fine mist in the cold air.

The sound of laughter from the *auberge* owner and his family drifted out from the dining room and they both turned around to listen and then smiled at one another.

'I know. This trip has brought back so many happy memories,' she whispered, her voice low as she scanned his face. 'I'm only sorry that I didn't come back to France sooner. But, after Aunt Margot died, I felt that I had to keep busy. It is too easy to mope on holiday.'

Rick raised his hand and stroked her cheek with his fingertips from temple to neck, then back again, forcing her to look into his eyes.

'I know what you mean. Listening to you talk about your aunt has helped me realise that I have never stopped in one place long enough to get over Tom's death and grieve his loss the way you have tried to do. One more point to you, Saskia Elwood. Miracle-worker. '

Saskia looked up into Rick's lovely eyes as he gently stroked her face, before replying. 'Me? Not a bit. I prefer to think that France has worked its magic on both of us. I have always loved it here. And if it wasn't for my dad… well, perhaps my life would have taken a different turn.'

Then she pressed her fingers to his lips, her eyes never leaving his. 'But then, we might never have met. And my world would have been a much sadder place.'

Rick's response was to draw her body closer to his, so that her head was resting on his broad shoulder, cuddling into his warmth, sensing and hearing the pounding of his heart as she slid her arms around his waist.

She had no need of hearing.

No need of sight.

The smell of his body, dancing sweat, and him, his own perfume, combined with the smooth texture of his fine shirt above the powerful muscles that lay below to create a heavenly pillow.

So that when she finally dared to break the silence her words were muffled in his chest. 'I plan to make some changes in my life when I get back to London. Even with managing Elwood House. I want to take time for short breaks. Life is so short. These past few days have made me realise just how much I miss being back in France. There are second cousins still here and I haven't seen my mother since April. I don't know how I'll manage it, but I need to make it happen.'

'You'll do it. And don't worry about Elwood House. If you allow me to invest in the business, you could train a wonderful deputy manager. No problem.'

'Really?'

'Really really.' He smiled. 'Family has to come first. I only wish that I had realised it earlier.'

There was a subtle change in the tone of his voice and Saskia looked up as Rick's gaze fixed on the movement of wind in the pine trees and the stars above them. He had a faraway look in his eyes as though he was talking to the sky itself. His softly spoken words had the power to penetrate her heart and bring burning tears to the back of her throat.

'I never had a chance to say goodbye to my brother Tom.'

Rick's hand moved in gentle circles on her back.

'I was climbing in the Andes and out of reach of the rest of the world. No Internet, no cellphones, no bombardment and clamour of the world. No constant noise and clutter. It had taken us three weeks to walk in and acclimatise to the altitude. Which was just how I liked it. We were a small team who knew what we were doing and what we were up against, working together and pitting ourselves against the best. We were the best!'

Rick slowly lowered his gaze so that they were facing each other and Saskia felt the air between them chill even further.

'Everything is so simple on a mountain. She strips you down to your most basic essence. No prisoners. It is a battle of you and your skills against nature and everything that she can throw at you. In theory, that should prepare you for anything in the outside world. But let me tell you, when I saw that helicopter coming up over the horizon at our base camp on the glacier? Suddenly I had a lot more to worry about than falling into crevasses and frostbite.'

He cleared his throat and shook his head.

'The minute I jumped into that helicopter I had this aching raw pit in my gut and every instinct that I ever had was screaming out a warning sign in big red letters. I knew that I was in trouble. But I had no clue about what I was about to face.'

His cheek rested on her head and she could feel the intensity of the vibration in his words through her skin.

'It had taken my parents three days to track the expedition down and pay a helicopter pilot to risk flying in at those altitudes. Three days was too long. Not even a private jet and police escorts could get me back to Napa Valley any faster. Tom never came out of the coma and died several times in the hospital, but it would have been nice to say something to him before he took his last breath.'

Rick's words were coming in jagged bursts as though he was holding back suppressed pain and she longed to help him express how he felt, but she dared not in case the flood waters engulfed her once she released the dam.

'He knew that you cared about him. I could see it in that photograph you showed me in the chalet. You were close.'

'Tom was my big brother and I thought that he was invincible and would always be there for me to fall back on. And I was wrong. Wrong about a lot of things.'

He smiled and rubbed his cold nose against hers. 'But not any longer. You've made a change in my life, Saskia. Helped me to get a few things straight in my head.'

'Me? How have I helped you?'

'Jean Baptiste and Nicole are on their way to a trade fair in California which Tom created so that independent producers could showcase what they do. I should be there right now to help and support my parents. Burgess Wine is the main sponsor. I need to be there. But there is always some great excuse why there's a burning problem in Europe that I have to solve in person or the world will end.'

He held up one hand. 'Oh, don't misunderstand. I want this London store to happen and I need to be based in Europe to see it through. But the truth is more basic than that. The more that I think about it, the more I realise that I have been so determined to prove to the world that I'm not the black sheep of the family any longer that I have been burning myself out running around the world, while all the time my parents needed me to be with them. To help them come to terms with losing Tom as a family. And I couldn't do it. I wasn't ready to try and didn't have the tools I needed to make it happen.'

He exhaled slowly and very gently released his arms from around her body, and stepped slightly back. 'Which makes me a fool. My parents are in their sixties. They need me to be their son and to work with them to carry on Tom's legacy. Instead of which, I am acting like a stubborn child who refuses to put on the hand-me-down clothes my older brother used to wear and resenting every second of having to change my identity to fit into his shoes.'

Rick shook his head slowly from side to side and tapped her gently on the end of her nose. 'Well, that stops today, gorgeous. I am going back to Napa to build bridges and this time it's because I want to, not because I am the only option that they have left.'

Saskia stared out past Rick and fixed her gaze on the gentle waving of branches to and fro in the light breeze, which was a perfect match to the tornado spinning inside her head.

It felt as though she had been strapped onto a horse on a childhood nightmare of a merry-go-round, which had started whirling faster and faster until all she could do was hang on for dear life, knowing that if she even tried to get off she would be seriously hurt.

Only to be slammed to a crushing stop into a large solid object called real life.

He was leaving. Just like her father had left her.

She had always known that this was a temporary arrangement. One week. Seven days out of her life.

It was just so hard to say goodbye.

'Then you have to go back to your parents and show them that you are the better man.' She smiled into his face and blinked away her tears. Her body yearned to lean closer so that her head could rest against that broad shoulder, but she fought the delicious sensation.

She had to.

He was so close she could drown in the heady mix of his scent and the warmth of a body that wanted to be with her as much as she needed him to stay with her.

It was almost a physical pain when his hands started to slowly move down her coat until they rested on her hips. Slowly, slowly, she looked up into the most amazing grey eyes she had ever seen.

And in that moment she could see there was something more. Something she had never seen before. Something different. His unsmiling eyes scanned her face for a few minutes, as though searching for an answer to some question he had not the words to ask.

Uncertainty. Concern. Doubt? That was certainly new.

His right hand came up and gently lifted a loose coil of her hair back behind her ear, in a gesture so tender and loving that she closed her eyes in the pleasure of it.

He slid his fingers through her hair until he found the base of her neck. Drawing her closer, he lowered his forehead onto hers so that each hot breath fanned her face with its intensity.

'Come with me.' The sides of his mouth twisted for a second, but this time there was no quick laughter. 'We could be back in London in a week. Come on, gorgeous. Take a risk on me and come to California. You won't regret it. After all, you have nothing to lose.'

CHAPTER ELEVEN

Must-Do list
- *Who am I kidding? This trip to France has opened my eyes to just how much I love having someone to talk to—about everything, not just the girl things.*
- *Need to take some big decisions about how I want to move forward in my life—difficult decisions. Scary decisions. Has to be done and I know who I want to help me make them—Rick.*

SASKIA LIFTED HER head and looked into those amazing blue-grey eyes which were gazing at her so lovingly that she almost, almost gave in to the temptation.

Inhaling a breath of cool air, she lifted one hand and stroked his cheek, feeling the stubble of his soft beard under her fingertips and watched his chest lift as he responded to her touch.

He meant it. He wanted her to come with him. He wanted her to leave London and come with him and meet his family and…she felt totally overwhelmed and terrified.

Suddenly her world felt totally out of control. She was whirling and whirling. Her heart was thumping so hard she was surprised that Rick couldn't hear it.

'Nothing to lose?' she repeated, and her shoulders slumped. 'Oh, Rick. Why did you have to say that? Why?'

'Because it is the truth. What is it? What's the problem?
Is it me? Or California? Talk to me. Tell me what is going
on inside that lovely head of yours. Help me understand.'

'It's all too much. Too soon. I only met you a few days
ago and now you want me to go to California with you? No.
I need to slow down and...and I need to breathe. Breathing would be good.'

She closed her eyes and tried to fight back an overwhelming sense of panic.

Her head was spinning and a strange dizzy sensation
swept over her. Cold, hot. Then cold again.

'Here. Come on. Sit down and exhale nice and slow.
That's it. Deep breaths, exhale slowly.'

Rick half carried her over to an old wooden bench and
she collapsed down on the hard rungs and felt the coat
wrapped tighter across her shoulders by Rick's strong arms
as he sat down beside her and hugged her tight.

'It's okay,' he murmured. 'It's fine. Everything is fine.'

'Fine?' she gasped in between gulping down air. 'How
can it be fine? I haven't had a panic attack like this in years.
Years! And it happens now. At the very time I am starting
to see some success in my crazy life. I am such a mess.'

'Hey, girls tell me that I am too much for them all the
time. I understand completely. '

She lifted her head and blinked at him, and Rick had
the cheek to grin and wink at her. But when she took another breath, the dizziness cleared a little and then a little
more until she could sit back against the hard bench and
look up at the sky without feeling nauseous.

'You must think that I am a complete idiot,' she whispered, not daring to look at Rick, who was still sitting
next to her so quietly with his arm around her waist. 'First
you offer to invest in my business and then...then you ask
me to fly off to California with you. I should be pinning

a medal to your chest and adding you to my Christmas card list. And how do I respond? By almost throwing up on you. I am so sorry.'

'Don't be.' He smiled and hugged her closer. 'I get it. These past few days have been quite a rush. I'm used to it. You're not. That's all.' His voice warmed and he shuffled around so that he could tip up her chin and gaze into her face. 'You did warn me about your fear of heights and this is quite a jump.'

'How do you know that? What if I let you down and let myself down at the same time? I don't want to disappoint you, and especially in California in front of your family and the wine trade. All I have going for me is my family name and some experience in running Elwood House. The last thing you need is to be ridiculed for investing in an unknown.'

'Not going to happen. And how do I know that I have hooked up with a star? I can see it in your face. Your voice. The way you meshed with Nicole and Jean Baptiste at their wedding and right here, tonight, in the love you have for this community. I watched you. You can speak the dialect and they are not fools. They know that you are the real deal, just as I do.'

Rick smiled. 'You. Are not capable of letting anyone down. I have been around long enough in sports to trust my gut instinct and I have never been wrong. Nope. No trying to wriggle out of it now. We are in this crazy project together.'

Someone inside the *auberge* started playing the piano and the sound of the music drifted out of the porch and into the garden, but Saskia barely heard the music. She was way too busy trying to remember to breathe while she processed what Rick was saying.

Which was even more difficult when he stretched out

his long legs in front of him, apparently oblivious to the cold and the way the fine cloth of his suit trousers strained under the pressure of the muscled thighs below.

One side of his face was lit by the warm golden light streaming out from the windows behind their heads, bringing the hard planes of those high cheekbones into sharp focus. His powerful jaw and strong shoulders screamed out authority and presence. He was a man who knew what he wanted and was not prepared to take no for an answer.

'What do you say, Saskia?' he said, his clear grey eyes locked onto her face, his voice low and intense, anxious. 'Are you willing to give us a chance?'

'Are you only talking about RB Wines or Elwood House?' she asked, her voice almost a whisper.

His response was to slide his long, strong fingers between hers and lock them there. Tight. The smiling crinkly grey eyes locked onto her and a wide open mouth grin of delight and happiness cracked his face. 'See. I knew that you would work it out. No, I'm not. But hey, doesn't that sound good?' He lifted one hand and wrote the words in the air. 'Burgess and Elwood. Wine Merchants to the stars. It's a winner. And Saskia and Rick isn't a bad combination either. Kinda like that. California and then London won't know what hit it.'

Saskia inhaled a deep breath, trying to process the words, while his body was only inches away from her own, leaning towards her, begging her to hold him, kiss him and caress him.

She swallowed hard and tried to form a sensible answer. 'I thought you couldn't wait to leave the city and head back to Chamonix and your chalet?'

'Angie has an excellent project team in London who are desperate to show me what they can do without my constant interference. My parents need me more right now.'

Saskia let out a long slow breath as his fingertips smoothed her hair back down over her forehead and into the back of her skull. Making speech impossible.

Then his voice softened to warm chocolate sauce capable of melting the coldest heart. 'I wouldn't want to start that journey with anyone else but the girl I am with right now.'

London. The wine store. Elwood House. And a chance for love.

This amazing man was offering her the chance to create something wonderful and make all of those fantastical plans she had dreamed up with Aunt Margot a reality. This man who she had only met a few days ago, yet she felt that she had known him all of her life.

He was holding her dream out to her, and all she had to do was say yes and it would be hers.

'Think of me as your personal guide to having some fun. You need to get out of the house and I'd like to introduce you to winemakers all around the world. Say yes. Say that you will trust me and come with me.'

Trust him? Trust him with her life, her future. Her love?

'Get out of the house?' She smiled and blinked a couple of times to help clear her head. 'I don't know about that part so much. I shall still need to invest a lot of time in Elwood House if I want to see it fly. Even if you do have your London office there.'

'Elwood House? Oh gorgeous, think bigger for a moment. My family company have a wine empire to run, and believe me, they could use your skills. You could work for the family, be part of the family. It could be great!'

What? Hold up! 'What are you talking about? I have been working for years to develop the skills to run my own private venue. That's what I want. That's what I have always wanted.'

The sound of laughter broke through her thoughts and Saskia pointed to the red geraniums still flowering in the window boxes behind her.

'I spent years learning the trade in a place just like this with my grandparents before I went to live with Aunt Margot. I can cook, clean, work behind the bar, manage, do everything. But don't you see? It has to be my own place. My mother thought that she could rely on my dad to take care of her and her family. He was a charmer and a chancer and I don't blame her a bit for falling fast and marrying him. But it was a disaster, Rick. We were left with nothing when he left. Nothing.'

She sucked in a breath, hoping that he would fill the empty silence, but he just sat there, looking at her as she dug an even deeper trench to separate them.

'I need Elwood House. It's my rock. The one place that I can call my own. I cannot walk away from it. Not even for a few weeks. That's why I agreed to think about buying from a London shop. So that I could be close to home. I cannot risk letting it go. Not on...'

As soon as the words left her mouth, she regretted them. The man who had been holding her so lovingly, unwilling to let her move out of his touch, stepped back. Moved away. Not physically, but emotionally.

The precious moment was gone. Trampled to fragments.

His face contorted with discomfort, pain, and closed down before her eyes. The warmth was gone, and she cursed herself for being so clumsy. She had lost him.

'Not on someone like me. Right. I've got the message.'

His back straightened and he drew back, physically holding her away from him. Her hands slid down his arms, desperate to hold onto the intensity of their connection, and her words babbled out in confusion and fear.

'Let's not talk about it now. You have such a lot to cel-

ebrate over the next few days when your family are all together for once in California. We can start work when you
are back in London.'

He turned away from her now, and sat back against the
bench, one hand still firmly clasped around hers.

'I am not your dad, Saskia. I have never taken a risk
with anyone else's money or time. Promises. Remember?'

Rick ran his fingers back through his thick dark hair
from his forehead to neck. 'No. I am not going to stop
jumping off mountains or pushing myself to the limits in
everything that I do. I thought that you understood that.'

The bitterness in his voice was such a contrast to the
loving man she had just been holding, Saskia took a breath
before answering. 'It's what makes you who you are. I do
understand that. Very clearly. It just takes some getting
used to.'

'Well, that is not going to change. No way.'

He paused and licked his lips and the world seemed to
still. 'Tom died of a brain haemorrhage. What I didn't tell
you was that he collapsed in an airport after a twelve-hour
flight after six days of back to back meetings and presentations at a trade fair. I saw his diary. He would have been
lucky to snatch a few hours sleep a night.'

He dropped his head back. 'Tom was a workaholic.
Thirty-six years old and single. He collapsed running to
collect his bag from the luggage carousel so that he could
catch a connecting flight home in time for a morning meeting. Isn't that the most ridiculous thing that you have ever
heard? I miss him every day and think about him every
day and I'm not ashamed of saying that out loud.'

Before Saskia could swallow down her tears in a burning throat and form her reply, Rick slid his fingers from
hers and got to his feet. He spun around to face her, blocking everything else out of her sight.

'Is that how you want me to live, Saskia? Is that the kind of man you want to be with? To work with? Because, if it is, then you are absolutely right. I am not the man for you. But I do know one thing.'

He stepped forward and took both of her hands and drew her to her feet in one smooth movement so that they were standing chest to chest, thigh to thigh, with only the cold night air separating them.

'I know that you are an amazing woman with so much compassion and intelligence and passion in your heart that I cannot get enough of you. We are two of a kind, Saskia Elwood, and I want you in my life—but you have to make that decision. You know who I am. You know where to find me.'

And, with that, he released her hands, tilted his head and kissed her lips with a touch that was so light and so warm and so heartfelt that she staggered under the weight of it. So that when he stepped back she had to lean against the bench for support.

'Goodnight. And thanks for a great day.'

'No problem. Goodnight, Rick…' she whispered as he turned and strode away. *Or was that goodbye?*

CHAPTER TWELVE

Must-Do list
- *I miss Rick so much and he has only been gone a few hours.*
- *Maybe I should make a list of all the ways that I don't need him and how very different we are?*
- *Stupid lists. Forget the lists. I don't need to write down what I want and who I want. Not any more.*

RICK SLOWED HIS car to a stop on the brow of a hill and looked out through the windscreen as dawn broke over the valley stretched out in glorious autumn colours.

He had been driving for almost an hour and was already bored of his own company. Every music track on the radio or CD reminded him of Saskia and the echoing silence in the car as he sat there only made it worse.

The laughter and excitement of the previous evening seemed such a long time ago but he wanted to keep hold of that feeling of happiness when he'd held Saskia in his arms and capture it for ever to keep him warm in the cold winter months ahead.

Rick dropped his head back against the leather seat and closed his eyes.

He should be grateful and happy that his plans were coming together.

Instead of which, his mind was in turmoil and he had spent most of the night tossing and turning, trying to work through what it was he truly wanted.

The more he thought about it, the more he admired Saskia for having the strength to know what she wanted and make the sacrifice to create something remarkable from what she had been given. He was lucky to have met her. Know her. Care about her. *Start falling for her.*

Oh yes. He was falling for Saskia Elwood—and falling hard and fast. *Avalanche speed.*

And now he was driving away from the woman he wanted because he was scared of not being worthy of her. Or not being the man she needed in her life.

He was actually *worried* that he would let her down.

Which made him the biggest fool in the world.

Sunshine flickered at the corner of his vision and he half opened his eyes with a smile and a snort. He had faced some amazing challenges in the sports world and only a week ago he would have shouted out that he was ready for anything life could throw at him.

Well, a pretty brunette had just shown him how wrong he could be. About a lot of things.

One thing he did know. Whenever he needed to prepare for a big sporting event, he called in a support team who would back him up at every stage. Maybe it was time to call in Team Burgess? The one team he had left behind to go solo for the past two years.

Rick flicked open his phone and dialled the number.

'Mum? Great to hear your voice. Me? Been better. Fact is, Mum, I need your help. And this time it's not about grape varieties.'

Saskia stepped out of the side entrance at the *auberge* and her gaze scanned out across the lawn, which was edged with bright flower beds to the low hills that lay beyond.

Her breath condensed in the cold damp air into a moist pale mist in front of her face, as she opened the gate and strolled out onto the narrow path that wound its way through the vineyard. The glistening frost which covered the hard and apparently dead wood of the harvested grape-vines was just visible in the early morning light.

She ran her fingers across one precious vine to the next, bracing herself with each step on the loose pebbles and stony ground of the slope beneath her feet. The earthy aroma of leaf mould, soil and sweet juice from crushed fruit wafted up as she slowly moved along the row, filling her senses in the damp air.

Some people loathed autumn, but she loved it. The chill damp of mornings like this one would open out into bright sunshine for a few precious hours later that day.

A shuffling noise and a cold wet nose pushing at her right hand broke the mood. 'Okay, Coco. Yes, I know it's breakfast time.'

Saskia strode back towards the house as the chocolate Labrador sniffed along the path ahead of her, looking for the rabbits, real and imaginary, with whom she shared the hillside. Sometimes she missed having a dog around, but it would be impossible in central London and with the kind of work she had chosen and the life she led.

She loved Alsace, she loved the culture and she loved the old family *auberge* where she had spent a sleepless night tossing and turning, her mind reliving every second of the time she had spent with Rick over the past few days.

Saskia shook her head and sighed. Stupid girl. She was getting too old to have crushes on hunky sportsmen…because that was all it could be. A crush.

But, lying in bed last night, trying to get some sleep and failing, Rick's words kept rolling around inside her head and simply would not go away.

Could she sell Elwood House and move to France? Or work for a company like Burgess Wine and employ a manager to run the venue? It would mean accepting Rick's offer to invest but it could open up all kinds of options that she had not even considered before.

Time was so short. The Christmas bookings were already coming in and then there was Amber's wedding and then Valentine's Day, mixed in with business meetings every week. Soon her life would be back to one long blur of activity and a holiday would seem like a distant dream.

No. She would make it happen. She could make the time for regular breaks. She had come a long way from the schoolgirl who was so terrified of drawing attention to herself in case the teasing about her father started up again.

It was time to start living a little.

Kate and Amber would be delighted and probably very creative when it came to setting up her social calendar!

Saskia picked up a small stick and threw it out to the stone wall of the terrace, watching Coco bound ahead to fetch it as she walked slowly back to the dew-frosted cobbled patio which circled the *auberge*.

Smoke from wood-burning stoves rose white and thick from the chimneys of the traditional timbered houses built along the path of the river valley below her. There was no breeze this morning to break the heavy cloud cover and chilling mist. That would come later with the seriously cold weather forecast for the rest of the week.

Coco ran back and forth into the vines and it was a few seconds before Saskia raised her head as her knees bent slightly to take the steeper sections of the slippery mesh of stones, worn smooth by generations of wine growers and their carts.

A warm smile blossomed on her lips as she grew closer to the house but the silence of her stroll was interrupted by the musical chime from her cellphone and for a moment she thought about answering it, before turning it off and indulging in a precious few moments of tranquillity before heading back to the long list of tasks that she had set herself to do today.

Just this once she would break her habit and ignore the siren call of her phone. And she knew just who was responsible for that.

Rick had already gone back to California to be with his family and she wished him well. He certainly had a lot of bridges to build. But she missed him so much already she had to keep busy or be a misery all day. His car was not in the car park so she had better make a start on working on transport back to London.

Saskia called out to Coco and they jogged down the path together. She had barely time to slip off her jacket and pet Coco when a very familiar voice echoed out from the warm country kitchen.

It couldn't be.

Stunned, Saskia wandered into the kitchen and stood frozen at the door.

Rick was wearing his smart casual denims and good shirt and his favourite boots, looking not only rested and handsome, but annoyingly chirpy.

How dared he stand there chatting to the breakfast cook? He must have driven to Chamonix and back again but he looked fresh and ready to take on the world. While she had tossed and turned half the night.

'Good morning, sweetheart,' Rick said. He picked up her hand and kissed it before winking at her. 'Look at you. Gorgeous as ever. You don't mind if I call you sweetheart, darling, do you? Excellent. That's my girl. Now—where can I find my breakfast?'

He pretended to look around, which was a joke since

the breakfast buffet table had already been laid out a few feet away in the dining room.

His girl? Gorgeous?

Saskia glanced down at her outfit and then narrowed her eyes at Rick.

She was wearing casual trousers which had picked up a thick layer of mud on the hems, her jacket was covered in dog hair from Coco and her hair was damp and limp around her shoulders. He couldn't have waited ten minutes until she had her shower?

'Oh, forget the breakfast. We can eat on the way.'

And then he launched himself at her.

Grabbing her around the waist, Rick pulled her to him as though she was water in the desert and kissed her so hard on the mouth that all sensible thought was wiped out.

There was nothing she could do except open her arms wide.

She didn't have any other choice. She was carrying Kate's gloves in one hand and a dog lead in the other. She couldn't even fight him off.

But then the kiss softened, one of his hands moved further up her back and his head tilted slightly so that he could lean in even closer.

This was it. This was the real thing.

This was Rick and it was everything that she had been hoping for.

As her eyes closed and she fell deeper and deeper into a hot kiss with each snatched breath, she was vaguely aware that the gloves and lead must have hit the floor because her hand slid up inside Rick's leather jacket and she returned the kiss.

His hands splayed out on her back as she poured into her kiss all of the passion and devotion, the fear and the doubts that came with giving your heart away to another human being.

It was total mind-numbing bliss. And felt so right it was crazy.

This was what she had been missing.

This was what she had been longing for since the moment he had said goodnight.

He was back and that was all that mattered.

Wait a minute!

He was back.

'Did they cancel your flight?' she whispered into the corner of his mouth.

Rick replied by bending his legs, grabbing her behind both knees and hoisting her over his right shoulder as though she weighed nothing at all.

'No time for that. I'll explain on the drive.'

'Put me down! Drive? What drive?' Saskia cried, clutching onto his jacket for dear life as her head bobbed up and down.

'The drive back to London, of course. It's time for you to meet my folks. They vet all of my girlfriends these days but they're fairly busy with a wine show this week so I am taking you to Napa to get some sun.'

'Wait! I haven't even packed my bag—and what do you mean—girlfriend? I thought you said that I was too set in my ways. Too much of a stay in one place kind of girl for an adventure junkie like you. Well, I have news for you— that hasn't changed. I'm still a home girl and I have no intention of changing that fact.'

'Great! Just what I need,' he replied and strode out down the hallway, much to the amusement of the family, who suddenly appeared out of nowhere as though they had been hiding. Even Coco wagged her tail—traitor!

'What? How can it be great? And can you please put

me down so that I can see your face when I am fighting with you?'

'Nope. From now on it's me and you against the world, gorgeous. I am not letting you out of my sight.'

Saskia looked up just as the *auberge* owner appeared at the door. 'Help! I'm being kidnapped.'

He replied by shaking his head slowly from side to side with a huge grin on his face before turning back inside.

'This is not funny,' Saskia called out in vain.

'Yes it is,' Rick replied and grinned around at her. 'Time to get you home, my sweet. We have a lot to do.'

'Wait a minute! I need my suitcase! And what do you mean, a lot to do?' Saskia replied as Rick bounced along the car park.

His feet slowed and she could see the back bumper of his four-by-four.

'I've had a busy morning. Apparently my parents are amazingly proud of what I have achieved so far. What's more, and you are going to like this, they are totally delighted that I am flying my new girlfriend out to meet them. That's you, by the way.'

'Girlfriend? Oh, Rick,' Saskia replied with way too much of a quiver in her voice. 'You told them that I am your girlfriend?'

'Absolutely. Because, incredible as it seems, I have come across a new extreme sport. It's all packaged in the shape of a girl called Saskia Elwood Mortimer. Dangerous? Hell, yes. But I am willing to take the risk.'

Rick stopped moving and took firm hold of her legs but when he spoke his voice was low and warm. 'So. This is the way it is going to be, Saskia. I am going to put you down, you are going to go inside and get packed. Then we are going to enjoy some excellent breakfast and drive to London together, before catching that flight. That's right.

I'm not letting you go. From now on I will be staying in one place. And that is where you are. No more running around the world. I am done with that. The Burgess and Elwood Show has come to town. Or...'

All she could hear was the birdsong in the pine trees either side of the road and the sound of Rick's breathing and the fast beat of his heart.

He was nervous. And she was heavy. Or both.

'Or...' she repeated with a quiver in her voice.

'Or you tell me that you don't want to be with me and I drive away and leave you here and I don't see you again.'

'Rick! No!'

His hands slid up her legs and gently, gently, gripped her around the waist and physically lifted her forward so that he was holding her under her bottom, taking her weight. And all the time his eyes were locked onto hers.

Then, and only then, did his grip relax so that she could slide down against the front of his shirt and jacket.

She didn't care that the front of her top had ridden up and was showing her pasty white midriff and back to the world on a cold frosty morning.

She cared even less that her trouser buttons seemed to have become snagged on his belt.

All she cared about was this man who was holding her and gazing at her face with such tenderness and love and devotion that it melted her heart just to look at him.

'Repeat after me,' he whispered in a voice that was hot chocolate sauce over home-made vanilla ice cream. 'I want to be with you, Richard Burgess, and the idea of being your girlfriend is growing on me. In fact I like it just fine.'

'I do like it,' she tried to say but her voice cracked and tears started streaming down her cheeks. 'Yes, I want to be with you so very much. Take me back to London, Rick. But only for as long as it takes me to get packed. I want to

see California. I want to meet your parents—and most of
all I want to see them with you.'

And then speaking was impossible because he had
swooped her up, her arms still around his neck, and was
twirling and twirling and twirling and laughing as though
he wanted the whole world to know that she loved him.

'I don't want you to stop but I am getting dizzy,' she
called out, deliriously happy.

'Best get used to that feeling.' He grinned and kissed her
and it was the kiss of a man who knew what he was doing.
'From now on your feet are not going to touch the ground.'

EPILOGUE

SASKIA STOOD IN the conservatory room at Elwood House and looked out onto the snow-covered patio winter wonderland where Amber and Sam would have their wedding photographs taken.

The snow had been falling for three days. It was fluffy, soft, crisp and beautiful and the air was cold enough to glaze the covering with a sparkling frost that would twinkle in the white fairy lights Saskia and Rick had finished just in time to drive back to Alsace to celebrate Christmas with his parents and her mother.

Inspired by the bower of fresh flowers and grape leaves that she had seen at the wedding in France, she had worked with the florist to create an extension to her garden pergola of wire and woven fir tree branches cut from the garden of the *auberge*.

Tall enough not to bash Sam on the head, the wide curve was smothered now in gold cones and red berries and fruit and dark shiny holly leaves interspersed with trailing golden blossoms which would only last the day in this chill but were worth it.

At dusk the lights hidden in the miniature conifers on each side of the cleared paving would create a secret pathway to the lover's bower.

She had always thought that Amber was ethereal, but

this was her chance to make Amber's day truly magical. It was exactly how she had imagined it would be. And Amber had cried for ten minutes when she'd seen it yesterday which, of course, set the other two off.

Thanks heaven that Sam, Heath and Rick had taken one look at their weeping ladies, who were hugging onto one another over chocolate ice cream and champagne, and decided to take off to their boutique hotel across the square in search of a solid Italian meal which involved lots of carbs washed down by copious quantities of good wine.

But that was okay. The girls were allowed to cry on the day before the wedding.

It had been a manic few days of post-Christmas hairdressers' appointments, manicures and facials—for all three of them. Final fittings at Katherine Lovat Designs, emergency phone calls around the world to check on flight times to arrange airport pickups, courtesy of Sam's dad and his wonderful limo service, daily crisis meetings in Saskia's kitchen over chocolate cake to cope with stressful family members from all sides, but at last it was done.

The first one of their little band was marrying the man she loved. Amber's wedding day had arrived.

Saskia strolled slowly back to the main entrance hall, smiling at the caterers and waiting staff who were putting the final touches to the wedding reception dinner. The dining tables had been dressed with lengths of bright scarlet and gold wedding sari fabric with gold decorations, candelabra and detailing. The marble hallway and wide wing staircase was gleaming and splendid. An army of florists had transformed this old house into something which was better than any grand hotel Saskia had ever been to. And, even better, it had taken Amber's breath away when she'd first seen it.

Pillar candles with rich gold and scarlet floral decoration spilling out from crystal vases. Rings of intertwined ribbon flowers and eucalyptus adorned every chair and Amber's favourite flower, the orchid, stood tall in stunning planters on the console table and bookcases.

The overall effect was warm and welcoming—just what Amber and Sam had asked for. No stuffiness. No hundreds of wedding guests they did not know. No formality of any kind. This was their very personal and private celebration of their love. And not even Amber's mother Julia had been able to make her move an inch.

Amber's bouquet was made of a trail of gold orchids and pastel blossoms and leaves. The girl who had once been too shy to wear anything but dark colours and school uniform had been transformed under the sunlight of Sam's love into a daring and beautiful woman who celebrated the new home she had made in India.

The house almost did her justice.

After the reception, when the candles were lit and the lights dimmed, it would be remarkable. It was already remarkable.

She had never seen the house looking so amazing—so happy and splendid.

Saskia blinked nervously and scanned the checklist. This was it. After so many months of work and planning. The first wedding Elwood House had ever seen, but not the last if her plans came to fruition. Kate was getting married at Jardine Manor but there was only place she wanted for her English wedding to Rick—right here. In her own home. With her family around her, old and new. They could celebrate later at the chalet in private.

'Hello, gorgeous,' a familiar voice whispered and she turned to see Rick strolling into the kitchen holding a substantial-looking sandwich. 'Nice place you got here.'

She closed her eyes and exhaled slowly before holding

out the sides of her sweater and making a short curtsey. 'I'm pleased that you like it.' She smiled, but then her smile faltered. 'I'm only sorry that Aunt Margot never got to see it like this. She would have loved it.'

'Hey,' he said, and wrapped his arm around one shoulder and planted a tender kiss on the top of her hair. 'She would have been proud of you. I am. Except for one tiny little thing.'

'Only one?'

He turned to face her and tipped her chin up with one finger. 'You have never stopped since we got back from France. Time to take five minutes and join in the fun.' He gestured with his head towards the stairs. 'Go on up and do some of that girly stuff with your pals.'

'But what about Sam…?'

Rick held up one hand. 'Heath Sheridan is as bad as you are with lists and timetables. He'll walk Sam over from the hotel in good time for the wedding. Fear not, for the sake of the lovely Amber, our boy Sam is even prepared to talk to his scary future mother-in-law so I don't think he'll make a run for it. He's been waiting a long time to claim his bride. And I'm not going anywhere. Not when you're around and there is enough food and most excellent wine to feed an army back there.'

'Good to know that your priorities haven't changed.' She laughed, and then checked her watch.

'Oh no,' she gasped. 'I can't believe it's that time already. The first guests will be here in half an hour and I need to change and… Speaking of which,' she added, glancing down at his well-worn denims and T-shirt, 'I like your outfit. It's so you!'

He turned her shoulders towards the stairs and patted her bottom. 'Go. Chill. I'll come and find you in ten minutes.'

* * *

Saskia walked into her bedroom, which had become the makeshift Bride's Suite, and stopped at the door and inhaled sharply.

Kate and Amber were lying on her wide bed in their dressing gowns. Giggling and making duvet angels.

They were her best friends in the world, and one of them was getting married today. In a few hours their lives and their relationship were about to change for good.

This was the last precious time to be together as three single girls.

And right now they both looked just the same as the first time she'd met them at high school. Twelve years old and mad as a bag of frogs.

She blinked happy tears from the corner of her eyes, but she flopped down at the bottom of the bed, untied her tennis shoes, then stretched out on the bed next to them with her arm around Amber's shoulder.

'Hello goddesses,' she said. 'What's new?'

'There is some crazy rumour going around that Amber is getting married. Just thinking how ridiculous this all is.' Kate giggled. 'Want to join us before the hysteria sets in?'

'Absolutely,' Saskia said, and took a good long sip out of the glass of champagne on the bedside cabinet which, judging from the lipstick stains, belonged to Amber.

'Why did I ever think that New Year's Day would be a good time to get married?' Amber asked with a glazed look in her beautiful eyes and perfect make up. 'Everyone is still stressed out from Christmas, my third stepdad is stuck in a snowbound airport and my mum never stops reminding me about all the important celebrity New Year parties that she sacrificed to be here with me. And I am so terrified that I will fluff my lines it's ridiculous. If it wasn't for Sam, I'd be on the next plane back to India.'

'What, and miss all the cake,' Kate laughed and turned on her side to look at them. 'Relax, gorgeous. Your diva mother is having the time of her life and wait until you see the over-the-top outfit she is wearing! The hat is so large we can all shelter underneath if it snows again.'

Amber squeezed her hand and chuckled. 'I know. It's horrendous. And I'm sorry for being such a nuisance. You would think that I should be used to performance anxiety by now. It's just that…I'm getting married today.'

Then she blinked. 'It's finally happening. I'm getting married. Today. Isn't that amazing? And I think I am going to cry again now.'

'Not post-mascara you don't,' Saskia replied, then sat up on the bed and turned towards Amber. 'Deep breathing. That's it. Pretend that you are about to play the piano in front of your family and friends and they all love you. Kate! I leave you alone for a few hours. How many glasses of champagne have you two had?'

Kate slid off the bed in her stockings and rattled the bottle and peered at the couple of inches left in the bottom. 'Oops. Perhaps this is a good time to get the camera out before we finish it off and everything goes a bit lopsided. Sam's journo pal might be doing the actual wedding photos but I would like one of the three of us getting ready.'

'Give that to me, you scamp,' Saskia called out and rushed around the bed to try and snatch the small digital camera. 'You are not to be trusted.'

'Oh no, you don't, Elwood. For the past few months you have been running yourself ragged and getting used to being adored by a handsome stud, which is exhausting enough for any girl. Well, as of right now, you have to turn off your compulsion to control the world and enjoy yourself. Tell her, Amber.'

'Kate's right. Put the organiser and the camera down

now, Saskia. And I am the bride so you have to do what I say.'

Saskia stopped playing with Kate and planted a hand on each hip, then shrugged at Amber, who was sitting up against the headboard with her hands in her lap.

'You are. And I do. Look—organiser in the drawer. There it goes. All gone.'

'Now you have to close the drawer,' Kate said, looking over her shoulder. 'Go on. It'll be fine on its own. Besides, it would never fit in that tiny bag I picked out for you.'

'This is true.' Saskia grinned and sat down on the corner of the bed with Kate sprawled next to her and she reached out and took Amber's hand.

'Are you ready to get married now, lovely girl?'

'No. But I am ready to get married to my Sam. I love him so much it's crazy.'

'Then it's a good thing that he has officially redeemed himself by worshipping you for the goddess that you are,' Kate sighed. 'In fact, Sam is almost worthy of you.'

'Wow. Now that is quite a compliment. Ladies, I think this calls for a toast. Oh—no spills on the duvet. Excellent. Wait. I'll prop the camera up on the desk and set the automatic timer. Smile please—cheesy grins all around.'

'Oh, I'm blinded!' Kate yelled a microsecond after the flash went off.

Amber lowered her forehead onto Saskia's shoulder and, as she smiled with a quivering upper lip, a single tear slid from the corner of her eye onto her beautiful cheek.

'This has been some year—and I couldn't have got through it without you two,' she whispered.

'We're so happy for you, Amber.' Kate sniffed and dabbed the tear away before blowing into the tissue. 'You have waited eleven years to find out that Sam is still madly in love with you. That's mega.'

'Mega.' Amber nodded and reached for another tissue. 'You have your Heath and now Saskia has found Rick. Who would have imagined so much could change since the high school reunion?'

'Now don't get me started,' Saskia said. 'The three goddesses will always be the goddesses, no matter where we are or what we are doing. Right? Of course right.'

Amber reached out and hugged each of the girls tight and then slid off the bed and jumped to her feet.

'Dresses! We need dresses. Shoes. Hair. Bijou. Let's go and show the world what we can achieve once we set our minds to it! Ready? Let's do this!'

As it was, Saskia was still zipping Kate into her dress when there was a sharp knock on the door and Rick stuck his head inside the bedroom, with his hand covering his eyes, and totally ignored the screams and shouts to go away.

'Hey, gorgeous ladies. Thought you ought to know that Heath and Sam are waiting downstairs in the library and there is a small blonde in a huge hat standing in the hallway demanding champagne. Shall I escort her up?'

'Mum!' Amber squealed and grabbed Saskia's hand in terror.

Saskia patted her on the hand. 'Nothing to worry about. Richard Burgess—your mission is to chat to the mother of the bride. She will be excited and nervous and is bound to have spotted Amber's dad and his other family by now and be spitting tacks. Can you spare some of that charm of yours?'

Rick widened the gap between his fingers and gave a low growl of appreciation at Saskia in her dress, winked once and then closed the door.

'Was Rick wearing a kilt? Oh my,' Kate gulped.

'I know. And just for me. Imagine that.'

* * *

Ten minutes later, and a whole thirty seconds ahead of schedule on her planner, Saskia adjusted the position of her bridesmaid posy and followed the direction of the gasps of awe and delight. Amber was standing at the top of the curved white marble staircase, holding hands with her father—her real father, a tall elegant man who had arrived from Paris with his entire entourage the previous day. They were chatting and laughing gently and it was wonderful to see.

Then Amber lifted her head and smiled at Saskia and gave her the gentlest of nods. She was ready.

This was it. This was her moment. And Amber had never looked more beautiful. She knew that she was loved and it shone out like a beacon.

Amber the fashion model. Amber the concert pianist. And now Amber the bride.

Saskia turned and gave the signal to Parvita and the string quartet of award-winning musicians who she'd pulled from all around the world on New Year's Day for the performance of a lifetime.

On the first beat of the music, Amber took her father's arm and he kissed her on the cheek one last time, before turning and taking the first step, and then the next, down the curving stately staircase.

Kate had created a long slender column of stunning hand-worked lace over flowing layers of silk which showed Amber's figure and tanned complexion to perfection. All topped by an antique lace veil and diamond tiara that her parents had provided as their wedding present.

Amber was the loveliest bride that Saskia had ever seen. As she turned slightly to pass down the aisle formed by chairs covered in rich red and gold sari fabric, she looked back at Saskia over one shoulder and mouthed the words "thank you".

Amber had caught her first glimpse of Sam. Who was waiting to claim her as his own.

And it melted Saskia's heart all over again.

Kate stepped in just behind the small train on Amber's dress, and then it was her turn to walk down the aisle behind her two best friends. There was Heath, grinning at Kate with such love. Rick sat next to him. In a kilt! And when she drew closer he flashed her a lusty look that almost made her drop her posy!

They were three girls in love with three remarkable men who loved them back.

The snow had stopped falling and beams of brilliant sunshine broke through the clouds, creating a carpet of sparkling silver crystals on the snow-covered pergola and conifers on the other side of the glass.

It was fairy tale perfect. Magical.

Red flower petals gathered by the girls at the orphanage in India were strewn on the path leading to the lover's bower.

And as Amber's father lifted his daughter's hand and gave it to Sam, the musicians and singers burst out in an almighty *Halleluiah* that made the roof of the conservatory ring with the energy of it. And she could not be happier.

* * * * *

MILLS & BOON®
By Request

RELIVE THE ROMANCE WITH THE BEST OF THE BEST

A sneak peek at next month's titles...

In stores from 20th October 2016:

- **Tempted by a Caffarelli** – Melanie Milburne

- **One Unforgettable Night** – Vicki Lewis Thompson, Debbi Rawlins & Candace Havens

In stores from 3rd November 2016:

- **Always On Her Mind** – Catherine Mann, Jules Bennett & Emily McKay

- **A Mistletoe Proposal** – Rebecca Winters, Melissa McClone & Abigail Gordon

Just can't wait?
Buy our books online a month before they hit the shops!
www.millsandboon.co.uk

Also available as eBooks.

Give a 12 month subscription to a friend today!

Call Customer Services
0844 844 1358*

or visit
millsandboon.co.uk/subscriptions

MILLS & BOON®

Why shop at millsandboon.co.uk?

Each year, thousands of romance readers find their perfect read at millsandboon.co.uk. That's because we're passionate about bringing you the very best romantic fiction. Here are some of the advantages of shopping at www.millsandboon.co.uk:

* **Get new books first**—you'll be able to buy your favourite books one month before they hit the shops

* **Get exclusive discounts**—you'll also be able to buy our specially created monthly collections, with up to 50% off the RRP

* **Find your favourite authors**—latest news, interviews and new releases for all your favourite authors and series on our website, plus ideas for what to try next

* **Join in**—once you've bought your favourite books, don't forget to register with us to rate, review and join in the discussions

Visit **www.millsandboon.co.uk**
for all this and more today!